THE
PURITY
OF
VENGEANCE

THE PURITY OF VENGEANCE

A Department Q Novel

Jussi Adler-Olsen

Translated by Martin Aitken

DUTTON
— est. 1852 —

DUTTON
— est. 1852 —

Published by the Penguin Group
Penguin Group (USA) LLC
375 Hudson Street
New York, New York 10014

USA | Canada | UK | Ireland | Australia | New Zealand | India | South Africa | China
penguin.com
A Penguin Random House Company

LIBRARY OF CONGRESS CATALOGING-IN-PUBLICATION DATA
Adler-Olsen, Jussi.
[Journal 64. English]
The purity of vengeance : a Department Q novel / Jussi Adler-Olsen;
Translated by Martin Aitken.—First Edition.
pages cm.
Translated from the Danish *Journal 64* with a variant title of
Journal fireogtreds by Martin Aitken
Previously published as *Journal 64* with a variant title of *Journal fireogtreds* in Danish.
ISBN 978-0-525-95401-9 (hardback)
I. Aitken, Martin, translator.   II. Title.
PT8176.1.D54J6813   2014
839.81'38—dc23   2013033253

ISBN 978-0-525-95401-9

Printed in the United States of America
1   3   5   7   9   10   8   6   4   2

Set in Apollo MT Std
Designed by Alissa Amell

Dedicated to my mother and father, Karen-Margrethe and Henry Olsen, and to my sisters, Elsebeth, Marianne, and Vippe.

PROLOGUE

November 1985

The feeling could get the better of her in an unguarded moment. The cool, delicate champagne glass between her fingers, the hum of voices, and the light hand of her husband at her waist. Apart from being in love, only brief flashbacks of a distant childhood reminded her of it. The security of her grandmother's chatter. Subdued laughter as she fell into a slumber. The laughter of people long since gone.

Nete pressed her lips together to stem the emotion. Sometimes it got the better of her.

She collected herself and gazed out upon the palette of colorful evening gowns and proud figures. The celebratory banquet in honor of the Danish recipient of the year's Nordic Prize for Medicine had drawn many guests. Scholars, physicians, pillars of society. Circles into which she certainly hadn't been born but in which she nevertheless had come to feel increasingly comfortable as the years passed.

She took a deep breath and was about to let out a contented sigh when she became acutely aware that a pair of eyes had latched onto her through the array of festive coiffures and men in tight bow ties. The inexplicable, unsettling charges of electricity only ever emitted by eyes that wished no good. Instinctively she moved aside, like a hunted animal seeking cover in undergrowth. She put her hand on her husband's arm and tried to smile as her gaze flickered across the elegantly dressed guests and the shimmer of the candelabra.

A woman tossed back her head in a moment's laughter, suddenly opening up a clear view to the rear end of the hall.

And there he stood.

His figure towered like a lighthouse above all the others. Despite the stooping posture and crooked legs, a great, strutting wild animal whose eyes swept over the crowd like a pair of searchlights.

Again she sensed his intense surveillance to the very core of her being and knew for certain that if she didn't react now her entire life would collapse in seconds.

"Andreas," she said, putting her hand to her throat, which was already sticky with perspiration. "Can't we leave now? I'm not feeling well."

Further entreaty was unnecessary. Her husband raised his dark eyebrows, nodded to those nearest, and turned away from the throng, taking her arm in his. It was typical of him, and she loved him for it.

"Thank you," she said. "I'm afraid it's my headache again."

He nodded, all too familiar with the affliction himself. Long, dark evenings in the drawing room, his migraine pounding.

It was yet another thing they had in common.

As they approached the majestic staircase the tall man stole forward and stepped in front of them.

He looked much older now, she noted. The eyes that once had sparkled had lost their luster. His hair was unrecognizable. Twenty-five years had taken their toll.

"Nete, are *you* here? You're the last person I would have expected to see in such company," he said bluntly.

She stepped to one side and drew her husband past, but her stalker was undeterred. "Don't you remember me, Nete?" came his voice from behind. "Of course you do. Curt Wad. How could you ever forget me?"

Halfway down the stairs he caught up with them.

"So you're Rosen's tart now, is that it? Imagine you, of all people, reaching such heights."

She tugged at her husband's arm to hasten him along, but Andreas Rosen was not known for turning his back on a problem. The present situation was no exception.

"Would you be so kind as to leave my wife alone?" he asked, his words accompanied by a glare that warned of rage.

"Oh, I see." The unwelcome guest took a step backward. "So you've actually lured Andreas Rosen into your web, Nete. Well done." He flashed what others might have taken to be a wry smile, but she knew better. "That piece of information seems to have completely passed me by, I'm afraid. But then I don't usually frequent such circles. Never read the gossip magazines."

In slow motion she saw her husband shake his head in disdain. Felt the grip of his hand on hers as he drew her on. For a moment she was able to breathe again. Their footsteps clattered, asynchronous echoes, urging them away.

They reached the downstairs cloakroom before the voice behind them spoke once more.

"Mr. Rosen! Perhaps you are unaware that your wife is a whore? A simple girl from Sprogø who isn't fussy about who she opens her legs for. Her feeble mind cannot distinguish between truth and lies, and—"

She felt a wrench of her wrist as her husband spun round. Several guests were trying to subdue the man who had interrupted their festivities. A couple of younger doctors leaned menacingly toward the tall man's chest, making it clear he was not wanted there.

"Andreas, don't," she shouted as her husband stepped toward the cluster of individuals that now surrounded her tormentor, but he was oblivious. Her alpha male was marking out his territory.

"I don't know who you are," he said, "but I strongly suggest you refrain from showing yourself in public again until you've learned how to behave in decent company."

The thin figure raised his head above the men who were holding him back and everyone present focused on his moistureless lips: the ladies behind the counter who were sorting the furs from the cotton coats, guests slinking their way past, the private chauffeurs waiting in front of the swing doors.

And then came the words that should never have been uttered.

"Why don't you ask Nete where she was sterilized? Ask her how many abortions she's had. Ask her what an isolation cell feels like after five days. Ask her, and leave lecturing me on social skills to your betters, Andreas Rosen."

Curt Wad extracted himself from those restraining him and stepped aside, eyes aflame with hatred. "I'm leaving now!" he spat. "And you, Nete!" He extended a trembling finger toward her. "You can go to hell, where you belong."

The room was a buzz of voices even before the swing doors closed behind him.

"That was Curt Wad," someone whispered. "An old student friend of the prizewinner, which is about the only good thing that can be said of him."

But the trap had sprung. She had been revealed.

All eyes were upon her now. Searching for signs of her true self. Was her neckline too plunging? Were her hips too vulgar? Were her lips?

They collected their coats, and the cloakroom lady's warm breath felt almost poisonous. You're no better than me, her expression said.

It happened that quickly.

She lowered her gaze and took her husband's arm.

Her beloved husband, whose eyes she hadn't the courage to look into.

She listened to the quiet purr of the engine.

They had not spoken a word to each other, staring past the swish of the windshield wipers into the autumn darkness through which they passed.

Perhaps he was waiting for her denials, but she had none to offer.

Perhaps she was expecting him to accommodate her. To help her out of her predicament. To look into her eyes and tell her it didn't matter, whatever it was, and that what counted were the eleven years they had been together.

Not the thirty-seven she had lived before that.

But he turned on the radio and filled the car with jangling remoteness, Sting accompanying them south across Sjælland, Sade and Madonna over Falster and the Guldborgsund strait to Lolland. Strange, young voices in the night. The only thing that bound them together.

Everything else was gone.

A few hundred meters before the village of Blans, still a couple of kilometers from the manor farm, he pulled in to the edge of the fields.

"Now tell me," he said, his gaze fastened to the darkness outside. His words were without warmth. He didn't even utter her name by way of comfort. All he had was *Tell me*!

She closed her eyes. Pleaded with him to understand there were underlying events that explained everything, and that the man who had confronted her was the very cause of her misfortune.

But apart from that, what he had said had been the truth. She admitted it, her voice a whisper.

It was true. All of it.

For an agonizing, all-consuming moment only his breathing was heard. Then he turned toward her with darkness in his eyes. "So that's why we've never been able to have children," he said.

She nodded. Pressed her lips together and told it like it was. Yes, she was guilty of lies and deceit. She came clean. As a young girl she had been committed to Sprogø, through no fault of her own. A chain of misunderstandings, abuse of power, betrayal. There was no other reason. And yes, she'd had abortions and had been sterilized, but the dreadful man they had just encountered . . .

He laid his hand on her arm, and its coldness went through her like an electric shock, prompting her to stop.

Then he put the car into gear, released the clutch, and drove slowly through the village before accelerating quickly past the meadows and the darkened view of the water.

"I'm sorry, Nete. But I can't forgive your allowing me to live all these years blindly believing we could become parents together. I simply can't. And as for the rest of what you've told me, quite frankly I'm disgusted."

He paused, and she felt an icy tingle at her temples, the muscles of her neck tensing.

He raised his head. Arrogantly, the way he did when negotiating with people he deemed unworthy of his respect. Confidently, as when ignoring poor advice.

"I shall pack some things," he said firmly. "In the meantime, you have a week to make other arrangements. Take whatever you need from Havngaard. You won't be left wanting."

She turned her face slowly away from him and stared out over the sea. Rolled the window down slightly and drew in the smell of seaweed borne by waves as black as ink, waves that might take her once and for all.

And the feeling returned to her of lonely, desperate days on Sprogø, when the same lapping sea had tried to lure her into putting an end to her miserable life.

"You won't be left wanting," he had said, as though it mattered.

He knew nothing about her.

She glanced at her watch and fixed the date in her mind, the fourteenth of November 1985, and felt her lips quiver as she turned to look at him.

His dark eyes were cavities in his face. Only the bends in the road ahead claimed his interest.

She lifted one hand slowly and grasped the steering wheel, wrenching it to the right as hard as she could just as he opened his mouth in protest.

The engine roared in vain as the road vanished beneath them, and as they hurtled through the windbreak the sound of rasping metal drowned out her husband's final protests.

When they hit the sea, it was almost like coming home.

1

November 2010

Carl had heard about the night's incident over the police radio on his way in from his house in Allerød. Under normal circumstances nothing could interest him less than vice cases, but somehow this felt different.

The owner of an escort service had been attacked with sulfuric acid in her flat on Enghavevej, leaving staff of the Rigshospital's burns unit with a job on their hands.

Now a call had gone out for witnesses, as yet without any luck.

A band of dodgy-looking Lithuanians had already been brought in for questioning, but as the night hours passed it had become clear that only one of the suspects could possibly be the perpetrator, and it was unlikely they would find out who. There was no evidence. On her admission to the hospital the victim had declared she would be unable to identify her assailant, and now they were going to have to let the whole lot of them go.

Hadn't he heard this before?

On his way through the courtyard of Police HQ he ran into Halmtorvet's Icicle, aka Brandur Isaksen from Station City, who was heading for the parking area.

"Off to make life difficult for someone, I hope?" Carl grunted in passing, whereupon the brainless oaf stopped as if it had been an invitation.

"It's Bak's sister this time," Isaksen said coldly.

Carl stared at him with bleary eyes. What the fuck was he talking about? "Tough shit," he replied. It was an all-purpose response adequate for most situations.

"You've heard about that acid attack over on Enghavevej, I take it? Not a pretty sight, I can tell you," Isaksen went on. "The doctors have been working on her all night. You know Børge Bak pretty well, don't you?"

Carl tossed his head back. Børge Bak? Of course he knew Børge Bak. The inspector from Department A who had applied for leave, then opted for early retirement. That sanctimonious git?

"We're about as much friends as you and I are," Carl blurted out.

Isaksen nodded, his teeth clenched. It was true: if there was any fondness at all between them it would fall apart at the flutter of a pair of butterfly wings.

"What about Børge's sister, Esther? You wouldn't know her, I suppose?" he asked.

Carl stared over at the colonnade along which Rose was now tripping with a handbag the size of a suitcase draped over her shoulder. What the hell was she planning to do, spend her holidays at the office?

He sensed Isaksen follow his gaze and tore himself away.

"Never met the woman. Doesn't she run a brothel?" Carl replied. "Anyway, that'd be more your domain, so keep me out of it, if you don't mind."

The corners of Isaksen's mouth succumbed to gravity. "You might as well be prepared. Bak'll be here before you know it, sticking his oar in."

Carl doubted it. Hadn't Bak chucked it all in because he hated his job and loathed Police HQ?

"He'll be welcome," he answered. "As long as he stays away from me."

Isaksen dragged his fingers through his early-morning tousle of jet-black hair. "Yeah, well, you've got enough on your plate shagging her, haven't you?"

He nodded in the direction of Rose as she vanished up the steps.

Carl shook his head and carried on walking. Isaksen could take a running jump with all his crap. Shagging Rose! He'd rather join a monastery in Bratislava.

"Just a minute, Carl," said the duty officer as he passed the cage half a minute later. "That psychologist woman, Mona Ibsen, left this for you." He thrust a gray envelope at Carl through the open door as though it were the highlight of his day.

Carl stared at it, nonplussed. Maybe it was.

The duty officer sat down again. "Assad was here at four this morning, so I heard. He sees to it he has plenty of time on his own, I'll say that for him. What's he up to down there, anyway? Planning a terrorist strike?" He chortled to himself for a moment, then thought better of it when he saw Carl's piercing gaze.

"Why don't you ask him yourself?" Carl said, recalling the case of the woman who had been arrested in the airport for merely uttering the word "bomb," a slip-up of front-page dimensions.

To his mind, what he'd just heard was a lot bloody worse.

Even from the bottom step of the rotunda stairwell he could tell this was one of Rose's better days. A heavy scent of cloves and jasmine assaulted his nostrils, reminding him of the old woman back in Øster Brønderslev who used to pinch the backsides of all the men who came to visit her. When Rose smelled like this, it gave him a headache, besides the one he always got on account of her usual grouching.

Assad's theory was that she'd inherited the perfume, while others reckoned this kind of putrefying blend was still available in certain Indian shops that couldn't care less if they ever saw another customer again.

"Hey, Carl, come here a minute, would you?" she bellowed from inside her office.

Carl gave a sigh. What now?

He walked stiffly past Assad's shambles of a cubbyhole, poked his nose into Rose's clinically disinfected domain, and immediately noticed the voluminous shoulder bag she'd just been toting. As far as Carl could tell, Rose's perfume wasn't the only disconcerting aspect of the day. The enormous wad of documents peeping out of her bag seemed just as disheartening.

"Erm," he ventured cautiously, indicating the reams of paper. "What's all that, then?"

She glared at him with kohl-rimmed eyes. It did not bode well.

"Some old cases that have been lying around various commissioners' offices this past year. Cases that should have been handed on to us. *You* of all people would know about that kind of slovenliness."

To the latter suggestion she added a kind of guttural growl that might have passed as a laugh.

"The folders here had been sent over to the National Investigation Center by mistake. I've just been to pick them up."

Carl raised his eyebrows. More work, so why the hell was she smiling?

"OK, I know what you're thinking: bad news of the day," Rose said, beating him to it. "But you haven't seen this yet. This one's not from the NIC, it was already on my chair when I came in."

She handed him a battered cardboard folder. She looked as if she expected him to flick through it on the spot, but on that count she had another thing coming. For Carl, bad news wasn't an option before a man's first smoke of the morning. There was a time and a place for everything, and he'd only just got here, for Chrissake.

He shook his head and wandered off into his own office, tossing the folder onto his desk and his coat over the chair in the corner.

The room smelled musty and the fluorescent light on the ceiling flickered even more frantically than usual. Wednesdays were always the worst.

He lit a smoke and trudged across the corridor to Assad's little broom cupboard, where everything seemed to be as usual: prayer mat rolled out on the floor; dense, myrtle-laced clouds of steam; transistor tuned in to something that sounded like the mating cries of dolphins interspersed with a gospel choir, played on an open-reel tape recorder with a dodgy drive belt.

Istanbul à la carte.

"Morning," Carl grunted.

Assad turned his head slowly toward him. A sunrise over Kuwait could not have been ruddier than the poor man's impressive proboscis.

"Jesus, Assad, that doesn't look too good," he exclaimed, retreating a step at the sight. If the flu was thinking of rampaging through the halls of Police HQ, he could only hope it would give him a wide berth.

"It came on yesterday," Assad sniffled. His runny eyes looked like a puppy's.

"Off home with you, on the double," Carl said, withdrawing even farther. No point in saying any more, given that Assad wasn't going to take any notice.

He went back to his safety zone and slung his legs up on the desk, wondering for the first time in his life whether it might be time to take a package holiday in the Canary Islands. Two weeks under an umbrella with a scantily clad Mona at his side wouldn't be half bad. The flu could cause as much havoc in Copenhagen as it liked while they were away.

He smiled at the thought, took out the little envelope from Mona, and opened it. The scent alone was almost enough. Delicate and sensual. Mona Ibsen in a nutshell. A far cry from Rose's dense, daily bombardment of his olfactory system.

My darling, it began.

Carl melted. Not since he'd lain incapacitated on a ward of Brønderslev Hospital with six stitches in his side and his appendix in a jar had he been addressed so with such affection.

My darling,

See you at my place at seven thirty for Martinmas goose, OK? Put a jacket on and bring the wine. I'll do the surprises.

Kisses, Mona

He felt the warmth rise in his cheeks. What a woman!

He closed his eyes, took a deep drag of his cigarette, and conjured up images to accompany the word "surprises." Not all of them would be deemed suitable for a family audience.

"What are you doing with your eyes closed and that big grin on your face?" came a harping voice from behind him. "Aren't you going to have a look in that case folder I gave you?"

Rose stood in the doorway with her arms folded and her head cocked to one side. It meant she was going nowhere until he did as she said.

Carl stubbed out his smoke and reached for the folder. Might as well get it over with or else she'd be standing there till she'd tied knots in her arms.

The folder contained ten faded sheets of paper from Hjørring District Court. He could see what it was at a glance.

How the hell did it wind up on Rose's chair?

He skimmed the first page, already knowing what he was about to read. Summer 1978. Man drowned in the Nørreå river. Owner of a large machine works, passionate angler, and a member of various clubs, accordingly. Four sets of fresh footprints around his stool and creel. None of his fishing tackle missing. Abu reel and rods at more than five hundred kroner apiece. Weather fine. Autopsy revealing nothing abnormal, no heart disease, no coronary thrombosis. Just drowned.

Had it not been for the river being only seventy-five centimeters deep at the spot in question, it would all have been written off as an accident.

But it wasn't the man's death in itself that had awakened Rose's interest; that much Carl knew. Nor was it the fact that the case had never been solved and hence now resided in the basement of Department Q. No, it was because attached to the case documents were a number of photographs, and Carl's mug appeared on two of them.

Carl sighed. The name of the drowned man was Birger Mørck, Carl's uncle. A jovial and generous man whom both his son, Ronny, and Carl himself had looked up to and often accompanied on excursions. Just as they had done that very day, to glean whatever they might about the mysteries of angling.

But a couple of girls from Copenhagen had cycled the length and breadth of the country and were now approaching their destination in Skagen, their flimsy tops arousingly moist with perspiration.

The sight of these two blonde beauties as they came toiling over the rises impacted on Carl and his cousin, Ronny, like a blow from a hammer, prompting them to put down their fishing rods and leg it across the field like a pair of young bulls setting their hooves on grass for the first time in their lives.

When they returned to the river two hours later with the contours of the two girls' tight tops forever imprinted on their retinas, Birger Mørck was already dead.

Many hours of questioning and many suspicions later, the Hjørring police shelved the case for good. And although they never succeeded in tracing the two girls from the capital who were the young men's only alibi, Ronny and Carl were released without charge. Carl's father was enraged and inconsolable for months, but apart from that the matter had no further consequences.

"You were quite a looker in those days, Carl. How old were you?" Rose intervened from the doorway.

He dropped the folder onto the desk. It wasn't a time he cared to be reminded about.

"Seventeen, and Ronny was twenty-seven." He sighed. "Have you any idea why this should turn up here all of a sudden?"

"What do you mean, *why*?" She rapped bony knuckles against her skull: "Hello, Prince Charming, anyone home? How about waking up a bit? That's what we do here, isn't it? We investigate unsolved crimes!"

"Yeah, but this one was closed as an accident. And apart from that, it didn't just emerge from out of your chair, did it?"

"You mean I should ask the police in Hjørring how come it's landed here?"

Carl raised his eyebrows. Ask a stupid question . . .

She turned on her heel and clattered off toward her own domain. Message understood.

Carl stared into space. Why the hell did this of all cases have to turn up now? As if it hadn't caused trouble enough already.

He looked once again at the photo of Ronny and himself, then shoved the folder over toward the other cases that lay piled up on his desk. Past was past but this was now. Nothing could alter that. Five minutes ago he'd read Mona's note. She'd called him "darling." He needed to keep his priorities straight.

He smiled, delved into his pocket for his mobile, and stared despondently at the minuscule keys. If he sent Mona a text message it would take him ten minutes to write it, and if he called her he could wait just as long before she answered.

He sighed and began to text. The technology of mobile keypads was seemingly the work of Pygmies with macaroni for fingers, and the average northern European male who needed to operate such a contraption could only feel like a hippopotamus trying to play the flute.

When he was finished he studied the result of his efforts and allowed a string of wrong spellings to pass with a sigh. Mona would understand well enough: the Martinmas goose had a taker.

Just as he put the mobile down on his desk, a head popped round the door.

The comb-over had been given a trim since he'd seen it last, and the leather jacket looked like it had been pressed, but the man inside it was as crumpled as ever.

"Bak. What the fuck are you doing here?" he inquired mechanically.

"As if you don't know already," his visitor replied, lack of sleep advertised by his drooping eyelids. "I'm going out of my mind. That's why!"

He plonked himself down on the chair opposite, despite Carl's obvious disapproval. "My sister Esther's never going to be the same again. And the bastard who threw acid in her face is sitting in a basement shop on Eskildsgade, laughing his head off. I'm sure you can understand why an old copper like me isn't exactly proud of his sister running a brothel, but do you think the scum should get away with doing what he's done?"

"I've no idea why you're here, Bak. Have a word with City, or Marcus Jacobsen, or one of the other chiefs if you're not happy with the way the investigation's proceeding. Assault and vice aren't my field, you know that."

"I'm here to ask you and Assad to come with me and force a confession out of the fucker."

Carl felt his brow furrow all the way up to his hairline. Was the man out of his mind?

"You've just had a new case turn up. I'm sure you've noticed," Bak went on. "It's from me. Old mate of mine up in Hjørring passed it on to me a few months back. I left it in Rose's office last night."

Carl scrutinized the man as he considered his options. As far as he could make out, there were three.

He could get up and punch him in the mouth. That was one. Another would be to kick his arse all the way down the corridor. But Carl chose the third.

"Yeah, that's it, there," he said, pointing toward the nightmarish pile on the corner of his desk. "How come you didn't deliver it to me? It would have been less devious, I'd have thought. More honest."

Bak smiled briefly. "When did honesty ever lead to anything with us two? Nah, I just wanted to make sure someone other than you down here laid eyes on it, so it wouldn't mysteriously disappear. Know what I mean?"

The two other options became attractive again. A good thing this dick was no longer around on a daily basis.

"I've been saving that folder until the right moment came along," Bak continued. "Do you get my drift?"

"No, I fucking don't. What moment?"

"The moment when I need your help!"

"Don't think I'm going to cave some potential perp's skull in just because you're waving a thirty-year-old drowning in front of my nose. I'm not interested, and I'll tell you why."

Carl extended a finger into the air for each point he made.

"*One*: The case is time-barred. *Two*: It was an accident. My uncle drowned. He took a turn and fell in the river, exactly as the investigators concluded. *Three*: I wasn't there when it happened and neither was my cousin. *Four*: Unlike you, I'm a decent copper who doesn't go around beating up his suspects."

Carl paused for a moment, the last utterance lingering in his throat. As far as he knew, Bak couldn't possibly have anything on him of that kind. His expression certainly didn't indicate it to be the case.

"And *five*." He extended all five fingers, then clenched his fist. "If I ever *do* get nasty with anyone, it'll most likely be with a certain ex-cop who doesn't seem to get the fact that he's no longer on the force."

Bak's expression hardened at once. "OK. But let me tell you this. Former colleague of mine from Hjørring likes to go to Thailand. Two weeks in Bangkok with all the frills."

"So?" said Carl, wondering what that had to do with anything.

"It seems your cousin, Ronny, has similar tastes. Likes a drink as well, he does," Bak went on. "And you know what, Carl? When your cousin, Ronny, gets tanked up, he starts talking."

Carl suppressed a deep sigh. Ronny, that bloody idiot! Was he getting himself into trouble again? It had been ten years at least since they'd seen each other at a fateful confirmation party in Odder, on which occasion Ronny had claimed more than his fair share of not only the booze but also the girls who'd been helping out as waitresses. Which would have been OK if only one of them hadn't been rather too willing, underage, and sister to the confirmand. The scandal had been contained, though remained an indelible blight on the Odder branch of the family. No, Ronny wasn't exactly the retiring sort.

Carl waved his hand dismissively. What did he care about Ronny?

"Go upstairs to Marcus and sound off as much as you like, Bak, but you know him as well as I do. You'll get exactly the same thing out of him as you're getting out of me. We don't beat up suspects, and we don't give in to threats from former colleagues with old history like this."

Bak leaned back in the chair. "In this bar in Thailand, in the presence of witnesses, your cousin was boasting to anyone who cared to listen that he killed his dad."

Carl's eyes narrowed. It didn't sound plausible.

"Oh, he was, was he? So report him and his rat-arsed confession, if you want. I know for a fact he couldn't have drowned his dad. He was with me."

"He says you were both in on it. Nice relative you've got there."

The frown that had appeared on Carl's brow plunged at once to the bridge of his nose as he rose to his feet, summoning all his poorly distributed body weight into his chest region. "Assad! Get in here, will you?" he bellowed at maximum velocity into Bak's astonished face.

Ten seconds later, Carl's feverish assistant stood sniffling in the doorway.

"Assad, my dear, flu-ridden friend. Would you be so kind as to cough all over this idiot here? Go on, take a deep breath."

"What else have you got in that pile of yours, Rose?"

For a second she looked like she was considering dumping the lot into his lap, but for once Carl had read her correctly: something had already grabbed her attention.

"That business about the madam who got attacked last night made me think of a case we just got in from Kolding. It was in the stack I picked up over at NIC."

"Did you know the woman is Bak's sister?"

Rose nodded. "Don't really know him myself, but word gets round, doesn't it? Wasn't it him who was here just now?" She jabbed a finger at the case folder at the top of the file, then opened it with a flutter of black-painted nails. "Now listen up, Carl, otherwise you can read it yourself."

"OK, OK," said Carl, his gaze skating about her uncluttered gray-white office. He almost felt a twinge of sadness as his mind went back to her alter ego Yrsa's inferno of pink.

"This case here's about a woman called Rita Nielsen, 'stage name'"—Rose drew quotes in the air—"Louise Ciccone. That's what she was calling herself for a time in the eighties when she organized so-called"—more quotes—"'exotic dancing' at nightclubs in the Triangle region of southeast Jutland. Several convictions for fraud, later for procuring prostitutes and running a brothel. Owned an escort service in Kolding up through the seventies and eighties, after which she disappeared into thin air in Copenhagen in 1987. Mobile Unit concentrated its investigation on the porn scenes in mid-Jutland and Copenhagen, but after three months they shelved the case with the suggestion it was most likely a suicide. A lot of serious crimes had come up in the meantime, so they no longer had the manpower to carry on the investigation, so it says."

She laid the folder on the desk and put on a sour expression. "Shelved, just like the Esther Bak case last night will be, most probably. Have *you* seen anyone rushing around in a frenzy upstairs so they can nail the bastard who did that to the poor woman?"

Carl gave a shrug. The only frenzy he'd seen that morning had been the one that had appeared in his stepson Jesper's sullen face when he woke him up at seven o'clock and told him he'd have to make his own way to college in Gentofte.

"The way I see it, there's absolutely zero to indicate suicidal tendencies in this case," Rose continued. "Rita Nielsen gets into her flash white Mercedes 500SEC and leaves home just like any other day! A couple of hours later she's disappeared off the face of the earth, and that's that." She pulled out a photo and tossed it onto the desk in front of him. It showed the car parked at a curbside, its interior stripped.

What a motor. Room for half the tarts of Vesterbro to sprawl and wriggle on its hood in the fake furs they'd scrimped and saved for. A far cry from his hand-me-down service vehicle.

"The last anyone saw of her was on Friday the fourth of September 1987. Looking at her credit-card transactions we can follow her movements from the time she leaves her home address in Kolding at five in the morning. She drives across Fyn, where she fills up with petrol, takes the ferry over the Storebælt, and then carries on to Copenhagen, where she buys a pack of cigarettes in a kiosk on Nørrebrogade at ten past ten. No one sees her after that. The Mercedes turns up stripped a couple of days later on Kapelvej. Leather seats, spare wheel, radio-cassette, the lot. They even half-inched the steering wheel. All that was left basically was a couple of cassette tapes and some books in the glove compartment."

Carl scratched his chin. "There can't have been many shops with direct-debit terminals back then, certainly not a kiosk in Nørrebro. Why go to all the bother of paying by card? Most likely it'll have been a paper transaction, and all for a lousy pack of smokes. Who'd have the bloody patience?"

Rose shrugged. "Maybe she didn't like cash. Maybe she didn't like the feel of it. Maybe she liked having her money in the bank and letting others pay the interest. Maybe she only had a five-hundred-kroner note and the kiosk didn't have change. Maybe—"

"Yes, all right, Rose, that'll do." Carl held up his hands. "Just tell me one thing. How come they reckoned it was suicide? Was she seriously ill? Or perhaps she *was* in financial difficulties? Was that why she paid for her ciggies by card?"

Somewhere inside her drastically oversized gray sweater, which looked suspiciously like it had been knitted by Yrsa, Rose shrugged again. "Who knows? It's all a bit odd, if you ask me. Rita Nielsen, alias Louise Ciccone, was quite a prosperous lady, and if her dodgy CV's anything to go by she certainly wasn't one to be knocked off her perch. According to her 'girls' in Kolding she was hard as nails, a survivor. She'd rather wipe out the entire world than risk going down herself, one of them said."

"Hmm!" The feeling had planted itself firmly in Carl's psyche. It annoyed him, but his interest had been awakened. The questions were beginning to pop up, one after another. Like those cigarettes. Would a person buy cigarettes right before committing suicide? Well, maybe, to calm the nerves.

His mind was churning now, and he hadn't even asked for it. Bollocks! If he got started on this one, he'd have more work on his hands than was good for him.

"So, unlike many of our colleagues," he went on, "you think we're dealing with a crime here. But is there anything at all to back that up?" He left the question in the air for a moment. "Apart from the case being shelved rather than closed, what more have you got to go on?"

Another shrug from her sweater. It meant she had nothing.

Carl stared at the folder. The photo of Rita Nielsen that was paper-clipped to the front showed a woman who exuded considerable strength. Broad cheekbones above more delicate facial features. Eyes sparkling with spirit and defiance. It was obvious she didn't feel embarrassed by the mugshot board she held against her chest. It probably wasn't the first time she'd had her photo taken for the police archives. No, women like her were immune to prison sentences. She was a survivor, like her girls said.

Why on earth would she take her own life?

He pulled the folder toward him across the desk, opened it, and ignored Rose's told-you-so smile.

Once again, the kohl-eyed beanstalk had set a new case in motion.

2

November 2010

The green van came at 12:30 P.M. on the dot, exactly as agreed.

"Still got five calls to do today, Mr. Wad," the driver said. "I hope you've got everything ready for me."

He was a good man, Mikael. Ten years in the job without a single question. Good-looking, presentable, and polite. Just the kind of man the Purity Party wished to see representing it among the general public. It was men like Mikael who made others want to join. Quiet and reliable. Strong, blue eyes and wavy blond hair, always neat and tidy. Calm even in the most hectic of situations, like the fracas in Haderslev a month before at one of the party's inaugural meetings. On that occasion, nine protesters bearing offensive placards had learned the hard way that upstanding men whose hearts beat for the fatherland were a force to be reckoned with.

Thanks to people like Mikael, it was all over by the time the police turned up.

They wouldn't be seeing those demonstrators again in a hurry.

Curt Wad opened the door to what once had been the stables of an old village school. He pushed aside an old metal fitting that hung from the wall above a small freezer and entered his nine-character code into the display as he had done so many times before. He waited a moment until he heard the familiar click and the sections of the end wall slid open.

Inside the room that was now revealed were all the things he kept secret from everyone but his like-minded confidants. The deep freezer with its illegally aborted fetuses, the filing cabinets full of documents and membership lists, the laptop he used for conferences, and the notes and records from his father's era, on which all their work was founded.

Curt opened the freezer and pulled out a box containing plastic bags, which he handed directly to the driver. "Here are the fetuses we're cremating ourselves. I hope the freezer in the van isn't full."

The driver smiled. "No, still plenty of room."

"And here's the courier mail for our people. You'll see who it's for."

"Right," said the driver, skimming through the envelopes. "I'm afraid I won't be at Fredensborg again until next week. I did the Nordsjælland area yesterday."

"It's not that important. As long as you do Århus. You're over there tomorrow, aren't you?"

The driver nodded and peered into the plastic box. "I'll get rid of these. Have we any for Glostrup Crematorium?"

Curt Wad closed the sliding door of the secret room and went over to the freezer in the anteroom. Mikael was allowed to look in that one.

"Yes, we've these ones here," he replied, lifting the lid and taking out a second box.

He put the box on the floor and took a plastic folder from the shelf above the freezer. "The documents relating to these fetuses are here." He handed the folder to the driver. "It's all by the book."

The driver checked off each bag in the box against the accompanying documents. "All in good order. Shouldn't be any bother," he said, then carried it all out to the van, where he put the contents of the two boxes into two mini-freezers, sorted the internal mail into pigeonholes for the various organizational sections, doffed his cap, and politely took his leave.

Curt Wad raised his hand and waved as the van disappeared down Brøndbyøstervej.

How fortunate, he thought to himself with satisfaction, that I can still serve the cause even at my age.

"It's hard to believe you're eighty-eight," people told him repeatedly, and they were right. When he looked at himself in the mirror, he, too, could see how easily he might be taken for a man fifteen years younger. What was more, he knew why.

"Life is about living in harmony with one's ideals," was his father's motto. Words of wisdom he himself had always upheld. It had its costs, of course, but as long as the mind was bright, so was the flesh.

Curt crossed the garden and went in through the back door as always during consultation hours. When his successor in the clinic was at work, the front part of the house was no longer Curt's. That was the agreement. Besides, he had plenty to do getting the party on its feet. The days were gone when he personally screened pregnant mothers and terminated lives. His protégé did it just as well and was every bit as zealous.

He put some coffee into the machine, drawing a finger over the measuring scoop to make sure he used just the right amount. Beate's stomach had become so sensitive of late, so this was important.

"Coffee time, eh, Curt?"

Karl-Johan Henriksen appeared in the doorway of the kitchen. Like his mentor, he set store by his appearance, and his white doctor's coat was always washed and ironed. For no matter how unfamiliar one might be to one's patients, they would regard anyone in a well-laundered smock as an authority to whom they would readily entrust their lives. They were simpletons, one and all.

"Dodgy stomach, myself," said Henriksen, taking a glass from the cupboard. "Hot chestnuts, butter, and red wine are all well and good at the time, though seldom the next day."

He smiled, filled the glass with water, and emptied a packet of antacid into it.

"The driver was here, so both freezers are empty, Karl-Johan. You can start filling them up again now."

Curt smiled at his pupil, knowing his instructions were superfluous. Henriksen was perhaps even more efficient than Curt himself had ever been.

"I'm just about ready. Three terminations today. Two regular and one special." Henriksen smiled back. The contents of his glass sizzled.

"And that would be?"

"A Somali woman from the Tåstrupgård flats, referred by Bent Lyngsøe. Pregnant with twins, I believe," Henriksen said, raising his eyebrows briefly before downing his bubbling remedy.

Karl-Johan Henriksen was a good man, no doubt about it. For the party as well as for The Cause.

"Are you not feeling well today, Beate, my dear?" Wad inquired cautiously as he entered the living room with the tray.

It had been more than ten years since she had been able to speak, but she could still smile, at least. Although she had become terribly frail and the beauty of her youth had long since left her, Curt was unable to bear the thought that one day, probably soon, he would have to live on without her.

"May we both live to see the day the party's gratitude to you can be expressed from the platform of parliament," he murmured, taking her featherlight hand in his.

He lowered his head and kissed her hand gently, feeling it tremble in his. It was all he needed to do.

"Here, my love," he said, and raised the cup to her lips after blowing on the surface of its contents. "Not too hot, not too cold. Just the way you like it."

She pursed her sunken lips, the lips that had kissed him and their two children so lovingly when they had needed it most, and sipped slowly, without a sound. Her eyes revealed that the coffee was good. These eyes that had seen so much and in which his own gaze had found solace when on rare occasions he had been consumed by doubt.

"I'm going to be on television later today, Beate. With Lønberg and Caspersen. They'll try to nail us up against the wall if they can, but they won't succeed. Today we shall win votes and reap the rewards of decades of work. The votes of a great many people, Beate. People who think like us. The journalists will take us for three old wrinklies," he chuckled, "which I suppose we are. They'll believe our minds are unsound. They'll think they can catch us out, being incoherent, spouting rubbish." He stroked his hand across her hair. "I'll put the TV on, so you can watch."

Jakob Ramberger was a highly competent and well-prepared journalist. Anything else would have been unwise in light of the criticisms that had lately been leveled against so many toothless television interviews. A shrewd TV journalist feared his viewers more than his bosses. Ramberger was both shrewd and able. He had speared top politicians on live television and stripped union bosses, motorcycle gang leaders, irresponsible business executives, and sundry criminals to the skin.

For this reason Curt was delighted that they were to be interviewed by Ramberger, because this time, for once, he would fail to tear his interviewees apart, a fact that would be destined to attract attention in tiny Denmark.

Ramberger and his studio guests greeted one another politely in an anteroom where the journalist's colleagues were preparing upcoming news stories, but as soon as Ramberger had released his victims' hands, the two parties prepared for trench warfare.

"Curt Wad, you have submitted to the Ministry of Home Affairs that the Purity Party has now collected the requisite number of signatures to make it eligible to stand in the next parliamentary election," Ramberger began, after a less than flattering introduction. "Congratulations are in order, and yet in the same breath I'll ask you what you believe the Purity Party has to offer the Danish voter that he can't already find in the existing political parties."

"You say 'he,' and yet the majority of the electorate is comprised of women," Curt Wad rejoined with a smile. He nodded toward the camera. "But to answer your question: Has the Danish voter any choice but to reject the established parties of old?"

The interviewer fixed his gaze on him. "The Purity Party isn't exactly represented here by fresh-faced youngsters, is it? An average age of seventy-one, I believe, and you, Dr. Wad, pushing the figure up with your eighty-eight years. Hand on heart, don't you think that in your own case it might be forty or fifty years too late to seek influence in running the country?"

"As far as I recall, Denmark's most influential figure is almost ten years my senior," Wad rejoined. "Everyone in the country shops in his supermarkets, heats their homes with his natural gas, and buys goods transported by his ships. When you are man enough to invite the fine individual in question into your studio and ridicule him on account of his age, then you will be welcome to invite me in again and ask me the same question."

The journalist nodded. "What I'm getting at is simply that it's hard to see how the average voter might consider themselves adequately represented in parliament by men who are at least a generation or two older. No one buys milk past its sell-by date, do they?"

"Just as no one buys fruit as unripe as the politicians who govern us at present. I suggest we drop the foodstuff metaphor, Mr. Ramberger. Besides, none of the three of us here today harbors any intention of standing for election to the Folketing. Our program states quite unequivocally that we shall be convening a first general assembly once the requisite number of signatures has been collected, and that the party's parliamentary candidates will be selected by that assembly."

"Now that we're on the subject of the party's program, the main thrust seems to concern moral norms, ideas, and ideologies that lead the mind back to an age most of us would be loath to return to. To political regimes that deliberately persecute minorities and society's weak: the mentally handicapped, ethnic minorities, the socially disenfranchised."

"But this is a fallacy; there's no comparison at all," Lønberg interjected. "On the contrary, our program is about assessing from a responsible and humanitarian point of view each individual case on its own terms and refraining from lumping things together in such a way as to preclude effective and comprehensive solutions. For that reason, our slogan is simple: *Change for the Better*. Change of quite a different nature from what you are suggesting here."

The interviewer smiled. "That all sounds well and good, but of course it presupposes that the party gets as far as gaining influence. Let me go on. This isn't my own allegation, but the newspapers have been full of articles concerning the Purity Party's platform, the main thrust being that its most obvious corollary would be the kind of racial anthropology that informed the programs of the National Socialists in Germany. Ossified dogmas in which the world is construed as comprising genetically different peoples in eternal conflict with each other. The notion of higher and lower races, the higher race being—"

"The higher race being wiped out if mixed with a lower one," Caspersen interrupted. "I sense that both you and the newspapers have been googling Nazism, Mr. Ramberger," he continued. "But our party does not condone discrimination, injustice, or inhumanity as the Nazis and like-minded parties once did and still do. On the contrary, we say only that we ought not to prolong life in cases where it has not the remotest chance of becoming even reasonably dignified. There has to be a limit to how much coercion doctors and ordinary citizens should be willing to accept from the authorities. A limit to how much suffering may be inflicted upon families, and how great a cost society is made to pay, simply because our politicians interfere in everything without making themselves aware of the consequences of their meddling."

The ensuing debate was long, followed by a phone-in where members of the public raised a whole variety of issues: compulsory sterilization of criminals and those who on account of mental illness or low intelligence were unable to take care of their offspring; social measures to strip families with large numbers of children of a range of benefits; criminalization of procuring the sexual services of prostitutes; closing national borders; denying entry into the country of uneducated immigrants, and a lot more besides.

Discussion was heated. Many viewers were unusually incensed, but just as many were appreciative of the viewpoints they had heard.

The program had indeed been a profitable exercise for the party.

"The decision-makers of tomorrow will be people of our own strength and conviction," said Caspersen on the drive home.

"Nothing ever stays the same," said Lønberg. "Let's just hope we've made an impression today."

"We most certainly have." Caspersen laughed. "You, Curt, definitely did."

Curt knew what Caspersen was thinking about. The journalist had asked Wad if it was correct that he had been taken to task by the authorities on various occasions over the years. The question had angered him, though he hadn't shown it. Instead he replied that if a doctor with a capable pair of hands and a good head on his shoulders did not at some point in his career find himself at odds with fundamental ethical principles, then he was not worthy of his role as God's obedient servant.

Lønberg smiled. "That shut Ramberger up for a minute, at least."

Wad did not return his smile. "The answer I gave was foolish. I was lucky he didn't pursue the matter further. We must be on constant guard as to what they might dig up. Are you listening? Give it the slightest morsel, and the press will do everything in its power to bring us down. We cannot expect to have any friends outside our own ranks. The present situation is exactly the same for us as it was for the Upsurge Party and the Denmark Party when no one reckoned with them. We can only hope the press and the politicians allow us as much leeway to establish ourselves as they did in those cases."

Caspersen frowned. "I can't see us not getting in at the next election, but it's no-holds-barred until we do. You both know my stance, of course. Even if it means sacrificing our commitment to The Cause, it will be worth it."

Wad studied him. Every group had its Judas. Caspersen was known for his work as a lawyer and from local politics, so with his organizational experience he certainly had his place among them. But the day he began to count his pieces of silver he would be finished. Wad would make sure of it.

No one interfered in the work of The Cause without his express permission.

Beate was sitting in front of the TV screen, where he had positioned her when he left. All the home help had needed to do was change her and make sure she had something to drink.

He stood for a moment and considered her from a distance. The way the light from the crystal chandelier fell made her look like she had diamonds sparkling in her hair. Her expression had an ethereal quality, like the first time she had danced for him. Perhaps she was dreaming of other days, when her life still lay ahead of her.

"Did you see the debate, my angel?" he asked in a soft voice, so as not to startle her.

Beate smiled for a second, though her gaze still seemed distant. He knew the lucid moments were few. That the brain hemorrhage was like a wedge between Beate's soul and the life that surrounded her. And yet he sensed she might have understood just a little.

"I'll put you to bed now. It's way past your time."

He picked up her fragile frame in his arms. When they were young he had lifted her up like a snowflake. Then came years when his strength had not sufficed against the ampleness of the mature woman. But now he again lifted her as though she weighed nothing at all.

He wondered if this ought to make him glad, but it didn't, and when he put her down on the bed he trembled. How quickly she closed her eyes now. Almost before she touched the pillow.

"I see it, my dear. Life ebbing out. Our turn soon to come."

When he returned to the living room he switched off the television, went over to the antique sideboard, and poured himself a brandy.

"In ten years I'll still be alive, Beate, I promise," he said to himself. "Before we meet again, all our visions will be fulfilled."

He nodded and emptied the glass in one.

"And no one, my dear, will stop us. No one."

3

November 1985

The first thing she registered was the foreign object in her nose. That, and the voices above her. Subdued voices, but authoritative. Gentle and mild.

Behind her closed eyelids, her eyes rolled in her head as though seeking a place in which to find greater awareness. Then she drifted once more into unconsciousness, wrapping herself into the darkness and the calm of her breathing, images of blissful summer and unworried play.

And then the pain struck hard, from the middle of her spine and down.

A spasm jerked back her head and everything in her lower body compacted in one long, agonizing discharge.

"We'll give her five notches more," said a voice, disappearing into a foggy distance, leaving her in the same void as before.

Nete was loved from the moment she was born. The family's little afterthought and the only girl in a flock of siblings who, despite lack of means, were never left wanting.

Her mother's hands were good and able. Hands that caressed and took care of domestic chores, and Nete became her mirror. Tartan skirt and a gleam in her eye, poking her finger into everything that took place on the small farm.

When she was four years old her father led a stallion into the yard and smiled as the oldest of her brothers walked the mare across the cobbles.

The twin boys sniggered as the stallion's long member began to quiver under its belly, and Nete drew back when the great beast mounted their sweet little Molly and thrust itself inside her.

She wanted to yell at it to make it stop, but her father grinned toothlessly and said that soon they'd be a draft animal the better for it.

Later, Nete understood that life often begins as dramatically as it can end, and the art is in doing one's best to enjoy what comes between.

"It's had a good life," her father always said when he put the knife to the throat of a writhing pig. He said the same about Nete's mother when she lay in her coffin, only thirty-eight years old.

The words weighed heavily on Nete's mind when she eventually awoke in the hospital bed and glanced around in the darkness, bewildered.

Blinking lights and apparatus surrounded her. She recognized nothing.

Then she turned her body. Ever so slightly, yet the effect was astonishing. Her head jerked back, her lungs expanded suddenly with air that caused her larynx to erupt.

She didn't perceive the screams as her own, for the pain in her legs made everything else immaterial. But the screams were there.

A door was flung open, and suddenly all was tumultuous light, flickering like fluorescent tubing, and resolute hands at work upon her body.

"Just relax now, Nete," said a voice, and then came the injection, soothing words, only this time she did not succumb to sleep.

"Where am I?" she asked, as her lower body drifted away into warmth that felt almost shimmering.

"You're in the hospital in Nykøbing Falster, Nete. And you're in good hands."

In a glimpse she saw the nurse turn her head toward her colleague and
raise her eyebrows.

That was when she remembered what had happened.

They pulled the oxygen tube from her nostrils and brushed back her
hair. As though she were being made ready to receive her sentence: that
life was over.

Three doctors stood at the foot of her bed when the consultant conveyed the news, gray eyes beneath trimmed eyebrows. "Your husband
was killed instantaneously, Mrs. Rosen," were the first words to pass his
lips. "We're so sorry" came only much later. It was a matter of putting
the right facts in the right places. Andreas Rosen was presumed to have
been killed by the cylinder block that had slammed into the driver's seat
on impact. Instead of helping him, a man beyond aid, rescuers had concentrated on extricating Nete from the vehicle, and the work of the emergency unit had been exemplary. He shaped this last word as though she
ought to smile when he said it.

"We've saved your legs, Nete. Most likely you'll walk with a limp, but
that's a lot better than the alternative."

And with that she stopped listening.

Andreas was dead.

Dead, without her having joined him on the other side, and now she
would have to live on without him. The only man she had ever loved
completely. The only person who had ever made her feel whole.

And now she had killed him.

"She's dozing off now," said one of the other doctors, but it wasn't
true. She was merely turning inward, to the place where despair, defeat,
and their reasons all merged into one and Curt Wad's face flared as clear
as the flames of hell.

Had it not been for him, everything in her life would have been different.

Curt Wad and the others.

Nete bridled the screams and tears that ought to have been given free rein, and promised herself that before she had given up her hold on life they would all be made to pay for everything of which they had robbed her.

She heard the footsteps as they left the room to continue the round. Even now she was forgotten, their attention already turned to others.

After they buried Nete's mother, the tone in the house became coarser. Nete was five years old and quick to learn. The word of God belonged to Sunday, her father said. And Nete learned vocabulary other girls did not encounter until later in life. The collaborators in Odense who worked for the German occupiers, repairing their equipment, were "filthy shitty-arsed swine," those who abetted them were "effin' bastards." In their house, a spade was now a spade, and "fuck" was a word like any other.

If people wanted to talk nice, they could go somewhere else.

On her first day at school Nete found out what a slap in the face felt like. Sixty pupils were lined up in rows outside the building, Nete at the front.

"I never seen so many bleedin' children!" she exclaimed out loud, thereby incurring the permanent wrath and resentment of the mistress as well as the effective lash of her right hand.

Later, when the blush on her cheek had become a bruise, she related, at the encouragement of a pair of lads of confirmation age, how her older brothers had told her boys could jiggle their dicks and make them squirt.

That same evening she sat crying in the parlor, trying to explain to her father where the marks on her face came from.

"No doubt you deserved it," said her father, and that was the end of it. He had been up since three in the morning and now he was tired. He had been so ever since the eldest son had found an apprenticeship in Birkelse and the twins had joined a fishing boat up at Hvide Sande.

Subsequently, the school's complaints about Nete would come in occasional bursts, though her father never took them seriously.

And little Nete understood none of it.

A week after the accident, one of the young nurses came to her bedside and asked if anyone should be contacted.

"I think you're the only one on the ward who doesn't get visitors," she said. Most likely it was meant to entice her out of the silent shell into which she had retreated, but all it did was make it more resilient.

"No, there's no one," Nete told her, and asked to be left alone.

That same evening a young lawyer from Maribo came and said he was the curator of her husband's estate and that he would soon be needing some signatures so that legal matters could get under way. He said nothing of her injuries.

"Have you thought about whether you'll be continuing your husband's business, Nete?" he inquired, as though it were something that had already been discussed.

She shook her head. How could he even consider that? She was a laboratory assistant. She had met her husband as an employee of his company in that very capacity. The matter was pursued no more.

"Will you be able to come to the funeral tomorrow?" he asked.

Nete bit on her lower lip. She felt her breathing stop, and the world with it. The light on the ceiling was suddenly far too bright.

"The funeral?" she repeated. The words were as much as she could muster.

"Yes. Your husband's sister, Tina, has made the arrangements along with our firm of lawyers. Your husband's wishes were already known to us: the service will be at Stokkemarke Church tomorrow at one o'clock. He asked for it to be a quiet occasion, so only those closest will be in attendance."

It was all she could bear to hear.

4

November 2010

The new phone in Assad's office was in a league of its own, ear-splittingly reminiscent of clanging Bohemian church bells, and if Assad wasn't there to answer it, the racket went on for an age before eventually dying out. Twice Carl had asked him to get rid of the infuriating contraption, but Assad maintained that the phone he'd had before was defective, and since he had this one lying around anyway, there was no sense in not putting it to use.

A person's worst enemies are among his friends, Carl thought, when the phone once again gave him the fright of his life, sending a jolt through his body that caused his legs to momentarily leave their resting place on the extended bottom drawer of his desk.

"I thought I told you to get rid of that bloody thing!" he yelled, as the mumble of Assad's voice reached him across the corridor.

"Didn't you hear me?" he inquired, when the sniffling moon of his assistant's face appeared in the doorway.

Assad didn't reply. Perhaps the inconvenience of his superior's question had prompted his ears to clog up.

"That was Bak on the phone," he said instead. "He says he is standing on Eskildsgade outside the basement flat where the Lithuanian who attacked his sister lives."

"What? Børge Bak? I hope you hung up on him, Assad!"

"No, he hung up on himself. But not before he said that if we did not come, it would be worst for yourself, Carl."

"For me? What was he doing calling you, then?"

Assad shrugged. "I was here last night when he came down and left the folder in Rose's office. His sister has been attacked, you know that, do you not?"

"You don't say."

"He told me he knew who did it, and I said that if it was me I would not stand around and do nothing."

Carl stared into his assistant's bleary dark eyes. What was inside that head of his? Camel's wool?

"For God's sake, Assad! He's not on the force anymore. In this country we call that taking the law into your own hands. It's a criminal offense. Do you know what that means? It means free board and lodging at Her Majesty's bed and breakfast. And when they let you out again there's nothing left to go back to. Adios, amigo."

"I am not familiar with this establishment you mention, Carl. And why are you talking about food now? I cannot eat a thing when I'm so cold."

Carl shook his head. "When you've *got* a cold, Assad. The expression is to *have* a cold." Had it now gone to his vocabulary?

Carl reached for his phone and pressed the number of the homicide chief, only to discover Jacobsen to be likewise bunged up.

"Yeah, all right," he said, when Carl informed him of Bak's call. "Bak was here in my office at eight this morning, wanting his old job back. Just a min—"

Carl counted eight sneezes in quick succession before the poor sod returned to the phone. Yet another infected area Carl would be giving a wide berth.

"The thing is, Bak's probably right. This Lithuanian, Linas Verslovas, has a conviction for a similar assault in Vilnius, and there's no doubt his income comes from prostitution. Unfortunately, we can't prove it at the moment," Jacobsen went on.

"OK. I heard on the police radio that she's saying she can't identify who attacked her, but I suppose we can assume she told her brother."

"Well, he swears she didn't. However, she's had trouble with this Verslovas before, and Bak knew that for certain."

"So now the former Børge Bak's snooping around Vesterbro, playing policeman."

There was another fit of sneezing at the other end. "Maybe you should get out there and talk some sense into him, Carl. We owe that much to an old colleague, at least."

"Do we?" Carl shot back, but Jacobsen had already terminated the call. Even a homicide chief could be forced to capitulate to nasal congestion.

"What now, Carl?" Assad asked, as if he hadn't already worked it out. He was already standing there in his mausoleum of a down jacket. "I told Rose we will be away for a few hours, but she heard nothing. She has only this Rita Nielsen in her head."

Funny bloke, Assad. How could he even consider venturing out on a sopping wet day in November in his state of health? Was there something wrong with his genes? Had the drifting sands of the desert engulfed his senses?

Carl sighed and picked up his coat from the chair.

"Just one thing," he said, as they trudged up the stairs. "How come you were here so early this morning? Four o'clock, a little bird tells me."

Carl had been expecting some simple explanation along the lines of: "I was Skyping with my uncle. It's the best time for him." Instead he got eyes that implored, like a man about to be subjected to all manner of torment.

"It doesn't matter, Carl," he said, but Carl wasn't the sort to let things go. "It doesn't matter" was crap people said when things mattered a lot. Along with such effervescent expressions as "Absolutely!" and "Awesome!," it was more than enough to put Carl in a very bad mood indeed.

"If you want to raise the standard of our future dialogues, Assad, I suggest you prick up your ears. When I ask you something, it *always* matters."

"Do *what* with my ears, Carl?"

"Just answer me, Assad," Carl replied with annoyance, pulling on his coat. "What were you doing here so early this morning? Is it to do with your family?"

"Yes, that is it."

"Listen, Assad. If you're having trouble with the wife, it's none of my business. And if it's because you're Skyping with that uncle of yours, or whoever the hell he happens to be, there's no need for you to be here at the crack of dawn, surely? Haven't you got a computer at home for that sort of thing?"

"Cracker dawn?"

Carl's arm got stuck in his sleeve. "For Chrissake, Assad! It's a figure of speech. Have you got a computer at home, or what?"

Assad gave a shrug. "Not at the moment. It's all difficult to explain, Carl. Can we not move on to Børge Bak now?"

Back at the beginning of time, when Carl would put on his white gloves and set off on his beat in that same part of Vesterbro, people would hang out of the windows of run-down tenements, baiting him in their flat Copenhagen dialect. Coppers like him from Jutland could get back in their wooden shoes and sod off to the hinterland where they belonged. At the time it had been a shock to him, but now he yearned for it. As he stood there, looking around at the neighborhood where talentless architects had deluded brainless local politicians into plastering the streets with ugly concrete blocks not even social class 5 could think of as home, it was an era that seemed light-years away. These days, people only lived here as a last resort. It was as simple as that. The residents of former times had been forced out into something even less desirable in Ishøj and other godforsaken outposts, where they now sat reminiscing about the good old days.

No, if you wanted to see classic redbrick buildings with cornices and sooty chimneys, you'd have a bloody job these days in the side streets off Istedgade. But if what you were looking for were concrete shells, baggy-arsed tracksuits, and junkies with empty sockets for eyes you'd come to the right place. Here were Nigerian pimps alongside East European con artists, and even the most humble and bizarre forms of crime found a fertile breeding ground.

More than anyone else in the homicide division, Børge Bak had served his time in these streets. He knew the dangers, the pitfalls, and the rules, one of which was that you never on any account entered an enclosed space around here without backup.

Now Carl and Assad stood in the pissing rain, analyzing this miserable, barren cityscape, and Bak was nowhere in sight. Which indicated he must have fallen foul.

"He said he would wait for us," said Assad, pointing to the basement steps of what had once been a shop and was now a vandalized ruin with whitewashed windows.

"Are you sure of the address?"

"As sure as eggs is eggs, Carl."

Carl stared at him incredulously, wondering where the hell he could have picked up a saying like that, then collected himself and turned to read the sun-bleached note in the window of the basement. *Kaunas Trading/Linas Verslovas*, it read. Innocuous enough, but firms like that tended to die as quickly as they were born, and more often than not their owners were shadier than a hundred-year-old tree in summer.

In the car Assad had quoted from Linas Verslovas's record. He had been pulled into HQ on several occasions, only to be released again. The man was described as a ruthless psychopath with a remarkable ability to talk gullible Eastern Europeans into taking the blame for his scummy activities in exchange for a pittance. Vestre Prison was full of them.

Carl tried the handle and gave the door a shove. A bell jingled as it opened to reveal a rectangular room containing absolutely nothing but packing materials and crumpled newspaper left behind by the previous occupant.

As they entered, they heard a dull thud from the back room. It sounded like the thump of a fist, but without the usual groan that followed.

"Bak," Carl called out, "are you in there?" He put his hand to his holster and made ready to draw his pistol and disengage the safety.

"I'm OK," said a voice from behind the flimsy, battered door.

Carl pushed it open with caution and assessed the sight he encountered.

Both men were beaten up, but the wiry Lithuanian was the worse off. The dragon tattoo that snaked around his throat and neck was set off by bruising, making it seem almost three-dimensional.

Carl felt his face contract into a grimace. He was glad someone else had been on the receiving end.

"What the hell are you doing here, Bak? Have you lost your mind, or what?"

"He stabbed me." Bak jerked his head toward the floor where a knife lay, its blade covered in blood. One of those vicious switchblades, the kind of thing that made Carl's stomach turn. If it was up to him, getting caught with one of those would cost a bundle in fines.

"You OK?" he asked, and Bak nodded.

"Flesh wound in the arm, I'll be all right. Fending off attack, so you can call it self-defense in the report," he said, then hammered his fist so suddenly against the bridge of the Lithuanian's nose that it made Assad jump.

"Arh, fuck you!" the pimp groaned, with an obvious accent. Carl stepped forward to intervene. "You saw that! I didn't do fuck all. Like when he came barging in. He came up and hit me. What was I supposed to do?" the Lithuanian lamented. He was hardly more than twenty-five years old and already up to his neck in shite.

Additional stuttered sentences from the mouth of the sinewy man proclaimed his total innocence. He knew nothing about any attack on anyone in any brothel. Indeed he had already told this to the police a thousand times.

"Come on, Bak, we're leaving. NOW!" Carl commanded, prompting Bak to follow up with another fist in the Lithuanian's face, knocking him backward over a table.

"He's not getting away with what he did to my sister." Bak turned to Carl, every fiber in his face tensed. "Do you realize she's going to lose her sight in one eye? That one side of her face is going to be scar tissue? This little scumbag's coming with us. Do you read me, Carl?"

"If you keep this up, Bak, I'm going to call City for assistance. In which case you'll have to take the punches as they come," Carl cautioned, and meant it.

Assad shook his head. "One moment," he said, stepping around his superior and yanking Bak aside so violently that a seam burst in the man's ubiquitous leather jacket.

"Get this crazy Arab away from me!" the Lithuanian screamed as Assad grabbed him and hauled him toward another door at the rear of the room.

The Lithuanian filled the air with threats. Everyone in the room was as good as dead if they didn't get the hell out immediately. Their stomachs would be split open and their heads torn off. Threats that would normally be taken seriously when issued by a man like him. Threats that were enough on their own to get him thrown into jail.

But Assad gripped the man's collar so hard that his invective could no longer escape his throat. He flung open the door of the back room and bundled the Lithuanian inside.

Bak and Carl exchanged glances as Assad kicked back his heel and the door slammed shut.

"Assad! You're not to kill him in there, do you understand?" Carl shouted, just to be on the safe side.

The silence was deafening.

Bak smiled, and it was obvious why, for Carl's options were all gone. There'd be no brandishing of the pistol now, no calls to Station City. He wasn't about to risk putting his assistant in an awkward position, and Bak knew it.

"Worried now, are you, Carl?" Bak nodded smugly to himself, then rolled up his sleeve to inspect the gash in his lower arm. He'd need a couple of stitches, but that was all. He produced a dirty handkerchief from his pocket and tied it tightly around the wound. Carl thought that probably wasn't a good idea, but who was he to intervene? A bout of blood poisoning might teach Bak some hygiene.

"Don't forget I know all about your past, Carl. You and Anker knew better than anyone how to squeeze shite out of swine. You were a right pair, the two of you. If Hardy hadn't joined you, you'd have ended up in the shit sooner or later, so leave out the holier-than-thou crap, all right?"

Carl glanced toward the back room. What the hell was Assad up to in there? He turned to Bak. "You know fuck all, Bak. I don't know what you're basing your assumptions on, but be sure of one thing: you've got it all wrong."

"I've been asking around, Carl. It's a miracle how you got away without disciplinary proceedings. Got to hand it to you, though, the two of you certainly knew how to get results out of your interrogations. Maybe that would explain it." He rolled his sleeve down. "I'd like my job back at HQ. I think you should help me on that one," he said. "I know Marcus is a bit reluctant, but it's common knowledge he listens to you. Christ knows why."

Carl shook his head. If sense of occasion was hereditary, the gene was completely absent from Bak's DNA.

He walked forward and opened the door of the back room.

The sight that met him was tranquil, to say the least. The Lithuanian was seated on the edge of a table, staring at Assad as though hypnotized. The face that had been so twisted and embittered now exuded the utmost gravity. It was a face washed clean of blood, and the man's shoulders had assumed a more normal latitude.

He got to his feet on a nod from Assad and walked past Bak and Carl without so much as a glance. Silently, he picked up a duffel bag from the floor, went over to a cupboard, and pulled out a drawer from which he took a few items of clothing, shoes, and a small bundle of banknotes, all of which he tossed into the bag.

Assad watched the man without speaking, red-nosed and runny-eyed, not obviously a sight that would frighten anyone.

"Can I have it now?" the Lithuanian asked.

Two photos and a wallet changed hands.

Verslovas opened the wallet and searched its compartments. They contained a fair amount of money as well as credit cards.

"Give me the driving license as well," he said, but Assad shook his head. The matter was already closed.

"Then I'm gone," said the Lithuanian. Bak was about to intervene, but Assad shook his head. He had this under control.

"You've got thirty hours, and not one second more! Do you understand?" Assad said with composure. The Lithuanian nodded.

"Hey, hang on a minute! You can't just let him go, for Chrissake!"

Bak protested, only to stop when Assad turned toward him and spoke calmly.

"He's *my* man now, Bak, can't you see? You don't think about him anymore, are you with me?"

Bak's face went white for a moment before the color returned. Assad exuded the air of a hydrogen bomb that had just been armed and prepared for release. The case was out of Bak's hands, and there was nothing he could do.

The last they saw of the Lithuanian as he opened the door was his dragon tattoo and the shoe he almost lost in the hurry. The transformation was total. The veneer scraped away. What was left was a boy of twenty-five, running for his life.

"Now you can tell your sister you have avenged her," Assad sniffled. "You will never see this man again, I promise you!"

Carl frowned, but said nothing until they were outside on the pavement by the car.

"What happened in there, Assad?" he asked. "What did you do to him? And what was all that about thirty hours?"

"I took him by the scruff of the neck, Carl, and mentioned some names. Names of people who could be let loose on him and his family if he did not leave the country immediately. I told him I did not care what he did now, but that he should hide himself away very carefully if they were not to find him." Assad nodded. "But they will, if they so wish."

There were years of accumulated distrust in the look Bak sent Assad. "There's only one thing people like him respect, and that's the Russian mafia," said Bak. "And you're not going to tell me you've got a say there." He waited for Assad's answer, but none was forthcoming. "Which means you've let him off scot-free, you idiot."

Assad tipped his head to one side and peered at Bak with bleary eyes. "I think you should say to your sister that everything is sorted now. Should we not be getting back, Carl? I feel the need for a cup of hot tea."

5

November 2010

Carl's gaze wavered back and forth between the case folder on his desk and the flatscreen on the wall. Neither was particularly appealing. On TV2's news channel the foreign minister teetered about on her high heels, trying to look competent while tame journalists nodded and deferred to the daggers in her eyes, and on the desk in front of him lay the folder concerning his uncle's drowning in 1978.

It was like choosing between plague and cholera.

He scratched behind his ear and closed his eyes. What a bloody awful day. Nowhere near as inactive and unstructured as he had hoped.

There was a whole meter of new unresolved cases on the shelf, two of which had already captured Rose's imagination. In particular the one about Rita Nielsen, the brothel owner who had disappeared in Copenhagen. It was a state of affairs that did not bode well. But to make matters worse, Assad was in his cubbyhole on the other side of the corridor, sniffling snot back up his nose every seven seconds and emitting multitudes of bacteria into the communal air. The man was at death's door, yet less than an hour and a half ago he'd smacked a hardened criminal up against a wall and issued threats so definitive the guy had fled for his life with terror written all over his face. What the hell was it with this Assad? Even his old mate Anker, who could scare the shit out of just about anyone, had been a Boy Scout by comparison.

And then there was the sudden echo from Carl's past. Why had his cousin, Ronny, been sounding off in a bar in Thailand about his uncle's death not being an accident, when Carl knew for a fact it was? And how come Ronny had claimed he had killed his father himself, when Carl knew he couldn't have? He and Carl had been together, ogling two pairs of tits up on Hjørringvej when it occurred, so it couldn't possibly have been Ronny. And now here Bak was, telling him Ronny had said *Carl* had been in on it.

Carl shook his head. He killed the TV images of the smug, empty-headed firebrand of a foreign minister and grabbed the phone.

He made four calls to four numbers, all in vain. He ran a check with the Civil Registration Office, then another couple of calls that were just as fruitless as the first. Ronny seemed to have an uncanny knack of being swallowed into oblivion by society's ever-accumulating piles of dross.

He'd have to get Lis onto it. She could find the scumbag for him, wherever the fuck he'd hidden himself.

Thirty seconds of busy tone followed before Carl got to his feet in annoyance, his entire system clogging up with frustration. What the hell were they doing upstairs that stopped them answering the phone?

On his way up to the third floor he encountered several red-nosed individuals all looking like death warmed up. The bloody flu was all over the place. He held his hand in front of his face as he passed. "Get thee behind me, satanic virus," he muttered to himself, nodding politely to coughing and sneezing colleagues with watery eyes and expressions so pained anyone would have thought the world was about to end.

Upstairs in homicide, however, all was quiet as the grave. As though all the killers the department's investigators had snapped into handcuffs over the years had joined forces to strike back with biological weaponry. The department's name suddenly seemed apt indeed. Had they all been wiped out, or what?

No steamingly libidinous Lis behind the counter with her flirty, flamingo-like poise, and even more surprisingly, no Ms. Sørensen, the miserable cow who only ever got up to go to the toilet.

"Where the hell is everyone?" he bellowed, making even the staplers rattle.

"All right, keep your fucking hair on, Carl," came a voice from an open door, halfway down the corridor.

Carl poked his head into the chaotic office whose timeworn furniture and mountains of documents made his own tip in the basement look like a luxury suite on a cruise liner.

He nodded to the head that was only barely visible behind the mounds of paper and repeated his question before Terje Ploug raised his flu-plagued face to peer at him.

"Where the hell is everyone? Have they all gone down in the epidemic?"

The reply said it all. Five well-delivered sneezes in quick succession, followed by assorted coughs and splutters, snot streaming from the man's nostrils.

"O-K!" said Carl, with emphasis on the second syllable, and stepped back.

"Lars Bjørn's in the briefing room with one of the teams and Marcus is out in the field," Ploug proffered between sniffles. "But now you're here, Carl, we've got a new lead in the nail-gun case. I was just about to give you a call."

"You don't say." Carl removed his gaze from the man's beacon of a nose, and his eyes drifted out of focus. It already seemed an age since he, Anker, and Hardy had been shot in that run-down shed in Amager. Would he ever be able to stop thinking about it?

"That allotment garden house where the three of you got hit after you found Georg Madsen with a nail fired into his brain was pulled down this morning," Ploug said drily.

"About time, and all." Carl stuck his hands in his pockets. They felt sticky.

"The bulldozers were very thorough. Took away the topsoil down to the clay."

"So what did they find?" Carl asked, already loath to hear more. Bastard case.

"A wooden box knocked together with Paslode nails. Inside was a sack containing body parts in various states of decay. They turned it up an hour ago and made the call straightaway. Marcus is out there now with the SOCOs."

Bollocks. He and Hardy would have no peace for a while yet.

"There's not much doubt this one's connected with the murders of Georg Madsen and those other two in Sorø who were done in with a nail gun, too," Ploug went on, dabbing his streaming eyes with a handkerchief that by rights ought to have been incinerated under expert supervision.

"And what makes you think that?"

"Whoever it was, there was a relatively long nail buried in his skull."

Carl nodded. Just like the others. It was a reasonable deduction.

"I'd like you to go with me to the scene in half an hour."

"Me? What for? It's not my case anymore."

If the expression on Terje Ploug's face was anything to go by, Carl could just as well have said that from now on he was going to wear nothing but pink camel-wool sweaters and deal only with cases involving three-legged Dalmatians.

"Marcus is of a different opinion," was all Ploug said.

Of course it was Carl's case, too. A pale scar at his temple reminded him of it on a daily basis. The brand of Cain that told of cowardice and an inability to act decisively at the most crucial moment of his life.

Carl passed his eyes over Ploug's walls. They were covered with photos from crime scenes, enough to fill a medium-sized packing case.

"OK," he said eventually. "But I'll drive myself," he added, an octave lower than normal. No way was he going to ride shotgun in Ploug's bacteriological blender. He'd even prefer to walk.

"What on earth are you doing here?" inquired Ms. Sørensen from behind the counter, when Carl passed by the secretaries' domain a few moments later, his head spinning with images from the fateful day when Anker lost his life and Hardy his mobility.

In an odd, portentous sort of way, her voice seemed almost mild and accommodating. Carl turned slowly, sarcastic jibes honed and ready to counter.

She was only a couple of meters away and yet she looked different somehow. He could just as easily have been looking at a dot in the distance.

It wasn't because she was dressed any differently than usual. She still looked like she'd wandered blindfolded into a secondhand shop. But her eyes, and her normally dry, now rather short hair, shone and glistened like patent leather shoes at a ball. Worst of all, two red blotches now spread across her cheeks, signaling not only excellent blood circulation, but also, and more alarmingly, that there might be more life in her than he had thought.

"Nice to see you," she said. As if life wasn't surreal enough as it was.

"Hmm," Carl grunted. Who would dare say more? "Don't suppose you know where Lis has got to? Is she ill like everyone else?" he asked with caution, prepared to be showered with invective and bile.

"She's over in the briefing room taking down notes, but she'll be down in the archive later. Do you want me to tell her to pop by?"

Carl swallowed. Did she say "pop by"? Did he really just hear Ilse the She-Devil, alias Ms. Sørensen, use such a breezy expression?

In this moment of bewilderment he sent her a crumpled smile and steered purposefully toward the stairwell.

———

"Yes, boss," Assad sniffled. "What did you wish to speak to me about?"

Carl's eyes narrowed. "It's very simple, Assad. You're going to tell me exactly what happened in that back room on Eskildsgade."

"What happened? Only that the man pricked up his ears."

"I see. But why, Assad? Who and what did you threaten him with? You don't frighten the pants off a hard-case villain from the Baltics by reading him Hans Christian Andersen's fairy tales, do you?"

"Oh, but they can be terrifying. Think for example about the one with the girl and the poisoned apple . . ."

Carl gave a sigh. "Andersen didn't write *Snow White*, Assad, OK? Now, who did you threaten him with?"

Assad hesitated, before taking a deep breath and looking Carl straight in the eye. "I just told him I was keeping his driving license so as to fax it on to some people I worked with before, and that he should go home to his family and get them away from their house, because if there was anyone home when my contacts came, or if he was still in Denmark at that time, the house would go up in smoke."

"The house would go up in smoke? Do you know what, I don't think we should mention that to anyone, Assad, are you with me?" Carl paused demonstratively, but Assad's gaze didn't waver.

"But the guy believed you, so it seems," Carl went on. "Why would he do that? Who did you tell him you were going to send that fax to? Who was he so afraid of?"

Assad pulled a folded piece of paper out of his pocket. Carl saw Linas Verslovas's name as Assad unfolded it. Beneath the name was a rather unflattering photo, albeit a good likeness, plus a few brief details and a lot of gibberish in a language Carl failed to recognize.

"I pulled some information before we went and 'had a word' with the man," Assad explained, scratching quotation marks in the air. "It's from some friends of mine in Vilnius. They can go into the police archives when they want."

Carl frowned.

"Are you saying you got this from people in Lithuanian intelligence?"

Assad nodded, detaching a dribble of snot from the tip of his nose.

"And these people read you a translation over the phone?"

Another dribble.

"I see. Not the most uplifting reading, I imagine. And then you threatened this Linas Verslovas with the secret police, or whatever they call themselves, saying they'd carry out reprisals against his family? Did he really have reason to believe they would?"

Assad shrugged.

Carl reached across the desk and pulled over a plastic folder of documents. "I've had your case file from the Danish Immigration Service lying around here ever since your first day in the basement, Assad. And now I've finally got round to having a look at it."

Carl felt a pair of dark eyes resting heavily on the top of his skull.

"As far as I can make out, everything you've told me about your background is here to the last detail." He looked up at his assistant.

"Of course, Carl. What did you expect?"

"But that's *all* there is. There's nothing here about what you did before you came to Denmark. Nothing about what made you eligible for residence here, or who took care of your remarkably swiftly approved asylum application. Nothing about your wife or children, when and where they were born, nothing about their backgrounds. Just the names, that's all. To my mind, this is an oddly unrepresentative and incomplete set of data we've got here. A person might think it had been subjected to a bit of editing."

Assad shrugged again. These were shoulders that were apparently the seat of some universal syntax comprising a veritable abundance of nuances.

"And now you're telling me you've got friends in the Lithuanian intelligence service, and that you can get them to help you by issuing threats and giving up confidential information, and all you've got to do is lift the receiver. But you know what, Assad?"

Another shrug, though this time his eyes were more alert.

"This means you can do things not even the head of our own intelligence service can do."

Yet another shrug. "This may be true, Carl. But what do you want to say by telling me so?"

"What do I want to say?" Carl straightened his back and tossed the folder back onto the desk in front of him. "What I want to say, Assad, is this: How come you've got so much fucking clout? *That's* what I want to know, and this case folder here is telling me nothing."

"Carl, listen. Are we not happy down here together? Do we not get along? Why should we go into this?"

"Because today you overstepped a mark beyond which ordinary curiosity no longer suffices."

"Say again?"

"For fuck's sake, Assad. Why don't you just tell me you worked for Syrian intelligence and that you got your hands dirty doing all sorts of shit for which they'll have your head on a plate if you ever go back? Tell me that here in Denmark you've been providing services for PET or FET, or some other similar bunch of snoops, so they felt they had to do the decent thing and let you stay on here, farting about in this basement so you could earn a decent wage. Come on, Assad, spill the beans, for Chrissake!"

"This I could do, Carl, if only what you say were true, but I'm afraid it is not quite correct. What is true is that in a way I have done some work for Denmark. That is why I am here, and also why I cannot tell you any more. Perhaps one day, Carl."

"But you've got friends in Lithuania. Where else have you got friends, can you tell me that? They might come in handy one day if we knew who they were."

"I shall tell you when the time comes, Carl. The whole ship hang."

Carl's shoulders drooped. "The whole *shebang*, Assad." He forced a weary smile in the direction of his flu-ridden helper. "But from now on you don't do anything like you did today without running it by me first, OK?"

"Running by you first?"

"Running *it* by me first. It means you have to ask before doing it, yeah?"

Assad thrust out his lower lip and nodded.

"There's another thing, Assad. I think it's about time you told me what you're doing here at HQ so early in the mornings. Is it something I'm not supposed to know about, seeing as how you have to steal about in the dark of night? And how come you don't want me stopping by to see you at home on Kongevejen? How come, while we're at it, that on more than one occasion I've seen you arguing with men who I'd hazard a guess come from the Middle East? And why are you and Samir Ghazi from the Rødovre police always trying to beat the shit out of each other every time your paths cross?"

"These are private matters, Carl."

He said it in a way that impacted immediately on Carl. It was an affront. Like a friend's rejection of an extended hand. An unequivocal accentuation to the effect that no matter how much they shared at work, Carl not merely came second, he simply didn't belong in his assistant's sphere from the moment Assad clocked out at the gate. Trust was the key concept here, and he didn't have it. Not by a long chalk.

"I thought as much. Two gorgeous guys having a cozy chat," came a familiar voice from the corridor.

Lis parked her pearly whites in a seductive smile and winked at them from the doorway. Her timing was miserable.

Carl looked at Assad, who had immediately resaddled and now seemed relaxed, his face beaming with delight.

"Oh, look at you, poor thing," said Lis, stepping forward and smoothing her hand over Assad's dusky cheek. "Have you come down with it, too? Your eyes are almost drowning. And you, Carl, forcing him in to work. Can't you see how helpless he is, the little dear?" She turned to face Carl with reproach in the blue of her eyes. "I'm to say from Ploug they're waiting for you out in Amager."

6

August 1987

It wasn't until she got to the end of Korsgade and sat down on the bench under the chestnut trees by the front door of the apartment building, her gaze directed toward Peblinge Lake, that she felt release from the city's disapproval and the prison of her own body.

The figures that graced the city streets of the 1980s were well shaped and comely. This she had noted, and on that point she was no longer able to compete.

She closed her eyes, put a hand to her lower leg, and rubbed it gingerly. As the tips of her fingers massaged the irregular contour of her shin bone, her thoughts wandered back to her old mantra: "I am *good enough . . . I* am good enough." But today it sounded hollow, no matter where she placed the emphasis. It had been a long time since she had repeated the words to herself.

She tipped forward, folded her arms around her knees, and pressed her forehead into her lap, her feet tapping out little drum rolls. It often helped against the excruciating jolts that ran through her body.

The walk to Daells Varehus department store and back to Peblinge Dossering was a tall order and led to pain. Pain in her shattered shin bone that forced her gait askew. Pain in the foot that for each step had to accommodate the centimeters by which her leg had been shortened. Pain in the hip that sought to relieve the pressure.

It hurt, but that wasn't the worst thing. Walking along Nørregade, she stared straight ahead, trying not to limp, knowing full well she would not succeed. It was hard to accept. Two years earlier she had been an attractive, nimble woman, and now she felt like a shadow of her former self.

But shadows live well in the shade, so she had told herself until now. The city was somewhere she could make a fresh start. It was why she had fled to Copenhagen almost two years earlier. Away from the shame and the grief, and the icy stares of the locals back on Lolland.

She had moved from Havngaard in order to forget, and now this.

Nete pressed her lips together as a pair of young women with prams walked by, faces and voices brimming with joy and abandon.

She looked away, first glaring at one of the neighborhood lowlifes who came strutting by with his ugly and unmanageable beast of a mongrel, then gazing out upon the flocks of birds that dotted the surface of the lake.

What an awful life. Twenty seconds in a lift at Daells Varehus forty-five minutes earlier had shaken her very foundation. That was all it took. Twenty seconds.

She closed her eyes and allowed her mind to replay what had happened. Her steps toward the lift on the fourth floor. Pressing the button. The relief at not having to wait more than a few seconds before the door slid open.

But what had been relief was now a malicious virus inside her.

She had taken the wrong lift. If only she had used the one at the other end she could have carried on with her life as before, letting herself be swallowed up among the edifices of Nørrebro, the bulwark of its streets.

She shook her head. Now everything was changed. After those fateful seconds the last remnants of Nete Rosen were no more. She was dead and departed. Deleted from this world. Now she was Nete Hermansen again. The girl from Sprogø was risen.

With all the consequences.

———

Eight weeks after the accident they had discharged her from the hospital without ceremony, and in the months that followed she lived alone at Havngaard. The lawyers were busy, for her husband had been a man of great means, and from time to time photographers lurked in the ditches and bushes. When one of Denmark's most prominent businessmen lost his life in a car crash, the newspapers and gossip magazines smelled new sales opportunities, and what could be better than a wealthy widow on crutches with a pained expression on her face? But Nete drew the curtains and let the world race on without her. She knew what people were thinking: the little mite who had wormed her way from the laboratories into the bed of the CEO didn't deserve to be where she was, and it was only because of her husband and his money that those around her had toadied to her all those years.

That was the way it felt still. Even some of the community nurses who tended her at home had difficulty concealing their disdain, but she soon had them replaced.

During these months the stories of Andreas Rosen's fatal accident became spiced with rumor and the anecdotes of witnesses. She felt the past squeeze like a python, and when they took her in to the police station in Maribo the people of the village stood at their windows and smiled smugly. It was common knowledge by then that the family who lived in the house opposite the spot where the accident had occurred had seen something that looked like a tussle inside the car immediately before it careered through the windbreak and plunged into the water.

But Nete did not break down and confess her sin, neither to the public nor to the authorities. Only inside.

They failed to knock her off balance, for she had long since learned to stand firm on her own two feet, even when storms were raging.

And then she left it all behind.

———

She undressed slowly in front of the windows facing the lake and sat down calmly on the stool before the bedroom mirror. The scar above her pubis was more visible now that her pubic hair was less pronounced. A faint lavender-colored line that marked the division between good fortune and bad, life and death. The scar of her sterilization.

She smoothed her hand over the loose skin of her barren abdomen and clenched her teeth. And then she rubbed until it hurt and her legs trembled, her breathing increasingly agitated as her thoughts ran aground.

Only four hours earlier she had been sitting in her kitchen with the department store catalog and had fallen for a pink sweater on page five.

Autumn Catalog 1987, the cover proclaimed, so full of promise. "Fashion knitwear" above the picture that grabbed her attention.

She had admired the item over her steaming coffee and thought to herself that a pattern-knit sweater like that would go so well with a shoulder-padded Pineta shirt blouse and give her a fresh start. For although her grief was immense, there was a life that remained to be lived, and she would soon feel ready again.

That was why she had stood in the lift almost two hours earlier, with her shopping bag in her hand and her heart full of cheer. Exactly one hour and fifty nine minutes earlier the lift had stopped at the third floor and a tall man had stepped inside and stood next to her, so close she could smell him.

He hadn't bothered looking at her, but she had seen him. Had studied him as she held her breath, retreating uncertainly into the corner, her cheeks flaming with rage. Hoping he didn't turn and catch her face in the mirror.

Here was a person who was clearly pleased with himself and the world around him. In control, as they said. In control of his life and, despite advancing years, of the future, too.

The scum.

An hour and fifty-eight minutes and forty seconds earlier he had stepped out of the lift on the second floor and left Nete gasping for air, hands clenched into fists. During the long minutes that followed she sensed nothing. Rode up and down in the lift without reacting to the concerned inquiries of other customers. It was all she could do to calm her pounding heart and gather her thoughts.

When once again she found herself outside on the street she no longer had the plastic bag in her hand. Who needed a pink sweater and a blouse with shoulder pads where life was taking her now?

And now she sat in her fourth-floor apartment, naked and desecrated in heart and soul, wondering how revenge could be taken, and against whom.

She smiled for a second, musing that perhaps she had not been the unfortunate one after all. Perhaps it was the despicable monster fate had sent into her path in this sublime chance encounter.

That was how she felt during the first hours after Curt Wad had once more entered her life.

When the summer came, her cousin Tage came, too. An unmanageable tyke neither the school nor the streets of Assens could contain. "Too much brawn, too little brain," said her uncle, but Nete loved it when he came to stay. It meant there was someone to help her while away the daylight hours for a few weeks. Feeding hens was fine for a small girl, but not the other jobs. Tage loved to get his hands dirty, so the pigsty and the little cowshed became his domain. Only when Tage was with them could she go to bed at night without her arms and legs aching from work, and for that she adored him.

Perhaps she adored him rather too much.

"Whoever taught you such foul language?" the schoolmistress barked, after the summer holiday. And it was always after the summer holiday that she was punished the hardest, for Tage's favorite words, like "fuck" and "shag" and "boner," were far removed from the lonely world the mistress inhabited.

It was words such as these, and Tage's freckled abandon, that laid the first stones on the path that led to Curt Wad.

Smooth, slippery stones.

She got up from the stool and put on her clothes as the list took shape in her mind. The list that opened the pores of her skin and smoothed the furrows of her brow.

There were people in the world who deserved not to breathe. People who strove only toward their own selfish goals and never looked back at the destruction they left in their wake. A few came to mind. The question was, what price should they be made to pay in consequence?

She walked down the long hallway and into the room at the end, where the table she had inherited from her father stood. At least a thousand meals had been consumed at that table, her father prodding at his food, silent and bitter, weary of life and all its pain. On rare occasions he had looked up to send her a fatigued smile. It was all he could muster.

Had it not been for her, he would have found himself a length of rope and hanged himself years before he eventually did. Such was the toll of arthritis, loneliness, and barrenness of mind.

She caressed the dark edge on which his arms had always rested and moved her fingers into the middle where the brown envelope had lain ever since she had moved in two years before.

It was worn and creased from the innumerable times she had opened it and studied its contents.

"Miss Nete Hermansen, Laboratory Assistant, Århus Technical College, Halmstadgade, Århus N," read the address on the envelope. The postal services had added the street number and the postcode in red pen. She had felt grateful to them many a time since.

She ran her fingers gently over the stamp and postmark. Almost seventeen years had passed since it had come through her mailbox. A whole life away.

Then she opened the envelope, took out the letter, and unfolded it.

Dearest Nete

In the most remarkable and unfathomable of ways, the veil has now been lifted on what has become of you since you got onto the train at Bredebro station and waved good-bye to us with such a happy smile.

I wish you to know that everything I have now learned about your passage through life these past six years has gladdened me more than I can ever express.

Now surely you must know that you are good enough. Am I right? Your reading handicap could indeed be overcome and there was a place for you in life after all. And such a place! I am so very proud of you, dear Nete. Grammar school with top marks. Your training as a laboratory assistant at the Aabenraa Technical College where you finished top of your class. And now soon to complete your course of study as a biological laboratory technician in Århus. So very well done indeed! Perhaps you are wondering how all this has come to my attention, in which case I can reveal to you the most singular coincidence that Interlab A/S, the company that has taken you into its employment as of 1 January, was founded by my old friend, Christopher Hale. Moreover, his son, Daniel, is my godson. We meet often, most recently on the occasion of our annual family get-together on the first Sunday of Advent, under the pretext of making decorations and baking cookies in preparation for the festive season.

I inquired of my friend what matters were occupying him at the time, and, would you believe, he informed me he had just finished reading through a for-

midable number of job applications, upon which he proceeded to show me the one he had selected. Can you imagine my surprise on seeing your name? And, if you will excuse my indiscretion, upon reading your letter of application and curriculum vitae? I must honestly admit to shedding tears of joy.

Now, Nete, I shall not burden you further with the sentiment of an old man. Suffice to say that Marianne and I are so very happy on your behalf. Know that you may now stand proud and declare to all the world that little sentence we composed so many years ago: I am good enough!

REMEMBER that, my dear!

We wish you all joy and happiness in your further passage through life.

Our most heartfelt greetings

Marianne and Erik Hanstholm
Bredebro, 14 December 1970

Three times she read the letter through, and three times she paused at the words: "Now surely you must know that you are good enough."

"I'm good enough!" she said out loud, picturing Erik Hanstholm's face lined by laughter. The first time she had uttered the sentence she had been just twenty-four years old, and now she was fifty. Where had all the years gone? If only she had got in touch with him before it was too late.

She breathed deeply, tipped her head, and noted the slant of the characters, the capital letters, and every little inkblot his fountain pen had left each time he paused.

Then she took a second sheet of paper out of the envelope and sat for a while, looking at it with tears in her eyes. There had been many diplomas and exam certificates since then, but this was the first and most momentous. Erik Hanstholm had made it for her, generous as always.

DIPLOMA, it read at the top, the word written in curly letters, and underneath it four lines covering the entire sheet: *No one who can read this can be called illiterate.*

That was all it said.

She dried her eyes and pressed her lips together. How thoughtless and selfish of her never to have got in touch. What would have become of her if it hadn't been for him and his wife, Marianne? And now it was too late. Passed away after a lengthy illness, the obituary notice had said three years ago.

"After a lengthy illness," whatever that meant.

She had written to Marianne Hanstholm to offer her condolences, only for her letters to be returned. Perhaps she was no more either, Nete had thought at the time. So who was left now, besides those who had destroyed her life?

Nobody.

Nete folded the letter and the diploma and put them back in the envelope. Then she went over to the windowsill where she put the brown envelope down on a tin plate.

When she set fire to it and the smoke rose up to the stucco molding on the ceiling she felt all shame to be gone for the first time since the accident.

She waited until the glow was extinguished and rubbed the remains to powder between her fingers. Then she carried the plate into the living room and stood for a moment at the windowsill there, regarding the plant with the sticky bristles. Its smell wasn't quite as pungent today.

She sprinkled the ashes into the flowerpot and turned to the bureau.

Atop this fine piece of furniture was a stack of envelopes and matching floral writing paper. The kind of hostess gift that was just as inevitable as candles and cloth doilies. She took six of these envelopes, sat down at the dining table, and wrote a name on each.

Curt Wad, Rita Nielsen, Gitte Charles, Tage Hermansen, Viggo Mogensen, and Philip Nørvig.

One name for each point of her life when things had gone off in the wrong direction.

As the names lay there in front of her they seemed anything but significant. Inconsequential, even. People who could be deleted from one's life by the stroke of a pen. But reality was another matter. The names were of the utmost substance. And their importance resided primarily in the fact that these individuals, to the extent that they were still alive, were walking around as free as Curt Wad. Not giving a moment's thought to the past and the slimy traces their passage through life had left behind them.

But she would make them stop and look back. And she would do it in her own devious way.

She picked up the phone and dialed the number of the Civil Registration Office.

"Good afternoon," she began. "My name is Nete Hermansen. Would you be kind enough to tell me how I can get in touch with some old acquaintances of mine? The addresses I have here seem to be rather out-of-date."

7

November 2010

The wind was capricious, and even from a distance Carl sensed the stench of a corpse hanging densely in the damp autumn air.

Behind a pair of bulldozers with lowered shovels, white-clad homicide police were conferring with forensic technicians.

It seemed they'd reached the point where they could hand over to the ambulance crew and orderlies from the Department of Forensic Medicine to cart off the remains.

Terje Ploug stood with a folder under his arm, puffing away on his pipe, and Marcus Jacobsen had a cigarette in his mouth. Not that smoke helped much. The poor bastard who had been laid so improperly to rest had long since reached a state of total decomposition, more malodorous than anything else on earth. As such it seemed somehow fortunate that the olfactory organs of the majority of those present were well and truly bunged up.

Carl stepped closer with nostrils pinched and stared at the box that was still in the ground, though almost fully excavated, its lid open. It wasn't as big as he'd imagined. Three-quarters of a meter square, but ample enough to contain a dismembered body. It was solidly made, put together from disused tongue-and-groove floorboards that had been varnished. Certainly a casket that could have stayed in the ground for years before disintegrating.

"How come they didn't just chuck the body straight in the hole?" Carl mused, as he stood on the edge of the excavation. "And why here, exactly?" He threw out his hands to indicate the surrounding area. "I mean, they weren't exactly short of options, were they?"

"We've had a look at the floor they pulled up from the shed." The chief drew his scarf tighter around the collar of his leather jacket and pointed toward a heap of boards behind some building workers in orange overalls.

"So now we've a fairly exact idea as to where they lowered the box down," Jacobsen went on. "Almost in the corner by the south wall, the hole cut out with a circular saw not that long ago. Crime scene boys reckon within the last five years."

Carl nodded. "OK. So the victim was killed and chopped up somewhere else and then transported here."

"Looks like it, anyway," said Jacobsen with a sniffle, his features momentarily shrouded in a cloud of cigarette smoke. "Maybe a reminder to Georg Madsen to behave himself a bit better than the poor sod lying there."

Terje Ploug nodded. "The SOCOs are saying the box was definitely buried under the area with the hole cut out, in the main room. As far as I can make out from the sketch in the report here"—he indicated a floor plan from his folder—"that would have been directly underneath the chair where you lot found Georg Madsen with the nail through his head. The spot where you got shot."

Carl straightened his back. It wasn't the kind of information likely to bring a Wednesday morning in November into the top flight. There was little doubt that ahead of them lay hundreds of hours of investigation and poking around in events Carl preferred to forget. If it was down to him he'd kick it into touch right now, drive out to the Airport Grill, get a couple of hot dogs and plenty of ketchup, and keep a nice, easy eye on the clock until three or four hours had passed and it was time for him to go home and get ready for his Martinmas goose at Mona's.

Ploug stood gawping at him as though he could read his mind.

"OK," said Carl. "Let's say we know the guy was killed somewhere else and most likely buried under Georg Madsen's floor with his knowledge. Now, what details might be missing?"

He scratched his head theatrically before proffering his own answer. "Oh, yeah, that's right. We don't know who he is, we've no idea why he got bumped off, and we haven't a clue who did it. Piece of cake, I'd say! But you'll have that sorted in no time, won't you, Ploug?" Carl grunted. He felt loathing kick in.

Here, two years earlier on this miserable patch of ground, he had nearly lost his life. Here the ambulance crews had driven away with Anker's dead body and Hardy's crippled one. Here Carl had fallen short and lain wounded on the floor, paralyzed by fear like some terrified animal, while their assailants made short work of his mates. And when this box made its final journey to forensics in just a short while from now, all tangible evidence of those events would be removed from the face of the earth. It felt right and wrong all at once.

"I think you're correct inasmuch as we can assume this took place with Georg Madsen's knowledge, but if burying the body was meant as a warning, I think we can take it for granted he didn't pay much heed," the chief commented.

Carl stared at the open box.

The skull was on its side on top of one of the black bin liners that still contained the rest of the body parts. Judging by the size of the cranium, the prominent jaw, and the healed fracture on the bridge of the nose, the victim was not only male, but also a man who had most likely seen his share of trouble. Now here he lay, toothless, his scalp a loose mat of rotten flesh, and from this slimy, decomposed mass protruded the head of a large galvanized nail. A nail seemingly of the same kind found in the skulls of Georg Madsen and the two mechanics at the auto repair shop down in Sorø.

Jacobsen pulled off his scene suit and nodded to the police photographers. "In a couple of hours we'll go through the contents of the box over at forensics. That should tell us if we've anything to go on that might help us identify the victim," he said by way of conclusion, and began making his way back to his car.

"You write the report, Ploug," he shouted back over his shoulder.

Carl withdrew a few meters and tried to filter out the stench of dead body with a couple of deep breaths in the close vicinity of Ploug's smoldering pipe.

"What the hell was the point of dragging me out here, Terje?" he asked. "To see if I was going to break down?"

Ploug returned the question with weary eyes. He didn't give a shit if Carl broke down or not.

"As far as I remember, the neighbor's place was just about there," he said, indicating an adjoining patch of ground. "He must have heard or seen people lugging a big box into next door's, not to mention the sound of a saw tearing Georg Madsen's floorboards apart, wouldn't you think? Do you remember him saying anything about it?"

Carl smiled. "Listen, Ploug. The neighbor had only had the place for ten days before Georg Madsen was done in, so he never knew the bloke. As far as I and the SOCOs can tell from that foul-smelling pile of flesh and bones there, the body's been in the ground at least five years. In other words, three years before Georg Madsen got knocked off. So how the fuck was the neighbor supposed to know anything? Anyway, weren't you the one who took charge of the investigation after they sent me off to the hospital? Didn't you speak to him yourself?"

"No, the bloke dropped dead from a heart attack the same day, didn't he? Popped his clogs right over there by the curb while we were packing up our gear. The murder and the circumstances surrounding it were too much for him, not to mention our lot milling about all of a sudden."

Carl thrust out his lower lip. Christ on a bike, was there no end to the lives these fuckers had on their conscience?

"You didn't know that, did you?" Ploug pulled his notebook out of his inside pocket. "In that case you probably haven't heard either that we've had information from the Netherlands about some similar killings. May and September of last year. A tower-block estate outside Rotterdam called Schiedam. Two blokes, both done in with a nail gun. They sent us a pile of photos."

He opened his folder and pulled out a series of images of the two men's skulls while a pair of officers cordoned off the scene with tape.

"Ninety-millimeter Paslode nail through the temple, same as here. I'll send you copies of the relevant documents once we get back. We can go through it when the report comes in from forensics."

OK, Carl thought to himself. Hardy's brains were in for some exercise.

He found Lis outside Rose's office with her arms folded beneath her bosom, nodding eagerly, fully engrossed in Rose's natter about life in general, and in the basement in particular. He picked up snippets—"like the bloody grave," "miserable as sin," and "thinks he's God's gift"—and was in total agreement until he realized she was talking about him.

"A-hemmm," he ventured, making a show of clearing his throat in the hope of startling his emo malcontent of a secretary into shame, but she didn't even bother to look up.

"Talk of the devil," she said without the slightest embarrassment, and handed him some papers. "Have a look at what I've highlighted in the

Rita Nielsen case and think yourself lucky you've got staff looking after the shop while certain others are off swanning about the countryside."

Oh, Christ. Was she back at this stage already? If they didn't watch out they'd have her so-called twin sister Yrsa turning up before they knew what had hit them.

"You were upstairs asking after me?" said Lis, as Rose's shadow vanished into her office.

"Yeah, I've been trying to track down my cousin, Ronny, without any luck and was wondering if . . ."

"Oh, that." For a moment she looked disappointed. "Bak told us the bare bones of it. What a performance. I'll see what I can do."

She flashed him a smile that turned his kneecaps into jelly, then headed for the archive.

"Just a minute, Lis," Carl blurted, stopping her in her tracks. "What the hell's the score with Ms. Sørensen up there? All of a sudden she's . . . well, I was going to say pleasant . . ."

"She's started on a course in NLP."

"NLP? Refresh my memory . . ."

But then Carl's mobile chimed. *Morten Holland*, the display read. What would his lodger be wanting him for now?

"Yeah, what is it, Morten?" he said, giving Lis an apologetic nod.

"Am I interrupting?" came Morten's cautious voice.

"Did the iceberg interrupt the *Titanic*? Did Brutus interrupt Caesar? What's up? Is Hardy all right?"

"Well, sort of, yeah. Nice one, by the way, the iceberg interrupting the *Titanic*. Ha, ha! Anyway, Hardy wants a word."

He heard the rustle as the phone was placed at Hardy's ear on the pillow. These calls were a bad habit Morten and Hardy had got into. It used to suffice for Carl and Hardy to have a bedside chat in the evenings when Carl got home, but apparently that was no good anymore.

"Can you hear me, Carl?" Carl pictured the big man paralyzed in his bed with Morten pressing the phone to his ear. Eyes half shut, a frown on his face, lips parched. Hardy was worried about something, Carl could tell by the sound of his voice. Most likely Terje Ploug had already been on to him.

"Ploug called," he said. "I suppose you know what about?"

"Yeah."

"OK, so what's the story, Carl? Tell me."

"It's about the bastards who shot us being coldblooded killers and stopping at nothing to ensure discipline in the ranks."

"You know that's not what I meant." There was a pause. The unpleasant kind. The kind that usually ended in confrontation.

"Do you know what I'm thinking? I'm thinking Anker was up to his neck in that shit. He knew there was a dead body in that allotment house before we went out there."

"OK. And what brings you to that conclusion, Hardy?"

"I just *know*. He changed so much in that period. Started spending more money than before. His personality changed. And he didn't go by the book that day."

"How do you mean?"

"He went over to the neighbor to question him before we'd even been inside Georg Madsen's place. But how could he know for sure there was a body?"

"The neighbor reported it."

"Come off it, Carl. How many times have people reported things like that, and how many times has it turned out the smell was a dead dog and the noise came from the television or the radio? Anker *always* went in to check if it was a false alarm before going out into the field. Only that day he didn't."

"How come you're telling me this *now*? Haven't you had time before, or what?"

"Remember when Minna and I put Anker up at ours when his wife booted him out?"

"No."

"It was only for a while, but Anker was in a bad way. He was sniffing coke."

"Yeah, that shrink, Kris, told me, the one Mona let loose on me. I had no idea at the time."

"He got into a fight one night he was out on the town. He had blood all over his clothes."

"And . . . ?"

"A lot of blood, Carl. He threw them in the bin."

"So now you see a connection between that and the body that turned up today?"

The same pause. Hardy had been one of the best detectives at Police HQ when he'd still able to stand up. "Insight and intuition" was how he explained it. Hardy and his bloody intuition.

"Let's wait and see what the autopsy says, Hardy."

"The skull in the box had no teeth, am I right?"

"Yeah."

"And the body was completely decomposed?"

"Something like that, yeah. Not soup, but almost."

"We're not likely to find out who he was, then, are we?"

"Can't be helped, I'm afraid, Hardy."

"That's easy enough for you to say, Carl. You're not the one lying here with a tube in his guts, staring up at the ceiling all day long, are you? If Anker was mixed up in that shit, then it's his fucking fault I'm here. *That's* why I'm calling you, Carl. So you keep a fucking eye on that case. And if Ploug starts arsing it up, you fucking owe it to your old mate here to make sure he gets it right, do you hear?"

When Morten Holland repeated his apologies and hung up, Carl found himself sitting on the edge of his chair with Rose's papers in his lap. How on earth he'd propelled himself into his office without noticing, he had no idea.

He closed his eyes for a moment and tried to picture Anker in his mind's eye, but his former colleague's features were already erased.

How could he possibly remember Anker's pupils and nostrils, his voice, and all the other things that gave away a cocaine habit?

8

November 2010

"**Have you seen Rose's** highlights in the Rita Nielsen case, Carl?"

Carl looked up and almost fell about laughing. Assad stood waving a handful of documents in front of him. Apparently he'd found a remedy for his dribbling nose. Protruding from each nostril was a bung of cotton wool of such dimension as to explain why his usual filtering out of all sibilants, conspicuous at the best of times, was now even more pronounced.

"What highlights? Where?" Carl replied, stifling a grin.

"The case about the woman who disappeared in Copenhagen. The brothel lady, Rita Nielsen." He tossed a handful of photocopies onto the desk. "Rose is making phone calls. In the meantime she wants us to look at these."

Carl picked up the copies and gestured toward Assad's cotton wool. "Take those plugs out, eh, Assad? I can't concentrate."

"But then I will dribble, Carl."

"Then dribble, if you must. Just make sure you do it on the floor." He nodded as the tampons were consigned to the bin, and turned his attention to Rose's documents. "What highlights?"

Assad leaned perilously close and flicked through the sheets. "Here," he said, pointing to a number of lines highlighted in red.

Carl skimmed the page. It was a detailing of the state in which Rita

Nielsen's abandoned Mercedes had been found, and Rose's red pen had underlined what few effects had been retrieved from the glove compartment. A tourist guide of northern Italy, some throat drops, a pack of paper handkerchiefs, a couple of brochures about Florence, and four cassette tapes of Madonna songs.

Nørrebro's purveyors of stolen goods obviously hadn't been confident of finding a market for Madonna, Carl thought to himself, noticing that Rose had doubly underscored the sentence "Cassette of *Who's That Girl* found to be without contents." Did they mean "contents" or "content"? Carl wondered with a smile.

"OK," he said eventually. "Not exactly earth shattering, is it? They found an empty Madonna cassette. Will you call the newspapers or shall I?"

Assad stared at him, perplexed. "On the next page there is some more. Oh, and I think the pages are back to front."

He indicated a couple more details Rose had found worthy of note. These concerned the phone call of 6 September 1987 that reported Rita Nielsen missing. It had been made by one Lone Rasmussen of Kolding, a woman who worked for Rita Nielsen, looking after the phone and managing her call girls' appointments. She had been concerned when Rita Nielsen failed to return to Kolding on the Saturday as expected. It had been noted that Lone Rasmussen was known to police on account of a number of cases involving prostitution and drugs.

The main sentence Rose had underlined ran: "According to Lone Rasmussen, Rita Nielsen had some particular appointment on the Sunday, because that day and those following were crossed out with diagonal red lines in the calendar Rita Nielsen kept in the massage parlor consistently referred to by Lone Rasmussen as 'the escort service.'"

"O-*K*," Carl repeated slowly as he read on through the text. So Rita Nielsen had taken time off and was going to be unavailable in the days after she disappeared. Investigators had looked into the matter and found nothing to indicate what these days off might have involved.

"I think Rose is trying to find this Lone Rasmussen as we speak," Assad sniffled.

Carl sighed. All this was twenty-three years ago. According to Lone Rasmussen's civil registration number she would now be in her mid-seventies, an advanced age for a woman with her history. And if, against all odds, she was still alive, what could she be expected to add to such vague statements after all these years?

"Look at this now, Carl." Assad flicked through the pages again, stopping at a sentence he read out loud, his diction a muffled monotone of nasal congestion.

"On searching Rita Nielsen's flat on the tenth day of her disappearance, officers discovered a cat in such a weakened state as to necessitate destruction by veterinarians."

"Bugger me," said Carl.

"And here, too." Assad pointed to the bottom of the page. "No evidence found to indicate any crime. Similarly, no personal documents, diaries, or anything else to suggest personal crisis. Rita Nielsen's home appears neat, though somewhat immaturely furnished with many knick-knacks and an unusual number of framed photo clippings of Madonna. In summary, nothing to suggest either suicide or homicide."

Again Rose had doubly underlined a passage: "unusual number of framed photo clippings of Madonna."

Why had she highlighted that? Carl wiped his nose. Was he coming down with it now as well? He bloody well hoped not. He was off to Mona's tonight.

"I'm not sure why Rose thinks all this Madonna stuff is so important," said Carl. "But that business about the cat might raise a few eyebrows."

Assad nodded. The stories people told about unmarried women and their pets were certainly not exaggerated. If they had a cat, they'd make certain it was taken care of before embarking on something as drastic as suicide. Either they went off together or else the animal was passed into good hands while there was still time.

"I'm assuming our colleagues in Kolding thought about that," he said, but Assad shook his head.

"They assumed she took her life on the spur of the moment," he replied with a sniff.

Carl winced, then nodded. It couldn't be ruled out, not by any means. She'd been a long way from both home and the cat, so you could never tell. People did all sorts of things.

Rose's voice rumbled through the corridor. "Get yourselves along here, you two. And make it sharpish."

Had he heard right? Was she bossing them about now? Was it no longer enough for her to decide what cases they were to pursue? If that was how she thought things worked around here she'd got another bloody thing coming, even if she did end up throwing a wobbler and mutating into Yrsa again. Rose's alter ego may not have been quite as bright, but she wasn't daft, not by a long chalk.

"Come along, Carl," said Assad, tugging at his sleeve. Apparently he was better trained.

Rose stood in the middle of her office floor, hand covering the telephone receiver and utterly unfazed by Carl's piercing glare of disapproval. Dressed in black from head to toe, she looked like a chimney sweep.

"It's Lone Rasmussen," she whispered. "I want you to listen to what she has to say. I'll explain afterward."

She put the receiver down on the desk and switched on the speaker function.

"Right, Lone, I've got my boss, Carl Mørck, and his assistant with me now," she said. "Can I ask you to repeat what you just told me?"

OK, she called him her boss, so maybe she *did* still know who was in charge. Carl gave her a nod of acknowledgment. She'd done well to find Lone Rasmussen. Not bad at all.

"Okaaay," came a drawling voice from the other end. A coarse, lazy voice, like the ones junkies ended up with if their drug abuse continued. Not that she sounded old, just wrecked. "Can everyone hear me now?"

Rose confirmed.

"Well, all I said was she loved that cat. There was another girl, I can't remember her name, who was supposed to look after it once, only she forgot and Rita got dead narked with her and gave her her marching orders. So whenever Rita was away after that, she got me to feed the thing. Tinned food, the good stuff. But it was only ever on its own when she was away for a very short time, a day or two at the most. Left its doings all over the place, it did, but Rita just cleaned up after it."

"So you're saying Rita would never have left her cat without making sure there was someone to look after it?" Rose asked, helping her along.

"That's right, yeah! It was odd at the time. I had no idea the cat was in the flat and she'd never given me a key. She never gave her key out unless there was good reason. Otherwise I'd have known the poor thing was starving to death. Are you with me?"

"Yes, we're with you, Lone. But the other thing you told me just before, would you say that again, about Madonna?"

"Oh, Rita was absolutely mad about her. Daft, she was."

"You said Rita was in love with her."

"Head over bloody heels. She never said as much, but we all knew."

"So Rita Nielsen was a lesbian?" Carl interjected.

"Ooh, we've got a man with us now, have we?" she cackled. "Yeah, well, Rita would shag almost anything that moved, wouldn't she?" At this point Lone Rasmussen paused suddenly and Rose's clinical habitat was filled with the sound of a person attempting to quench a boundless thirst. "I don't think she ever said no, to be honest," she continued after prolonged gulping. "Only in the days she was doing it for money, and the bloke, or whoever it was, didn't have any."

"You don't think Rita committed suicide, then?" Carl went on.

Lone's reply was a guttural eruption of laughter, followed by prompt dismissal: "You must be bloody joking."

"And you've no idea what might have happened to her?"

"None whatsoever. Weird, it was. But my guess is it was to do with money, even if she did have loads in the bank when the lawyers finally finished sorting out the estate. Took them eight years, if I remember right."

"And she left everything including her flat to Cats Protection, isn't that right?" Rose said.

There you go, Carl thought to himself. A woman like that would never leave her pet to die of starvation.

"Yeah, what a waste that was. I could have done with a couple of her millions myself," said Lone wistfully.

"OK," said Carl. "Just to sum up. Rita drove to Copenhagen on the Friday, and your impression was she'd be home again the next day, the Saturday. That's why she hadn't asked you to look after the cat. After that, you assumed she slept at home in Kolding on the Saturday night, that she was going to be otherwise engaged during the days that followed, and that you *might* have to look after the cat, though you were unsure as to whether the cat was actually in the flat. Is that right?"

"Yeah, pretty much."

"And was this a usual kind of occurrence?"

"It was, yeah. She'd often go off for a few days. A trip to London, maybe, to see the musicals. She liked that. I mean, who wouldn't? But then she was the one with the money, wasn't she?"

The last couple of sentences were rather unintelligible. Assad concentrated with his eyes squinched together as though he'd been surprised by a sudden sandstorm, but Carl had little difficulty picking out the words.

"One more thing. Rita bought a packet of smokes on her debit card in Copenhagen the last day anyone saw her alive. Would you have any idea why she didn't pay in cash? Bearing in mind the small amount."

Lone Rasmussen guffawed. "The taxman nailed her once with a hundred grand in a drawer at home. Came down hard on her, they did. She couldn't explain where it came from, could she? After that, every penny went into the bank and she never made a cash withdrawal. Paid for *everything* with her Dankort or Diners. Course, a lot of shops didn't accept plastic then, but if they didn't, she'd just go elsewhere. No way she was going to make the same mistake again. And she never did."

"OK," said Carl. So that was *that* sorted. "A shame you didn't get any of her money," he added, and almost meant it. Most likely it would have been the death of her, but at least she'd have gone out with a bang.

"Well, I did get her furniture and all the stuff from the flat. Cats Protection didn't want any of it, and all I had was cheap rubbish."

He could imagine.

They thanked her and concluded the call. They were welcome to get in touch again, she told them.

Carl nodded. It'd give her something to talk about.

Rose scrutinized their expressions and could tell she'd got them interested. There was substance to this, a case that cried out for fresh investigation.

"OK, what else have you got, Rose?" Carl asked. "Out with it."

"You don't know much about Madonna, do you, Carl?"

He looked at her wearily for a moment. In the eyes of someone like Rose, who had been a part of this world a good many years less than himself, it seemed that anyone over thirty had already descended into a rut, while being over forty meant never having been young at all. He shuddered to think how eyes like hers perceived a person who was fifty, sixty, or more.

He shrugged. Despite his advanced age he of course knew quite a lot about Madonna. But Rose didn't need to know how one of his former girlfriends had driven him up the wall with "Material Girl," or how Vigga had danced in the nude for him, writhing her hips sensually as she wailed the words to "Papa Don't Preach." It wasn't the kind of performance he felt inclined to share with anyone.

"What's there to know?" he said. "Hasn't she gone religious these days?"

Rose was far from impressed. "Rita Nielsen set up her call-girl business and massage parlor in Kolding in 1983. She called herself Louise Ciccone on the local porn scene. Doesn't that ring a bell?"

Assad raised a tentative finger in the air. "Ciccone is a kind of pasta, I think, with meat inside. Very nice."

She glared at him, indignant. "Madonna's real name is Madonna Louise Ciccone. Lone Rasmussen told me they played her records all the time in the massage parlor, nothing else would do, and Rita was always trying to copy Madonna's makeup and hair. At the time she disappeared she had the same Marilyn Monroe peroxide job Madonna sported on her Who's That Girl tour. See for yourselves!"

She clicked an image onto her computer screen. A provocative photo of Madonna in fishnets, black corset, and unmistakable eighties makeup, with dark eyebrows and fluffy blonde hair, mike in hand and her arm dangling limply at her side. Carl remembered it well, like it was yesterday. Only it wasn't.

"That's exactly how she looked, Lone Rasmussen told me. Dark eyeshadow and bloodred lips, the works. This is Rita Nielsen the day she disappeared. Older, perhaps, but still a bit of a stunner, apparently."

"My goodness," said Assad, master of the succinct.

"I checked out the contents of Rita's glove compartment," Rose continued. "All Madonna's LPs on cassette. Including the sound track of *Who's That Girl*, though the tape was missing. Most likely it was in the cassette player that got nicked. And then there were the brochures about Florence, and the guidebook of northern Italy. It got me wondering if it all might fit together. Have a look at this."

She clicked an icon on the desktop and the same image of Madonna came up. Exactly the same, apart from a series of dates listed down one side of the page. Rose pointed at them.

"June the fourteenth and fifteenth, Nashinomiya Stadium, Osaka, Japan," Assad read out loud. It couldn't have sounded less Japanese. Absolutely abominable.

"The stadium's actually called Nishinomiya, according to all my other sources, but who's counting," said Rose, a ring of superiority passing through black-painted lips. "But look at the bottom of the list and you'll be in for a surprise."

Carl heard Assad read out loud again. "September the sixth, Stadio Comunale, Florence, Italy."

"OK," said Carl. "Let me guess what year we're talking about here: 1987, by any chance?"

Rose nodded vigorously. Now she was in high gear. "The same Sunday Rita Nielsen had crossed out in her calendar. If you ask me, she was going to the last concert on Madonna's world tour. I'm positive. Rita wanted to get home from Copenhagen as quickly as possible so she could pack her things and get off to Florence to see her idol."

Assad and Carl exchanged glances. The brochures, the pet-sitting, the Madonna obsession. It all matched up.

"Any way of checking if she booked a flight from Billund that day?"

Rose gave him a look of disappointment. "I've already done that, and their system doesn't go back that far. They didn't find anything in the flat either, so we'll have to assume she had the tickets for the flight and the concert with her when she disappeared."

"In which case it's hardly likely to be suicide," Carl concluded, and gave Rose a very gentle pat on the shoulder.

Carl read through Rose's notes on Rita Nielsen. Checking Rita's merits seemed to have been a relatively straightforward matter, for since childhood she had been under the watchful eye of vigilant public authorities. They'd all been involved at some point. Child welfare and the psychiatric services, the police, hospitals, and the prison system. Born 1 April 1935, to a prostitute mother who went on working the streets while Rita was brought up by family at the arse-end of the social scale. Caught shoplifting at five, minor crime throughout her six-year education. Approved school, children's home, more crime. Prostituted herself for the first time at age fifteen, pregnant at seventeen, abortion, then a period under observation for social deviance and subnormal intelligence. The family had disintegrated long before.

After a time in foster care came more prostitution, followed by a spell at the Keller Mental Asylum in Brejning where she was diagnosed as subnormal. Repeated attempts to abscond and episodes of violence led to several terms at the Women's Home on the island of Sprogø in the years 1955–61. There was another placement in a foster home and more crime, after which she disappeared from the system for a period extending from the summer of 1963 to the mid-1970s, when she seemed to have been earning a living as a dancer in various cities throughout Europe.

Next she set up a massage parlor in Aalborg, and was later convicted of procuring. After that, her social problems seemed to come to an end. Apparently she'd learned her lesson and managed to accumulate a considerable amount of money running a brothel and escort service without interference from the authorities. She paid her taxes and left liquid assets amounting to three and a half million kroner, the equivalent of at least ten million in today's money.

Carl mused as he read. If Rita Nielsen had been mentally challenged, he knew quite a few others who were, too.

It was then that he leaned his elbow into something wet on his desk and realized his nose had been running. There was enough to fill a cup.

"Bollocks," he exclaimed, throwing his head back and fumbling for something to use as a handkerchief.

Two minutes later he was out in the corridor, interrupting Rose and Assad as they fastened copies of Rita's case documents to the smaller of their two expansive bulletin boards.

Carl glanced at the other board, a composite of soft particleboard panels extending from the door of Assad's cubbyhole all the way to Rose's office. On it was affixed one sheet of paper for each of the unsolved cases that had come in since Department Q had been set up. Arranged chronologically, several of them were joined by colored string to indicate a possible connection. The system was Assad's, and it was simple. Blue string matched up cases Assad felt had something in common; red string joined those in which a connection had actually been established.

At the moment they had a couple of blues, but no reds.

There was no doubt this was a state of affairs Assad intended to do something about.

Carl ran his eyes over the cases. There were at least a hundred sheets of paper now. No doubt much of it was rubbish that didn't belong. It was like finding a needle *and* a thread in a haystack, and then trying to thread the needle blindfolded.

"Right, I'm off home," he said. "If I'm not mistaken, I'm coming down with the dreaded lurgy like you, Assad. If either of you are planning on hanging around for a while I'd suggest getting hold of the newspapers from the time Rita Nielsen disappeared. Try from the week leading up to the fourth of September and as far as the fifteenth. It'll give us some idea of what was going on at the time. Buggered if I can remember."

Rose planted her hands on her hips. "Like we're just going to fall over something they overlooked in all that painstaking police work?"

She said "painstaking." An odd word, Carl thought, for someone of such relative youth.

"Whatever," he rejoined. "I've got some shut-eye and a goose to be thinking about." And then he turned and was gone.

9

August 1987

Nete's mother always told her she had good hands. In her view there was no doubt whatsoever that Nete would one day be appreciated for the work they could do. Apart from having a good head on one's shoulders, small, diligent hands were the most important tool God could give a person, and her father reaped the benefits of her gift after the death of his wife.

When fence posts collapsed it was Nete who put them up again. Nete caulked the feeding troughs when the wood began to rot. She nailed things together and broke them apart when the time came.

And these same able hands were to be her curse during her time on the island of Sprogø. Scratched until they bled when the scrub encroached upon the fields. Laboring all through the day with nothing in return. Nothing good, at least.

Then came better years when they were left in peace. But now they were to be put to use again.

She measured up the back room at the end of the hallway with the same tape measure she used in her sewing, precisely charting its height, width, and length. The window alcoves and the door were subtracted from the total surface area, and then she wrote up her order. Tools, paint, filler, silicone sealant, laths, nails, rolls of plastic sheeting, weather stripping, mineral wool, floorboards, and plasterboard enough for two layers.

The timber outlet on Ryesgade promised delivery the next day. It suited her well, for circumstances demanded she wait no longer.

And when everything had been brought up into the apartment, the room was insulated and the joinery completed during the day while her downstairs neighbor was at work and the woman in the adjoining apartment was out shopping or traipsing round the city lakes with her little Tibetan rug pisser of a Lhasa apso.

No one was to hear what was going on in the flat to the left on the fourth floor. No one was to see her with a hammer or a saw. No one was to appear with prying questions, for she had lived anonymously in the apartment for two years now and intended to go on doing so until the end of her days.

No matter what else she was planning.

When the room was finished she stood in the doorway and admired her work. The ceiling had been the difficult part to insulate and clad, but also the most important along with the door and the floor, which she had raised and insulated with two layers of plastic sheeting and thick slabs of mineral wool. Then she had adjusted the door so it could still be opened inward, even though she had laid carpet over the new flooring.

Apart from the difference in floor level compared with the hallway, there was absolutely nothing that called attention to itself. The room was ready. Joins filled, walls and ceiling painted, chunky weather stripping around the doors and windows. The furnishings were arranged exactly as before: the same pictures on the walls, the same knickknacks on the windowsills, and of course the dining table in the middle with its lace tablecloth and six chairs. Her own chair, the one with the armrests, she placed at the head of the table.

She turned to the plant in the window and rubbed one of its leaves gently between her fingers. The smell was pungent, though not unpleasant. It was this smell of henbane that made her feel safe.

All the girls of Sprogø whispered about Gitte Charles when she arrived with the mail boat in the summer of 1956. Some said she was a trained nurse, but it wasn't at all true. An auxiliary, perhaps, but not fully qualified, for besides the matron, none of the staff on the island had any formal training whatsoever. But Nete already knew that.

The new arrival caused a stir, and the reason was the girls now had something pretty to look at. Swinging her arms coquettishly, striding along with a gait some said reminded them of Greta Garbo, Gitte Charles was in a league of her own. Nothing at all like the other miserable old crones who were either spinsters, divorcees, or widows, and for that reason had felt obliged to seek employment in this diabolical place.

Gitte Charles carried herself proudly. She was blonde like Nete, her hair alluringly put up in a fashion not even the matron allowed herself. Feminine and with a spring in her step, the kind of woman Nete and many of the others dreamed of becoming.

The girls cast envious, in some cases libidinous, glances in the direction of Gitte Charles, but soon they discovered that behind the delicate exterior, a demon lurked. And apart from Rita, they kept their distance.

When Charles, as they called her, grew weary of Rita's company, she turned her blue eyes on Nete, promising to ease her daily burdens, offering security and perhaps even the chance of getting away from the island altogether.

It all depended on how nice Nete was to Charles. And Charles let her know that should Nete ever happen to let the cat out of the bag as to what the two of them had together, she would do well never to drink anything ever again if she wanted to go on living. Because who knew if there might be henbane in her cup?

With this abominable threat, Charles introduced Nete to henbane and its ghastly properties.

"*Hyoscyamus niger*," she said, dramatically and deliberately, so as to emphasize the gravity of the matter. The name alone made Nete shudder.

"They say witches used it for their flying ointment," Charles went on. "And when they were caught, the priests and persecutors used the same plant to dull the witches' senses during their torture. "Witches' Herb," they called it, so a person should be cautious indeed. Perhaps it would be better to do as I say, don't you think?"

Nete came to heel and remained there for months, and the time was in every way her worst on Sprogø.

When Nete looked out over the sea she saw waves that could not only carry her away from the island to freedom, but also pull her down. Down into the darkness where no one would ever find her or do her harm again.

The seeds of the henbane plant were the only thing Nete took with her from Sprogø when she finally left the island. Nothing more, after four years of toil and torment.

Much later, after qualifying as a laboratory assistant, she heard of monastery excavations where centuries-old henbane seed had been activated, and immediately she planted her own seeds in a pot and set it in a sunny spot.

Presently a healthy green plant appeared like a reincarnation to greet her, as if it were an old friend who'd been gone a long time and had now returned.

For some years it had flourished in the soil of Havngaard, and the plant that now stood in the window of her Nørrebro apartment was directly descended from those original seeds. She had dried the plants and stored them with the clothes she wore on the day she finally returned to freedom. They were relics of a bygone age. Leaves, seed capsules, desiccated stalks, and the moistureless remnants of what had once been the loveliest white flowers with dark veins and a gleaming red eye in the middle. She had gathered two bags of the plant's various parts and knew exactly how to use them.

Perhaps it had been henbane and its unrevealed secrets that had prompted Nete to continue her studies and become a biology lab technician. Perhaps it was what made her immerse herself in chemistry.

Whatever the reason, with her upgraded knowledge of substances and their effects on the human body she was more able to comprehend what a singularly lethal implement nature had allowed to grow so freely in Sprogø's earth.

After a few experiments she succeeded in producing extracts of the three most important active ingredients of the plant in her kitchen on the fourth floor, and she tested the results on herself in tiny, mild doses.

The hyoscyamine made her constipated and dried up her saliva; small bumps appeared on her face and in her mouth, and her heart became strangely arrhythmic, without actually making her ill.

She feared the scopolamine more. She knew just fifty milligrams was a lethal dose. Even in the smallest amounts, scopolamine was highly soporific and at the same time a euphoriant. No wonder it had been used as a truth serum during World War II. A person with scopolamine in their blood became oblivious to whatever they might say in the dreamy, somnolent state the substance induced.

And then there was the atropine, a colorless crystalline alkaloid found in all plants of the nightshade family. Maybe Nete hadn't been as careful ingesting this as she had with the two other substances. In any case, it impaired both her vision and her ability to speak, caused a fever and flushes, made her skin burn, and gave her hallucinations that very nearly delivered her into unconsciousness.

There was little doubt that a cocktail of these three ingredients would be lethal if sufficiently concentrated. Nete knew what would happen if she heated them up together and boiled away ninety-five percent of the water.

Thus, she now held a sizable bottle of henbane extract in her hands, with all the windows steamed up and the air inside the apartment heavy with its bitter smell.

All that remained was to find the right dosage for the right body.

Nete had not used her husband's computer since she moved in. Why should she? There was no one to write to, nothing to write about, no accounts to be kept, no business correspondence to conduct. No spread-sheets or word processing. Those days were gone.

But that Thursday in August 1987 she switched on the computer and listened to its whirring as the screen slowly became green. A tingling sen-sation ran through her body, and her stomach knotted with apprehension.

When the letters were written and sent there would be no turning back. The path of Nete's life was narrowing and would come to a dead end. That was how she looked at it, and it was how she wanted it to be.

She wrote several drafts of the letter she would send, but the final version was this:

COPENHAGEN, THURSDAY 27 AUGUST 1987

Dear . . .

Many years have passed since we last saw each other. Years I can proudly say have slowly evolved into an agreeable and gratifying life.

Throughout this time I have reflected upon my destiny and have come to the conclusion that events of the past were unavoidable and now, at the end of the day, I finally realize that I was not without blame for their occurrence.

Whatever took place then, whatever harsh words were spoken, whatever misunderstandings occurred, I am no longer tormented. In fact, quite the contrary. Looking back provides me with peace of mind and the knowledge that I survived it all, and now is the time for reconciliation.

As you may know from the press, I was for some years married to Andreas Rosen, and my husband's inheritance has made me a very wealthy woman.

Now fate has decreed that I undergo hospital treatment. Regrettably, I have been diagnosed as suffering from an incurable illness, for which reason the time I have left for what follows is short indeed.

Since I have been unable to give birth to children who might inherit my estate, I have now decided to share my wealth with some of the individuals I have encountered for better or worse on my journey through life.

Thus I would hereby like to invite you to come to my home address at Peblinge Dossering 32, Copenhagen, on

FRIDAY 4 SEPTEMBER at . . .

For the occasion, my lawyer will be present to ensure that the sum of 10 million kroner be transferred to you. Naturally, this gift is subject to taxation by the authorities, but the lawyer will instruct you further on this matter, so you have no reason for concern.

I feel certain that, following these proceedings, we shall be able to speak freely of times past. Sadly, my future has little to offer. However, I would be highly appreciative of the opportunity to perhaps make comfortable your own. Such occasion would indeed give me pleasure and peace of mind.

I realize this comes at short notice, but regardless of whatever plans you might have for the day in question, I am certain you will find it worth your while to make the journey here.

I would ask you to bring this invitation with you and to arrive promptly at the time indicated, since the lawyer has been given a rather busy schedule that day.

I enclose 2,000 kroner in the form of a crossed check in order to meet your travel expenses.

I look forward to seeing you again in the conviction that our meeting will be beneficial to us both.

> *Yours faithfully,*
> *Nete Hermansen*

It was a good letter, she decided, and saved it in six versions, each with a different name and appointment time, after which she printed them out and added her signature at the bottom. A meticulous, confident signature, not at all the kind the recipients had previously seen from her hand.

Six letters. Curt Wad, Rita Nielsen, Gitte Charles, Tage Hermansen, Viggo Mogensen, and Philip Nørvig. For a moment she considered writing to her two surviving brothers, only to dismiss the notion. They'd been so young at the time and had hardly known her. Besides, they were at sea when it happened, and Mads, their older brother, had died. No, they couldn't be blamed for anything.

So now there were six envelopes in front of her. By rights there should have been nine, but she knew death had stolen a march on her on three occasions, and those particular chapters had already been closed by time.

Her schoolmistress, the consultant physician, and the matron from Sprogø were already gone. They were the ones who got away. Three people for whom it would have been the easiest thing in the world to show mercy. Or perhaps rather to let justice prevail. All three committed grievous wrongs and made terrible mistakes, and all three went through life staunchly believing the opposite to be true: that their work and their lives had benefited not only society, but also the poor individuals in their charge.

And this in particular preyed on Nete's mind. Preyed on her mind and tormented her.

"Nete, come with me," the schoolmistress snarled. And when Nete hesitated she dragged her by the car all the way round to the back of the building so that dust whirled in their wake.

"You contemptible little monster. You silly, half-witted child, how dare you?" she spat, striking Nete in the face with a bony hand. And when Nete yelled back at her with tears in her eyes and demanded to know why she was being punished, the mistress struck her again.

She looked around her as she lay on the ground with the incensed figure standing over her. It occurred to her that her dress would be dirty now, and that her father would be sorry on account that it had cost him so much money. She tried to shield herself and wished only to be consumed by the apple blossom that fluttered from the trees, the song of the skylark that chirped high above them, the cheerful laughter of her schoolmates on the other side of the building.

"This is the end. I've had enough of you, you despicable little beast, do you understand? Immoral hussy!"

But Nete did not understand. She had been playing with the boys and they had asked her to lift up her dress. And when she had done so and gigglingly revealed a pair of voluminous pink knickers handed down from her mother, they had all howled with delight because it had been so natural of her, so carefree and exuberant. Until the mistress had forced her way among them and slapped their faces one by one, causing the group to disperse, leaving only Nete behind.

"You little whore!" the mistress barked, and Nete knew what it meant, so she answered back and said she most certainly was not, and if anyone accused her of being one, then they must be one themselves.

The mistress's eyes rolled in their sockets as Nete spat the words.

And that was why she struck Nete so hard behind the school building, and it was why she kicked gravel in her face and screamed at her and told her that from now on she was no longer a pupil at the school, and if she ever had the chance she would make sure to teach an underling such as her never to answer back again. The way Nete had behaved ever since she first came to the school, she deserved nothing good in life. And what she had done now could never, ever be made up for. Of that the mistress would make certain.

And so she did.

10

November 2010

Three and a half hours, and then hopefully he'd be presenting himself at Mona's, ironed and pressed and looking like a man she'd want to spend a night of bliss with.

Carl glanced despondently at his ashen face in the rearview mirror as he parked the car outside his house at the end of the row in Allerød. Hope could hardly have been more forlorn.

Two hours of shut-eye might do the trick, he thought to himself, only then to see the figure of Terje Ploug striding toward him.

"What now, Ploug?" he barked, getting out of the car.

Ploug gave a shrug. "The nail-gun case. I needed to hear Hardy's version."

"You've heard it five times already, at least."

"True, but I thought perhaps he might remember something new, now there's been a development."

The bloodhound in Ploug had picked up a scent, that much was obvious. He was one of the more thorough investigators at HQ. No one would more gladly drive thirty-five kilometers to gather twigs for what later might turn into a bonfire of suspicion.

"And did he?"

"Maybe."

"Maybe? What the hell's that supposed to mean?"

"Ask him yourself," Ploug said, then raised a couple of fingers to his temple in farewell.

Morten Holland came scurrying toward Carl the moment he came in. Any thoughts he might have entertained of having a private life were made futile by the eternal presence of his fat lodger.

Morten glanced at his watch. "A good thing you're home early today, Carl. There's been so much going on here. I'm not even sure I can remember it all." He sounded out of breath, his sentences rattled off with urgency. No peace for the wicked.

"All right, hold your horses," Carl said, though stopping a hundred and twenty kilos of blubber in its tracks was never going to be easy, especially with a sore throat coming on.

"I've had Vigga on the phone for a whole *hour*. She's in a foul mood and you're to ring her *up* as soon as you get in."

Carl's head lolled. If he hadn't felt lousy before, he certainly did now. How the hell could his wife, who he hadn't lived with for years, still impact so drastically on his immune system?

"What did she want?" he asked wearily.

But Morten merely held up his chubby hands defensively, campily fluttering them about as if to stave off impending interrogation. Carl would obviously have to find out for himself.

Another job to add to the list.

"Anything else, apart from Terje Ploug coming round?" he forced himself to ask. Might as well get it over with before he passed out from fatigue.

"Yeah, Jesper called home from college. He says his wallet's been stolen."

Carl shook his head. His brainless stepson! Almost three years at Allerød Gymnasium School only to drop out just before his final two

exams. Crap marks across the board. Now on his second year at prepara-
tory college in Gentofte, flitting back and forth in fits of protest between
Vigga's allotment garden house in Islev and Carl's place in Allerød. A new
girl in his room every other day, nonstop partying, and general arsing
about. Par for the course at that age.

"How much money was in it?" Carl asked.

Morten rolled his eyes. Not *that* much, surely?

"He can sort it out himself," said Carl, stepping into the front room.

"All right, Hardy?" he said quietly.

Maybe the worst thing was how he never stirred in his hospital bed
when someone came in. An outstretched hand to shake, or just a finger
raised in greeting would have done no end of good.

He smoothed his hand over the forehead of his quadriplegic former
colleague as he always did, and was greeted by two blue eyes full of a
yearning to see more than just their immediate surroundings in Carl's
living room.

"News channel, eh?" Carl noted, nodding toward the flatscreen in the
corner.

Hardy's mouth twisted. What else was there for him to do? "Terje
Ploug's just been here," he said.

"Yeah, I ran into him outside. He seemed to think you might have
something new to add to the case, is that right?" Carl stepped back, feeling a sneeze coming on, but the tickle in his nose went away again.
"Sorry, best keep my distance, I reckon. Think I'm coming down with
something. They're all dropping like flies at HQ."

Hardy tried to smile. Catching a cold was the least of his worries these
days. "Ploug told me some more about that body they found today."

"Yeah, it was in a poor state. Dismembered and put into rubbish bags.
Decomposition had been impeded by the plastic, of course, but it was still
what you'd call advanced decay."

"Ploug says they found a smaller bag that had almost formed a vacuum inside," said Hardy. "They reckon there was warm air in it to begin with and then it must have cooled quickly. At any rate, the flesh inside seemed relatively well preserved."

"OK. In that case they might have some decent DNA to go on. Maybe it's a step forward, eh, Hardy? I think we both could do with a break-through there."

Hardy looked him straight in the eye. "I told Ploug they should try and find out if the guy had an ethnic background."

Carl cocked his head and immediately felt his nose start to dribble. "What for?"

"Because Anker told me he'd had a run-in with some fucking for-eigner that night he came home with blood on his clothes the time he was staying with Minna and me. And I'm not talking about bloodstains you'd normally see after a fight. Not the kind of fights I've ever seen, at any rate."

"What the hell would that have to do with the case?"

"I've been asking myself the same question. But something tells me Anker was up shit creek, OK? We've already talked about that."

Carl nodded. "Let's talk about it in the morning, Hardy. I'm off upstairs for some shut-eye, see if I can kick this bloody virus into touch. Mona's invited me over tonight for Martinmas goose and surprises."

"Well, have a nice time," Hardy said. He sounded bitter.

Carl flopped down heavily on his bed and recalled the hat remedy. As far as he was aware, this was something his old dad still swore by in times of illness.

"Lie down on a bed that's got two bedposts," he always said. "Hang a hat on one post and reach for the bottle of booze you should always have on your bedside table. Keep drinking until you see a hat on both posts. I promise you, you'll be right as rain the next day. And if you're not, you won't care."

It never failed, but what if you had to drive a car a couple of hours later? What if you didn't want to turn up where you were going stinking of booze? Arriving pissed was something Mona definitely wouldn't reward with kisses and cuddles.

He heaved a couple of sighs and felt sorry for himself, then reached out for his Tullamore whisky regardless, and took a couple of swigs. It couldn't do any harm, surely?

A moment later he pressed Vigga's number on his mobile, inhaled deeply, and waited with bated breath.

"Oh, I'm so glad you called," Vigga twittered. It was a sure sign things would go belly-up any minute.

"Out with it, Vigga. I'm too ill and too knackered to beat about the bush."

"Are you ill? In that case it can wait."

Bollocks! She knew perfectly well he knew she didn't mean it.

"Has it got to do with money?" he asked.

"Carl!" Too delighted by half. Carl took another swig from the whisky bottle. "Gurkamal's proposed to me."

Whisky-filled nostrils can be a rather unpleasant affair, Carl discovered. He spluttered a couple of times and wiped the slime from the tip of his nose, ignoring his furiously streaming eyes.

"But that's bigamy, Vigga, for Chrissake. You're still married to me, remember?"

She laughed.

Carl sat up straight and put the bottle down on the night table.

"Listen, is this your way of asking for a divorce? Do you think I'm going to sit here in bed on a perfectly decent Wednesday and have a good laugh while you tell me the roof's falling down on me? I can't fucking afford to get divorced, Vigga, you know that. There's no way I can keep the house if we're going to be dividing things up between us now. The same house your son lives in and which is the home of two lodgers. You can't be serious, surely? Can't you and this Gherkin bloke make do with shacking up together? Why go the whole hog and get married?"

"Our Anand Karaj is going to be held in Patiala, where his family lives. Isn't it fantastic?"

"Hey, hey, hey, hold on a minute, Vigga. Didn't you hear what I just said? How do you expect me to deal with a divorce now? Didn't we say we had to agree before taking things that far? And what the fuck's this 'ham and carriage' you're talking about? I'm not with you."

"Anand Karaj, you daft thing. It's where we bow before the Guru Granth Sahib to solemnize the nuptials."

Carl's eyes panned quickly across the bedroom wall on which small tapestries still hung from the time Vigga had been infatuated with Hinduism and the mysteries of Bali. Was there any religion left with which she had not flirted outrageously over the years?

"I'm not with you *at all*, Vigga. Are you seriously expecting me to cough up three or four hundred grand to get you married off to some bloke with half a mile of hair in his turban who's going to keep you under his thumb all day long?"

She laughed like a schoolgirl who'd just talked her parents into letting her get her nose pierced.

If she kept on like this he was going to pass out. He reached for a tissue on the bedside table and blew his nose. Oddly enough, nothing came out.

"Carl! You obviously know absolutely nothing about the teachings of Guru Nanak. Sikhism goes in for equality of the sexes, for meditation, and earning an honest living. Sharing with the poor and setting store by hard work. You can't find a purer way of living than what's practiced by the Sikhs."

"Well, if they *have to* share with the poor, then this Gherkin of yours can start off by sharing with me. Let's say two hundred grand and we're quits, shall we?"

More laughter, as if she'd never stop. "Relax, Carl. You can borrow the money from Gurkamal, then give it to me. He'll give you a low rate of interest, so you'll have no worries there. I've had an estate agent value the house. Anything of that standard in Rønneholtparken is going for 1.9 million at the moment. We still owe six hundred thousand, so you get off with half of the 1.3 that's left *and* you can keep the furniture into the bargain."

Six hundred and fifty thousand kroner!

Carl leaned back and slowly closed the flap of his mobile.

It was like the shock had driven the virus out of his body and replaced it with thirty-two lead weights somewhere in his chest region.

He smelled her scent even before she opened the door.

"Come in," said Mona, taking his arm and drawing him inside.

Bliss lasted a further three seconds until she veered off to the dining room and left him standing before a young woman in a clinging micro-dress who stood leaning over the table, lighting candles.

"This is Samantha, my youngest daughter," Mona announced. "She's been looking forward to meeting you."

The eyes of this clone of a twenty-year-younger Mona did not, however, exude quite as much pleasure as her mother's introduction seemed to warrant. She gave him the once-over, clearly noting his receding temples, his rather crumpled posture, and the knot in his tie that suddenly felt far too tight. It was obvious she wasn't impressed.

"Hi, Carl," she said, already revealing resentment of her mother's latest dip into the bottomless pit labeled "Men the Cat Dragged In."

"Hi, Samantha," he replied, struggling to produce something resembling an enthusiastic smile. What the hell had Mona been telling her about him that made him such a disappointment in real life?

The situation took a further nosedive when a small boy came charging in and gave him a whack over the legs with a plastic sword.

"I'm a dangerous robber!" shouted the flaxen-haired monster they referred to as Ludwig.

The flu was nothing on this. Any more surprises today and he'd be cured in no time.

He endured the starter with a smile and the kind of look on his face he'd picked up from countless reruns of Richard Gere films, but when the goose came in, Ludwig's eyes nearly popped out of his head.

"Your nose is dripping into the gravy," he said, pointing at Carl's runny protuberance and thereby activating a burst of barely contained muscle spasms in his mother's abdomen.

When the boy started blathering on about the scar at Carl's temple, announcing that it was horrible and then refusing to believe Carl could possibly have his own real pistol, Carl realized he was out of options.

Please, he prayed silently, eyes turned heavenward, if you don't help me now, there's a child here who's going to be slung over my knee in ten seconds.

The bell that saved him was neither an attractive grandmother's sense of occasion nor a young mother's reprimand. Instead, it was the buzz of the mobile phone in his back pocket, signaling, thank God, that the evening might be over.

"Excuse me just a second," he said, raising one hand in an appeal for silence and reaching into his pocket with the other.

"Assad, what is it?" he said, seeing his assistant's name on the display. Right now he would answer any question whatsoever in any way imaginable, if only it could get him out of here.

"I am sorry for my disturbance, Carl, but can you tell me how many people are reported missing every year in Denmark?"

A cryptic opener, to say the least, and one that could only provoke an equally cryptic response. It was perfect.

"About fifteen hundred, I'd say. Where are you now?" The latter utterance always sounded good.

"Rose and I are still in the basement here. And how many of these fifteen hundred do you think are still missing at the end of the year, Carl?"

"It varies. But about ten, I reckon."

Carl got up from the table and tried to look totally immersed.

"Has there been a new development in the case?" he asked. Another excellent line.

"I'm not sure," Assad replied. "You must tell me. But in the same week when this brothel woman Rita Nielsen disappeared, two others were also reported missing, then another the week after, and none of them have ever been found again. Don't you think this is very strange? *Four* in such a few days, Carl. What do you say? This is just as many as normal for half a year."

"Right, stay where you are, I'm on my way!" A fantastic exit line, though Assad was probably a bit bewildered. When had Carl ever reacted so promptly?

He turned back to the table. "I'm really sorry," he said. "You've probably noticed I'm a little preoccupied today. For one thing, I've got a dreadful cold, so I hope I haven't passed it on to anyone." He sniffled once for emphasis, only to discover his nostrils to be completely dried out. "The other thing is we've got four missing persons on our hands, as well as an exceptionally grisly murder out in Amager that we need to get a handle on. I do apologize, but I'm afraid I have to be on my way, otherwise there's no telling what kind of mess we're going to end up with."

He locked his eyes onto Mona's. She seemed genuinely worried. Not at all like when she was counseling him.

"Is it the shooting again?" she asked, ignoring his lavish compliments on a lovely evening. "Do be careful, won't you? You're still very much affected by all that, Carl."

He nodded. "Yeah, same old case. No need to worry on my account, though. I'm not planning on getting mixed up in anything. And I'm *fine*, really."

Mona frowned. What a crap evening. Two steps backward was what it was. An unfortunate entry into the family, to say the least. Her daughter hated him. Carl hated the grandson. He'd hardly even tasted the goose before dribbling his snot into the gravy, and now Mona was bringing up the nail-gun case again. No doubt she'd have that twerp of a shrink called Kris on his back again now.

"I'm *fine*," he reiterated, then popped a parting finger-gun shot at little Ludwig and flashed him a smile.

Next time he'd have to make sure to be more informed as to the nature of Mona's surprises.

11

August 1987

Tage heard the snap of the letter box and swore. Ever since he had affixed the *No Junk Mail* sticker, all he ever received were letters from the tax authorities and it was seldom they wished him well. He'd never understood why they couldn't leave him alone with the small change he picked up on the side mending bicycles and stripping down the carburetors of young punks' mopeds. Would they prefer him to go cap in hand to the social services in Middelfart, or maybe start doing break-ins in the summer houses at Skårup Strand like the blokes he did his drinking with?

He reached down and picked up one of the wine bottles between the bed and the upturned beer crate he used as a bedside table, checked to see if he'd used it during the night, then held it to his crotch and pissed until it was full. Then he wiped his hands on the duvet cover and slowly got to his feet. He was getting tired of having stuttering, mousy Mette lodging with him. The bathroom was behind her room in the main house, and here in the workshop where he was bedded down, the boards were rotten and the wind whistled in through all the cracks, and winter would be back in no time.

He gazed around the room. There were old, crumpled pin-ups of topless girls with engine grease smeared across their breasts. Wheel hubs, tires, and assorted moped parts were dumped all over the place, and the concrete floor was blackened with the crud of old motor oil. It wasn't the kind of place most people would be proud of, but it was his.

He reached up and found the ashtray on the shelf on the wall full of good stubs. He selected the best of them, lit up, and inhaled deeply. The red glow raced the final millimeters toward his begrimed fingers before he stubbed it out.

Hitching up his underpants, he tiptoed across the cold floor to the door. One step out and his fingers could just reach the letter box. It was a decent box, knocked together out of particleboard, with a lid that had ballooned to twice the thickness compared to when he'd made it back at the dawn of time.

He looked up and down the road, but no one was there. He didn't want anyone kicking up a fuss again about him standing in the middle of Brenderup with his beer gut and filthy undies on show. "Bourgeois cows who couldn't cope with the sight of a full-grown man in the prime of his life," as he told his drinking mates on the bench. It was a good word and he liked to use it. Bourgeois. French, it was.

To his surprise, the letter he retrieved from the box wasn't a bill from the taxman or anything official from the local authority, just an ordinary white envelope with a stamp on. He hadn't received a letter like that for years.

He straightened his back. As though at this very moment he was being watched by the sender, or perhaps rather as though the letter itself had eyes and could tell if the receiver was worthy of its message.

He did not recognize the hand but saw his name written with meticulous, curly letters that lifted themselves elegantly from the paper. It suited him fine.

Then he turned it over, immediately sensing the surge of adrenaline in his veins. Like a person in love, he felt his cheeks blush. And like a hunted man, his eyes grew wide.

Nothing could have been more unexpected than this. A letter from Nete. Nete Hermansen, his cousin. With her address and everything.

Nete, who he never thought he would ever hear from again. And with good reason.

He took a deep breath and for a moment considered dropping the envelope back in the letter box. As if the elements and the box itself would be able to consume it, tear it from his hands in order that he might escape being confronted by its contents.

Such was the effect.

From his practical experience working on their father's smallholding, Nete's older brother, Mads, had learned that, like all other living creatures, human beings could be divided into two kinds, male and female. And as long as a person knew that, there wasn't much more to learn. Everything else would come of its own accord. The fundamentals of life were divided between these two groups. Matters of work, and all that went on within the four walls of the home. It was all designed so that one group or the other would take care of any given issue.

Mads gathered his younger siblings and his male cousin in the yard in front of the farmhouse, pulled down his pants, and pointed to his member.

"If you've got one of these, you're one sort. And if you've got a slit instead, then you're another. That's all there is to it."

His brothers and cousin Tage had laughed, whereupon Nete had pulled her knickers down as though to demonstrate some kind of child-like solidarity and understanding.

Tage in particular found this uplifting. Where he came from, undressing was something that took place in private, and if truth be told he had never quite grasped this singular way in which men and women differed.

It was Tage's first summer spent at his uncle's. So much better than hot days by the harbor in Assens and in the narrow lanes where he and the other boys could hide with their Eiffel cigarettes and dream of one day heading off to sea.

They got on well, Nete and Tage. The twins were his good friends, too, but Nete was his favorite, even though she was almost eight years his junior. She was so easy to get along with, laughing if only he pulled a face, and throwing herself with abandon into the daftest of situations at the drop of a hat.

It was the first time in Tage's life a person ever looked up to him, and he loved it. For that reason he worked hard to help Nete with whatever was asked of her.

When Mads and the twins eventually moved out, Nete was left with only her father and summer days with Tage, and he vividly recalled how hard it impacted on her. Not least in view of the recurring smear campaigns in the village, and her father's increasingly unpredictable moods and occasionally unjust behavior.

They were not in love, Tage and Nete, only close friends, and yet in the intimacy between them lingered all the tantalizing questions about the two groups into which human beings could be divided, and how they sometimes behaved in each other's company.

Thus it was Tage who taught Nete how humans mate, and therefore it was he who, without intention, took everything away from her.

He sat down heavily on the bed, glanced at the bottle on the workbench, and wondered for a moment what would help him more, drinking the cherry wine before or after he read the letter.

As he sat, he heard the sound of his lodger, Mette, coughing in the front room. It wasn't the kind of noise usually associated with a woman, but he had got used to it. She was all right under the duvet, too, on a cold winter's day, as long as the social services didn't get any ideas about them living together as a couple and fiddling their benefits.

He weighed the envelope in his hand and pulled out the contents. A fine sheet of writing paper folded twice with flowers on it. He was expecting to see the handwriting again when he unfolded it, only to find the letter to be machine printed and easily legible. He read it quickly through to get the anguish over with, and was about to succumb to the temptation of the cherry wine when he got to the place where it said she would give him ten million kroner if at a given time he would come to her address in Copenhagen.

He let go of the letter and saw it descend to the concrete floor. It was only then that he saw the check attached to the bottom of the page with paper clips, made out in his name to the amount of two thousand kroner.

Never before had there been so much money in his hands at this time of the month. It was all he could think of. The rest was just too unreal. The millions. Nete's illness. The whole situation!

Two thousand kroner! Not even when he'd been at sea had he ever had so much money at the end of the month. Not even when he worked at the trailer factory before it moved to Nørre Aaby and got rid of him because of his drinking.

He pulled the check from the letter and felt it between his fingers.

It was bloody real and all.

Nete was fun and Tage was game. When the bull was drawn over to the smallholding's only cow she asked if he could get a boner just as big, and when he showed her, she fell about laughing as if at one of the jokes her twin brothers were always rattling off. Even when they kissed she was unceremonious and amenable, and Tage was pleased. He was there to try himself out on her, for this was how he thought about her all the time, even though she had only just begun to take shape. He looked smart in his brown soldier's uniform, garrison cap tucked under his shoulder strap, narrow in the waist. And it worked, thanks to the bull and the cow performing their inescapable annual ritual.

Nete found Tage to be all grown up and just as she wanted, and when he asked her to take off her clothes in the hay loft and make him happy, she didn't hesitate. Why should she? Everyone had said this was how it worked, that such was the way of the male and the female.

And when nothing bad happened, they did it again on other occasions, repeating what they had learned: that nothing could compete with the joy of human bodies close together.

When she was fifteen she became pregnant. And although she was glad and told Tage that now they would be together for the rest of their days, he refused to acknowledge his paternity. If he really was the father of her bastard child, he shouted, it would get him into trouble because she was underage and their liaison had been against the law. No way was he going to prison for her.

Nete's father believed her explanation, until he thrashed the daylights out of Tage with no effect but her cousin continuing to deny his part in Nete's predicament. Since his own sons had always succumbed to such brutal interrogation, he naturally supposed the young man to be speaking the truth.

After that, Tage never saw Nete again. He heard about her on occasion, and from time to time he felt ridden by deep feelings of shame.

Eventually, he chose to forget everything.

He spent two days getting ready. Bathing his hands in lubricating oil and rubbing and scrubbing until the chapped skin was pink and vital. He shaved several times until his cheeks once again became smooth and bright. At the barber's they received him like a prodigal son, washing and cutting his hair, dabbing him with scent as only professionals are able. He polished his teeth with bicarbonate of soda until his gums bled, and when all was done he looked at himself in the mirror and saw the echo of better days. If he was going to receive ten million kroner, he would do so in style. Nete was to look upon him as though he had led a worthy life. He wanted her to see him as the young man who had once made her laugh and to approach him with pride.

He trembled still at the thought. That he, at the age of almost fifty-eight, could rise from the very bowels of society and stand erect, a complete human, the eyes that came to rest on him no longer afraid that he would do them harm.

In the night he dreamed of respect and envy, of brighter times in new surroundings. Only a bloody masochist would stay on in this miserable place, where they squinted at him as if he had the plague. No fucking way was he going to hang about in a village of fourteen hundred inhabitants, where even the railway was dying out and whose pride and joy was a trailer factory that had long since moved, making way for nothing more than a knobhead institution called The Nordic School for Peace.

He picked out the biggest gentleman's outfitters in Bogense and bought himself a glistening, blue-flecked suit that the assistant, with a wry smile, informed him was the highest fashion and which, being significantly marked down, left him with just enough money for some petrol for his moped and a return train ticket from Fjby to Copenhagen.

It felt like the moment of his life as he got on his VéloSoleX and chugged off through the town. The looks he attracted seemed quite unlike those he was used to.

Never before had he been so ready to meet the future.

12

August 1987

Much to his satisfaction, Curt Wad had seen the political right increase its hold on the population throughout the eighties, and now, at the end of August 1987, the media were predicting almost without exception that the conservative bloc would stay in power after the election.

These were truly favorable days for Curt Wad and those who shared his opinions. The Upsurge Party railed against immigration, and gradually an increasing number of Christian groups and nationalist organizations had gathered around shrewd populist agitators who skillfully cracked the whip over depravation and moral decay, without demonstrating the slightest sensitivity to basic principles of human rights.

The general gist was that people were not born equal, nor were they meant to be, and the voters might just as well get used to the fact.

Favorable days indeed. Such thoughts had now wormed their way into parliament and certain NGOs, and at the same time funds came flowing in to Curt's cherished Purity Party, which he worked hard to ensure would one day develop into a bona fide political party with a wide network of local branches and parliamentary representation in the seat of government, Christiansborg. With this moral shift in the population, it was almost like returning to the thirties, forties, and fifties. Certainly, it was a far cry from the depravity of the sixties and seventies when youngsters marched noisily in the streets, preaching free love and socialism. A time when wretched individuals, the dregs of society, had their pockets lined by the state and antisocial behavior was explained away as being the failure of both government and society.

Happily, such days were gone. Here, in the 1980s, every man was the architect of his own fortune. And many were indeed industrious, so much was evident, for each day new contributions to Curt Wad's Purity Party came pouring in from upstanding citizens, foundations, and trusts.

The results showed. Two office ladies had already been taken on to deal with the party's accounts and distribution of information, and at least four of the party's nine branches were growing at a rate of five members a week.

At long last, aversion to homosexuality, drug addiction, juvenile crime, promiscuity, immigration, political asylum, and the propagation of poor genetic material had begun to sweep through large segments of the population. As if to underline the point, the AIDS virus had arrived, and served to remind of what Christian communities referred to as "the finger of God."

The leverage such issues provided in helping do away with these evils had been superfluous in the fifties, but in those days there had been much better means by which to strike back.

No matter. These were promising times indeed. Though not uttered aloud, the guiding ethos of the Purity Party spread like wildfire: bad blood should never be mixed with good.

The association for the defense of the nation's unblemished blood and moral values had gone by three different names since Curt's father had founded the movement in his stubborn endeavors to ensure racial purity and the raising of public morals. In the 1940s he had called it the Anti-Debauchery Committee. Later it became the Community of Danes, then eventually the Purity Party.

What had been conceived in the mind of a general practitioner from

Fyn, and since refined by his son, was no longer a private matter. The association now numbered some two thousand members, all of whom were only too happy to pay a tidy annual subscription. These were respected citizens ranging from lawyers, doctors, and police officers to care workers and priests. People who in their daily work were witness to much that was deplorable and possessed the insight and ability to do something about it.

Had Curt's father still been alive he would have been proud to see how far his son had carried these thoughts and gratified by the way in which he had administered what the two of them eventually began to refer to as "The Cause." This was the framework within which he and like-minded supporters clandestinely carried out the illegalities they were striving to legitimize through the activities of the Purity Party, most notably the separation of fetuses deemed not to be deserving of life from those that were.

Curt Wad had just completed a recorded radio interview in which he again expounded upon the official version of the Purity Party's fundamental ideas, when his wife placed a pile of letters in front of him in a shaft of sunlight that shone on the middle of his oak wood desk.

The mail was always a mixed bag.

The anonymous letters went into the wastebasket without further ado. Which took care of about a third of what came in.

After that came the usual hate mail and threats. In such cases Curt carefully noted down the names and addresses of the senders, subsequently passing the letters on to the office in town. If the ladies there noticed repeated harassment by the same individuals, Curt would call local branch spokesmen, who would then make sure that no further correspondence ensued. Since most people had secrets they didn't want to get out, there were many ways by which to tackle such matters, and local lawyers, doctors, and priests had access to a large number of archives. Some would call it blackmail. Curt called it self-defense.

Then there were those applying for membership, and these cases called for particular alertness. Infiltration could be a tricky matter once it had occurred, and for that reason one had to proceed with caution from the start. Which was why Curt Wad opened his mail himself.

Finally came the more typical expressions of opinion spanning a broad spectrum, from kudos to whining and rage.

Among the last of the day's batch Curt Wad came upon the letter from Nete Hermansen. He couldn't prevent himself from smiling when he saw the sender's name on the back of the envelope. Not many cases over the years had turned out as successfully as hers. On two separate occasions in his life he had put a stop to this woman's immoral behavior and depravation. The whore.

But what did this miserable specimen want with him now? Would it be tears or rebuke? If truth be told, he didn't care. To him, Nete Hermansen was a nobody. Always had been and always would be. The fact that she was now on her own after that stupid husband of hers had got himself killed in a car crash the same night he'd bumped into her last prompted little more than a shrug.

She deserved no better.

He tossed the unopened envelope onto the pile of unimportant mail. He wasn't even curious. Not like he'd been all those years ago.

The first time he heard about Nete was when the chairman of the school board came to Curt's father's surgery with reports of a girl who had fallen into the mill stream at Puge and suffered abdominal bleeding as a result.

"She may have aborted. Much would seem to indicate so," said the chairman. "Any talk of schoolboys being responsible should not be taken seriously. It was an accident, and should you be called out to the home, Dr. Wad, please note that any sign of violence is due only to the girl's falling into the stream."

"How old is she?" his father asked.

"Just turned fifteen."

"Hardly natural to be pregnant at that age," said his father.

"Well, she's hardly a natural girl," the chairman rejoined with a snort. "She was thrown out of school years ago on account of various depravities. Lewd behavior, inviting fornication with the boys, foul language. Simple of mind and action, and violent toward her fellow pupils and schoolmistress."

At this, Curt's father leaned back his head and nodded in full understanding.

"Ah, one of those," he said. "Retarded, I imagine."

"Most certainly," said the chairman.

"Would the good children whom this contemptible child might wish to accuse by any chance include a personal acquaintance of the chairman among their number?"

"Yes, as it happens," the chairman replied, reaching to accept one of the cigars that lay neatly arranged in the box on top of the doctor's desk. "One of the boys is the youngest child of my brother's sister-in-law."

"I see," said Curt's father. "A clash of social categories, if ever there was one."

Curt was thirty years old at the time and already on his way to taking over his father's practice, but he had yet to encounter a patient such as the girl in question.

"What does she do, this girl?" Curt inquired, receiving an encouraging nod from his father.

"Well, I'm not that informed, I'm afraid. But it seems she helps her father out on his smallholding."

"And the father is?" Curt's father asked.

"As far as I recall, his name's Lars Hermansen. A common man, rather the brawny type, I believe."

"I know him," said Curt's father. Of course he did. He had even assisted when the girl had been born. "A bit funny in the head, exacerbated by his wife's death. In any case a strange, insular sort. No wonder if the girl's a bit odd, too."

And that was that.

As expected, Dr. Wad was called out to Nete's father's smallholding, there to conclude that the girl had foolishly slipped and fallen into the stream and then thrashed around in the current, thereby injuring herself on branches and rocks that lay beneath the embankment. Any other explanation she might provide could only be down to shock and distress. Her bleeding, however, was regrettable. Had she perhaps been pregnant? he asked the father.

Curt had been present, as on all his father's house calls of late, and he clearly remembered how the girl's father paled at the question and slowly shook his head.

Police involvement would be unnecessary in that respect, the father had said.

And thus the case was pursued no further.

Toward evening the association's activities were again in motion and Curt Wad was looking forward. In ten minutes he would be meeting with three of the Purity Party's most diligent members who were not only in close touch with prominent figures in the right-wing parties, but also well connected with civil servants in the ministries of justice and internal affairs who looked dimly upon the way the country was progressing, particularly when it came to immigration and family reunification policies. And the motivation for their involvement was the same as for all other members: far too many foreign elements, undesirable and lower-standing individuals, had already wangled their way into the country.

"A threat to society and the public in general," came the cry from several quarters, and Curt Wad could not have agreed more. It was all a matter of genes, and people with slanting eyes or brown skin had no part in the idealized narrative of flaxen-haired girls and boys with strong, muscular frames. Tamils, Pakistanis, Turks, Afghans, Vietnamese, all had to be stopped in the manner of any other invasive impurity. Effectively and without hesitation.

They spoke at length that evening about what measures the Purity Party might take, and when two of the men had left, Curt remained with the one he knew best. An excellent man indeed, a doctor like himself with a lucrative practice north of the capital.

"We've talked about The Cause many times now, Curt," the man said, studying him with a firm gaze before continuing. "I knew your father, of course. He made me aware of my responsibility back when I was a young physician at the university hospital in Odense. He was a fine man, Curt. I learned a great deal from him, professionally as well as in regard to ethical issues."

They nodded to each other. It had been a source of considerable gratification to Curt that his father had lived until Curt's sixty-second year. Now it was already three years since he had finally succumbed to advanced age, ninety-seven years old. Time passed so quickly.

"Your father told me I should come to you if ever I wanted to become active," said his guest, pausing for a moment as though aware that whatever step he took next would lead him directly into a complex of difficult questions and treacherous pitfalls.

"I'm glad," said Curt eventually. "But why *now*, if I may ask?"

The man raised his eyebrows and allowed himself time before answering. "For several reasons. Our talk here, tonight, is one. Another is that we've more than our fair share of foreigners in Nordsjælland, too. Immigrants, often closely related, and still they intermarry. As we know, unhealthy offspring are far from seldom in cases of inbreeding."

Curt nodded. This was true. They were all over the place.

"Basically, I'd like to do my bit as far as that's concerned," the man said quietly.

Curt nodded again. Another able and upstanding citizen had joined the fold.

"You realize you'll be taking on work which under no circumstances may be discussed with anyone other than those we've specifically approved, and that this restriction will apply for as long as you live?"

"Yes," said the man. "I'd imagined that would be the case."

"Little of what we do within the framework of The Cause can bear the light of day in present circumstances, but you'll be aware of that, obviously. We've a lot at stake."

"Indeed."

"Many would prefer to see a person vanish from the face of the earth rather than put up with him carrying out his work without due care and discretion."

The man nodded. "Understandably so. I'd feel the same way, I'm sure."

"So you're willing to be initiated into our selection procedures with regard to pregnancy termination and sterilization?"

"I am."

"We employ special terminology in such instances. We have lists of addresses and our own specially developed methods of abortion. If we initiate you into these procedures you will become a full-fledged member. Do you understand?"

"Yes, I do. What is required before I can be approved?"

Curt scrutinized the man. Was the will present? Would these eyes remain as calm if he faced prison and disgrace? Did he have enough backbone to resist pressure from without?

"Your family and friends are to be kept in the dark, unless they take active part in our work."

"My wife takes no interest in what I do, so there's nothing to worry about on that account." His guest smiled. It was just the reaction Curt had hoped for at this point in their discussion.

"Very well, let's go into my surgery. You'll take off your clothes and allow me to check for listening devices. After that I want you to write down some facts about yourself, things you'd want no one in the world to know besides us. No doubt you've a couple of skeletons in your cupboard much like the rest of us, am I right? The points in question should preferably concern your medical work."

Here his guest nodded. Not everyone did.

"You want secrets. To be used against me if I get cold feet?"

"I'm sure you've got some."

The man nodded again.

"Plenty."

Afterward, when Curt had searched him and watched as he signed his statement, he issued the obligatory strict exhortations to loyalty and silence in respect of The Cause's activities and fundamental principles. And when this didn't seem to discourage the man either, Curt delivered a brief introduction to how spontaneous abortions could be provoked without giving rise to suspicion, before informing him, by way of conclusion, of the intervals required between such treatments to ensure the attention of health inspectors and the police would not be aroused.

When finally they said their good-byes, Curt was left with the splendid feeling of once again having contributed to the good of his nation.

He poured himself a brandy and sat down at the oak desk, trying to recall how many times he had performed the procedure himself.

The cases had been many. Nete Hermansen had been one.

His gaze fell once more on her letter on top of the pile. Then he closed his eyes in pleasant recollection of that very first and most memorable occasion.

13

November 2010

In the late hours of evening on a dark November day such as this, there was something magical about the windows of Police HQ. Like eyes lit up, they seemed almost to be keeping watch. Offices were always awake somewhere in the imposing building, their occupants dwelling on cases that wouldn't rest and couldn't keep. This was the hour when the city bared its teeth: the streetwalker was beaten, drinking mates fell out and drew knives, gangs sought confrontation, and wallets were plundered.

Carl had spent thousands of hours in this building with the street-lamps winking while decent citizens slept in their beds, but he had to admit it had been a while ago now.

If only his evening with Mona hadn't been so excruciating. If only he could have sat down on her bed and gazed into her gorgeous brown eyes instead. If only it had been like that, he would never have bothered to see who was calling him so late. But it hadn't, and Assad turned out to be his savior.

And now he was stuck with the consequences. He went down the stairs to the basement and shook his head in disbelief as Rose and Assad came toward him.

"What the hell are you two doing here?" he asked, continuing along the corridor without stopping. "You do realize you've been here for nineteen hours now, Assad?"

He glanced over his shoulder. Rose's traipsing feet behind him didn't exactly sound like she was full of beans. "And what about you, Rose? How come you're still here? Scraping up overtime for a day off, is that it?" He threw his coat over the chair in his office. "Something new in the Rita Nielsen case that can't wait till tomorrow?"

Assad raised his bushy eyebrows sufficiently for the redness of his eyes to give Carl a start. "Here are the newspapers we have examined," he said, dumping a pile onto Carl's desk.

"Only we haven't had that close a look," Rose added.

Knowing Rose, this was a rather modest statement. He noted the grin on Assad's face. They'd almost certainly pored through the pages until the paper had worn thin. Of course they had. First the missing persons department's files of all reported cases in September 1987, then the newspapers. He knew perfectly well how they operated.

"There's nothing in that period to suggest any kind of trouble on the drugs scene or other episodes that could be linked to rape or anything similar in the area," Rose said.

"Anyone considered the possibility of Rita Nielsen having left the car somewhere else, and that it wasn't her who parked it on Kapelvej?" Carl asked. "Maybe we shouldn't be looking at Copenhagen at all. If she didn't park the car herself, she could have disappeared anywhere at all between here and the Storebælt ferry."

"They already thought of that," Rose replied. "The thing is, though, that according to the police report, the kiosk owner in Nørrebro remembered her when they turned up to ask about her credit card transaction. So she *was* in Nørrebro that morning."

Carl pressed his lips together. "Why did she leave home so early? Have you thought about that?" he asked.

Assad nodded. "Definitely because she had an appointment, I think."

Carl agreed. The time of her departure had been bothering him. No one leaves home at five in the morning without good reason, certainly no one of Rita Nielsen's profession, which was mostly conducted during the night. And it was hardly likely to do with Saturday shopping hours either, so what explanation could there be, other than she had an appointment to keep?

"Either someone met her when she got to Copenhagen, in which case whoever it was knows more about her disappearance than we do, or else she never arrived, in which case someone must have realized as much," Carl said. "What sort of an effort was made to find her? Was it enough, do you reckon?"

"Enough?" Assad looked at Rose, who seemed just as blank. The pair of them had obviously run out of blood sugar.

"Yeah, enough for anyone who'd been in touch with her, or was supposed to have been, to have known about her disappearance," said Rose.

"But listen, Carl," she went on, "police spent three days going from door to door. It was in all the papers. The call was put out on TV and on local and national radio, and not a soul came forward, other than that kiosk owner."

"So you reckon someone knew about her going missing, but kept it to themselves? And whoever knew about it might have been involved in her disappearance, is that right?"

Rose smacked her heels together and saluted. "Indeed, sir."

"And now the two of you are telling me there was an unusual number of missing persons reported at about the same time and that none of them have ever been found, is that right, Assad?"

"Yes, and now we have one more who was never found," Assad replied. "We have asked for a whole more week of newspapers, just to be certain we are not missing something that is not on the lists we have from the police districts."

Carl pondered Assad's information for a moment. "So now we've got a total of, what, five persons, including Rita Nielsen, who've never turned up? Five people in two weeks, vanished without a trace, is that what you're saying?"

"Bull's-eye. In the country as a whole there were fifty-five persons reported missing during the two weeks we've been concentrating on, and ten months later five still hadn't been found. And they still haven't, twenty-three years on," Rose said with a nod. "I'd say that must be a record, so many disappearances in such a few days."

Carl tried to assess the dark shadows under her eyes. Was it fatigue, or had her mascara simply been redistributed during the course of the day?

"Let's have a look," he said, running his finger down Rose's list.

He got out a pen and crossed out one of the names. "We can forget about her, at any rate," he said, indicating the woman's age and the circumstances of her disappearance.

"Yes, we think she is too old," said Assad. "And this I say even though my father's sister is older by two years, eighty-five this Christmas, and still she chops firewood all day long."

What a lot of bollocks about nothing, Carl thought to himself. "Listen, Assad! This woman here was senile. She went missing from her care home, and I'm sure she didn't chop firewood, OK? What about the others on the list? Have you checked them out? Is there anything that might connect them with Rita Nielsen's disappearance?"

Here they grinned. Like a pair of bleeding kids.

"Come on, then, let's have it."

Assad gave Rose a nudge with his elbow.

"There's this lawyer by the name of Philip Nørvig from a law firm called Nørvig and Sønderskov in Korsør," she began. "The day before his teenage daughter's most important handball match of the year, Nørvig told her she'd have to take her mother along instead of him, despite the fact he'd promised to be there. All he said by way of explanation was that he had an important meeting in Copenhagen that couldn't be put off."

"And then he disappeared?"

"Yeah, he took the train from Halsskov later that same morning and would have got in to Copenhagen Central about nine thirty. After that, nothing. Vanished off the face of the earth."

"Anyone see him get off the train?"

"A couple of other passengers from Korsør recognized him. He was involved in quite a number of associations in the town, so a lot of people knew who he was."

"I think I remember now," said Carl, ignoring the snot he felt sliding lazily down his nostril. "Prominent lawyer in Korsør. Fairly big thing in the papers at the time. Didn't he turn up floating around in one of the canals here in Copenhagen?"

"No, he disappeared totally, Carl," said Assad. "You must be thinking of another man."

"Was that case up on our bulletin board already, Assad?"

Assad nodded. In which case a length of red string most likely now connected it to the Rita Nielsen case.

"You've got something about it on that sheet there, I see. What's it say about this Nørvig bloke, Rose?"

"He was born in 1925 . . ." was as far as she got.

"In 1925? Bloody hell!" Carl blurted out. "He must have been in his early sixties in 1987. Pretty old for the father of a teenage handball player."

"How about listening to the rest before butting in?" said Rose wearily. The way her eyes were beginning to blink, she reminded him of an aging female rock star trying to come on sexy from beneath a boatload of mascara. Any minute now she'd probably fall asleep.

"Born in 1925," she repeated. "Law degree from Århus in 1950. Junior lawyer with Laursen and Bonde in Vallensbæk, 1950 to 1954. Set up his own firm in Korsør in 1954, right to plead before the High Court in 1965. Married to Sara Julie Enevoldsen, 1950. Divorced, 1973. Two children by first marriage. Married his secretary, Mie Hansen, 1974. One child by her, a daughter by the name of Cecilie, born the same year."

She looked up, a suggestive expression on her face. There was the explanation for his late fatherhood. The bloke had knocked up his secretary. Philip Nørvig seemed to be a man who knew what he wanted.

"He stood for chairman of the local association of sports clubs and was voted in for three terms. After a while he joined the parish council, too. Until 1982, when he got forced out because of accusations of fraud in his law firm. He had to go to court, but got off due to lack of evidence. Still lost a lot of clients, though, and by the time he disappeared five years later, he'd had his driving license revoked because of a drunk driving conviction. Financially, he'd gone down the drain as well. It was all in the red."

"Hmmm." Carl thrust out his lower lip and felt the urge for a smoke. A ciggie would do the world of good for his ailing health *and* his powers of concentration.

"Hey, don't you be lighting up now, Carl," Rose said.

Carl stared at her in astonishment. How the . . . ?

"Wouldn't dream of it, Rose." He cleared his throat. It had started to itch. "You got any tea in that urn of yours, Assad?"

His assistant's brown eyes lit up for a moment, only to be extinguished again. "I'm afraid not, Carl. But I can offer you a good cup of coffee. What do you say?"

Carl swallowed. Assad's coffee was enough to put the wind up any virus.

"As long as it's not too strong, Assad," he replied with an imploring look. Last time it had cost him half a toilet roll. He didn't want that again.

"So the only thing connecting the two cases is that both individuals disappeared under pretty much the same circumstances," he reasoned. "Both were going to Copenhagen that day. We don't know why Rita Nielsen was, but Nørvig said he had a meeting. It's not much to go on, Rose."

"You're forgetting the time, Carl. They disappeared on the same day and almost at the exact same time. That's what *I* call weird."

"I'm still not convinced. What about the other two cases on the list?"

She looked down at the sheet of paper in her hands. "There's a Viggo Mogensen who we don't know anything about. He just vanished. Last seen down by the harbor in Lundeborg, setting out over the Storebælt in his little boat."

"Was he a fisherman?"

"Don't think so. It was just a little boat he had. He did have a fishing boat at one point, but it was broken up. Probably on account of all that EU fishing quota crap."

"Was the boat ever found?"

"Yeah, in Warnemünde. It was nabbed by a couple of Poles who claimed it had been left moored for ages in Jyllinge before they took it. They didn't consider it stealing, in any case."

"What did they say in Jyllinge?"

"They said it wasn't true. There'd never been a boat."

"Sounds to me like the Poles half-inched it, then tipped him overboard."

"They couldn't have. They had a job on in Sweden from August until October 1987, so they weren't in Denmark at all during the time he disappeared."

"How big was this boat? Could it have been moored somewhere with no one noticing?"

"We shall find this out, Carl," said Assad. He was standing in the doorway with the finest little tray made from genuine imitation silver. Carl considered the minuscule cups with trepidation. The smaller the cups, the more ferocious the contents. And these ones were small.

"Bottoms up, Carl," said Assad, with fever-plagued eyes. He looked like someone in need of resuscitation.

Carl downed his coffee in one and found himself thinking it wasn't so bad after all. It was a feeling that lasted all of four seconds before his systems began to react as if he'd imbibed a blend of castor oil and nitroglycerin.

"Good, eh, Carl?" Assad commented.

No wonder his eyes were red.

"OK," Carl spluttered. "We'll put Viggo Mogensen on the back burner for now. I'm not sure there's any link with Rita Nielsen there. Have we got him on the board, Assad?"

Assad shook his head. "The conclusion was he probably drowned in an accident. He was a jolly man who liked a drink. Not an alky, just a tiddler."

"A *tippler*, Assad. The word is *tippler*, just don't ask me why, that's all. What more have we got?" He looked at Rose's list and tried to suppress the discomfort that arose as the coffee substance reached his stomach.

"Then there's this one," said Rose, pointing to another name. "Gitte Charles, it says here. Born 1934 in Tórshavn. Daughter of a grocer, Alistair Charles. The father went bankrupt at the end of the war and the parents divorced. He went back to Aberdeen where he came from, and Gitte and her mother and younger brother moved to Vejle. Trained to be a nurse for a while, but dropped out and wound up working at the mental asylum in Brejning. After that, a few spells as an auxiliary nurse at various places around the country before ending up at the hospital on the island of Samsø."

Rose nodded slowly to herself as she scanned through the text.

"What comes next is just so typical for people who disappear from one day to the next," she said. "Listen to this. She works at Samsø's hospital in Tranebjerg from 1971 to 1980. Seems to be well liked, although she's caught drunk on the job a couple of times. She goes into therapy for alcohol abuse and all's well, until one day they catch her stealing surgical spirits. It turns out her drinking problem's out of control and she gets sacked on the spot. After a few months she's taken on by the community home health care where she bikes around the island to the elderly and infirm, only then they find out she's stealing from them, too, so she gets the boot again. From 1984 till the time she disappears, she's out of work and living on benefits. Not exactly a shining career."

"Suicide?"

"That's what they reckoned. She's seen taking the ferry to Kalundborg and disembarking at the other side, and that's it. She was dressed nice, but no one spoke to her. Case shelved."

"So she won't be on our board either, Assad?"

Assad shook his head. "It's a strange world we live in," he said.

So true. And strange, too, that Carl's flu seemed to be going away, whereas his guts were now on their knees, begging for mercy.

"Back in a minute," he said suddenly, and shot off down the corridor toward the toilet. Short, shuffling steps with buttocks clenched. This was the last time *ever* he was going to drink that muck again.

He plonked himself down on the toilet seat with his pants round his ankles and his forehead resting against his knees. How could it be possible to get rid of something so quickly that had taken him so long to eat? It was one of those mysteries he had absolutely no desire whatsoever to delve into.

He wiped the sweat from his brow and tried to think about something else. It was all still there, conveniently retrievable from short-term memory. A fisherman from Fyn, an auxiliary nurse, a tart from Kolding, and a lawyer from Korsør. If there was anything at all to link these cases together they could call him Donald Duck. Statistics could be pretty peculiar, so it wasn't entirely inconceivable that four people could disappear for good the same weekend, completely independently of one another. Why not?

Stranger things had happened. And coincidences occurred by definition when you were least expecting them.

"We've found something, Carl," came a voice from the other side of the cubicle door.

"All right, Assad, hang on. Be with you in a minute," he replied, knowing full well it wasn't true. No way was he getting up until his guts had stopped churning. You never knew what might happen.

Carl heard the door shut again and sat for a while, breathing deeply as his peristaltic predicament seemed to ease. They'd found something, Assad had said.

His thoughts went into overdrive. There was something niggling here, and he didn't know what it was. Something to do with that Gitte Charles woman, if only he could put his finger on it.

One thing he'd noted about the four cases was the ages of those who had disappeared. Rita Nielsen was fifty-two, Philip Nørvig was sixty-two, Gitte Charles was fifty-three, and Viggo Mogensen fifty-four. Not the most typical age for people to vanish without a trace. It happened before that, when you were young and wild and emotional, yes. And later, when illness, loneliness, and life's disappointments weighed heavy. But these people were neither young nor old, yet still nothing could be derived from the fact. Statistics were indeed unpredictable.

Half an hour later he eventually pulled up his pants and fastened his belt. Sore in the arse and what felt like a couple of kilos lighter.

"That coffee of yours is too strong, Assad," he said, plonking himself wearily on his office chair.

The cheeky sod laughed. "It's not my coffee, Carl. You've come down with what the rest of us have got. Coughing, sneezing, shitting like a machine gun, and maybe red eyes, too. Two days it lasts, but you are ahead, Carl. Everyone at HQ has been on the crapper, apart from Rose. She has the iron constitution like a camel. You can feed a camel with Ebola and cholera, and all that happens is it gets fatter."

"Where is she now, Assad?"

"Looking at the Internet, but she'll be back in a minute."

"So what is it the two of you have found out?" Carl was skeptical with regard to Assad's take on his stomach upset, for all he had to do was look at his coffee cup and he felt the spasms return. Which was why, to Assad's bewilderment, he covered the cup with a sheet of paper.

"Well, you see it's this Gitte Charles woman. She worked at a place for mentally challenged people. That is what we found out."

Carl cocked his head. "And . . . ?" he inquired, hearing a clatter of footsteps in the corridor.

Rose burst into the office, mouth wide open, as if she really were brainless.

"We've got a connection between Rita Nielsen and Gitte Charles, and it's right here," she said, planting an index finger slap in the middle of a printout map of Denmark.

Sprogø.

14

August 1987

She sat as if stuck to the bench, staring in the direction of the old bunker off Korsgade. It wouldn't be long before the drug addict came shuffling by with his ugly mongrel.

Satan, the dog was called, a fitting name if ever there was one. Yesterday the canine monster had got hold of a cocker spaniel, and only a swift kick from a man in wooden clogs had prompted the beast to let go. The addict had of course threatened to do the bloke in and set the dog on him, but nothing had come of it. There were too many onlookers, and Nete had been one of them.

A dog like that didn't deserve to strut about in her city, she had thought to herself, and now she had decided to kill two birds with one stone.

The sausage she'd placed at the bottom of Korsgade, at the foot of the old concrete bunker left over from the war, had been injected with henbane extract, a sufficient dose for present purposes. The slobbering mongrel wouldn't be able to resist once it began sniffing around where it always did its business and happened upon an unexpected meal. A dog like that with its jaws around a treat couldn't be stopped by any man. Not that she thought its master would bother to try. He was certainly not as fussy as other dog owners when it came to what his pet stuck its nose into. But still, one could never tell.

She waited only a few minutes before she caught sight of the panting beast dragging its owner along the path called Peblinge Dossering. It took less than ten seconds for it to pick up the scent of the bait, and in one quick lunge the sausage was wolfed.

As far as she could see, it went down in one.

When they passed by her bench, she stood up calmly, noting the time on her watch and limping on behind.

She knew the man couldn't be bothered doing the whole circuit around all four lakes, but she also knew it wouldn't take that long. The walk around Peblinge Lake would take about fifteen minutes at the pace they were going, and with the concentrated dose she'd injected into the meat she felt sure they wouldn't get that far.

As they approached Dronning Louise's Bridge, the dog suddenly seemed unable to maintain its direction. Its owner kept jerking the leash, only for the animal to continue veering erratically.

On the other side of the bridge the man steered his dog down to the path that ran along the opposite side of the lake and began to chastise it for its stubbornness. He stopped when it began to growl and turned to face him, teeth bared.

They stood in a motionless face-off for a minute, perhaps two. Nete leaned against the elaborate railing of the bridge, as if entranced by the view across the lake to the Pavilion restaurant.

But she was absorbed in something else entirely. Out of the corner of her eye she saw the dog sit down heavily and look around in bewilderment, as though it no longer knew which way was up or down. Its tongue flopped out of its mouth. She knew it was a symptom.

Any second now it'll jump in the lake to drink, she thought to herself, but it didn't. It was already too late for that.

Not until the dog fell onto its side, panting and eventually becoming still, did it dawn on the moron at the other end of the leash that something was terribly wrong.

With a look of both perplexity and impotence he jerked the leash and yelled, "C'mon, Satan," but Satan wasn't going anywhere. The sausage and the henbane had made sure of it.

Ten minutes was all it took.

For an hour she sat listening to classical on the radio. It soothed her mind and allowed her to think constructively. She had seen the effects of the henbane and had no further worries in that respect. Now it was all a question of whether people could stick to the times of their appointments. She was in no doubt they would come. Ten million kroner was a great deal of money indeed, and was anyone in the kingdom unaware that she was good for it, and a lot more besides? Oh, they would come all right, she reassured herself as the radio news time approached.

The headlines were uninspiring. The Minister for Church Affairs was in the GDR, and proceedings had just begun against an Israeli citizen who had leaked secrets about nuclear weapons.

Nete got up to go to the kitchen and prepare some lunch when she heard Curt Wad's name mentioned.

She felt herself shudder, as though she had been prodded with something sharp, and held her breath as if it was the only remedy.

The voice was the same as two years before. Clear, self-assured, and arrogant. The theme, however, was new.

"The Purity Party stands for much more than countering the soft stance of our politicians on immigration. The issue of childbirth in the lowest and weakest social groups is also of paramount concern to us. Whether they are born retarded, grow up to be substance abusers, or are genetically predisposed to delinquency, children born of parents with severe social problems are often a considerable burden on society, and one that costs us billions of kroner every year," Wad opined, allowing his interviewer little chance to get a word in edgeways. "Imagine how much we would save if criminal parents were stripped of the right to have children. The welfare authorities would become almost superfluous. Prisons would be depopulated. Or what if we were relieved of the astronomical expense of looking after unemployed immigrants who come here with the sole purpose of draining public coffers, dragging entire families with them, and filling our schools with children who understand neither our language nor our customs? Imagine the effect if large families living on public benefits and allowing their hordes of children to fend for themselves were suddenly no longer permitted to multiply with such tenacity and produce offspring they are incapable of looking after. This is a matter of . . ."

Nete slumped down in her chair and looked out over the tops of the chestnut trees. Her stomach turned. What man would be the judge of whether a person was eligible to live or not?

Curt Wad, of course.

For a moment she thought she would throw up.

Nete was standing before her father. There was a darkness about him, a bitterness she had never seen before.

"All through school I defended you, Nete. Do you realize that?"

She nodded, knowing it to be true. More times than she cared to recall they had been summoned to the dismal classroom, where her father had protested against the headmaster's and the schoolmistress's threats. But each time, he had softened up sufficiently to listen to the charges and promise she would mend her ways. He would teach her to abide by the word of God and to think twice about what words she took in her mouth. He would lead her onto a better path and correct her licentious behavior.

But Nete never understood why he could swear so profusely himself, and why it was so wrong to talk about what males and females did, when it was all around them every day on the farm.

"They say you're foulmouthed and stupid, and that you contaminate everything around you," her father told her. "You were expelled from school, so I found a lady to teach you instead, though she didn't come cheap. If only you'd at least learned to read and write, but you couldn't even manage that. Everywhere I go, people look at me with resentment. I'm the smallholder whose daughter brings shame to the village. The pastor, the school, everyone speaks against you, and thereby against me. You've yet to be confirmed, and now you're pregnant besides. And you tell me it's your cousin who's the father."

"He is. We did it together."

"No, he is *not*, Nete! Tage says he's had nothing to do with you. So who's responsible?"

"Me and Tage together."

"Get down on your knees, Nete."

"But . . ."

"DOWN ON YOUR KNEES!"

She did as she was told, watching as he stepped across the floor and reached into the bag on the table.

"Here," he said, depositing a fistful of rice grains on the floor in front of her. "Eat!"

He placed a jug of water next to her. "And drink!"

She glanced around the room, her eyes passing over the picture of her mother, delicate and smiling in her bridal gown, over the glass-fronted cabinet with the porcelain inside and the clock on the wall that had long since stopped. And nothing in the room could comfort her, nothing suggested there was any way out.

"Tell me who you cavorted with, Nete, or else eat."

"With Tage. Only with him."

"Here," her father snarled, forcing rice into her mouth with hands that trembled from rage.

The grains caught in her throat, though she drank all she could. Each time she swallowed she thought she would choke on these small, pointed grains heaped on the floor.

When her father buried his face in his hands and began to sob and beg her to tell him who had made her pregnant, she flew up at once, breaking the water jug in the process. Four strides to the door and she was out. In the open she was quick and nimble, and she knew the landscape like no other.

She heard her father's cries behind her, and later his screams in the distance, but they didn't stop her. What brought her to a halt was the pain in her abdomen as the rice began to swell with the water and her bile. She felt her stomach expand and it made her throw back her head and gasp for breath.

"It was Taaaaaggggeee!" she screamed, out across the reeds and the stream that flowed in front of her. Then she fell to her knees and pressed her fists against her abdomen as hard as she could. It helped momentarily, but her stomach was swelling still. She put a finger down her throat in an effort to regurgitate, but nothing could assuage her pain.

"It was Tage! Why can't you tell him, Mother?" she wept, her eyes turned to the heavens. But her mother didn't answer. Instead she found herself confronted by five boys with fishing rods.

"Nete, the willy wanker!" one of them cried.

"Willy wanker, willy wanker!" the others joined in.

She closed her eyes. Everything inside her felt wrong, her diaphragm and abdomen, and places she had never been aware of before. She felt a throbbing behind her eye, in her temples, inside her skull. She could smell her own sweat. Her whole being tried to scream away the pain and make the body whole again.

But she couldn't scream, no matter how much she wanted to. Nor could she answer when the boys asked if she'd lift up her dress so they could see what she looked like down below.

She heard the expectation in their voices, revealing them for what they were: silly little boys without a clue, who'd only ever done what their fathers told them. Her refusal to answer made them not only angry, but embarrassed, which was the very worst anyone could make them feel.

"She's a dirty pig," one of them yelled. "Throw her in the stream and wash her clean."

And without warning they took hold of her arms and legs and cast her into the water with all their might.

They heard the splash, and the thud as she landed stomach-first on a submerged boulder, and they saw how she flailed her arms as blood colored the water between her legs.

But none of them did anything to help. Instead they ran away.

And there, in the cold water, came the scream.

The scream saved her, because her father followed the sound, hauled her ashore, and carried her home. Strong arms, suddenly gentle. He, too, had seen the blood and realized she could no longer defend herself.

He put her to bed and laid a cool cloth across her stomach, and asked for forgiveness for losing his temper. But she said nothing. The stabs of pain in her head and abdomen made it impossible to speak.

After that, he never again raised the issue of who had made her pregnant. The fetus was no longer, so much was obvious. Nete's mother had also had miscarriages, it was no secret, and the signs were unmistakable. Even Nete knew.

That evening, when Nete's brow became hot with fever, her father called Dr. Wad. An hour later Wad arrived with his son, Curt, apparently unsurprised by Nete's condition. He noted her father's explanation that she had slipped and fallen into the stream. Others had already told him as much, and now he could see it must have been the case. It was too bad the girl had begun to bleed, Wad said, and asked her father if she was pregnant, not even bothering to examine her himself.

She watched her father as he shook his head, paralyzed by shame and indecision.

"That would be unlawful," her father said in a quiet voice. "So of course not. There's no need for the police on that account. An accident is an accident."

"You'll be all right again," said the doctor's son. He stroked her arm, his touch rather too prolonged, the tips of his fingers surreptitiously brushing against her small breasts.

It was the first time she saw Curt Wad, and even then she felt uncomfortable in his presence.

Afterward her father scrutinized her for some time before eventually collecting himself and announcing to her the decision that would destroy her life and his.

"I can't have you here any longer, Nete. We must find you a foster family. I shall speak to the authorities in the morning."

After the radio interview with Curt Wad she sat frowning in her chair in the middle of the living room. Not even Carl Nielsen's *Springtime on Funen* or Bach's preludes could bring her peace.

A monster had been allowed to speak over the airwaves. The interviewer had tried her best to halt his flow with her penetrating questions, but he had utilized his allotted time to the full, expertly and with sickening effect.

Everything he had stood for back then was not only intact but now seemingly reinforced to such an extent that she was appalled. Curt Wad had made public the aims of his work and that of the organization he had founded and which so plainly belonged to a bygone age. A time when people raised their arms in Nazi salutes and clicked their heels, murdering in the insane belief that some people are born better than others and that the right to divide humanity into those who are worthy and those who are not belonged to them and them alone.

She would do everything in her power to make sure the monster rose to her bait, no matter the consequences.

Her body trembled as she found his number, her fingers fumbling at the dial until she got it right.

It took three tries before the line was no longer busy. He'd probably been inundated after the interview. She hoped his callers were people who despised him for what he was.

But when she finally got through, there was nothing in Curt Wad's voice to indicate this was the case.

"Purity Party, Curt Wad speaking," he announced directly, and without shame.

When she introduced herself he indignantly demanded to know what on earth she thought she was playing at, wasting his time with that letter of hers and now phone calls.

He was about to hang up on her when she mustered all her strength and calmly informed him of her business.

"I'm terminally ill and I want you to know I have come to terms with what happened between us. The letter I sent you informs you of my intention to release a large sum of money to you or the organizations you have founded. If you haven't already done so, I suggest you read it and seriously consider its content. I fear time may be short."

And with that she put down the receiver. Her eyes wandered to the bottle of poison as she felt a migraine coming on.

Only five days to go now.

15

November 2010

With his cheek stuck to the wall and a pungent, exotic pong in his nostrils, Carl awoke to see a pair of scrutinizing eyes and a mat of prickly stubble in front of his face.

"Here, Carl," said Assad, offering a steaming glass of scalding-hot liquid.

Carl recoiled immediately and felt a jab of pain in his neck as though a vice had suddenly tightened on a muscle. To think tea could have such a foul smell.

He glanced around and remembered it had been a late night and that at some point he'd felt he couldn't manage the drive home. He sniffed his armpits and wished he hadn't.

"Genuine Ar Raqqah tea," said Assad hoarsely.

"Ar Raqqah," Carl repeated. "Sounds nasty. What is it, a disease? An accumulation of catarrh?"

Assad smiled. "Ar Raqqah is a very fine city on the Euphrates."

"The Euphrates? Whoever heard of tea from the Euphrates? What country are we talking about, anyway?"

"Syria, of course." Assad shoveled a couple of teaspoons of sugar into the glass and handed it to him.

"Assad, as far as I know they don't grow tea in Syria."

"Herbal tea, Carl. You've been coughing all night."

Carl stretched the muscles of his neck, but it only seemed to make things worse. "What about Rose, did she go home afterward?"

"No, she has been busy on the toilet most of the night. It's her turn now."

"She wasn't ill last time I saw her."

"It came on later, then."

"Where is she now?" Hopefully miles away.

"At the Royal Library, looking at books about Sprogø. When she was not shitting she was on the Internet, reading. This is some of it here," Assad said, handing Carl some stapled sets of printouts.

"Just give us a minute to freshen up a bit, Assad, yeah?"

"Of course, Carl. And while you're reading you can eat as many of these as you can. They come from the same place as the tea. They are very, very, very good indeed."

Three "verys" too many, I shouldn't wonder, Carl thought to himself as he studied the packet that was decorated with Arabic lettering and a picture of a cookie even a castaway would turn his nose up at.

"Thanks, Assad," he mumbled, stumbling out toward the toilets to take care of stop-gap ablutions. After that he could sort out his own breakfast. Lis usually had something tasty stashed away in her desk up on the third floor.

He was looking forward already.

"Funny you should turn up now," said Lis, her wonky front teeth showing in a devastatingly delicious smile. "I've found your cousin, Ronny, and it wasn't easy, I can tell you. That man changes address the way the rest of us change nightclothes."

Carl pictured the two faded T-shirts he took turns sleeping in, before shaking the image from his mind. "Where is he now, then?" he asked, doing his best to appear less disheveled than he looked.

"He's taken over the lease on a flat in Vanløse. Here's his mobile number. It's a pay-as-you-go SIM, just so's you know."

Vanløse! He drove past the bloody place every day. Small world.

"Where's old misery guts, then? She off sick as well?" he asked, with a nod toward Ms. Sørensen's chair.

"Nah, she's like me. Can't keep a good woman down," Lis replied, gesturing toward the depopulated offices of the homicide division. "Unlike the wimpy male specimens we've got around here. No, Cata's off on her NLP course. Last day today."

Cata? The old hag couldn't be called Cata, surely? Was she winding him up or what?

"Cata—is that Ms. Sørensen?"

Lis nodded. "Catarina, actually. But she prefers Cata."

Carl staggered back down the stairs to the basement

It was a madhouse up there.

"Have you read my printouts?" Rose asked, the second she noticed Carl's presence. She looked like death warmed up.

"Not yet, no. Don't you think you should go home, Rose?"

"Later, maybe. There's something we need to talk about."

"I was afraid you might say that. What's all this about Sprogø?"

"Gitte Charles and Rita Nielsen were there at the same time."

"And . . . ?" he said, sounding like he didn't grasp the importance, though he most certainly did. This was fucking ace work, and all three of them knew it.

"So they must have known each other," Rose said. "Gitte Charles was on the staff and Rita was an inmate."

"Inmate? How do you mean?"

"You don't know much about Sprogø, do you, Carl?"

"Well, I know it's a little island between Sjælland and Fyn, that the

Storebælt Bridge crosses over it, and you could see it from the ferries back in the days when you had to sail over the strait. There's a lighthouse there. And a hill, and lots of fucking grass."

"And some buildings as well, yeah?"

"Right. Since they built the bridge you can see them pretty clearly, especially if you're coming from Sjælland. Yellow, aren't they?"

Assad came over to them. This time neatly combed and shaved, albeit bleeding from nicks on his chin and throat. Maybe they should have a fund-raiser and get him a new razor.

Rose tilted her head. "I take it you've heard of the women's home on the island, Carl?"

"Course I have. A place where they sent fallen women for a while, wasn't it?"

"Let me enlighten you. I'll make it brief, so listen up, Carl. You, too, Assad."

She raised a finger in the air like a schoolmistress. This was Rose in her element.

"It all started in 1923 with a certain Christian Keller, who was a doctor who worked with the mentally deficient. For some years he'd been in charge of a number of institutions for the mentally challenged, among them the one in Brejning. Together they were known as the Keller Institutions. He was the kind of doctor who firmly believed in his own infallibility and reckoned it qualified him to pick out people who hadn't the ability to occupy what they called a 'suitable role' in society.

"His theories, which resulted in the setting up of the institution on Sprogø, were based on the eugenic concepts of social hygiene that flourished at the time. Ideas about 'poor genetic material,' the propagation of degenerate offspring, that sort of bollocks."

Assad smiled. "Eugenics! Yes, I know all about this. It's when you cut off the testicles of boys so they can sing the high notes. We had many of these in the old harems of the Middle East."

"Those are *eunuchs*, Assad," Carl said by way of correction, only then noticing the cheeky grin on his assistant's face. Bloody comedian.

"Carl, I am making fun now. I looked this up last night. 'Eugenics' comes from the Greek language and means 'well born.' It's a theory that divides people up according to their origin and environment." He gave Carl a hearty slap on the shoulder. It was obvious he was rather more in the picture on this than his superior.

But then his smile vanished. "And do you know what? I hate it very much," he said solemnly. "I hate how some people think they are better humans than others. Racial superiority, you know? The idea that some people are worth more than others." He looked straight at Carl. It was the first time Assad had ever spoken of such matters.

"But many people are like this, yes?" he went on. "They feel they are better. They think this is what it's all about. To be human is trying to be better than the rest, am I right?"

Carl nodded. It sounded like Assad had had his own firsthand dealings with discrimination. Of course he had.

"What went on then was quackery," Rose continued. "The doctors hadn't a clue. If a woman's behavior was deemed to be antisocial she'd be in their spotlight in no time. Especially women who were considered to be of 'easy virtue.' They were classed as having 'low sexual morals' and stigmatized as being responsible for spreading venereal disease and giving birth to degenerate children. They could be sent to Sprogø indefinitely without being convicted of any crime. The doctors thought they could do that. They thought it was their right and duty to do so, because these women weren't part of the 'normal' society to which everyone else belonged."

Rose stood silently for a moment, lending weight to what she said next.

"The way I see it, they were a bunch of bigoted, self-righteous, self-indulgent charlatans who came running to the rescue every time some parish or other wanted to get rid of a woman who'd offended the morals of the local squire. These doctors thought they were God."

Carl nodded. "Yeah, or the Devil himself," he mused. "But I honestly thought the women who got sent to the island were feeble-minded. Not that it justifies the treatment they were given," he added in a hurry. "Rather the opposite, I'd say."

"Tsssk," Rose exclaimed scornfully. "Feeble-minded, yeah, that's what they called it. And maybe they *were*, according to the idiotic and primitive so-called intelligence tests the doctors subjected them to. But who the hell were they to call women feeble-minded, just because the women may have gone through life without the right kind of input? Most of them may well have been social cases, but they were treated like criminals and inferior beings. Of course, a few *were* actually mentally ill or backward in some way, but not all of them, not by a long chalk. And since when has being stupid been a crime in Denmark? If it was, there wouldn't be many of our politicians walking around on the loose today, would there? What took place then was a completely unacceptable infringement of human rights. Amnesty International and the Court of Human Rights would have had a field day with it, and the worst thing is, the same kind of thing's still going on in our little kingdom. Just think of how often limb restraints are used in psychiatry. Think of all the people they drug up to the eyeballs with pills and crap, so all they can do is shrivel up and die. Think of how many people can't get citizenship here just because they can't get the answers right to a load of stupid fucking questions of no relevance to anything." Rose almost spat out the words.

Either she's short on sleep or else it's a bad case of PMS, Carl found himself thinking, as he dug into his pocket for the cookies Lis had supplied him with.

He offered Rose one, but she shook her head. He'd forgotten all about her dodgy stomach. Assad didn't want one either. Great. All the more for him, then.

"Listen, Carl. There was no escape from Sprogø. It was hell on earth for these women, do you understand? They were considered to be ill, but there was no treatment because it wasn't a hospital. And it wasn't a prison either, yet they were there indefinitely. Some of them spent nearly their whole lives without contact with their families or anyone else for that matter outside the island. And this went on right until 1961. That's during your lifetime, Carl, do you realize that?" Clearly the case had roused Rose's sense of justice.

He was about to protest, but realized she was right. It *had* happened in his lifetime. Only just, but he was surprised nonetheless.

"OK." He nodded. "So this Christian Keller had all these women deported to Sprogø because he reckoned they weren't fit to lead a normal life, is that it? And that's why Rita Nielsen landed there, too?"

"Yeah. I sat up all night reading up on these horrible people. Keller and his successor, Wildenskov, from Brejning. The two of them ruled the roost on Sprogø from 1923 until two years before the place closed down in 1961. That's almost forty years, and in all that time more than fifteen hundred women got sent to the island indefinitely, and it was no picnic, I can tell you that much. Rough treatment and hard work. Poorly trained staff who looked on 'the girls,' as they were called, as inferior. They ran a brutal regime of discipline and kept them under surveillance day and night. There were punishment cells for when the girls got out of line. Isolation for days on end. And if any of them got their hopes up about getting away from the place again, they first had to reconcile themselves with being sterilized. Forced sterilization! They were robbed of their sexuality *and* their reproductive organs, Carl." She tossed her head angrily and kicked the wall. "The bastards! It's beyond fucking belief!"

"Are you OK, Rose?" asked Assad, cautiously putting a hand on her arm.

"Abuse of power, that's what it was. The worst kind imaginable," she said, with a look on her face that Carl hadn't seen before. "Imagine being deported to an island and left there to rot. We Danes are no fucking better than those we claim to despise," she hissed. "We're as bad as those who stone unfaithful women or the Nazis who murdered anyone who was mentally or physically disabled. As far as I can see, what happened out there on Sprogø was the same as what happened to dissidents in the Soviet Bloc during the Cold War. We're no fucking better at all, I'm telling you!"

And with that she turned and marched off toward the toilets. Apparently her stomach was still playing up.

"Phew," said Carl.

"She was on her high horse about it all night, Carl," said Assad, almost in a whisper. No way was he about to risk Rose overhearing him. "In my opinion she is acting strange about it. Maybe soon she will send Yrsa to us instead."

Carl's eyes narrowed. The nagging suspicion returned. "You reckon Rose has personal experience of that kind of treatment, is that what you're suggesting, Assad?"

Assad shrugged. "All I'm saying is that there is something grating inside her like a stone inside a shoe."

Carl paused and stared at the phone for a second before picking it up and dialing Ronny's number.

It rang for a while and he hung up, waited twenty seconds and called again.

"Yeah?" said a gravelly voice, worn out by age, alcohol, and late nights.

"All right, Ronny?" Carl said.

No response.

"It's Carl."

Still no response.

He spoke a bit louder, then louder again, eventually noting some form of activity at the other end, a strangled snort like someone snapping for air in their sleep, the rattle of mucus in a throat after the sixty cigarettes whose stubs most likely filled his cousin's ashtray.

"Come again?" the voice finally said.

"It's your cousin, Carl. How's it going?"

More coughing, then: "What's the time?"

Carl looked at the clock. "Quarter past nine."

"*Quarter past nine!* You're kidding me, aren't you? Not a word in ten years and here you are calling at quarter past fucking nine?" And then he hung up.

Nothing new under the sun. Carl could picture him. No clothes on, most likely, apart from the socks he never took off. Probably sporting the world's longest toenails, too, with stubble unevenly distributed about his face. A big man who preferred dingy back rooms and as little sun as possible, no matter where in the world he happened to be. If he was fond of Thailand, it certainly wasn't because he wanted a tan.

Less than ten minutes went by before he called back.

"What number's that, Carl? Where are you?"

"My office at Police HQ."

"Fucking hell."

"I'm hearing things about you, Ronny. We need to talk, OK?"

"What sort of things?"

"You spouting off in shady bars around the world about your dad's death, and mixing me up in it."

"Who says?"

"Other police officers."

"They're sick in the head."

"How about you stopping by?"

"Police HQ? You must be fucking joking. You gone senile since I saw you last? Nah, if we're going to talk, you'll have to make it worth my while."

Any second now he would make a proposal involving money. Money Carl was to provide and which would be spent on drink.

"You can get the ale in, and some food. Tivoli Hall, just round the corner from where you are."

"Never heard of it."

"Opposite the Rio Bravo. You know where *that* is. Corner of Stormgade."

If he knew Carl was familiar with the Rio Bravo, why the hell didn't he suggest meeting there, the imbecile?

They arranged a time and Carl sat for a moment after he'd hung up, thinking about what he could say that might seep into his idiotic cousin's thick skull.

That'll be Mona, he thought to himself when the phone rang again. He looked at the time. Half nine. He wouldn't put it past her. Just thinking about her made his stomach flutter.

"Hi," he said, but the voice at the other end wasn't Mona's, and it certainly wasn't sexy. More like a kick in the teeth.

"Can you come upstairs for a minute, Carl?" It was Tomas Laursen, the finest forensics officer west of Copenhagen until loathing got the better of him and a lottery jackpot subsequently consumed by dodgy investments gave him his ticket to freedom. Now he was back, running the cafeteria on the fourth floor and making a fine job of it, so Carl had heard, and it was about time he got his arse up there and found out for himself.

Now was as good a time as any.

"What's on your mind, Tomas?"

"That body they found out in Amager yesterday."

————

The only thing reminiscent of the cafeteria before the powers that be decided they needed something more up to date was that the place was still cramped as hell.

"All right?" Carl asked his brick outhouse of a former colleague, receiving a kind of sideways nod in reply.

"Well, you know how it is. I probably won't be able to pay for the Ferrari I ordered yesterday in one go, but apart from that . . ." Laursen said with a grin as he hauled Carl off into the kitchen.

There his expression became solemn. "Do you have any idea how loud people actually talk when they're sitting here filling their faces, Carl?" he asked, in a subdued voice. "I certainly didn't, not until I took the place on."

He popped open a beer and handed it to Carl.

"Listen. What if I overheard someone going on about you and Bak being at each other's throats over the Amager case, would that be true?"

Carl took a swig from the bottle. As if he hadn't enough to be getting on with. "Not about that case, exactly. Why?"

"Bak was in here yesterday making it sound like there was something fishy about the way you came out of that shooting in Amager, when Anker was killed and Hardy was left paralyzed. He seemed to reckon you just wanted it to *look like* you were shot at. Said the flesh wound you got in the temple never could have knocked you unconscious, and that anyone could fake a shot like that at close range."

"The fucking bastard. This must have been just before I helped him out with that business about his sister. The fucking ungrateful bastard. And who was he mouthing off to? Who's going to be passing it on?"

Laursen shook his head. He wasn't saying. Apparently it would be bad for business if his customers in the cafeteria felt they couldn't give vent. Which Carl thought was OK, as long as the gossip wasn't about him.

"It seems to be the word round here, I'm afraid, but that's not all, Carl."

"What else?" Carl put his beer down on top of a fridge. He didn't want to be reeking of lager when he stood before the chief two minutes from now to play hell.

"Forensics found a number of significant items yesterday that had been in the pockets of that corpse. One was a coin that had been stuck in a fold, apparently. A one-krone coin, to be more exact. In fact, they found five Danish coins in all, but this one was the most recent."

"When was it from?"

"The date was 2006. So the body was in the ground four years at most. But there's more."

"Seems reasonable. What else did they find?"

"Two of the coins were wrapped in plastic wrap, and there were prints. Two right index fingers, different individuals."

"OK. And what do they make of that?"

"The prints are very clear and well preserved, so wrapping the coins up like that served the intended purpose, I'd say."

"And whose prints were they?"

"One was Anker Henningsen's."

Carl's eyes widened. He recalled the look of suspicion on Hardy's face, heard his embittered voice telling him about Anker's cocaine habit.

Laursen handed him back his beer before studying him with searching eyes.

"The other one was yours, Carl."

16

August 1987

Curt Wad sat for a moment, weighing Nete's letter in his hand before tearing it open with the same lack of expectation as he would have opened unsolicited mail from a drug company.

Once, Nete had been the girl who aroused his abusive urges, but there had been dozens after her. So why even bother with this insignificant little peasant now? What possible interest could he have in her opinions or thoughts?

He read through the letter, then put it aside with a smile.

The little hussy. Charity and forgiveness, who would have thought it? And why should he believe a single word?

"Nice try, Nete Hermansen," he said out loud. "But I shall check up on you."

He opened the top drawer of his desk, pulling it out as far as it could go until he heard the click, then pushed the desktop gently sideways until it revealed the shallow compartment in which lay his indispensable address book with all its phone numbers.

He opened it at one of the first pages, dialed a number, and introduced himself.

"I need a civil registration number. Can you help me? A Nete Hermansen, possibly registered in her married name, Rosen. The address is Peblinge Dossering 32, fourth floor, in Nørrebro, Copenhagen. Yes, that's her. You remember her? Indeed, her husband was such a clever man, though I believe his judgment may have been failing him in later years. You've found the number? Excellent, that was very quick, I must say."

He noted it down and expressed his thanks, reminding his contact that the favor would be returned with pleasure whenever required. It was the way of all brotherhoods.

Then he flicked through his address book again, dialed another number, put the book back in its place, and clicked the desktop shut.

"Svenne, Curt Wad here," he said. "I need some information on a Nete Rosen, I've got the civil registration number here. I believe she's receiving hospital treatment and I need to have that confirmed. In Copenhagen, I assume. How long before you can let me know? All right, if you can get back to me today I'd be most grateful. You'll try? Excellent, thank you so much!"

When he'd finished he leaned back in his chair and read through the letter one more time. It was astonishingly well written, devoid of spelling mistakes and errors of grammar. Even the punctuation was impeccable, so there was no doubt that someone must have helped her. A slow-witted dyslexic like her with no schooling to speak of. As if she could fool him.

He smiled wryly. The most immediate assumption was that the lawyer had helped her with it. Hadn't it said something about a lawyer taking part in the meeting if Curt decided to accept her invitation?

He laughed out loud. Did she really imagine he would come?

"What are you laughing about all on your own, Curt?"

He turned to face his wife and shook his head dismissively.

"I'm in a good mood, that's all," he replied, putting his arms around her waist as she came to him at the desk.

"You deserve it, my dear. You've done such splendid work."

Curt Wad nodded. He was rather pleased with himself, too.

———

When eventually his father retired, Curt took on his practice, patients, medical records from a lifetime's work, and various files pertaining to the Anti-Debauchery Committee and the Community of Danes. Important documents to Curt and poison in the wrong hands, though not nearly as toxic as the work he was asked to carry on: the work of The Cause.

This involved not only seeking out pregnant women whose unborn children were deemed undeserving of life, but also meticulous recruitment efforts to secure a continued influx of qualified individuals. People who would rather die than reveal what this clandestine organization stood for.

For some years Curt's surgery on Fyn worked well as the hub of The Cause's activities. But with an ever-increasing number of the organization's abortions being carried out in the capital region he eventually decided to break with the past and move to Brøndby, an uninspiring suburb to the west of the city, and yet an epicenter with respect to his work. Here the major hospitals were near at hand, there was easy access to the most skilled general practitioners and specialists with considerable practices, and not least of all, the location was in close proximity to the clientele that were the organization's primary focus.

Here in this concrete hinterland he met his wife, Beate, in the mid-1960s. A marvelous woman, a nurse with good genes, a sense of nation, and a winning mentality from which Curt derived much advantage in the years that followed.

Even before they were married he initiated her into his work and the benefits of devoting oneself to the organization and its aims. He had anticipated a certain reluctance or at best trepidation, yet she had shown both understanding and initiative. In fact, she soon proved invaluable in establishing bonds among nurses and midwives. Within a year she had brought into the fold more than twenty-five scouts, as she called them, and from there things took off. She it was who coined the name Purity

Party, proposing that the political aspect of The Cause be intensified parallel to its day-to-day practical work.

She was the ideal woman and mother.

"Have a look at this, Beate." He handed her Nete's letter, giving her time to read it through. She smiled as she did so. The same winsome smile she had passed on to their two magnificent sons.

"Well, I must say. How will you answer her, Curt?" she asked. "Do you think she means it? Does she really have that kind of money?"

He nodded. "There's no doubt she does. But she's up to something more than simply lining our pockets, of that we can be certain."

He stood up, drawing back a curtain that hung in front of the wall behind him, thereby revealing five large filing cabinets in olive-green metal that he'd been guarding for years. In a month's time the fireproof strong room in the old stables that now served as storage space would be finished and everything would be moved out there. No one outside the inner circle would have access.

"I remember the number even now," he chuckled, pulling out a drawer from the second cabinet.

"Here," he said, and tossed a gray suspension file onto the desk in front of her.

It had been a long time since it had seen the light of day. There had been no reason until now. But on seeing the file he nonetheless tipped his head back slightly and for a brief moment allowed his gaze to drift out of focus.

The sixty-three files before it, containing the medical records of as many individuals, had been his and his father's in tandem, but this one was his and his alone. His first solo accomplishment for The Cause.

FILE NO. 64 it read on the front.

"Born 18 May 1937. That makes her just a week older than me," said his wife.

He laughed. "The difference is that you're fifty and look like you're thirty-five, whereas she almost certainly looks more like she's sixty-five."

"I see she was sent away to Sprogø. How on earth can a person like that express herself so well?"

"I imagine she had help."

He drew his wife toward him and gave her hand a squeeze. What he'd said wasn't entirely true. Beate and Nete resembled each other a great deal. Both were just the type he preferred. Blonde, blue-eyed, and Nordic, with all the curves. Women with smooth skin and lips that could take a man's breath away.

"What makes you think she's up to something? According to your file on her she was given a D and C in 1955. Nothing out of the ordinary in a woman having her womb scraped, surely?"

"Nete Hermansen has always been a woman of split personality, exhibiting a strong tendency to take on different personas as she sees fit. The result of a feeble mind, not to mention psychopathic tendencies and utterly warped self-perception. I can deal with her, of course, but I shall be taking precautions."

"How?"

"I've put out an inquiry through the organization. Soon we'll know if she really is as ill as she'd like us to believe from her letter."

Curt Wad received an answer to his inquiry the next morning. It was an answer that confirmed his suspicions.

No person with that civil registration number had received treatment in any public hospital since Nete's road accident in which her husband lost his life in November 1985, nor did such a person figure in the records of any private clinic. Since her hospitalization at Nykøbing Falster General and a couple of biannual check-ups both there and later at Copenhagen's Rigshospital, nothing else was to be found.

What the devil was she up to? Why was she lying about being ill? Plainly she was trying to lure him into a trap with kind words and plausible explanations as to the reason for her sudden approach. But what did she intend to do if he didn't turn up? Was he to be punished? Or was she simply trying to find a chink in his armor? Did she really not think he knew how to protect himself? Did she think she could catch him off guard with a tape recorder, spilling secrets and making admissions?

He laughed.

The silly little cow. What on earth could make her believe he would rise to the bait, that she could expose what he had done to her all those years before? Especially after Nørvig, the lawyer, had refuted her claims once and for all.

Again he laughed at the thought. In less than ten minutes he could muster a crew of strapping young men brimming with national pride who were used to applying the thumbscrews when necessary. If he accepted the invitation and turned up at Nete Hermansen's home on Friday with such supporters at his side, she'd soon find out who was going to be punished and who was in for a surprise.

The prospect was tempting indeed, but on that particular day he was scheduled to take part in the inaugural meeting of a new branch of the organization in Hadsten, so entertainment would have to yield to more important matters.

He shoved her letter across the desktop into the wastepaper basket, resolving that next time she tried a similar stunt he would teach her a lesson once and for all about who ruled whom and exactly what that involved.

He went into the consulting room and took his time putting on his doctor's coat, smoothing out the creases and making sure it was just right. After all, this was his uniform. In it he exuded the greatest authority and professional expertise.

Then he sat down at the glass-topped desk, pulled his appointment diary toward him, and glanced through it. Today was not going to be

busy. A referral for abortion, three fertility consultations, another referral, and then the day's only case from The Cause.

His first patient was a presentable, rather subdued young woman.
According to her GP she was a healthy, well-bred student seeking abortion on account of her boyfriend's desertion, which in turn had sparked
off a bout of depression.

"And you're Sofie, is that right?" he asked with a smile.

Her lips tightened. She was already on the verge of tears.

Curt Wad studied her for a moment without speaking. The girl had
clear blue eyes. A noble brow. Neat, symmetrical eyebrows and ears positioned nicely, close against the skull. She was well proportioned and in
good shape, her hands fine and slender.

"I understand your boyfriend left you. That's very sad, Sofie. You
were fond of him, I take it."

She nodded silently.

"He was a decent chap, and good-looking, am I right?"

She nodded again.

"And yet everything would seem to indicate that he was rather silly,
wouldn't you say? Choosing the easy way out and leaving you in the
lurch?"

She protested, just as he thought she would.

"He's not silly at all. He goes to the university, like I was going to."

Curt Wad fixed his eyes on her. "You're not happy about this, are you,
Sofie?"

She stared at the floor and shook her head. Now she was crying.

"At present you're working in your parents' shoe shop. Don't you
like it?"

"It's all right, but it's only for the time being. Like I said, I'm planning
to go to university at some point."

"What do your parents think about you wanting to have an abortion,
Sofie?"

"They keep it to themselves. They say it's my decision. They don't interfere. At least not in a negative way."

"And you're quite sure this is what you want?"

"Yes."

He went over and sat down on the chair next to her and took her hand in his. "Listen, Sofie. You're a healthy young woman, and the child you want to have removed is completely at the mercy of your decision. I know you would be able to give this child the most wonderful life, if you changed your mind. Would you like me to call your parents and have a word with them, see how they feel about the matter? It sounds to me like you have very good parents indeed, not the sort who would force you into doing something you didn't want. Don't you think we should hear what they have to say? What do you think?"

She raised her head and looked at him, as though he had pressed a button. Reluctant, on her guard, and very much in doubt.

Curt Wad said nothing. He knew this was the moment to hold back.

"How's your day been, Curt?" Beate asked as she filled his cup. Three o'clock tea, she called it. These moments together were the best thing about having the practice and their private residence in the same house.

"Fine. Managed to talk a lovely young girl out of an abortion this morning. She broke down in tears when I assured her that her parents would give her all the support they could. That she could have the baby and go on working in their shop to the best of her abilities. I told her they'd help look after the child and that it wouldn't affect her going on to university."

"Well done."

"Yes, she was a fine girl. So very Nordic. She'll have a lovely child, a credit to the country."

Beate smiled. "And what's next? Something completely different, I shouldn't wonder. Did Dr. Lønberg refer the patients out there in the waiting room?"

"That obvious, is it?" He smiled. "Yes, he did. Lønberg's still a good man for us. Fifteen cases in just four months. Your scouts are always so very efficient, my dear."

Fifteen minutes later the door of the consulting room opened as Curt sat reading the referral. He glanced up at the couple who entered and nodded a friendly greeting, comparing what he saw to what was written on the paper in his hand.

The accompanying description was brief, though no less vivid on that account.

Mother, Camilla Hansen, 38 yrs, 5 wks pregnant, it began. *Six children by four different men. Welfare recipient. Five of children receiving remedial education, eldest currently institutionalized. Father of unborn child, Johnny Huurinainen, 25 yrs, welfare recipient, three times sentenced for offenses against property, drug abuser receiving methadone treatment. Neither parent educated beyond statutory minimum.*

Camilla Hansen presenting with pain during urination. Cause: chlamydia, patient not yet informed.

Suggest surgical intervention

Curt nodded to himself. A good man indeed, this Lønberg.

He raised his head and considered the dismal couple in front of him.

Like an insect whose only purpose was to breed, the pregnant woman sat in the chair, overweight, fidgeting for want of a cigarette, hair greasy and unkempt, confident in the assumption that he would help her give birth to yet another utterly useless runt of the kind she had already given life to six times before. That he would allow new individuals of the same miserable genetic inheritance to populate the streets of the country's capital. But he would not. Not if he could help it.

He smiled at them, a gesture met only by vacant expressions and appallingly maintained teeth. Not even a decent smile could they muster. It was pathetic.

"I understand you're having trouble when you go to the toilet, Camilla. Let's have a look, shall we? You can sit in the waiting room, Johnny. I'm sure my wife will bring you a nice cup of coffee if you want one."

"I'd rather have a Coke," he said.

Curt smiled. He could have his Coke. He could have five or six, and by the time he'd drunk them Camilla would be done. She would be tearful because the doctor had seen no option but to perform a D&C, but happily ignorant of the fact that it would be the last time she'd be needing one.

17

November 2010

Once Carl had got over the shock of a coin with his fingerprints on it having been found in the festering remains of a corpse, he gave Laursen a friendly squeeze on the arm and asked to be tipped off if he happened to get wind of similar information. Anything that might be of interest. New forensic leads the department conceivably wanted Carl to remain in the dark about, or snippets of information people might inadvertently let slip. Whatever it was, Carl wanted to be kept in the know.

"Where's Marcus?" he asked Lis, down on the third floor.

"Briefing a couple of the units," was all she said. Was she avoiding his gaze, or was it his paranoia kicking in?

Then she lifted her head and fluttered her eyelashes at him. "Did you get that goose stuffed all right last night, Carl?" she asked, with a grin that would have been censored by the film board back in the fifties.

Good sign. If all she was interested in was whether or not he got off, the rumor of the coin with his prints on it probably wasn't the talk of the department yet.

He barged into the briefing room, ignoring the thirty-odd eyes that latched onto him like leeches.

"Sorry about this, Marcus," he announced to the pale and weary man with the raised eyebrows, loudly enough to make sure everyone heard him. "But as I understand it there are certain matters we need to address before things get out of hand."

He turned to the assembled faces. A number of them were visibly marked by recent days of nasal discharge and sprinting to the lavatory, sunken-cheeked and bleary-eyed, and rather aggressive-looking.

"There's a rumor going round as to my involvement in the Amager shooting that puts me in a bad light. So I'm saying this now, and then I want no more of it, all right? I haven't the faintest idea why coins with our prints on them—mine and Anker's—happened to be in the pockets of that corpse out there. But if you put those fever-ridden brains of yours to use, you'll realize it's more than likely because you were intended to find them if and when the body turned up. Get the drift?"

He looked around the assembly. It would be an exaggeration to say the response was overwhelming. "OK. We agree the body could just as well have been buried somewhere else, yeah? And whoever buried it could have just dumped it straight in the ground as it was. But they didn't, did they? Which indicates they weren't *that* bothered if we found it and dug it up again, because then the investigation would be focused on all the wrong things, wouldn't it?"

His audience remained nonplussed.

"For Chrissake, I know you've all been wondering what the fuck happened out there and why I've kept well out of it since then." He looked straight at Terje Ploug, who was seated in the third row. "But listen, Ploug, the reason I don't want to be doing with that case is because I'm ashamed of what happened, OK? And if you only stopped to think, you'd realize that's why Hardy's laid out in my living room now. That's *my* way of dealing with it, OK? I'm not leaving Hardy in the lurch this time, but I will concede I may have botched up that day in Amager."

A couple of investigators now shifted uneasily on their chairs. Maybe it was a sign that something was beginning to dawn. On the other hand, it could just be hemorrhoids. Bloody public servants, you could never tell.

"One last thing. What do you think it's like, having your best mates piled on top of you all of a sudden with blood gushing out of them, and then realizing you've just been shot yourself? I reckon you should have a ponder about that. Suffice to say it fucks you up."

"No one's accusing you of anything, Carl," said Ploug. A reaction at last. "Anyway, that's not what we're here to discuss."

Carl scanned the room. What was going on in those thick heads of theirs? Several of them couldn't stand the sight of him, he knew that. It was mutual, too. Bloody morons.

"Right, then. In that case, I suggest that from now on you lot keep your shit-spouting mouths shut and think before you fucking open them again. End of fucking message!"

He slammed the door so hard that it echoed through the building, and he didn't break stride until he flung himself down on his chair in the basement, fumbling for a match to light the cigarette that trembled between his lips.

They'd found a coin with his prints on it in the pocket of a corpse, and he had no idea how it had got there or why. What a pile of shit.

His thoughts churned. Why, why, why? It was impossible for him to turn his back on the case now. The mere thought of it made him feel sick.

He inhaled deeply through clenched teeth and felt his heartbeat rocket again. Think about something else, he told himself. No way did he want to find himself writhing on the floor again with pains in his chest that could do away with hardier men than him.

"Switch focus," he muttered under his breath, closing his eyes.

Right now there was one person more deserving than any other of being flattened by the tornado that raged inside him, and that person was Bak.

"I'll teach you, you fucking twat," he growled, searching for his number.

"What are you doing, Carl, sitting alone here talking to yourself?"

said Assad from the doorway. The man had so many furrows in his brow, his face looked like a washboard.

"Nothing for you to worry about, Assad. I'm about to give Bak the bollocking of his life for the shite he's been spreading round the place about me."

"I think you should listen to this first, Carl. I've just been on the phone to a man called Nielsen from the police academy. I talked to him about Rose."

What a bloody time to pick. Just when he'd got himself worked up into a nicely constructive rage. Was it just going to fizzle out?

"All right, tell me, if it can't wait. What did he say?"

"When Rose came to us the first time, do you remember Marcus Jacobsen telling us she was not a police officer, because she failed her exams and drove a car like a blind man with no arms?"

"Something like that, Assad, yeah. So what?"

"It is true that she was no good at driving. Nielsen said she turned over on a bend and smashed three very fine vehicles to figurines."

"I think that'd be *smithereens*, Assad. But pretty impressive, all the same. Three, you say?"

"Yes. The one she was in, the instructor's from the training facility, and one more that was in the way."

Carl tried to picture the scene. "Pretty good going, that. I don't reckon we should lend her the keys to the pool car for the time being, though," he grunted.

"That's not all, Carl. Rose had her Yrsa turn up in the middle of it all. With the cars still upside down."

Carl sensed his jaw drop, but the words that came out of his mouth were beyond his control: "Holy jackpot!" he spluttered, unsure of what it meant. If Rose had morphed into her twin-sister alter ego Yrsa in that situation, it certainly wasn't for the fun of it. It meant she'd completely lost touch with base.

"OK, not so good. What did the instructors at the academy do about it?"

"They had a psychologist take a look at her. By that time she was Rose again."

"Good grief, Assad, have you spoken to Rose about this? And please say no."

Assad gave him a look of disappointment. Of course he hadn't.

"There's more, Carl. She had an office job at Station City before coming to us. Do you remember what Brandur Isaksen said about her?"

"Vaguely. Something about her reversing into a colleague's car, and then something else about her destroying some important documents."

"Yes, and about drinking."

"Yeah, she shagged a couple of her colleagues at a Christmas do that got out of hand. Brandur, that little puritan, told me to be wary about giving her alcohol."

For a brief moment Carl's thoughts went back longingly to the Lis he'd known before she met that Frank bloke of hers. In her case he reckoned a bit of a frolic at the Christmas do wouldn't be half bad. He smiled to himself.

"Brandur was just jealous of the blokes Rose had cast her oddly cloaked womanhood upon, don't you think? Anyway, what Rose does at a Christmas party is her own concern and that of whoever else happens to be involved. Nothing to do with Brandur, me, or anyone else, surely?"

"I don't know anything about Christmas dos, Carl, or any other spicy matters. But I do know that when Rose did what she did at that party, she was all of a sudden Yrsa again. I just spoke to two people from Station City, and everyone remembers it." Assad raised his eyebrows. Carl took it to mean "What do you think of *that*?"

"She most definitely was not Rose, that much is certain, because she spoke in a different voice and behaved quite differently, they said.

Perhaps there is even a third person inside her," Assad mused, his words trailing away as his eyebrows plunged again.

The idea was mind-boggling. A third personality? Christ on a bike!

Carl sensed that the steam had gone from the bollocking he'd planned for Børge Bak. The feeling riled him. The twat deserved all that was coming to him.

"Do we know what's actually wrong with her?" he asked.

"She has never been admitted to the hospital, Carl, if that's what you mean. But I've taken down the number of Rose's mother, so maybe you can ask her."

"Rose's mother?" Assad certainly wasn't daft. Straight to the heart of the matter, why not?

"Good idea, Assad. Why don't you call her yourself?"

"Because . . ." He gave Carl a pleading look. "Because I just don't want to, that's all. If Rose finds out, it will be better if it's you she's angry with, OK?"

Carl threw up his hands in resignation. This was apparently one of those days over which he had no control whatsoever.

He reached out for the number Assad handed him and gestured for his assistant to leave him to it, dialed the number, and waited. It was a phone number from the good old days with a 45-prefix. Lyngby or Virum, as far as he remembered.

It may have been a crap day, but at least his call was answered.

"Yrsa Knudsen," said the voice at the other end.

Carl didn't believe his own ears. "Yrsa?" For a moment he was in doubt, until he heard Rose call out to Assad farther down the corridor. So she was still there. "Er, yes, I'm sorry," he went on. "This is Carl Mørck, Rose's boss. Is this Rose's mother?"

"I hope not." She laughed, a deep, resounding laugh. "No, I'm her sister."

This was a turn-up. So Rose really did have a sister called Yrsa? The voice sounded fairly close to Rose's interpretation of Yrsa's, but was different nonetheless.

"Rose's twin sister?"

"No." Yrsa laughed again. "There aren't any twins among us, but we're four sisters in all."

"Four?" Carl spluttered, perhaps rather too audibly.

"Yeah. Rose, me, Vicky, and Lise-Marie."

"Four sisters . . . and Rose is the eldest. I had no idea."

"There's only a year between us. Mum and Dad tried to get it all over with as quickly as possible, but when no boys appeared, Mumsy eventually decided to stick a cork in it." She guffawed, a throaty cackle that could have been Rose any day.

"I see. Well, I'm sorry, but the reason I was calling was to speak to your mother. Would that be OK? Is she there?"

"I'm afraid not. Mum hasn't been home in over three years. Her new bloke's apartment on the Costa del Sol suits her better, apparently." She laughed again. The jolly type, it seemed.

"OK, then I'll get to the point. Can I speak to you in confidence? What I mean is that Rose mustn't know I'm calling until I tell her personally."

"No can do!"

"You mean, you'll tell Rose I rang? I'd much rather you didn't."

"No, that's not what I'm saying. We don't see Rose at all these days. But I'll tell the others. We've no secrets from each other."

This was weird. Utterly off the map.

"Oh, I see! Then I'll just ask you, then. Has Rose ever suffered from psychiatric problems? A personality disorder, perhaps? Has she ever undergone treatment for anything like that?"

"Well, I don't know if you'd call it treatment, but she guzzled most of the pills our mother was prescribed when our dad died. Not to mention getting out of her head on weed, snorting her brains out on various substances, and boozing herself up to the eyeballs. So in a way you could say she's been on medication, I suppose. Don't know if it's helped much, though."

"Helped in respect of what?"

"In respect of her not wanting to be Rose anymore when she was down. She wanted to be one of us instead, or someone else altogether."

"So what you're actually saying is she's not well, right?"

"Not well? I wouldn't know, to be honest. What I do know is she's off her rocker."

This, at least, came as no surprise. "Has she always been like this?"

"As long as I can remember, yeah. Only it got worse after our dad died."

"I understand. Any particular reason? I'm sorry, that sounds wrong doesn't it? What I meant was, were there any unusual circumstances surrounding your father's death?"

"Yes, there were. He was killed in an accident at work. He got pulled into a machine. They had to gather him up in pieces in a tarpaulin. Apparently when the ambulance crew dropped him off for the postmortem, all they said was: 'See if you can put this back together.'"

She spoke with surprising coolness. Cynically, almost.

"I'm sorry to hear it. Sounds like a dreadful way to die. I can see how that must have affected you all very deeply indeed. But Rose lost her grip, is that what you're saying?"

"She had a summer office job at the steelworks in Frederiksværk where our dad worked. She saw them drag him out. So, yeah, Rose was the one who lost her grip."

It was a terrible story. Who wouldn't have cracked up?

"All of a sudden she just didn't want to be Rose anymore. It's as simple as that. One day she was a punk, the next an elegant lady, or one of us sisters. I don't know if I'd call her ill, but Lise-Marie, Vicky, and I don't want to be with her when she keeps changing into one of us. I'm sure you can understand that."

"Why do you think it's affected her like this?"

"Like I said before, she's off her rocker. You must have realized that, seeing as how you're calling."

Carl nodded. Rose wasn't the only one in her family with keen powers of deduction.

"One last thing, just to satisfy my curiosity. Is your hair blonde and curly? And do you like pink and wear pleated skirts?"

There was an eruption of laughter at the other end. "You mean she's already done that one on you? The blonde hair and curls is right enough. The pink, too, for that matter. I'm wearing pink nail polish and lipstick right now, as a matter of fact. But I definitely haven't worn the pleated skirt for years."

"A tartan pleated skirt?"

"That's it, yeah. It was all the rage around the time I got confirmed."

"If you have a look through your wardrobe or wherever you might have put it last, Yrsa, I think you'll discover you no longer have full possession of that skirt."

After he'd hung up he sat for a while with a smile on his face. He didn't know much about these sisters, but he reckoned he and Assad could deal with them if suddenly they happened to turn up looking suspiciously like their Rose.

The Tivoli Hall was indeed situated on the corner opposite the Rio Bravo, but a hall it was not. Not unless you could call a low-ceilinged cellar a hall.

Carl's cousin sat toward the back of the room in comfortable proximity to the men's toilets. Once Ronny planted himself in a place like this, he wasn't going anywhere in a hurry apart from the gents, so his bladder could keep abreast of activities at the other end of his all-consuming anatomy.

Ronny waved his hand in the air, as if Carl wouldn't be able to recognize him. He was looking older and had put on weight, but other than that he regrettably didn't seem to have changed a bit. His hair was Brylcreemed into a quiff of sorts, though hardly rock 'n' roll, more like a has-been crooner in an Argentinian soap for yearning suburban housewives. Vigga would have called him vulgar. Kitted out in a tight-woven, shiny mafioso jacket and a pair of jeans that fitted neither the rest of his getup nor Ronny's fat-arsed, skinny-legged frame. It all might have seemed becoming had he been a flirtatious signorina from Napoli, but he was Ronny. Right down to his winklepicker shoes. It was pathetic.

"I've already ordered," Ronny announced, indicating two empty beer bottles.

"I'm assuming one of them was mine," Carl ventured, only for Ronny to shake his head.

"Two more," he called out, then leaned toward Carl.

"Nice to see you again, cuz." He reached out to clasp Carl's hands, but Carl pulled them away in time. It gave a couple of the other clients something to talk about.

He looked his cousin in the eye before condensing into two sentences Børge Bak's claims about Ronny's mouthing off in a Bangkok bar.

"So what?" was his only response. He wasn't even denying it.

"You drink too much, Ronny. Do you want me to put a word in for you, get you into rehab? Not that I'd pay, you understand, but if you keep on making noises in public about bumping off your dad and me being in on it, you might just end up getting colonic irrigation for free in one of those nice prisons the courts will make available for you."

"Bollocks, that case lapsed years ago." Ronny flashed a smile to the woman who appeared with two more bottles and a plate of food. He'd ordered dried cod.

Carl cast a glance at the menu. Ronny's fish cost a hundred and ninety-five kroner. Probably the most expensive dish they had, but he was going to pay for it himself if Carl had any say in the matter.

"Thanks, but the beer's not for me," said Carl, shoving the two bottles across the table to his cousin. No doubt now about who was to pick up the tab.

"And there's no time-bar on murder cases in Denmark," he continued drily, ignoring the start the waitress gave on hearing his words.

"Listen, mate," said Ronny, once they were alone again. "No one can prove anything, so lighten up. The old man was a bastard. He may have been nice to you, but he wasn't to me, in case you didn't know. Those fishing trips were just a smoke screen to impress your dad. Truth was, he couldn't be arsed. As soon as we buggered off up the road to those girls, he was going to get himself comfy in his camping chair with his ciggies and a dram, and the fish could kiss his backside. Most of those he 'caught' were ones he'd brought with him. Didn't you suss that out?"

Carl shook his head. It didn't at all fit his image of the man his father had been so fond of, and from whom Carl had learned so much.

"Not true, Ronny. The fish that day were fresh, and your dad hadn't touched a drop. The autopsy was very clear about that. So why all the crap?"

Ronny raised his eyebrows and finished chewing before answering. "You were just a big kid at the time, Carl. You only saw what you wanted to see. And the way I look at it now, you're still a kid. If you don't want to hear the truth, you can pay the bill and sod off."

"So tell me, then. Tell me how you killed your dad and how I was mixed up in it."

"All you have to do is think of all those posters in your bedroom."

What kind of fucking answer was that? "What posters?"

Ronny laughed. "Funny *I* should remember, when you've forgotten."

Carl took a deep breath. All that supping had obviously addled the man's brains.

"Bruce Lee, John Saxon, Chuck Norris." He executed a couple of karate chops in the air. "Pow! Pow! *Way of the Dragon. Enter the Dragon. Fist of Fury. Those* posters, Carl."

"The kung fu posters? I only had them a short while, and I'd taken them down again *long* before then. What are you getting at, anyway?"

"JEET KUNE DO-ooo!" Ronny burst out suddenly, spraying chewed-up cod all over the table and causing the other guests to almost choke on their lager. "That was your battle cry, Carl. Aalborg, Hjørring, Frederikshavn, Nørresundby. If there was a Bruce Lee film on in any of those places, you'd be there. You can't have forgotten, surely? As soon as you weren't underage anymore you were there at the front of the queue. So it can't have been *that* long before. As far as I'm aware, the age limit's sixteen, and you were seventeen when the old man died."

"What the fuck are you talking about, Ronny? What's this got to do with anything?"

His cousin leaned across the table again. "You taught me kung fu, Carl. And as soon as you eyeballed those girls up on the road, you saw fuck all else. That's when I gave him a chop to the throat. Not hard, but hard enough to break a bloke's neck, just like you showed me. I'd been practicing on the sheep at home, so I just aimed at his jugular and let him have it. Followed up with a heel kick and finished him off. Just like that!"

Carl saw the tablecloth jerk. The moron was even going to demonstrate.

"All right, no need to draw a picture. And I'd rather not have you spitting your lunch all over my clothes, if you don't mind," he said. "But do you know what, Ronny? There's not a shred of truth in any of what you just told me, so why are you spouting such shite? I told your dad we'd catch him later, and then you and me went off together. Are you so traumatized by his death that you need to fabricate a pack of lies just to go on living? It's sad, that's what it is."

Ronny smiled. "Believe what you want. You up for dessert?"

Carl shook his head. "If I ever hear you going on about your dad's accident like this again, I'll give you 'Jeet Kune Do,' or whatever he calls himself, are you with me?"

And with that he got up and left his cousin with the remains of his fish and most likely some serious considerations as to how he was going to get out of paying the bill.

No doubt he'd already gone off the dessert.

"Marcus Jacobsen wants to see you, pronto," said the duty officer when he got back.

If I'm in for a bollocking now, I'll give him one, too, he thought to himself as he went up the stairs.

"I'll get right to the point," said Marcus, even before Carl had closed the door behind him. "And I want you to answer me straight. Do you know anyone by the name of Pete Boswell?"

Carl frowned. "Never heard of him," he replied.

"We've received an anonymous tip-off this afternoon about that body out in Amager."

"I hate anonymous tip-offs. What's the score, then?"

"Seems the victim's a Brit. Pete Boswell, twenty-nine years old, Jamaican origins. Disappeared in autumn 2006. Registered as staying at the Hotel Triton at the time, employed by a trading company calling itself Kandaloo Workshop, dealing in Indian, Indonesian, and Malaysian artifacts and furniture. Ring any bells?"

"None whatsoever."

"Odd, then, wouldn't you say, that our anonymous friend says you, Anker Henningsen, and this Pete Boswell had a meeting the day he disappeared?"

"A meeting?" Carl felt the furrows tighten on his brow. "Why the hell would I have a meeting with someone who imports furniture and bric-a-brac? I've had the same furniture ever since I moved into the house in Allerød. I can't *afford* new furniture, and what I need I get from IKEA like everyone else. What the fuck's this about, Marcus?"

"You may well ask. But let's wait and see, shall we? Anonymous calls of this nature are rarely one-off occurrences," said Jacobsen.

Not a word about Carl barging in on his briefing earlier on.

18

August 1987

Gitte Charles was like a painting that had once delighted its creator, but which had now been discarded, stuffed away in a corner of some junk shop with the signature obliterated by time. Up in Tórshavn in the Faroe Islands her name alone had been enough to make her feel special, and in adolescence she had promised herself that if ever a suitor should enter her life and marriage ensue, she would not give up her name. The child they called Gitte Charles was a rugged, swaggering girl who remained a mainstay in Gitte's memory. The time since wasn't worth talking about.

When a father goes bankrupt and abandons his family, the world of a child goes to pieces and grand designs diminish. And so it was for Gitte, her mother, and her younger brother.

Back in Denmark, in Vejle, they found a secure, albeit less favorable, substitute for their former home, a flat with no view of the sea or water of any kind, and before long the family comprised three members striving in different directions and with little interest in one another's lives. She had not seen her mother or her brother since she was sixteen, thirty-seven years ago now, and it was a fact with which she was perfectly content.

Thank God they've no idea how seedy my life has become, Gitte thought to herself, taking a deep drag on her cigarette. She'd had nothing alcoholic to drink since Monday and it was driving her up the wall. Not because she was dependent. She wasn't, not at all. But the kick, the blast it gave her brain, the sharp bite on the tongue and in the back of the throat somehow raised her out of the void. If there were funds in her account, which there weren't, it being the end of the month, then a bottle of gin could work miracles for a couple of days. It took no more than that, so she wasn't an alcoholic. She was just a bit down, that's all.

She thought about cycling to Tranebjerg to see if there might be anyone left who could remember her for doing good when she was with the community home-health care. Maybe she could wangle a cup of coffee and a glass of cherry wine. There could be liqueur or tawny port.

She closed her eyes and could almost taste it.

Just one glass, it didn't matter what, and waiting for her benefit to come would be that much easier. Why did there have to be so long between payments?

She'd tried to get them to pay out once a week instead, but the social workers had cottoned on. Once a week and she'd be there again after a couple of days, pockets empty and cap in hand, whereas a monthly payout meant they only saw her at the end of the month.

It was the most practical solution for them, she realized that. She wasn't stupid.

She gazed out over the fields and caught a glimpse of the postman's van on its way along Maarup Kirkevej from the church in Nordby. At this time of year the island was dead. The tourists had all gone home, the brothers who owned just about the whole island had gone into semi-hibernation in their tractor sheds, and everyone else sat around waiting for the evening news and spring to come.

For almost two years she had lived in this outbuilding belonging to a farm whose owner never gave her the time of day. It was lonely, but she was used to it. In many respects she was the quintessence of an islander. Her years in the Faroe Islands, on Sprogø, and now Samsø, had been far better than those she had spent in the big towns where everyone busied about and yet had no time for one another. No, islands were made for people like her. A person was in charge. Life was manageable.

The van pulled into the yard and the postman got out with a letter in his hand. It wasn't often the farm owner received letters. Flyers from the cooperative store in neighboring Maarup were more than enough for him to get on with, and the rest of the island seemed to have acknowledged the fact.

But then she was taken aback. Didn't he just drop the letter into her box? A mistake, surely?

As the van drove off she put on her dressing gown, then scurried out in her slippers and opened the postbox. The address on the envelope was handwritten. She hadn't received that kind of letter in years. She took a deep breath in anticipation, turned the envelope over in her hand, and felt a surge of surprise and astonishment run through her body, her stomach knotting immediately. It was from Nete Hermansen.

She read the name and address of the sender once more, and then again to make sure, sitting down at the little table in the kitchen, fumbling for her cigarettes. For some time she simply stared at the envelope, wondering what it might contain.

Nete Hermansen! It was all such a long time ago.

In the late summer of 1956, six months to the day after Gitte's twenty-second birthday, she boarded the mail boat from Korsør to Sprogø, full of expectation, but with little knowledge of the place that would be her home for several years to come.

She had personally sought the advice of the senior doctor at Brejning in order to ascertain whether the place might be suited to her, and he had peered at her over his horn-rimmed glasses with eyes that were warm and wise as ever. It was all the answer she needed. A young, natural, healthy girl like her could only do good in such a place, he told her. And that settled it.

She was familiar with the feeble-minded. Some could be rather a handful, but most were no trouble. The girls out on the island were not quite as simple as those who'd been in her section at Brejning, so she was told, and she was happy at the thought.

They stood waiting for her in a huddle on the jetty in their long tartan dresses, with big smiles and eager waves, and Gitte thought only that their hair was ugly and their smiles too broad by half. Later she learned that the woman she was replacing had been despised more than any other and that the girls had been counting the days until the mail boat came and took the dreaded woman away.

Perhaps that was why they received her with such warm embraces and hearty pats on the back.

"I like you!" exclaimed one of the girls, who was three times the size of the others, hugging Gitte almost until she was black and blue. Viola was her name, and her overwhelming presence would soon become rather tiresome.

But Gitte was welcomed and appreciated.

"I gather from your dossier that you've grown fond of referring to yourself as a nurse over there in Brejning. I won't support your using that designation, but, I won't protest either if you continue to do so. We've no fully trained staff here on the island, so it may be quite beneficial to us if the other wardens believe they've something to live up to."

There were no smiles in the matron's rooms, but out in the courtyard a group of giggling girls stole glances at her through the window. Scarecrows with pudding-basin haircuts, standing in a huddle and pulling faces.

"Your records are satisfactory, but I should like you to note that your long hair may trigger unwanted desires in the girls, so I must ask you to put it up under a hairnet whenever you are among them.

"I've made sure your room has been cleaned and made ready. From now on that will be your own responsibility. Here on Sprogø we set greater store by order and neatness than I'm sure you're used to from Brejning. Clean clothes at all times. The same applies to the girls, and morning hygiene is obligatory."

She nodded to Gitte, clearly expecting a similar sign of agreement in return. Gitte obliged.

The first time she saw Nete was a couple of hours later when she was led through the girls' dining room into the one used by the staff.

The girl was seated at the window, gazing out over the water as though it were the only thing that existed. It was a state of calm wholly undisturbed by the chatter of the other girls in her proximity, the hulking Viola who screeched a greeting to Gitte, or even the food on the table. The light fell on her face and made shadows that seemed almost to wrench her innermost thoughts from her mind. In that most fleeting of moments Gitte fell for her completely.

When the matron presented Gitte to the girls, they clapped their hands and waved, calling out their names and trying to draw attention to themselves. Only Nete and the girl who sat opposite her reacted differently. Nete, by turning her head and looking Gitte straight in the eye as though some invisible armor had to be penetrated first, and the girl opposite, with fluttering eyes that seemed almost to caress Gitte's body.

"What's the name of that quiet girl, the one who was sitting over by the window?" she asked later, as she sat down at the dinner table with the rest of the staff.

"I'm not sure I know who you mean," said the matron.

"The one who was sitting opposite that other girl, the provocative one."

"Opposite Rita? That'd be Nete," said the woman next to her. "She always sits over there in the corner, just staring out at the sea and the gulls. She likes to watch them break open the mussels. But if you think she's the quiet type, I'm afraid you're much mistaken."

Gitte opened Nete Hermansen's letter and began to read, her hands trembling increasingly as she did so. When she got to the place where Nete said she was intending to make Gitte a gift of ten million kroner, she gasped for breath and was forced to put the letter down. She paced the floor in the kitchen area for several minutes, not daring to look at it. She rearranged her tins of tea, ran a cloth across the tabletop, and wiped her hands dry against her hips before turning her attention once more to the matter at hand. Ten million kroner. And then she read that a check was enclosed. She snatched up the envelope and looked inside. It was true. She hadn't seen it until now.

She sat down heavily and gazed around the shabby room, her lips quivering.

"It's from Nete," she said to herself repeatedly, before taking off her dressing gown.

The check was in the amount of two thousand kroner. Much more than the ferry and the train to Copenhagen and back would cost. She wouldn't be able to cash it at the bank in Tranebjerg, because she owed them more than the check was worth, but the farm owner could give her fifteen hundred for it. And then she would cycle to the little co-op in Maarup as fast as she could.

This was a situation that required assistance. And the co-op's selection of spirits would be more than sufficient.

19

September 1987

Nete gathered the brochures that had been laid out neatly on the coffee table and put them on the windowsill. Alluring brochures presenting comfortable apartments in Santa Ponsa, Andratx, and Porto Cristo, a couple of terraced houses in Son Vida and Pollenca, and a penthouse in San Telmo. The prices were reasonable and there were plenty to choose from. Her dreams were queuing up, and now they would be fulfilled.

She wanted to be away from Denmark when winter set in, and Mallorca seemed like the ideal place. There, in that delightful countryside, she would enjoy the fruits of her husband's hard work and grow old with grace.

The day after tomorrow, when everything was over, she would book her ticket to Palma de Mallorca and decide on the right property. And a week from now she would be gone.

Again she took out the list of names and ran her eyes down the page, going through the entire procedure in her mind. Nothing could be left to chance.

Rita Nielsen 11:00–11:45
* Tidy up: 11:45–12:30

Tage Hermansen 12:30–13:15
* Tidy up: 13:15–13:45

Viggo Mogensen 13:45–14:30
* Tidy up: 14:30–15:00

Philip Nørvig 15:00–15:45
* Tidy up: 15:45–16:15

Curt Wad 16:15–17:00
* Tidy up: 17:00–17:30

Gitte Charles 17:30–18:15
* Tidy up: 18:15–

She nodded to herself, picturing the arrival of each of the invited names. Yes, everything seemed to be right.

As soon as one of them was inside the apartment she would press the button to shut off the entry phone downstairs. When the victim could no longer put up a struggle, she would switch it on again. If the next in line arrived early and called up, she would ask them to leave and come back at the appointed time. Should anyone arrive late, she would put them at the back of the queue and suggest they go down to the Pavilion and have something to eat at her expense. Given the situation and the prospect of such rich rewards, she was in no doubt they would follow her instructions.

And if chance should dictate that whoever it was happened to bump into the next in line outside the front door, it would hardly matter. She had been careful enough to arrange the order of arrivals so that sequential callers had never met before. Curt Wad and Gitte Charles might conceivably have run into each other at some hospital or other institution, but the risk of a man like Curt Wad not arriving on the dot was presumably minimal indeed.

"Wise to put Gitte last," she said out loud. One could never know with Gitte. Punctuality had never been a matter of much concern to her.

Yes, the plan was good, and the timing looked like it was going to work just fine.

None of the other residents would ever let anyone into the building apart from their own visitors, she was sure of that. The thieving drug addicts down on Blågårds Plads had demonstrated on several occasions that doing so would be foolhardy indeed.

When everything was done, she would have the whole evening and night to take care of what remained.

The only thing she needed to do now was make sure the room really *was* airtight. It called for a test.

She fetched her shopping bag and a screwdriver from the toolbox, went out onto the landing, and kneeled down in front of her door. The groove on top of one of the screws was worn, but she persevered and eventually succeeded in removing the nameplate. She dropped it in her shopping bag, descended the stairs, and went out into the street.

First the heel bar and key-cutting shop on Blågårdsgade, then the paint store on Nørrebrogade, she decided.

"Leave it with me and I'll see what I can do," said the key cutter, as he examined the nameplate. "But it won't be ready for an hour and a quarter. I've got some shoes that need heeling first."

"I'll come back in an hour and a half. Make sure the engraving's the same as the original. And do spell the name correctly, won't you?"

That's done, she said to herself, as she walked down the street. The name on the entry phone was still Nete Rosen, but she would fix that with a sticky label and a permanent marker. From now on she was Nete Hermansen; the documents were already signed and sent in. The other residents might wonder, but she didn't care.

"I need something with a strong smell," she told the paint dealer. "I'm a biology teacher and the children are working on the olfactory system tomorrow. I'm all right for things that smell nice, but what I need is something pungent."

The paint dealer gave her a wry smile. "In that case I'd say turpentine, ammonia, and paraffin. That should be enough to bring tears to anyone's eyes."

"Right, and I'll be needing some formalin. Four or five bottles."

She smiled as he handed the plastic bags over the counter, and then she was done.

Two hours later the new nameplate bearing the name NETE HERMANSEN was fixed to the door. It would be wrong indeed for these imminent acts of vengeance to occur behind a door bearing the name of Rosen.

She went out into the kitchen and collected eight bowls, taking them with her to the room at the end of the hallway.

She spread newspapers out over the dining table just in case, and on top of them she placed the bowls, filling each with strongly scented or malodorous liquids. Eau de cologne, lavender water, turpentine, paraffin, benzine, vinegar, methylated spirits, and finally ammonia.

The latter gave off an invisible cloud that impacted suddenly, stabbing at her nostrils and throat and making her gasp with discomfort.

She left the bottles where they were and backed out of the room as quickly as she could, closing the door behind her.

Groaning, she dashed into the bathroom and rinsed her face over and over in cold water. The fumes of these combined substances were truly abominable. It felt almost as if they were corroding her flesh, seeping into her brain through the membranes of her nose.

She hobbled through all the rooms of the apartment, opening the windows wide to let out the fumes that had escaped when she had left the airtight room or which still clung tenaciously to her clothes.

After an hour she closed the windows again, placed the bottles of formalin in the cupboard underneath the sink, left the apartment, and went down to sit on the bench by the lake.

A little smile curved the corners of her mouth.

This was going to work.

After another hour she was ready to go back. Her breathing was now unencumbered, her clothes aired by the gentle breeze of late summer. It was good to have come this far. She felt serene.

If, against all expectation, even the slightest trace of fumes still lingered in the stairwell or the apartment, she would have to work all night to rectify it. Her task now was clear. She had no way of knowing for certain if the formalin would work according to plan, so the room *had* to be completely airtight. If it wasn't, she wouldn't be able to go to Mallorca, no matter how much her mind was set.

She entered the hall of the building and stood for a long time at the bottom of the stairs, sniffing the air. There was a slight scent of the neighbor's dog, but that was all. Her sense of smell had always been good.

She repeated the procedure on every landing with the same result, and when finally she came to the fourth floor she got down on her knees in front of her door, pushed open the letter box, and inhaled deeply.

She smiled. Still nothing.

Then she entered the apartment and was met by the same fresh air that had wafted in through the windows an hour before. She stood for a moment, eyes closed, concentrating on this one sense that could mean the difference between success and failure. But still there was nothing.

Another hour passed without a trace appearing, and finally she let herself into the room at the end of the hallway.

In less than a second her eyes were streaming. Like a veritable nerve-gas attack, the overwhelming fumes seemed to penetrate every exposed pore. She closed her eyes tight and held a hand in front of her mouth as she fumbled her way to the window and managed to fling it open.

Like a person about to drown, she stuck her head out into the air and gasped for oxygen, coughing and spluttering as if she would never stop.

After fifteen minutes the contents of all eight bowls had been poured into the toilet and flushed away repeatedly to make sure. Then she once again opened wide all the windows in the apartment before washing the bowls thoroughly. By the time evening came, she knew her work had stood the test.

She laid a white cloth over the dining table in the airtight room, took out her finest porcelain, and set the table. Crystal glasses, silver cutlery, and a meticulous little place card for each of her guests.

It was to be a festive occasion.

When she was done she looked out at the tops of the chestnut trees, whose leaves were already turning yellow. Happily, she would soon be gone.

She remembered to close the windows of the airtight room before going to bed, sealing them with clear silicone. And then at last she stood back and admired her work.

It would be a long time indeed before these windows were opened again.

20

November 2010

It was like a curtain of cloud had descended to darken Carl's thoughts, black and ominous, crackling with electricity: the nail-gun case, Hardy's suspicions and the coins with Anker's and his own prints on them, Vigga's wedding plans and how they would impact on his financial situation, Assad's past, Rose's oddities, Ronny's idiotic blatherings, and the total backfire of his evening with Mona. Never before had he felt so many different issues weighing him down all at once. He could hardly shift buttocks before the next disaster came crashing down. Such brooding was in no way befitting for an otherwise competent servant of the state employed to solve mysteries confounding to all others. He found himself wondering if they might set up a department whose prime function was to solve *his* mysteries.

Carl sighed, lit a smoke, and switched on the news channel. It helped a bit to see that others were in deeper shit than himself.

A single glance at the flatscreen on the wall and he was down to earth again with a bang. Five grown men arguing about the government's pocket philosophies on matters economic. Could anything be more inconsequential? What was the point?

Carl picked up the sheet of paper Rose had placed on top of the report while he'd been upstairs with Marcus. Half a page, written by hand. Was that really all she could dig up on Gitte Charles?

He read it through, finding it to be anything but encouraging.

Though Rose had inquired extensively, no one from Samsø's community home health care unit could remember anything about a Gitte Charles, and for that reason no one had the slightest recollection of her thefts from the elderly whom she had visited on her rounds. Her spell at the hospital in Tranebjerg likewise drew a blank, the place having been closed down in the intervening years and the staff dispersed to all corners. Her mother was long since deceased, and her brother, who had emigrated to Canada, had also died a few years back. The only real connection was the man who had rented out a room to her on Maarup Kirkevej twenty-three years ago.

Rose's description of him was a hoot. *The bloke was an idiot, or maybe just a grumpy old git. After Gitte Charles, he's rented out his dwarf-sized flat (21 m²) to 15 or 20 others. He remembers her well, but had nothing intelligent to say. One of those yokels with cowshit on his shoes and tractors left to rust round the back of the house, who thinks undisclosed earnings are the only income worth having.*

Carl put the paper down on his desk, then began studying the summary of the investigations into the Gitte Charles case. Here, too, pickings were meager.

The picture changed a couple of times on the flatscreen, cutting quickly between a couple of large gatherings in congress halls and the faces of a pair of aging men beaming smiles at anyone who might care to notice.

The reporter relating the story accorded them little respect in his voice-over:

"Now that the Purity Party, after a succession of failed attempts, has finally managed to gather enough signatures to be eligible to stand in the next parliamentary elections, many will be asking themselves whether Danish politics has finally hit rock bottom. Not since the days of the Upsurge Party have we seen a party running on such a controversial and, in many people's opinion, contemptible platform. At today's inaugural general assembly, the party's founder, the fanatical and often disparaged fertility doctor Curt Wad, presented the party's parliamentary candidates, and in contrast to the days of the Upsurge Party these included several prominent men and women with scholarly backgrounds and high-profile careers. With the average age of their candidates being forty-two, accusations by political rivals that the Purity Party consists solely of geriatrics have been clearly refuted, despite Dr. Wad himself being eighty-eight and many of the party's executive committee having long since retired from professional life."

The TV producer then cut to a tall man with white sideburns who looked considerably younger than eighty-eight. *Dr. Curt Wad, Physician and Party Founder,* read the caption.

"Have you had a look at my note and the report on Gitte Charles's disappearance?" Rose interrupted.

Carl turned to look at her. After having spoken to her real sister, Yrsa, it was hard to know what to make of her persona. Was this, too, just an artificial facade? These black expanses of material, the kohl, and the shoes that could skewer a cobra?

"Er, yeah. Sort of, anyway."

"There's not much to go on apart from the first report we got from Lis. Seems there was nothing the investigators could get a handle on at the time, so all they did was issue a description. Gitte Charles's drinking was emphasized, and even though the term 'alcoholic' funnily enough isn't mentioned directly, it's obvious their logic was telling them she most likely died on a binge somewhere or other. There was no next of kin and no work colleagues, so it all got shelved. Exit Gitte Charles."

"There's something about her being seen boarding the ferry to Kalundborg. Any theory of her maybe having fallen overboard?"

Rose gave him a look of irritation. "No, Carl, she was seen disembarking, I've already told you that. How many seconds did you spend going through it, anyway?"

It was a question he chose to ignore. Sarcasm was his own specialty. "What did her landlord have to say about her disappearance?" he asked instead. "He must have wondered, once his rent stopped coming in."

"It didn't. The social services paid it directly, otherwise she'd have boozed it all away. So the landlord, that shite, wasn't going to tell anyone she was gone as long as the money kept coming in. In the end it was the manager from the local co-op store who reported it. He said Gitte Charles had come into the shop all cocky on the last day of August with fifteen hundred kroner in her pocket. She told him she'd inherited a lot of money and now she was off to Copenhagen to collect. He laughed at her, and she got miffed."

Carl recoiled in his chair. "An inheritance? Was there any truth in that?"

"None whatsoever. I've already been in touch with the probate court about it, and there wasn't a thing."

"Hmm. It'd have been too good to be true, wouldn't it?"

"Yeah, but listen. There's a sentence here that might make you wonder."

She picked up the folder from the desk and found a place about half-way through the report.

"Here it is. The co-op manager reported her missing a week later because she'd put a five-hundred-kroner note in his hand and said if she didn't come back ten million better off the next week, the money was his. And if she did, he could give it back to her along with a cup of coffee and a dram. He had nothing to lose, did he? Which was why he entered the bet."

"Ten million!" Carl whistled. "But a pipe dream all the same?"

"Most probably, yeah. But listen to this. The co-op manager found her bike down by the harbor a week later and thought something might be up."

"Seems like a reasonable assumption. He still had his five hundred kroner. And from what we know, it sounds like she wasn't one to throw money away," said Carl.

"Exactly. The report says this: *Co-op manager Lasse Bjerg stated that unless Gitte Charles really had collected her ten million kroner and left her old life behind once and for all to start afresh, something terrible had most likely happened to her.* And here comes the bit I want you to take note of: *Five hundred kroner was a considerable sum of money for Gitte Charles. Why would she give so much away of her own free will?*

"Maybe we should make the trip to Samsø, have a chat with our man from the co op and the landlord, check out the lay of the land," Carl mused. The break would do him good.

"That won't turn anything up, Carl. The manager's in the nursing home with advanced dementia and I've already spoken to the landlord. The man's a meathead and Gitte's stuff's long since gone. Would you believe he sold it all off at a flea market when she didn't come back? Talk about making the most of a situation."

"So what we've got is nothing, basically?"

"In spades!"

"OK, what do we do now, then? We know that two people who must have known each other disappeared without a trace the same day. Gitte Charles and Rita Nielsen. Gitte Charles leaves nothing behind, and in Rita Nielsen's case her former employee, Lone Rasmussen, still has some of her personal effects, though nothing with any bearing on the case." He was about to tap a smoke from the packet, only for his fingers to remain suspended in the air at the sight of Rose's arctic glare. "We could pay a call on Lone Rasmussen and have a rummage round in what Rita left behind, but who could be arsed driving all the way to Vejle for that?"

"She doesn't live in Vejle anymore," said Rose.

"Where, then?"

"Thisted."

"Even farther away. Brilliant."

"Like I said, she doesn't live in Vejle."

Carl fished out his cigarette and was about to light up when Assad came in through the door, wafting the air to get rid of smoke that had yet to materialize. Had they all gone soft, or what?

"Have you discussed this Gitte Charles woman?" Assad wanted to know.

Both nodded.

"I haven't got round yet to that fisherman, Viggo Mogensen," he went on. "But we are coming along nicely with this Philip Nørvig. I've made an appointment with his wife. She still lives in their house in Halsskov."

Carl recoiled. "Not now, I hope?"

Rose hoisted her eyelids slowly to a level marginally above her pupils. The girl looked knackered. "Use your head, Carl. Don't you think we've been here long enough for one day?"

He looked at Assad. "So it's tomorrow, then?"

Assad gave him the thumbs-up. "Perhaps I can drive the car?" he ventured.

If that's what he thought, he could bleeding well think again.

"Your mobile's ringing, Carl," said Rose, indicating the rotating contraption on his desk.

He glanced at the display without recognizing the number before answering.

It was a rather less-than-friendly female voice. "Hello, would this be Carl Mørck?" it inquired.

"It would."

"In that case I'd ask you to come over to the Tivoli Hall and pay the bill your cousin left behind."

Carl held his breath and counted to ten. "What's it got to do with me?"

"I'm standing here with an order slip and a load of spiel scrawled on the back. It says: 'Sorry, must dash to catch a flight. My cousin, Detective

Inspector Carl Mørck of the homicide division at Police HQ, has promised to come over in a bit and pay the bill. You know who he is. The bloke who was sitting here with me at the table. He asked me to give you his mobile number in case he got caught up on the way, so you can make arrangements for payment.'"

"You what?" Carl exclaimed. It was all he could muster.

"We found it on the table after he'd gone."

Carl felt like a new cub scout whose pack leader had sent him off on a fool's errand to fetch sparks for the campfire.

"I'll be right over," he said, resolving on the spot to stop off in Vanløse on his way home and pay a certain freeloading cousin of his a social visit.

Ronny's rented dwelling wasn't exactly impressive. To call it a slum would have been a compliment. A rusty iron stairway led up the side of a building, whereafter the visitor arrived on a filthy concrete platform in front of a steel door that seemed to have been put in about halfway between the first and second floors. A bit like the access to a projector room in a disused cinema, only a shoddy prototype. He hammered a fist against the door a couple of times, hearing a voice shout from within, followed eventually by the rattle of the lock.

This time Ronny was dressed rather more homogeneously in his undies, briefs and wife-beater both embellished with the same roaring dragon.

"There's a beer if you want one," he said, leading Carl into an incense-filled room dimly lit by lava lamps and colored rice-paper lanterns bearing steamy erotic motifs.

"This is Mae, as I call her," he said, nodding in the direction of an Asian woman small enough to fit inside Ronny's carcass three or four times over.

The woman didn't turn to greet him. She was busy at the stove, tiny hands fluttering over saucepans, the air filled with aromas of Pattaya and something that reminded Carl of his barbecue back home in Allerød.

"Little gem, she is. Won't be long before the food's ready," Ronny said, sitting down on a bombed-out sofa camouflaged by saronglike pieces of cloth in various shades of saffron.

Carl sat down opposite him and accepted the bottle of lager Ronny placed on the ebony coffee table between them.

"You owe me six hundred and seventy kroner, as well as an explanation as to how you can possibly be eating again so soon after the meal you shoveled down your neck at the Tivoli Hall."

Ronny smiled and patted his gut. "All a question of training," he said, prompting the Thai woman to turn round with the whitest smile Carl had ever seen. She wasn't the usual twenty-five-year-old with skin as smooth as a mirror, like most other imported Thai girls. This one was weathered, her face creased with laughter lines, eyes keen and bright.

One–nil to Ronny.

"You were picking up the tab, Carl, I told you so on the phone. You scheduled a meeting during working hours, so the rules say you pay."

Carl took a deep breath. "Scheduled a meeting? Working hours? May I ask what you actually do for a living, Ronny? No, let me guess. Professional stretcher of undershirts, perhaps?"

He saw the Thai woman shudder with stifled laughter over by the stove. Not only did she understand Danish, she had a sense of humor, too.

"Cheers, Carl," said Ronny, with a smile. "Good to see you again."

"So I shouldn't bank on getting my money back, then?"

"Nope. But I can offer you the most delicious Tom Kha Gai you could ever wish for."

"Sounds like something poisonous."

The Thai woman chuckled again.

"It's a spicy chicken soup made with coconut milk, kaffir lime leaves, and galangal," Ronny explained.

"Listen here, Ronny," Carl sighed. "You did me for six hundred and seventy kroner today, but we'll let that go. It'll be the last time you pull one over on me. Right now I'm up to my eyeballs in work, but our little chat today has got me rather concerned. Are you lining up to blackmail me, Ronny? Because if you are, I can guarantee your feet won't touch before you and little Mae here are in front of a judge in the district court or on a plane back to Chow Mein City or wherever the fuck it is you like to hang out, do you get my drift?"

The woman turned and began to berate Ronny in Thai. He shook his head a couple of times before his face suddenly became livid with rage. His bushy eyebrows seemed to take on a life of their own.

Then he glared at Carl. "I've got two things to say to you. First, you were the one who came to me this morning, like I said. And second, my wife, Mae-Ying-Thahan Mørck, just struck you off the guest list."

Less than a minute later he was out the door. Apparently Ronny's diminutive spouse had found out that if she rattled her kitchen utensils loud enough, people tended to beat a hasty retreat.

So our paths diverge again, Ronny, he said to himself, with a sneaking feeling that he might be wrong. He felt his mobile vibrate in his pocket and knew it was Mona before he saw the display.

"Hi, gorgeous," he said, trying to sound like he had a cold, though not enough to prevent him from taking up an invitation.

"If you fancy giving it another try with my daughter and Ludwig, you can come round tomorrow," she said.

A rather reluctant peace offering, by the sound of it.

"I'd love to," he said, as if he meant it.

"Good. Seven o'clock, then, at mine. And I ought to remind you you've got an appointment with Kris tomorrow afternoon at three, in his office. You've been there before, so you know where it is."

"Have I? Can't say it rings a bell," he said, lying through his teeth.

"Yes, you have. And Carl? You need it. I know the signals."

"But I'll be in Halsskov tomorrow."

"Not at three o'clock, you won't!"

"Mona, I'm doing fine. There isn't the slightest bit of panic left in me after that nail-gun case, I can assure you."

"I spoke to Marcus Jacobsen about your hysterics in the briefing room today."

"Hysterics? What hysterics?"

"Besides, I'd like to be sure the man I'm on the verge of selecting to be my regular lover is mentally up to the job."

Carl racked his brains to find the right rejoinder, only to sense all semblance of verbal dexterity slipping away. Expressing his feelings properly right now would mean resorting to tango steps, if he could.

"The way things are looking, you're in for a rough time, I'm afraid. Marcus has asked me to tell you there's been a development. They've turned something else up in the box that body was buried in."

So much for ballroom dancing.

"They found a piece of paper underneath the body. A xerox of a photograph, wrapped up in plastic. It shows the victim, this Pete Boswell, standing between you and Anker with his arms around your shoulders."

21

November 2010

"You're looking tired, Carl. Perhaps I should do the driving?" Assad said the next morning.

"I *am* tired, and no, you're *not* doing the driving, Assad. Not as long as I'm with you, anyway."

"Were you unable to sleep?"

Carl didn't answer. He'd slept all right, albeit only for two hours. It had been a night of churning thoughts. The evening before, Marcus Jacobsen had e-mailed him the photo of the victim standing shoulder to shoulder with Carl and Anker, thereby confirming what Mona had told him earlier on.

"We've got the lab looking into it to see if they can ascertain whether or not it's a fake. I'm assuming we agree that would be the best outcome," the chief had written.

Understatement of the year. Of course it'd be best if they could conclude it was a fake, because it *was a fake*. Was Jacobsen angling for some kind of confession here?

He'd never been anywhere near the deceased, didn't even know him, and yet this was costing him precious fucking sleep. If forensics was unable to prove the photo had been manipulated, Carl could expect a suspension any day now. He knew as well as anyone how Marcus operated.

He gazed out at the tailback of cars in front of them, working his jaw muscles. If he'd been thinking straight they'd have waited half an hour.

"A lot of traffic on the road," said Assad, ever observant.

"Yeah, and if they don't get their fucking arses moving, we won't be in Halsskov before ten o'clock."

"We have the whole day ahead of us, Carl."

"No, we don't. I've got to be back by three."

"Ah, in that case we should put this away," he said, pointing at the GPS. "We can leave the motorway and be there in no time if I read the map for you, Carl."

It was a proposal that cost them another hour before they eventually turned into the driveway of Philip Nørvig's house just as the eleven o'clock news started on the radio.

"Demonstrators are gathering this morning outside the home of Curt Wad in Brøndby," said the newsreader. "A protest action initiated by grass-roots organizations seeks to highlight what they refer to as the antidemocratic principles on which Dr. Wad's Purity Party is founded. Curt Wad stated . . ."

Carl switched off the engine and stepped out onto the gravel of the driveway.

"If it hadn't been for Herbert . . ."

Mie Nørvig nodded in the direction of the man who had just entered the living room to introduce himself. Like Mie, he seemed to be somewhere in his seventies.

". . . well, Cecilie and I would never have been able to keep the house on at all."

Carl greeted the man politely as he sat down.

"I can well understand. It must have been a trying time indeed," Carl said with a nod. Another understatement. Not only had her husband gone bust, he'd done a bunk on her and left her to sort out the mess herself.

"I'll be very direct, Mrs. Nørvig." He hesitated, suddenly in doubt. "That *is* still your surname, isn't it?"

She rubbed the back of her hand nervously. The question was obviously an embarrassment. "Yes, it is. You see, Herbert and I aren't married. The courts declared me bankrupt when Philip disappeared, so it wasn't the sensible thing to do."

Carl forced a smile to show he understood, though he couldn't have cared less whether they were married or not. "Is it conceivable your husband just couldn't cope, and decided to put it all behind him?"

"Not if you mean did he commit suicide. Philip was too much of a coward for that." It sounded harsh, but maybe she would have preferred him to have taken a length of rope and hanged himself in one of the trees in the garden. Maybe it would have been better for her.

"No, what I mean is whether he might simply have run away from it all. Perhaps he managed to put some money aside and then settled down somewhere abroad where no one would find him."

She looked at him with surprise. Had the thought never occurred to her?

"Impossible. Philip hated traveling. Sometimes I used to pester him for us to go on a trip. Nothing special, just a bus trip to Germany, that sort of thing. A couple of days at most. But he never would. He hated going anywhere new. Why else would he set up his practice in a dump like this? Because it's where he grew up, that's why!"

"Perhaps he felt he had no option but to disappear, the way things stood with the business. A mountain village in Crete, maybe, or somewhere in Argentina. A place where a person running away from problems at home could settle down nicely with no questions asked."

Mie Nørvig snorted and shook her head. The idea was clearly unthinkable.

The man she called Herbert broke in.

"I'm sorry, but perhaps I ought to add at this point that Philip was an old schoolfriend of my elder brother. He always used to say Philip was a sissy." He sent his partner a knowing look, most likely to reinforce his position as a considerably more appropriate match than his predecessor. "Once, when there was a school trip to Bornholm, Philip refused to go. He said he wouldn't be able to understand a word of the local dialect, so there was no point. His teachers huffed and puffed, but he stuck to his guns. He wasn't one to be forced into doing what didn't suit him."

"Hmm. Doesn't sound like what I'd call a sissy, but maybe you're made of hardier stuff here. OK, let's put that theory aside for the time being. It wasn't suicide, and he didn't settle abroad. Which means we're left with an accident, manslaughter, or murder. Which do you reckon would be most likely?"

"In my opinion it was that damned organization he belonged to that killed him," Mie Nørvig said, looking at Assad.

Carl glanced at his assistant, whose dark eyebrows had suddenly relocated to the northern extremity of his corrugated brow.

"Come now, Mie," said Herbert, from the sofa. "We don't know that."

Carl fixed his gaze on the elderly woman. "I'm not sure I'm with you. What organization?" he asked. "There's no mention in the case file of him belonging to any organization."

"I never mentioned it before."

"I see. Then perhaps you might put us in the picture?"

"They called themselves The Cause."

Assad reached for his notepad.

"The Cause? A bit melodramatic, isn't it? Sounds like a Sherlock Holmes whodunnit." He ventured a smile, but the information had triggered quite a different reaction inside him. "And what might this 'Cause' involve?" he asked.

"Mie, I don't think you ought to . . ." interrupted Herbert, but Mie Nørvig ignored him.

"I don't know much about it, to be honest, because Philip never mentioned it. Apparently he wasn't allowed. But I couldn't help but pick up little snippets through the years. I was his secretary, after all," she said, dismissing her partner's protest with a wave of her hand.

"What sort of snippets?" Carl went on.

"About some people deserving to have children and others not. Philip sometimes assisted in passing compulsory sterilizations through the system. He'd been doing it for some years before I began working for him. There was an old case they sometimes mentioned when Curt was here. I—"

"Curt?" Carl interrupted.

"Curt Wad. He's in politics now."

Carl tried to place the vaguely familiar name and failed.

"The Hermansen case, they called it," the woman continued. "I think it must have been the first one they collaborated on. In later years Philip also served as a contact for doctors and other lawyers. There was a whole network he was in charge of."

"I see. But that sort of thing wasn't unusual at the time, was it? I mean, why should your husband have been in danger on that account? The authorities must have allowed the sterilization of lots of mentally challenged individuals in the old days."

"Yes, but quite often they sterilized people who *weren't* mentally challenged, and had them committed, too. It was the convenient thing to do if they wanted them out of the way. Gypsy women, for instance. And women with big families who relied on social benefits or else prostituted themselves. If The Cause could coax these women into the surgeries, they often came out again with their tubes tied, and certainly without the unborn children in their womb if they were pregnant."

"OK, let me get this straight. You're saying that radical surgical operations were performed illegally on these women without their consent?"

Mie Nørvig lifted her teaspoon and stirred her coffee, regardless that it was long since cold. That was her reply. They'd have to figure out the rest for themselves.

"Does any information exist on this organization, The Cause? Dossiers, reports of any kind?"

"Not as such, no. But I do have Philip's files and newspaper cuttings in the basement where he had his office."

"Honestly, Mie, do you think this is wise? Will it help matters?" Herbert inquired. "What I mean is, aren't we better off letting sleeping dogs lie?"

Mie Nørvig didn't answer him.

And then Assad raised his hand in the air, slowly and with a pained expression on his face. "Excuse me, may I use the toilet, please?"

Carl didn't care much for rummaging through piles of documents. He had staff for that. But with one answering a call of nature and the other holding the fort back at HQ, he didn't have much choice.

"Where should we start?" he asked Mie Nørvig, who stood gazing around the basement office as if she were a stranger in her own home.

Carl gave a sigh as she pulled out a couple of drawers from a filing cabinet to reveal a seemingly endless series of suspension files, all stuffed to bursting point. Poring through all this lot looked like it would take forever. Definitely something he could do without.

Mie Nørvig shrugged. "I haven't concerned myself with any of this for a great many years. I don't like to come down here since Philip disappeared. I've thought of just getting rid of it all, of course, but these are all confidential documents that need to be disposed of in the proper manner. It'd be such a bother. Much easier to lock the door and forget all about it. It's not as if we need the space." She paused and stared vacantly around the room once more.

"It's a daunting task, I must say," Herbert ventured. "Perhaps Mie and I ought to sift through and see if there's anything that might be of interest to you. If anything turns up we could pass it on. Would that be all right? Of course, we'd need to know what we were looking for first."

"Oh, I know," Mie Nørvig exclaimed suddenly, indicating a large roll-front cabinet of light-colored wood, on top of which were cardboard boxes heavy with preprinted envelopes, business cards, and an assortment of forms.

She turned the key and the roll-front descended promptly like a guillotine.

"There," she said, picking out a blue spiral scrapbook in A3 format. "Philip's first wife kept it. After 1973, when Philip and Sara Julie were divorced, the cuttings were no longer stuck in, just placed between the pages."

"You've been through it, I take it?"

"Certainly. After Sara Julie, I was the one who put the articles in that Philip asked me to cut out of the papers."

"And what was it you wanted to show me?" Carl asked, noting that Assad had now entered the room, no longer paler than was healthy-looking for the average Arab. Maybe he was in better fettle now he'd been for a groaner.

"You all right, Assad?" he asked.

"Just a minor relapse, Carl." He patted himself cautiously on the stomach, hinting that his peristaltic woes might not be over.

"Here," said Mie Nørvig. "A cutting from 1980. And there's the person I was telling you about," she went on, pointing at the article. "Curt Wad. I couldn't stand the man. Whenever he'd been here, or whenever my husband spoke to him on the phone, it was as though Philip was a different person. He could become so callous. No, callous isn't quite the word. More impassive, as though he had no feelings left inside him. All of a sudden he could be so cold toward my daughter and me, as though he'd taken on a completely different personality. Normally he was kind enough, but often when this happened we would argue."

Carl studied the article. *Purity Party Sets Up Korsør Branch*, the headline ran. Below it was a press photo. Philip Nørvig in a tweed jacket, the man at his side elegant in a dark suit, a tight knot in his tie.

Philip Nørvig and Curt Wad led the meeting with authority, read the caption.

"Well, fuck me," Carl muttered, glancing apologetically in the direction of his hosts. "This is the bloke who's all over the news. The Purity Party, I recognize the name now."

The photo showed a rather younger version of the Curt Wad he'd seen on TV the day before. Jet-black sideburns, a tall, handsome man in his prime, and by his side a thin, wiry man with sharp creases in his trousers and a smile that seemed false and infrequently used.

She nodded. "Yes, that's him. Curt Wad."

"He's trying to get this Purity Party into parliament at the moment, is that right?"

She nodded again. "It's not the first time, not by a long way. But this time it seems he might succeed, perish the thought. Curt Wad is a man with a lot of influence and no scruples, and his ideas are sick. One can only hope they're given short shrift."

"You don't know what you're talking about, Mie," said Herbert, interrupting again.

Officious git, Carl thought to himself.

"Oh, but I do," Mie Nørvig replied with some annoyance. "And you know fine well I do! You've kept up with the papers just as much as I have. Think of what that Louis Petterson was writing at one point; we've talked about it. Curt Wad and all his yes-men have been in the thick of all sorts of dreadful cases, abortions he referred to as necessary curettages, and sterilizations. Interventions the women didn't even know they'd been subjected to."

Herbert protested more emotionally than seemed called for. "My wife . . . Mie, that is, has got it into her head that Wad is to blame for Philip's disappearance. Grief can be a terrible thing, and . . ."

Carl frowned and watched the man's expression closely as Mie Nørvig went on, firm in her conviction. It was as though his arguments had long since worn thin.

"Two years after this photograph was taken, after Philip had put in thousands of hours working for that Purity Party of his, Wad kicked him out. That man, there"—she jabbed a finger at the image of Curt Wad—"came down here personally and kicked Philip out without the slightest warning. They claimed he'd been embezzling funds, but it wasn't true. Just like it wasn't true that he'd committed fraud in his law practice. He wouldn't dream of such a thing. He just wasn't all that good with figures, that's all."

"I really can't see any obvious grounds for linking Curt Wad and this incident to Philip's disappearance, Mie," said Herbert, rather more subdued now. "Bear in mind the man's still alive. He could sue you for—"

"I'm not afraid of Curt Wad anymore, I've told you that!" It was an emphatic outburst, her cheeks flushed beneath the fine layer of powder on her face. "You keep out of this for once, Herbert, and let me speak up. Do you hear me?"

Herbert retreated. It was plain that the matter would be the subject of continued debate behind closed doors.

"Perhaps you are also a member of this Purity Party, Mr. Herbert?" Assad ventured from the corner of the room.

The man's jaw twitched, though he let the question pass. Carl sent his assistant an inquiring look. Assad nodded toward a framed diploma on the wall. Carl stepped closer. *Diploma of Honor*, it read. *Awarded to Philip*

Nørvig and Herbert Sønderskov of Nørvig & Sønderskov Lawyers for their
sponsorship of the Korsør Scholarship Award 1972.

Assad's eyes narrowed as he directed a second discreet nod toward
Mie Nørvig's partner.

Carl returned the gesture. Well spotted, Assad.

"So you're a lawyer, too, Herbert?" Carl asked.

"Well, used to be," he replied. "I retired in 2001. But yes, I represented in the High Court until then."

"And you and Philip Nørvig were partners, is that right?"

Herbert Sønderskov's voice deepened a notch. "Indeed, we enjoyed a
long and fruitful professional partnership until deciding to go our separate ways in 1983."

"That would be in the wake of the accusations leveled against Philip
Nørvig and the rupture between him and Curt Wad?" Carl went on.

Sønderskov frowned. This rather round-shouldered pensioner had
years of experience clearing clients of charges brought against them.
Experience he was now taking advantage of to protect himself.

"It certainly was, yes. Philip had got himself mixed up in something
of which I did not approve, but the dissolution of the partnership was
more for practical reasons than anything else."

"Very practical indeed, it would seem. You got all his clients and his
wife in one go," Assad commented drily. "Were you still friends when he
disappeared? And where were you at the time anyway?"

"Oh, so we're shifting the focus now, are we?" Sønderskov turned to
face Carl. "I think you should inform your assistant here that I have come
across a great many policemen in my time and am more than accustomed
to hearing exactly this kind of insinuation and scurrilous suggestion on an
almost daily basis. I am not on trial here, nor have I ever been, is that understood? And besides, I was in Greenland during the time in question. I
had a practice there for six months and didn't return home again until after
Philip disappeared. A month after, as I recall. I can prove it, of course."

Only then did he turn back to Assad, anticipating the appropriately sheepish expression this eloquent counter must surely have brought to the man's face. Assad, however, was nonplussed.

"And of course Philip Nørvig's wife had become available in the meantime, isn't that right?" Assad continued.

Oddly, Mie Nørvig refrained from commenting on Assad's audacity. Had the same thought occurred to her, too?

"Now you listen here, this is outrageous!" Herbert Sønderskov seemed suddenly to age, though the venom that had no doubt made him a formidable opponent in former years was plain enough. "We open the doors of our home and welcome you inside, only to be met by insult. If this is the way the police do their job these days, then it seems I shall have to look up the commissioner personally and have a word with him. What was it you said your name was? Assad, was it? And the surname?"

Buttering-up time, Carl thought to himself. With the shit he was in at the moment the last thing he needed was an irate lawyer putting his oar in.

"I do apologize, Mr. Sønderskov, my assistant overstepped the mark. He's on loan from another department and used to dealing with individuals less upstanding than your good self." He turned to Assad. "Would you mind waiting for me by the car, Assad? I'll be along in just a minute."

Assad gave a shrug. "OK, boss. But remember to check if there's anything on a Rita Nielsen in all these drawers." He gestured toward a filing cabinet. "This one here says 'L to N.'" Then he turned on his heel and walked stiffly out, looking like he'd either just spent twenty hours on horseback or else wasn't quite finished on the crapper.

"That's right," said Carl, looking now at Mie Nørvig. "As Assad just said, I'd very much like to see if your archives here might include information concerning a woman who disappeared on the same day as your husband. A woman by the name of Rita Nielsen. May I?"

Without waiting for an answer he pulled out the drawer marked "L to N" and peered at its contents. There were an awful lot of Nielsens.

At the same instant, Herbert Sønderskov came up from behind and closed the drawer.

"Here we are going to have to stop, I'm afraid. These documents are confidential and I cannot under any circumstances allow you to breach the anonymity of the company's clients. I must ask you to leave at once."

"Well, I'll just have to get a warrant, then, won't I?" Carl countered, pulling his mobile from his pocket.

"By all means. But first you are to leave."

"I'm not sure that's such a good idea. If there *is* a file on Rita Nielsen in that drawer, who knows if it'll still be there in an hour's time? You'd be surprised how things like that can sprout wings all of a sudden."

"I'm asking you to leave now, do you understand me?" Herbert Sønderskov reiterated in an icy voice. "You might be able to secure a warrant, but we'll just have to cross that bridge when we come to it. I know the law."

"Oh, stop it, Herbert," Mie Nørvig broke in firmly, making it abundantly clear which of them wore the trousers. Carl pictured Sønderskov exiled in front of the telly, dreaming about the dinners she definitely wouldn't be serving him for the next week at least. Here was proof that cohabitation was the form of human interaction that involved by far the most numerous opportunities of sanction.

She pulled out the drawer, flicking through the files with the digital dexterity that came from years of practice.

"Here," she said, extracting a folder. "This is the closest we get to a Rita Nielsen." She showed Carl the front cover. It read SIGRID NIELSEN.

"OK, so now we know. Thanks." Carl sent a nod in the direction of Herbert, who glared at him. "Could I ask you, Mie, to check and see if there's anything on a woman by the name of Gitte Charles, too, by any chance? And a man called Viggo Mogensen? That'll be all for now, I promise."

Two minutes later he was out of the door. No Gitte Charles and no Viggo Mogensen.

"I don't think Herbert's going to remember you too fondly, Assad," Carl grunted, as they turned the car toward Copenhagen.

"Maybe not. But when a man like him starts to panic, he acts like a hungry camel eating thistles. He keeps on chewing without daring to swallow. You saw how uncomfortable he was? I think he was acting strange."

Carl looked at him. Even in profile it was easy to see the smile that reached to his ears.

"Did you really go to the bathroom, Assad?"

Assad laughed. "No, Carl, I didn't. I poked around upstairs and found this, full of photos." He arched his midriff upward, reached under his belt, and plunged a hand into the most intimate depths of his trousers.

"Here," he said, retrieving an envelope. "I found it in Mie Nørvig's wardrobe in the bedroom. In the kind of cardboard box that so often has interesting things inside. I took the whole lot thinking it might be less obvious than only taking a few," he said, as he began to peruse the contents.

Logic for dummies.

Carl pulled over and took the first of the photos Assad handed him.

It was a group picture, clearly taken on some festive occasion. Champagne glasses raised to the photographer and smiles all round.

Assad planted a stubby finger in the middle. "This is Philip Nørvig with a woman who is not Mie. I think we should assume it's his first wife. And look at this . . ." He slid his finger to the edge of the group.

"Here is Herbert Sønderskov and Mie, not as old as now. Don't you agree he seems to have been rather fond of her even then?"

Carl nodded. Sønderskov's arm was certainly well wrapped around Mie's shoulders.

"Look on the back, Carl."

He turned the photo in his hand. *July 4 1973. 5 years of Nørvig & Sønderskov.*

"And look at this other one I found."

The colors were faded, and the photo had clearly not been taken by a professional. A wedding photograph, taken outside the town hall in Korsør. Mie and Philip Nørvig, Mie bulgingly pregnant, Philip wearing a triumphant smile in stark contrast to Herbert Sønderskov's thin-lipped expression a little farther back on the steps behind the happy couple.

"Do you see what I mean, Carl?"

He nodded. "Philip Nørvig knocks up Herbert Sønderskov's lady love. The secretary's shagging the both of them, but Nørvig ends up with the prize."

"We need to check and see if Sønderskov really was in Greenland when Nørvig went missing," said Assad.

"Yeah, but I'm pretty sure he's telling the truth on that. What I'm more interested in is his defense of this Curt Wad bloke, whose guts Mie Nørvig obviously can't stand. Not that I blame her, he sounds like a creep, if you ask me. My feeling is we should follow Mie Nørvig's female intuition and take a fine toothcomb along with us."

"A fine toothcomb?"

"Yes, Assad. Or a fine-toothed comb. Whatever. We'll get Rose onto it, if she can be arsed."

When they'd got as far as the McDonald's sign that beckoned to the motorway traffic at Karlstrup, Rose called back.

"You don't honestly expect me to be able to give you the lowdown on this Wad wanker off the top of my head, do you? He's a million years old at least, and he hasn't stood still once, I can tell you."

Her voice grew increasingly shrill, until Carl realized he'd better step in and calm her down before things got out of hand.

"No, of course not, Rose. Just give me the bare bones, that's all. We'll get to the details later, if needs be. Just find out if there's any source that can give us a summary. A newspaper article, something like that. What we want to know to begin with is if there's any dirt on him. As far as I understand it, he's rather a controversial character."

"If you want dirt on Curt Wad you should speak to a journalist called Louis Petterson. *He's* definitely been on his back, believe me."

"Yeah, his name already cropped up earlier on. Has he written anything on him recently?"

"Not really, no. Most of it was five or six years back, then it seems like he stopped."

"Maybe there was nothing left to dig up."

"That's not the impression *I* get. As far as I can see, there's been quite a lot of journalists trying to find out what Curt Wad's been up to. But this Louis Petterson was the one who got the headlines."

"OK, where does he live, this Louis Petterson?"

"In Holbæk. What for?"

"Just give me his number, there's a good girl."

"Oooh, say that again, would ya? I didn't quite catch it."

Carl contemplated riposting with something sarcastic, but stifled the urge. "I said, 'there's a good girl.'"

"I thought that was it. Wonders never cease, do they?" she retorted, before giving him the number. "But if you're thinking of having a word with him, you'd do best to go to Café Vivaldi on Ahlgade, number 42, because that's where he drinks and that's where he is now, according to his wife."

"How do you know that? Have you already called him?"

"Of course I have! Who do you think you're dealing with here?" she snorted, and hung up.

"Bollocks," said Carl, and pointed a finger at the GPS. "Assad, enter Ahlgade 42, Holbæk. We're going for a drink," he instructed, picturing Mona's face when he called her in a minute to cancel his session with her psychologist friend, Kris.

She would not be amused.

Maybe he'd been expecting a dingy little dive impenetrable to the harsh light of day, to which weary reporters for reasons unfathomable retired to recharge their batteries. But Café Vivaldi was nothing like it.

"This is not what I expected, Carl," said Assad, as they entered what looked like the handsomest building on the street. It even had a tower.

Carl glanced around the packed room, only to realize he had no idea what the man they'd come to see looked like.

"Get on the phone to Rose. Maybe she can give us a description," he said, scanning the decor. Opalescent glass, stucco work on the ceiling. Tastefully done out, with pleasant lighting, comfy chairs and benches, and little details all over.

Any money that's him over there, Carl thought to himself, eyeing a man who was sounding off at the center of a group of late-middle-aged men who had gathered on a raised area in the middle of the room. Typically blasé, weary features, and eyes forever on the lookout.

Carl turned to Assad, who stood nodding into his mobile with Rose on the other end.

"So what do you reckon, Assad? Is that him over there?"

"No." Assad ran his gaze over the variegated collection of salad-consuming young ladies who lunched, enamored couples sipping cappuccinos with fingers entwined, and others who were on their own, immersed in newspapers, full glasses of lager in front of them.

"I think that's him over there," he said eventually, pointing to a youngish sandy-haired guy seated on a bench in a corner by the window, playing backgammon with a man of about the same age.

Carl knew he wouldn't have clocked him in a hundred years.

They went over and stood for a moment as the two men shoved their counters around the board, seemingly oblivious until Carl cleared his throat.

"Louis Petterson? Can we speak to you for a minute?"

The man looked up, instantly bridging the gap from deep concentration to adrenaline-charged reality. In less than a second Petterson registered the two men's disparate appearance and gauged them for what they were: cops. His eyes went back to the backgammon board for a moment, and after a couple of quick moves he indicated a time-out.

"I don't think these two are here to watch us play, Mogens."

The man's cool was rather surprising, Carl thought. Petterson's opponent nodded and disappeared into the throng on the other side of the raised floor area.

"I don't do crime anymore," he said, turning his glass of white wine slowly in his hand.

"Fine. But we're here because you've done a lot of stuff on Curt Wad," Carl explained.

Petterson smiled. "You'll be from intelligence, then. Long time since PET have been round to see me, I must say."

"No, we're from homicide in Copenhagen."

The man's expression went from casual supercilious to wide-eyed and alert with the appearance of just a single line in his brow. Without his years of experience, Carl might not have even noticed. This wasn't the reaction of a journalist on the lookout for a story, in which case his face would have lit up. The prospect of well-paid copy in a major paper was ever-present whenever the word "homicide" was mentioned. But that wasn't what this guy was thinking, which told Carl a lot.

"Like I said, we want to know about Curt Wad. Can you give us ten minutes?"

"Sure, but I haven't done anything on the man in five years. Ran out of steam, you could say."

Ran out of steam, my arse. The rate you're twirling that wineglass tells another story, Carl thought to himself.

"I checked up on you," Carl lied. "You're not on the dole, so how are you earning a living these days, Louis?"

"I work for an organization," Petterson replied, trying to gauge how much Carl really knew.

And for that reason Carl nodded. "Right answer. Care to tell us about it?"

"Maybe. Or you could start by telling me which murder you're investigating."

"Did I say we were investigating a murder? Don't think I did, did I, Assad?"

Assad shook his head.

"Relax," said Assad. "You're not under suspicion for anything in particular."

It was true, but Petterson was alerted nonetheless.

"Who is, then, and for what? Oh, and maybe you could show me some ID while we're at it?"

Carl held his badge high enough for everyone in the vicinity to get a good look.

"Would you like to see mine, too?" Assad inquired boldly.

Thankfully, Petterson declined. Perhaps it was about time they fabricated some form of ID for Assad. A business card with something that looked like a police logo would probably do the trick.

"We're investigating four cases involving missing persons," said Carl. "Does the name Gitte Charles mean anything to you? She was an auxiliary nurse, lived on Samsø."

Petterson shook his head.

"Rita Nielsen, then? Or Viggo Mogensen?"

"Nope. When did they go missing?"

"Beginning of September 1987."

Petterson put on a smirk. "I'd have been twelve at the time."

"So it wasn't you, then," Assad smirked back.

"How about Philip Nørvig? Ring a bell?"

Petterson leaned his head back and pretended to rack his brains, but Carl saw right through him. The journalist clearly knew full well who Philip Nørvig was. He might just as well have put it up in lights.

"He was a lawyer in Korsør, lived in Halsskov," Carl said, applying a smile of his own. "Formerly active in the Purity Party, excluded in 1982. But you were only seven then, so that won't have been your fault either."

"Can't say I've heard of him. Should I have?"

"Considering the amount of copy you've put out on the Purity Party, let's say I'd be surprised if you hadn't."

"OK, I may have done. Just not certain, that's all."

And why not? Carl thought.

"We can always check up in the newspaper archives. The police are good at that sort of thing, or maybe you didn't know?"

Petterson paled.

"What have you written about The Cause?" asked Assad. A bit prematurely, but still.

The man shook his head. It was supposed to mean "nothing," and maybe it was the truth.

"You realize we're going to check this, don't you, Louis? And let me say this: your body language tells me you know considerably more than you're letting on. I don't know what, and it may even be immaterial, but I think you should start talking right now. Are you working for Curt Wad?"

"Everything OK, Louis?" asked his friend, Mogens, who'd cautiously approached them again.

"Yeah, I'm fine. But these two are barking up the wrong tree." He turned back to Carl. His voice was calm. "I've nothing to do with that man, nothing at all. I work for an organization called Benefice. It's an independent body run on voluntary funding. My job is to gather information on the mistakes of the Denmark Party and the government coalition over the past decade. Let's just say there's enough there to keep me going."

"Yeah, you must be a busy man. OK, so we'll drop that angle. But who would that information be for?"

"Anyone who asks for it." Petterson straightened up. "Listen, I'm sorry I can't be more helpful. If you want to know about Curt Wad, you can read up on him. It sounds like you've got all my articles, but I've moved on since then. So unless you've got any specific questions about these missing persons of yours, I'd be grateful if you'd let me enjoy what's left of my day off."

"Bit of a turn he took there," Carl mused, when they were back on the street a few minutes later. "All we asked him for was a quick briefing on this Curt Wad. What the fuck's he up to, I wonder?"

"I will tell you in a short time, Carl. Right now the man is making a whole lot of phone calls. Don't look, because he is watching us through the window. But I think we should get Lis to find out who he is calling."

22

September 1987

That Friday morning Nete awoke in her apartment with a thumping headache. Whether it was due to her olfactory experiments the day before, or the knowledge that on this momentous day she would be killing six individuals within twelve hours, she had no idea.

All she knew was that if she didn't take her migraine tablets, everything would go down the drain. Two tablets may have been sufficient, but she took three, and for the next hour or two she sat staring at the clock until the capillaries of her brain finally relaxed and light could strike her retinas without it feeling like an electric shock.

Then she put the teacups out on the mahogany sideboard in her stylish living room, laid out the silver teaspoons in a neat row, and placed the decanter of henbane extract at the ready so when the time came she could pour her guests the correct amount with a minimum of fuss.

She went over the procedure in her mind for the tenth time before sitting down once more to wait, the English grandfather clock ticking away behind her. Tomorrow afternoon she would fly to Mallorca, and Valldemossa's luscious green would fill her senses and expel the past and all its demons from her mind.

But first the burial chamber was ready for occupation.

————

The family to whom her father had been referred following her miscarriage in the stream received Nete as an outcast, and an outcast she would remain.

The maid's room was set apart from the rest of the house and the work she was expected to do during the day was demanding, so the only time she was together with the family was at meals, and these passed in the deepest silence. On the few occasions she ventured to open her mouth, they shushed her, though she did her utmost to speak nicely. Even the daughter and son, who were almost the same age as she, tended to ignore her. She was a foreign body, a stranger, and yet they treated her as though they had the power of life and death over her. Apart from work, her life offered nothing in the way of distraction, and a fond word was never uttered. Sternness, admonishment, and rules were the order of the day.

Twenty kilometers separated Nete from her childhood home, a mere hour by bicycle. But Nete had none and her days were spent hoping her father would stop by to visit. He never did.

After she had been with the family for a year and a half she was summoned to the drawing room, where the local policeman stood conversing with her foster father. He was smiling, but the moment he caught sight of Nete his expression changed.

"Nete Hermansen, I'm sorry to have to inform you that your father hanged himself in his home last Sunday. The authorities have therefore decided that the good family here be named as your permanent guardians. That means they'll have full authority over you until your twenty-first birthday. Think yourself lucky. Your father left only his debts."

It was as matter-of-fact as that. No condolences, nothing about any funeral.

They nodded curtly to her by way of conclusion. Nete's life had collapsed. The audience was over.

She cried in the fields, and the farm workers whispered like people do about those outside the fold. Sometimes she felt so lonely the pain of it became physical. At other times she was totally indifferent.

If only there had been kindness, an occasional pat on the cheek. But Nete learned to live without.

When the fair came to the nearby town that weekend, the other girls on the farm took the bus without telling her. That was why she stood at the side of the road with two kroner in her pocket, jerking her thumb at any vehicle that happened to pass.

The one that stopped was hardly a sight for sore eyes. A beaten-up truck with moldering seats, but the driver smiled.

Obviously, he had no idea who she was.

He said his name was Viggo. Viggo Mogensen, all the way from Lundeborg. He was carrying smoked fish in the back for a stallholder who would sell them at the market. Two full crates smelling of smoke and the sea, and she could hardly recall so much excitement.

When the other girls saw her strolling among the merry-go-rounds and shooting galleries with an ice cream in her hand and a good-looking young man at her side, their eyes grew wide with something she had never seen before. Later she would think of it as envy, but at the time she was simply taken aback, and for good reason.

The weather was hot, like her summers with Tage, and Viggo spoke so vividly of the sea and the free life that Nete almost felt it to be her own. An increasing sense of happiness warmed her being and made everything so much easier for Viggo than might otherwise have been the case.

She let him put his arm around her shoulders as he drove her home, and she looked at him with hope in her heart, cheeks blushing when he stopped the truck behind some trees and drew her toward him. And she felt no alarm when he put on the rubber and told her it meant that everything would be pleasure and there would be no worries.

But afterward, when he withdrew from her and saw the condom had burst, his expression changed. She asked if she would now become pregnant, perhaps hoping he would say she might, and that he would at least take her home with him.

While the latter was wishful thinking, she had indeed become pregnant, and the other girls were quick to find out.

"Sick in the cornfield means a bun in the oven," one of them shouted after her. And they laughed until their headscarves came undone under their chins.

Half an hour later she stood before her foster mother, who in a trembling voice threatened to bring the house down on her, not to mention the police, if she did not agree to have the fetus removed.

The same day, a taxi drew up in the yard and the son was sent away, the family wishing to spare him from being exposed to the vileness Nete had imposed upon their lives. Nete declared the culprit to be a decent young man from Lundeborg whom she had met at the fair, but the girls who had seen them together insisted he was just the kind of reprobate who took advantage of young girls for his own pleasure and nothing but.

The upshot was an ultimatum. Either she went back to her former physician to have it removed or else the family would have to ask the social authorities to hand the matter over to the police.

"You've got rid of them before, you know what it's like," said her foster mother, without the slightest sympathy, whereafter the woman's husband drove her in the car and dropped her outside the surgery. She could take the bus home when it was done, he said, for his time was too precious for him to hang about all day. He refrained from wishing her luck, though he may have smiled sheepishly, perhaps to conceal his glee.

Nete never knew what was on his mind.

She sat for some time, slapping her knees together, rocking gently back and forth in the green waiting room. The smell of camphor and medicine made her feel queasy and afraid. The fear of medical instruments and the doctor's couch descended upon her, the minutes dragging by as coughing patients were treated one by one behind the closed door of the consulting room. She heard the sound of the physician's voice. It was deep and calm, but in no way soothing.

When at last her turn came, the final patient of the day, a doctor younger than the one she had been expecting took her hand and greeted her with what sounded like kindness in his voice. It was because of his voice that she let go of her most immediate reservations. And when he added that he remembered her well and then asked if she was happy in her new family, she nodded quietly and placed herself in his hands.

She found no cause for concern when he sent the secretary home, nor when he locked the door, though she wondered why it was the son and not the father who now looked upon her as though they had met on many occasions before. They had only ever seen each other the time the old doctor had come to their home after her miscarriage.

"You have the honor of being my very first gynecological patient, Nete. My father only recently handed on his practice to me, so now I'm the one you should address as 'Doctor Wad.'"

"But when my guardian called, it was your father he spoke to, Doctor. Do you know what's supposed to happen?"

He stood for a moment and looked her up and down in a way she didn't care for. He went over to the windows and drew the curtains, turning to face her with an expression that indicated to her that his white coat concealed interests more private than professional.

"I most certainly do," he replied after a while, sitting down opposite her and finally taking his eyes off her body. "Regrettably, the law in this country imposes certain restrictions on induced abortions, so you can thank your lucky stars I'm as compassionately disposed as my father in that respect. But then I assume you know all that," he said, placing his hand on her knee. "Just as I assume you know that you and I can get into a lot of trouble indeed if what we're going to do today should be divulged."

She nodded silently and handed him the envelope. In it were all her savings from the last two years, minus the five two-kroner coins in her pocket, plus a hundred-kroner note donated by her foster mother. Four hundred kroner in all. She only hoped it was enough.

"Let's leave that for a moment, shall we, Nete? First we need to get you onto the examination couch. Leave your knickers on the chair here."

She did as she was told, staring at the metal stirrups and thinking she would never be able to lift her legs that high. She giggled, despite being afraid. It all seemed so unreal and comical.

"Now, if you'd just lie back," he said, helping her legs into place. And there she lay with her genitals exposed, wondering how long it would take.

She raised her head for a moment and saw him peering darkly between her legs.

"Keep still now," he said, with a slight jiggle of his lower body, as though he were dropping his trousers.

And a second later she realized that was exactly what he had done.

First she felt his hairy thighs against hers. It tickled, and then came the thrust against her groin, causing her to arch her back like a bow.

"Ow," she cried. He drew away only to thrust again and again, holding her knees tightly, making her unable to close her legs or twist away. He said nothing, simply stared down between her thighs, eyes wide.

She tried to protest, to make him stop, but her windpipe seemed only to contract, allowing no words to pass. Then he bore down on her with all his weight, eyes now glazed and empty. It wasn't at all nice, as it had been with Tage and Viggo. Not even remotely. Just the smell of him made her feel sick.

After a short while he raised his head toward the ceiling and his mouth opened to expel a groan.

When he was finished he buttoned his trousers and ran his fingers slowly up and down her tender, wet crotch.

"You're ready now," he said. "That's how it's done."

Nete bit her lower lip. A feeling of shame planted itself inside her and had been there ever since. The feeling that her body and her mind were two separate things, and each could be played off against the other. She felt disconsolate and angry, and very, very alone.

She watched as he prepared the anesthesia mask and felt the sudden urge to flee. But before she knew it, the sickly smell of ether filled her nostrils. Her head spun in the haze, her final thought being that when it was all over she would spend the ten kroner she had left on a train ticket to Odense, where she would find the place they called the Council for Unwed Mothers. She'd heard they could help people like her. And what Curt Wad had done to her she would avenge.

Thus the foundation of a lifelong catastrophe was laid.

The following days brought one disappointment after another. The women at the council were at first accommodating. They gave her tea and held her hand, and she felt there was nothing they wouldn't do to help her. But when she told them the details of her rape, the subsequent abortion, and the money she had paid, their faces turned grave.

"To begin with, Nete, you must realize that such charges are serious indeed. Furthermore, we don't quite understand why you first have an abortion and *then* come to us. It seems so back-to-front. I'm afraid we shall have to hand the matter over to the authorities. You understand, I hope? We must do things by the book here."

Nete thought about telling them it was her guardians who wanted it that way. That what they most certainly did *not* want was a girl in their charge who flaunted her depraved and despicable ways in front of their children and the young farmhands in their employ. But Nete said nothing, feeling some loyalty for their at least having taken her in. It was a loyalty that was far from reciprocated, as she later discovered.

Shortly afterward two uniformed officers appeared in the office and asked her to accompany them. She was to make a statement at the police station, but first they would have to go to the hospital so they could determine whether she was telling the truth.

When they were done she could stay the night in the city under the council's watchful eye.

They examined her thoroughly and found evidence of a gynecological intervention. Men in white coats put their fingers inside her and women with nurses' badges wiped her clean.

Questions were put. She answered truthfully and to the best of her ability. The doctors' faces were solemn, and their whispers when they withdrew to a corner of the room seemed laden with concern.

She felt in little doubt these people were on her side, and for that reason her sudden confrontation with a free and smiling Curt Wad in the interview room of the police station filled her with fright. He seemed chummy with the two uniformed officers, and the man at his side, who introduced himself as Philip Nørvig, a lawyer, was clearly prepared to give her a hard time.

They asked Nete to sit down and nodded to the two women who entered the room. One of them she knew from the council, the other was not introduced.

"We've spoken to Dr. Wad here, and he has confirmed to us that he performed what's technically known as dilation and curettage on you, Nete," the second woman said. "We have Dr. Wad's case record here."

She placed the folder on the table in front of her. On the cover was a word she couldn't read, and underneath it the figure "64." That, at least, she could understand.

"This is what Dr. Wad wrote down after you left his surgery," the lawyer explained. "It states quite unequivocally that you received a

D and C following heavy, irregular bleeding, and that this in all proba-
bility relates back to a miscarriage you suffered almost two years ago.
Moreover, it states that in spite of your young age you have admitted to
having had sexual relations with strangers, a claim supported by your
guardians. Would that be correct?"

"I don't know what a D and C is, but I do know the doctor did things
to me that were wrong." She pressed her lips together to control their
trembling. She wasn't going to let them make her cry.

"Miss Hermansen, as Dr. Wad's lawyer I must advise you to be very
careful indeed about putting forward allegations that cannot be corrob-
orated," Nørvig said, his face ashen yet composed. "You have stated that
Dr. Wad performed an induced abortion on you, and yet the physicians
here in Odense have been unable to confirm this. Curt Wad is a consci-
entious and highly competent doctor. His work is to help people, not to
carry out unlawful abortions. A curettage was given, yes, but it was for
your own benefit, is that not correct?"

He leaned forward, as though about to leap at her throat, but Nete was
no more frightened by it than she was already.

"He got on top of me and had sex with me, and I shouted at him to
stop. That's what happened, I'm telling you."

She glanced at the faces that surrounded her. It was like talking to
trees in the woods.

"I think you should be very careful about saying such things, Nete,"
said the woman from the Council for Unwed Mothers. "It doesn't help
matters."

The lawyer looked around smugly. Nete didn't like him one bit.

"Indeed. Now, you claim that Dr. Wad violated you," he went on. "To
which Dr. Wad graciously responds that the anesthetic ether you were
given had a rather powerful effect on you, and that in such instances
patients very often suffer from hallucinations. Are you familiar with the
word, Nete?"

"No, and it doesn't matter if I am or not, because he did something he shouldn't have and it was before he put the mask on me."

The assembled parties exchanged glances.

"Let me suggest something to you, Nete. Supposing a doctor *were* to rape a patient in a situation such as that, don't you think he would wait until *after* she was anesthetized?" the woman Nete hadn't seen before interjected. "I have to say that what you're telling us now is very hard to believe."

"But that's what happened." Nete looked around her, realizing that none of those present were on her side.

She stood up, again feeling the discomfort in her abdomen, the wetness in her knickers. "I want to go home now," she said. "I'll catch the bus."

"I'm afraid it's not that easy, Nete. Either you retract your allegations or else we shall have to ask you to stay," said one of the policemen. He shoved a piece of paper across the table toward her. She stared at it, uncomprehending, and he pointed to a dotted line at the bottom.

"Just write your name there and you can go."

It was easy enough for him to say. But she could neither read nor write.

Nete's gaze moved from the sheet of paper to the tall man seated opposite her. Their eyes met and she saw what she took to be an appeal to confidentiality in Curt Wad's eyes. But she was having none of it.

"He did what I said he did," she reiterated.

They asked her to take a seat at a table in the corner while they conferred. The women seemed to take the matter seriously indeed, and Curt Wad shook his head a couple of times when they addressed him. Finally, he stood up to his full height and shook hands with each of them by turn.

He was allowed to go.

Two hours later she was seated on the edge of a bed in a small room in a house whose location was unknown to her.

They told her the case would proceed quickly and that she would be assigned a lawyer to act on her behalf. They said her guardians would be sending on her things.

She was no longer wanted on the farm.

Some weeks passed before the charges against Curt Wad were brought before the court, but in the meantime the authorities and Wad's lawyer wasted little time. Philip Nørvig proved especially proficient when it came to parrying accusations, and the court listened to him eagerly.

They tested her intelligence, called witnesses, and duplicated documents.

A mere two days before the case was due, Nete was finally contacted by her appointed lawyer. A convivial man in his mid-sixties, which was about all that could be said of him.

It wasn't until she sat in the courtroom that she fully realized no one intended to believe her and that the case had become too serious to be simply ignored.

Not one witness turned to face her from the stand. The air between them felt like ice.

Her despicable former schoolmistress told of skirts uplifted, lewd language, dim-wittedness, laziness, and general promiscuity. The pastor who had confirmed her schoolmates related tales of ungodliness and diabolical tendencies.

And thus the conclusion was formed early in the proceedings: here, surely, was a clear-cut case of "antisocial retardation."

On this account Nete was deemed not only morally but also mentally deficient. A runt of society, whose presence among normal people they could expect to be spared. Mendacious and sly, despite her lack of schooling. They spoke repeatedly and without mitigation of her "loose and flighty character." They accused her of actively displaying contrariness, even rebellion. They claimed her offensive, brazenly erotic behavior had never been less than a source of great distress to all those around her and that since puberty she had become a menace. When it transpired that her IQ had been measured at 72.4 on the Binet-Simon scale, all were in agreement that Curt Wad had been the victim of disingenuous defamation and relentless mendacity despite his good intentions.

Nete protested, maintaining that the questions put to her in the IQ test had been silly beyond belief, adding that she had paid Curt Wad exactly four hundred kroner to terminate the pregnancy. Confronted with this latter information, her foster father stated under oath that she couldn't possibly have put so much money aside. Nete was shocked. Either he was lying or else his wife had not informed him of the sum she had donated. She shouted out to the judge that if they wanted to know if she was speaking the truth, they could ask the wife themselves. But the woman was not present in court, and apparently the will to get to the bottom of the matter was similarly absent.

Later came the head of the parish council, who was related to one of the boys who had thrown her into the mill stream at Puge. The man took the stand and declared that a girls' home—or better yet, a reformatory— would be a more appropriate form of placement than another foster family. This had been obvious, he stated, ever since she had begun cavorting with whoever took her fancy and had provoked a miscarriage by throwing herself onto jagged rocks. The girl was a disgrace to an otherwise peaceful parish.

One by one, the charges brought against Curt Wad were dismissed by the court. From the self-satisfied look in Philip Nørvig's eye it struck Nete that these proceedings were meant to catapult his career into the higher courts, and all the while Curt Wad sat with a smug smile stuck to his dependable, trustworthy face.

And then, on one of the final, freezing days of February, the judge, having weighed up the pros and cons, conveyed to Curt Wad the court's regrets that he had suffered the indignation of being dragged through the mire by such a mendacious and despicable child.

As he passed Nete on his way out, Wad nodded briefly to her in order that the court might note his magnanimity while remaining unaware of the triumph and scorn in his eyes. At the same moment the judge instructed that this seventeen-year-old minor be placed in the charge of the National Authority for the Mentally Handicapped in order that they might work for the rehabilitation of this defective individual so that she in years to come might return a better person, fit to be a part of the community.

Two days passed, and then she was sent to the Keller Institution at Brejning.

The consultant there informed her that he did not at first blush consider her to be retarded in any way and that he would write to her parish council to tell them she would be discharged from the institution should tests indicate that she was normal.

But things turned out differently.

Rita made sure of it.

23

November 2010

The First National Congress of the Purity Party was a resounding success. Curt had looked out on the assembly with pride, misty-eyed, as he was only on rare occasions.

Here, in the winter of his life, the task of setting up a political party with realistic parliamentary aspirations had finally been accomplished, and now almost two thousand fervently upstanding Danes were giving him an ecstatic ovation. Finally, there was hope for the native land of his sons. If only Beate had been able to stand at his side.

"A good thing you stopped that journalist before he finished his nasty tirade," said one of the local chairmen afterward.

Curt nodded. If one was prepared to fight for beliefs that spawned resistance and created enemies, it was important to have strong men who could step in when the situation demanded. This time he had managed without, but if it happened again, as it surely would, he would make certain there were people around him to take care of unpleasantness.

Fortunately, the situation had been dealt with swiftly and the rest of the meeting had gone off without a hitch and with excellent presentations of the party's election platform and parliamentary candidates.

"This is a fascist party you're trying to build here, isn't it, Dr. Wad?" the journalist had shouted, pushing his way through the throng with his Dictaphone aloft.

Curt had shaken his head and smiled. It was what to do when people got too close.

"Certainly not," he'd shouted back. "But let's talk under more amenable circumstances. I'll put you straight and tell you all you want to know."

He sent a quick, reproachful glance in the direction of security, holding them off just in time, allowing the throng to close around the troublemaker once more. Parrying the jibes of hecklers and fending off everyday loonies was acceptable, but physically assaulting a journalist doing his job wasn't. He would have to make sure his people knew.

"Who was that man?" he asked Lønberg, once the doors of the old assembly hall had been closed behind them.

"No one of any note. He's from the Free Press, gathering ammunition for his base. His name is Søren Brandt."

"In that case I know him. Keep an eye on him."

"We already are."

"I mean *really* keep an eye on him."

Lønberg nodded and Curt gave him a brief pat on the shoulder before opening the door to a smaller conference room. Here sat an exclusive gathering of some one hundred men, waiting for him.

He stepped up onto a little podium and looked out on his loyal supporters, who sat up in their chairs and began to applaud. "Well, gentlemen," he began, "here sit the nation's elite, ignoring the smoking ban."

There were broad smiles all round and someone in the front row reached out to offer him a cigar from a small leather case. Curt Wad smiled and held up his hands deprecatingly. "Thanks all the same, but a man has to look after his health. Especially once he's past eighty."

His audience laughed heartily. It was good to be among them. These were the initiated. People he could trust. Able men who had devoted themselves to The Cause, the majority of whom had been with him for a good many years. What he had to say to them now would not go down well.

"Our meeting today went off magnificently, and if the atmosphere in there in any way reflects the sentiments of the population, I think we can look forward to securing a significant number of seats at the next election."

The cheering assembly rose in a standing ovation.

Curt savored the gesture for a moment, then raised his hands to silence them, breathing in deeply before continuing to speak. "Please, be seated. We are all equal here. We who are in this room now are the Purity Party's very backbone. We manned the barricades over the years and carried out the work. We have been the moral vanguard, always ready to step into the breach discreetly and in confidence. 'He who wisheth only to serve the Lord shall reap the greatest reward,' as my father used to say."

More applause.

A smile passed over his face. "Thank you. My father would have been proud to be here today." He bowed his head slightly to look down on those sitting closest. "Our work forestalling the birth of offspring unworthy of our nation, and preventing conception in women who might produce them, is the continuation of a long and honorable endeavor, and through this work all of us present have come to understand that indifference leads to nothing good." He raised his hands to the audience in acknowledgment. "We who are gathered here have never been indifferent." A ripple of applause went round the room. "And now from our founding ideas a political party has emerged that will strive toward a society in which the work we hitherto have carried out in secret and with the law of the land against us might soon be brought forward into the light. Not only made lawful, but also lauded."

"Hear, hear!" shouted several at once.

"However, until this happens I am afraid the activities of this circle must cease."

His words triggered consternation and alarm. Many froze in their seats, cigars smoldering between their fingers.

"You all witnessed the efforts of that journalist to cast aspersions upon us earlier. There will be more like him, and our most imperative task is to keep them in check. For that reason, the work carried out by those present must for a time be curtailed." There was a murmur of voices that died away when Wad held up his hand. "Only this morning we received the sad news that one of our finest friends, Hans Christian Dyrmand of Sønderborg—and I note that many of you knew Hans Christian personally—has taken his own life."

He looked down on the faces before him. Some were devastated, others pensive.

"We know that for the past two weeks Hans Christian had been the subject of investigations by the health authorities. An instance of termination and subsequent sterilization allegedly performed so ineptly that the girl in question was forced to seek treatment at Sønderborg General Hospital. Hans Christian opted to take the consequences, destroying all his records and personal documents and then proceeding along the ultimate path." Again, this sent a murmur through the assembly, though Curt was unable to gauge its more exact nature.

"If Hans Christian's membership of The Cause had come to light, I'm sure you can imagine how it would have impacted on our work. Hans Christian obviously realized this himself. All that we now strive to achieve within the framework of the Purity Party would have been destroyed."

There was a long silence.

"Such weaknesses cannot be accepted in the present climate, at a time when the Purity Party needs to be marketed and firmly anchored in the minds of the Danish people," he said.

Afterward, he was approached by several members who informed him that they would continue their clandestine efforts despite his appeal, though with assurances that they would scrutinize all their records to make sure nothing could compromise The Cause.

Which was exactly what he had wanted. Safety first.

"Will you be attending Hans Christian's funeral?" Lønberg asked as they were leaving.

Curt smiled. He was a good man, Lønberg. Always on the lookout for flaws in other people's powers of judgment, including Curt's own.

"Of course not, Wilfrid. But we shall miss him, don't you agree?"

"Indeed." Lønberg nodded. It had surely been far from easy for him to convince an old friend that sleeping pills were his only remaining option.

Far from easy indeed.

By the time he got home, Beate was already asleep.

He switched on the iPhone his son had given him and saw the abundance of text messages he'd received.

They'll have to wait until morning, he thought to himself. He was too tired now.

He sat down for a moment on the edge of the bed, gazing at Beate's face with eyes narrowed, as if to soften the harsh workings of time. To him she was beautiful regardless, and he preferred to dwell on the fact rather than how frail she had become.

He kissed her brow, then went into the bathroom and undressed.

Under the shower he was an old man. Only there was he unable to ignore his own body's decline. When he looked down at himself he could see how his calves had withered away to almost nothing, his skin white and bare where once it had been covered by vigorous dark hair. His stomach was no longer firm as in former days, and his arms could hardly reach to scrub his back.

He leaned his head back to wash away this sudden melancholy, feeling the jets of hot water stabbing at his face.

Growing old was hard, releasing the reins likewise. While he had indeed received the tributes of the assembly today, it had been a man stepping down, a man whose work was done. He was a figurehead now, destined to sit in state and nothing more. As from today, others would speak on behalf of the party. He would retain an advisory role, of course, but the congress had selected those who would represent them in the public eye, and who was to say they would always choose to follow his advice?

Always. He repeated the word ruminatively. Such a strange word to utter at the age of eighty-eight. How empty it suddenly seemed.

He toweled himself dry, taking care not to slip on the floor, when the iPhone rang in the pocket of his trousers on the toilet seat.

He took it and said his name, a puddle of water at his feet.

"Herbert Sønderskov. I've been trying to reach you all day."

"I see," said Wad. "Herbert, it's a long time since I've heard from you, my friend. And yes, I'm sorry, but my phone's been switched off on account of the congress in Tåstrup."

Sønderskov congratulated him, though he sounded anything but happy. "Curt, we've had the police here looking into some missing persons cases, among them Philip's. A Carl Mørck from Police HQ in Copenhagen. Mie mentioned your name in a couple of contexts. I'm afraid she mentioned The Cause, too."

Curt stood still for a moment. "What does Mie know?"

"Nothing much. Not from me, at any rate, and probably not from

Philip either. She seems to have picked up a few snippets here and there, that's all. She mentioned Louis Petterson as well. She kept on, though I tried to stop her. I'm afraid she's become rather headstrong of late."

This was not good. "What did she say, exactly; can you remember?" Curt shivered with cold, goose bumps appearing on his skin, his few remaining body hairs standing on end.

He listened without comment to what Herbert Sønderskov had to tell him. Only when he was finished did he speak.

"Do you know if this detective has been in touch with Louis Petterson?"

"No, I was going to check, but I haven't got Louis's mobile number. Not exactly available on the Internet, is it?"

There was a silence as Curt tried to assess the damage. No, it was not good. Not good at all.

"Herbert, our work has never been so much in jeopardy, so please try to understand what I'm now going to ask of you. You and Mie are to go on holiday, are you with me? I'll pay. Go to Tenerife. On the west of the island there are some cliffs called Acantilado de Los Gigantes. They're very steep and they face the sea."

"Oh, God," said Sønderskov faintly.

"Listen to me, Herbert! There is no other way. It must look like an accident, do you hear me?"

He heard the sound of Sønderskov's labored breathing at the other end.

"Herbert, much is at stake. Consider your brother, good friends, colleagues, and acquaintances. Not to mention yourself. It could mean years of effort wasted and political ruin. Many will be brought down if Mie isn't stopped. We're talking court cases, long and protracted. Lengthy jail sentences. Disgrace and downfall. All the work we've done to establish ourselves as an organization will be in vain. Thousands upon thousands of hours and donations to the tune of millions. Today was the Purity

Party's First National Congress. After the next election we'll be represented in parliament. You and Mie will be jeopardizing all of this if you fail to act."

Still Sønderskov was unable to speak.

"I take it you destroyed Philip's files as we agreed. Are all his records gone?"

There was no answer. Curt was mortified. Now they'd have to take care of it themselves.

"I can't do it, Curt. Can't we just go away until it all dies down?" Sønderskov begged. As if he didn't know his pleas were hopeless.

"Two distinguished pensioners with Danish passports, Herbert? Do you seriously believe you could just blend into the crowd? The police would find you in no time. And if *they* didn't, *we* would."

"Oh, God," Sønderskov said again.

"You've got twenty-four hours. Book with Star Tour tomorrow. If they're sold out, take a scheduled flight to Madrid, then on to Tenerife by domestic airline. Once you're there, take photos of your location every five hours and e-mail them to me so I know where you are. This will be the end of the matter, are you with me?"

The reply came hesitantly. "I understand."

And then Curt hung up.

We'll check that you do, he said to himself. And then we'll get those bloody files out of the house and burn them.

He scrolled through his missed calls on the iPhone's display. Sønderskov had been telling the truth. He'd been calling him every half hour since twelve thirty. And later Louis Petterson had been doing likewise, fifteen calls in all.

This did not bode well at all.

An investigation into Philip Nørvig's disappearance didn't worry him in the slightest. He'd had nothing to do with it. The thing that concerned him was what Mie had told the police.

Hadn't he warned Philip about that damned woman? Hadn't he warned Herbert?

He had, had he not?

Half an hour of crisis passed, during which time he called Louis Petterson's mobile repeatedly before the young journalist called back.

"Yeah, sorry, it's just that I turn my mobile off every time I've called you, so I can't be traced," he explained. "I don't want that Carl Mørck bloke and his creepy assistant calling me up either."

"Give me a quick briefing," Curt demanded. Petterson complied.

"Where are you now?" Curt asked, when he was done.

"A lay-by outside Kiel."

"And where are you going?"

"You don't need to know."

Curt nodded.

"And you needn't worry. The Benefice files are all with me."

Good man.

They concluded the conversation and Curt got dressed. Sleep would have to wait.

He went upstairs to the hobby room with its little kitchenette, pulled out a drawer under the worktable, removed a plastic tray full of nuts and bolts, and retrieved the old Nokia phone that lay hidden underneath.

He inserted a pay-as-you-go SIM card, plugged the phone into the charger, activated it, and dialed Caspersen's number. His call was answered in less than twenty seconds.

"You're up late, Curt. How come you're calling from this number?"

"A crisis," he replied. "Note down the number and call me up from your pay-as-you-go. In exactly five minutes."

Caspersen did as he was instructed, listening to Curt's briefing in deep silence.

"Who have we got at Police HQ that can be trusted?" Curt asked, when he had finished explaining.

"No one. But we've a man at Station City," Caspersen replied.

"Get in touch with him, tell him there's a police investigation we need to have stopped. Tell him it'll be worth his while, as long as this Carl Mørck is pacified."

24

November 2010

Carl glanced at the time as he turned into the parking lot with his wipers going full whack. A quarter to four, three-quarters of an hour late for his stupid appointment with Kris, the shrink. Mona would give him hell for this tonight. Why the fuck did everything have to go belly-up all the time?

"Better take this with us," said Assad, digging a folding umbrella out of the storage pocket in the car door.

Carl killed the engine. "I'm not in the fucking mood for sharing umbrellas," he grumbled, then found himself regretting his words as he stood at the entrance to the grim concrete building and realized someone had pulled the plug out of the sky and all he could see was a curtain of rain.

"Get in under this, Carl. You've just been ill, remember?" Assad shouted.

He stared disapprovingly at the polka-dot umbrella. What the hell could possess a full-grown man in the prime of life to purchase such a monstrously ridiculous item? It was *pink*, for Chrissake.

He huddled underneath it nonetheless, scuttling through the puddles with Assad until a colleague suddenly appeared from out of the deluge and walked past them with a grin on his face as if he'd suspected all along the two of them had something going on between them besides police work. Fucking embarrassing, it was.

Carl stepped out into the pouring rain with his chin up. Men with umbrellas were pathetic, almost as bad as men who stripped to the waist on picnics. He couldn't be doing with them.

"You look like a drowned rat," the duty officer said as Carl squelched by in a hurry, sounding like a sink plunger gone berserk.

"Check who's behind this Benefice organization, will you, Rose?" he said, ignoring her comments about beached whales and upturned bathtubs.

He dabbed at his clothes with toilet paper in a feeble attempt to dry off, promising himself to get an automatic hand dryer installed in the lavs. One of those things would have his body temperature back to normal in no time.

"Have you spoken to Lis, Assad?" he asked, three-quarters of a roll later, as Assad unfurled his prayer mat on the floor of his cubbyhole.

"All in good time, Carl. Prayers first."

Carl glanced at his watch. Half of HQ would be heading home in a minute, Lis among them. Somebody had to stick to normal working hours, even if it wasn't him.

He plonked himself down on his office chair and called her number.

"Department A. How can I help you-u-u?" sang a voice he could have sworn belonged to Ms. Sørensen.

"Er, Lis?"

"Lis is at the gynecologist's. This is Cata speaking."

Too much information, on both counts.

"Oh, I see. Carl Mørck here. Did either of you check up on who this Louis Petterson character called at about three this afternoon?"

"Yes, love, we did."

"Love?" Was he hearing right? What kind of a course had she been on anyway? Arse-lickers' proficiency?

"He called that Curt Wad in Brøndby. Do you want his address?"

———

Two calls to Louis Petterson yielded nothing but a message telling him the number was unavailable at the moment, but then what had he expected? He would have rather enjoyed confronting Petterson with why he'd called someone he claimed he had nothing to do with.

He looked up at his bulletin board with a sigh, picking out the scrap of paper with Kris's number on it. It wasn't one he'd considered writing in his little phone book, but using it now was certainly a more attractive option than wading through the weather to Anker Heegaards Gade.

"Kris la Cour," said the voice at the other end. So he had a pretentious surname to boot.

"Carl Mørck," he replied.

"I can't speak to you now, Carl, I'm just about to receive a client. Call me back tomorrow morning."

Bollocks. Mona would definitely not be pleased.

"I do apologize, Kris," he blurted out, before the guy hung up. "It turned out there was just no way I could make it today. As you know, my path is woeful and paved with corpses. Can't you fit me in on Monday instead? Please? I know it'll be good for me."

The pause that followed was as excruciating as the one between the executioner's "Aim" and "Fire!" There was no doubt in his mind that this self-important fountain of eau de cologne would be reporting directly back to Mona.

"Hmm. Are you sincere about that, I wonder?"

Sincere about what, Carl was just about to ask, only then to grasp what he was getting at.

"I most certainly am. I'm convinced our sessions will prove highly beneficial to me," he replied, thinking more in terms of access to Mona's gorgeously accommodating body than any attempts Kris might make at straightening out his cerebral convolutions.

"All right, Monday it is, then. Three o'clock, same as today. OK?"

Carl turned his eyes to the ceiling. Yeah, for fuck's sake.

"Thanks," he said, and hung up.

"Two things for you, Carl," said a voice behind him.

He could smell the perfume before she even spoke. Like a shimmering shroud of fabric softener suspended in the air. Impossible to ignore.

He turned and saw Rose in the doorway with a pile of newspapers under her arm.

"What's that perfume you're wearing?" he asked, knowing full well that what she said next could be tantamount to lethal stab wounds if he didn't watch out.

"That? Oh, it's Yrsa's."

Enough said. It seemed they wouldn't be allowed to forget Yrsa in a hurry.

"First off is I've checked this Herbert Sønderskov who you had a chat with down in Halsskov. Seems he's on the level when he says he can't have had anything to do with Nørvig's disappearance, because he was in Greenland from the first of April to the eighteenth of October 1987. He was under contract as a jurist with the home government there."

Carl nodded, feeling the disturbing rumblings of a tempest brewing in his colon.

"And second, this Benefice thing is a privately funded think tank. Besides a couple of political analysts working freelance, they've got one journalist on the permanent staff, this Louis Petterson. They work according to what they call 'the briefcase technique,' which means they produce short copy that busy politicians can scan in a few seconds. Populist, tendentious crap, if you ask me."

Carl didn't doubt it for a second. "Who's behind it?" he asked.

"A Liselotte Siemens. She's chair of the board and her sister's the managing director."

"Hmm. Never heard of her."

"Me neither, but I checked up on her background. I went back twenty-five years through all her various registered addresses, before I turned up something that might be a lead."

"Go on."

"In the late eighties she was living at the same address as a well-known fertility doctor out in Hellerup by the name of Wilfrid Lønberg. He's the father of the two Siemens sisters. Which is pretty interesting, I'd say."

"Yeah?" Carl leaned forward slightly. "Why's that, then?"

"Because Wilfrid Lønberg is one of the founders of the Purity Party. Haven't you seen him on telly?"

Carl tried to think back, only to find that his turbulent guts seemed to have severed all connection to his cerebral cortex.

"OK. And what are the newspapers for, then?" he went on, indicating the pile under Rose's arm.

"Assad and I are sifting through the period our missing persons disappeared again, just different newspapers this time. We need to be certain we've covered everything."

"Nice work, Rose," he said, calculating how many strides it would take him to get to the bathroom.

Ten minutes later he stood in front of Assad looking decidedly pale. "I'm off home, Assad. Dodgy stomach."

Now he's going to say "Told you so," Carl thought to himself.

But instead Assad reached underneath the desk, producing his umbrella and then handing it to him.

"Pity the camel that cannot cough and shit at the same time," he said.

Whatever the fuck that was supposed to mean.

The drive home was a tap dance on the accelerator, sweat dripping from every pore, his stomach in utter turmoil. If he got stopped by the traffic police he'd have no option but to plead force majeure. He even considered turning on the blue light and the siren. It'd been decades since he last shit his pants, and he was banking on keeping up the good run for some while to come.

So when he got home and found the front door locked he almost tore it down. What the hell were they playing at in there?

Five minutes of relief on the crapper and he was feeling rather better. In two hours he was due to present himself and his Colgate smile at Mona's, ready to play favorite uncle for her beast of a grandson.

Hardy was awake when he came into the living room, watching the rain spill over the roof gutters.

"Fucking weather," he said, hearing Carl enter. "What I wouldn't give to be out in it just for half a minute."

"Nice to see you, too, mate." Carl sat down by Hardy's bed and ran his hand over his friend's forehead. "There's a downside to everything, you know. I've just got myself a dose of bloody stomach flu because of that weather."

"Straight up? I'd give anything for stomach flu."

Carl smiled and followed Hardy's eyes downward.

There was a letter open on his duvet, and Carl recognized the address of the sender immediately. He was expecting one himself any day now.

"Ah, so your divorce from Minna came through. How do you feel about it, Hardy?"

Hardy clenched his teeth and made a heart-rending attempt to avoid noticing Carl's sympathetic expression.

"Don't think I can talk about it, Carl," he replied, after a minute or so in the deepest silence.

Carl understood him better than anyone. It had been a good marriage. Probably the best in Carl's circle of acquaintances. It'd have been their silver wedding in a few months, but the bullet Hardy caught had scuppered that, too.

Carl nodded. "Did Minna come round with it herself?"

"Yeah. Our boy was with her. They're all right."

Hardy understood, of course he did. Why should the life of the woman he loved stop just because his had?

"The funny thing is I gained a little bit of hope today."

Carl raised his eyebrows, a reflex. He smiled apologetically, but too late.

"Yeah, I know what you're thinking, Carl. You think I'm a plonker who refuses to face facts. But half an hour ago Mika did something to me that hurt like fuck. Enough to have Morten dancing a jig round the room, anyway."

"Who the hell's Mika?"

"OK, you sure haven't been home much lately. If you don't know who Mika is, you better ask Morten. Only remember to knock first. They're in the intimate phase at the moment." He emitted a gurgling sound that could pass for a chuckle.

Carl stood quiet as a mouse outside Morten's basement door until muffled laughter provided him with a cue to knock.

He went in hesitantly. The thought of seeing blubbery Morten in a close encounter with someone called Mika was enough to give anyone pause.

The two men were standing innocently in front of the open door of what had once been a sauna, their arms draped around each other's shoulders.

"Hey, Carl. Just showing Mika my Playmobil collection."

Carl sensed the lame expression on his face. If Morten Holland really had got this swarthy hunk down here on the pretext of inspecting his Playmobil collection, it beat hands down all his own ruses for luring unsuspecting women into his lair.

"Hullo," said Mika, extending a hand hairier than Carl's chest. "Mika Johansen. I'm a collector, like Morten."

"Aaa," muttered Carl, suddenly devoid of consonants.

"He doesn't collect Kinder Eggs or Playmobil like me, but look what he gave me."

Morten handed Carl a little cardboard box. 3218-A BAUARBEITER, it read. And sure enough, inside was a little blue man in a red hard hat, holding what was presumably an oversized broom.

"Very nice," said Carl, and handed it back.

"Nice?" Morten snorted, and gave his guest a big hug. "It's not nice, it's awesome, Carl. Now I've got a complete set of workmen from 1974, when it all started, right through to now. And the box is mint. Awesome, it is."

Carl hadn't seen his lodger sparkle like this since he moved in three years ago.

"So what do you collect, then?" Carl asked Mika, not really wanting to know.

"Antiquarian books on the central nervous system."

Carl struggled in vain to find a fitting expression. The dark Adonis laughed.

"Funny thing to collect, I know. But I *am* a trained physiotherapist and certified acupuncturist, so maybe it's not all that odd."

"We met each other two weeks ago when I did something to my neck. My head was all stuck, don't you remember, Carl?"

Was there any time when Morten's head *wasn't* stuck? If there was, he'd missed it.

"Have you talked to Hardy?" Morten asked.

"Yeah, that's why I came down. He said something had hurt like fuck." He turned to Mika. "What did you do, stick a needle in his eye?"

He tried to laugh, but was on his own.

"Not quite. I put needles into some nerves that still seem to be active."

"And he reacted to that?"

"Too right," said Morten.

"We need to sit him up," said Mika. "He's got feeling in a number of places. There's an area on his shoulder, and two around the base of his thumb. It's very encouraging."

"How do you mean, encouraging?"

"I don't think any of us can fully appreciate how hard he's struggled to stimulate these sensations. But there seem to be indications that if he keeps working at it, he might be able to move his thumb."

"His thumb? And what good's that going to do him?"

Mika smiled. "A lot. It means contact, work, transport, the ability to take charge of himself."

"Are you talking about a power wheelchair now?"

There was a pause, during which Morten gazed in admiration at his new conquest, while Carl felt his body temperature getting warmer, his heart beginning to pound.

"That, and a lot more besides. I've got loads of contacts in the health sector, and Hardy's definitely a patient worth investing in. I'm absolutely convinced his life can change radically in the foreseeable future."

Carl stood rooted to the spot. He felt like the ceiling was coming down on him, with no sense of where his feet were planted or where to direct his gaze. In short, he was flabbergasted, like a kid suddenly making sense of the world. It was a feeling largely unknown to him, and all he could do was step forward and draw this man toward him in a hug. He wanted to say thank you, but the words stuck in his throat.

Then he felt a pat on the back. "Yeah," said Mika, an angel. "I know how you must feel, Carl. It's major. Major indeed."

Luckily it was Friday, so the toy shop on Allerød town square was still open. Just time to find some crap or other for Mona's grandson, something that *couldn't* be used as a weapon.

"Hi," he said a short while later, as the boy stared up at him in Mona's entrance hall, looking like someone who could do a person a lot of damage even without anything to hit them with.

He handed the boy his present, keeping a safe distance. An arm shot out like a striking cobra.

"Nice reflexes," he said to Mona, as the boy disappeared with his prize. He drew her toward him, holding her so tightly not even a blade of grass could get in between. She really was exceptionally gorgeous, fragrant and appetizing almost beyond belief.

"What did you get him?" she asked, then kissed him. How the hell was he supposed to remember, with her lovely brown eyes so close?

"Erm . . . a Phlat Ball, I think it was called. You can press it flat and then it pops into a ball again. It's got a timer on it . . . I think."

She gave him a skeptical look as if to say Ludwig would have little trouble finding any number of uses for the toy that Carl most likely wasn't anticipating.

This time Mona's daughter, Samantha, seemed more prepared. She shook his hand and refrained from staring at his less flattering physical attributes.

She had her mother's eyes. How the hell anyone could leave a goddess like her alone with a kid to bring up, he had no idea. At least, not until she opened her mouth.

"Hope you're not going to dribble in the gravy again," she said, bursting into resonant and highly inappropriate laughter.

Carl tried to go along with her, though his own laughter was rather less hearty.

They went straight in and sat down at the table. Carl was prepared for battle. Four tablets from the chemist's had plugged his peristaltics, and his mind was clear and ready for the worst.

"How do you like the Phlat Ball, Ludwig?"

The boy didn't answer. Maybe because he had two handfuls of fries stuffed sideways in his mouth.

"It went out of the window, first try," answered his mother. "You go down and fetch it in the courtyard after we've eaten, do you hear me, Ludwig?"

Still no answer. The lad was consistent, at least.

Carl looked at Mona, who simply shrugged. Apparently his probationary period wasn't over yet.

"Did any of your brains come out of that hole when you got shot?" the boy eventually asked, after shoveling a couple more handfuls of fries down his throat. He pointed at the scar on Carl's temple.

"Some," he replied. "So now I'm only twice as brainy as the prime minister."

"That doesn't say much," his mother grunted from the sideline.

"I'm good at maths, are you?" the boy asked, his bright eyes looking directly at Carl for the first time. Contact.

"Brilliant at it," Carl lied.

"Do you know about 1089?" the boy asked. Carl was surprised he could even name such a big number. How old was he, anyway? Five?

"You might need some paper for this, Carl," said Mona, digging a notepad and a pencil out of a drawer in the chest behind her.

"OK," said the boy. "Think of a three-digit number and write it down."

Three-digit number. Where the hell did a five-year-old learn a phrase like that?

Carl nodded and did as he was told. 367.

"Now turn the number round."

"Turn it round? How do you mean?"

"Write it back-to-front. Are you sure it was only *some* of your brains that leaked out?" asked the boy's enchanting mother.

Carl wrote 763.

"Now subtract the smallest number from the biggest," instructed the curly-headed genius.

763 minus 367. Carl covered the page with his hand, so they wouldn't notice he still did sums like he was in year three.

"What's the answer?" Ludwig's eyes were wide with anticipation.

"Erm, 396, I think."

"Now turn the number round and add it to 396. What does that give you?"

"You mean 693 plus 396? Like, add them together?"

"Yes!"

Carl concentrated on his addition, again using his hand to shield his scribble.

"Ten eighty-nine," he said, after a bit of bother carrying his figures.

The boy howled with laughter as Carl raised his head, sensing how gobsmacked he looked.

"Nice one, Ludwig. Is it always going to be 1089, no matter what?"

The boy looked disappointed. "Yes, wasn't that what I said? But if you start with 102, for example, you'll get ninety-nine after the first subtraction. Then you have to write 099 rather then ninety-nine, because it always has to be a three-digit number, remember?"

Carl nodded as if he'd got the drift.

"Clever lad," he said drily, sending Samantha a smile. "Gets it from his mum, I'm sure."

She didn't reply, so obviously he was right.

"Samantha's probably one of the most gifted mathematicians in the country. But it looks like Ludwig's going to be even better," Mona informed him, then handed him the salmon.

OK, so mum and spawn were two of a kind. Part genius, part ball of fire, part impoliteness personified. Some mix. Not the easiest of families to join.

———

After another couple of intellectual challenges, Carl was finally let off the hook. Two more portions of fries were rounded off with three scoops of ice cream, by which time the boy was exhausted. Samantha and Ludwig called it a day and said their good-byes, leaving Mona standing in front of him with sparks in her eyes.

"I've made an appointment with Kris for Monday," Carl said, wanting to get this part over with quickly. "I called him to apologize for not being able to make it today. Honestly, Mona, it's been all go since this morning."

"Don't worry about it," she said, drawing him into a tight embrace, so tight Carl was almost at boiling point.

"I think *you're* ready for a bit of nooky," she said, sliding her hand down the front of his trousers.

Carl sucked in air through his teeth. She certainly was perceptive, he'd give her that. Maybe she'd inherited it from her daughter.

Following the obligatory initial maneuvers that resulted in Mona popping off to the bathroom to powder her nose, Carl was left sitting on the edge of the bed with blazing cheeks, swollen lips, and a pair of briefs that suddenly felt far too small.

And then his mobile rang.

It was Rose's number at HQ. Bollocks.

"Yeah, what is it, Rose?" he said bluntly into the receiver. "Make it short, I'm in the middle of something important," he added, sensing his pride and joy slowly beginning to wilt.

"We came up trumps, Carl."

"What are you talking about? And how come you're still at work?"

"We both are. Hi, Carl!" Assad chirped in the background. What were they doing, having a dance party down there, or what?

"We've found another missing persons case. It wasn't reported until a month after the others, so we didn't see it to begin with."

"OK, and what makes you think they're linked?"

"They called it the VéloSoleX case. Bloke from Brenderup on Fyn gets on his moped and heads off for Ejby, leaves it outside the railway station, and no one ever sees him again. Vanished into thin air."

"And what was the date?"

"Fourth of September 1987. But there's more."

Carl glanced toward the bathroom, where the woman of his erotic dreams was already making cooing noises.

"Come on, make it quick. What else did you turn up?"

"His name was Hermansen. Tage Hermansen."

Carl frowned. "And?"

"Hermansen, Carl!" Assad cried out in the background. "Don't you remember? That was the name Mie Nørvig mentioned in connection with the very first case her first husband handled for Curt Wad."

"OK," Carl replied. "We'll have to look into it. Nice work. Now go home, the pair of you."

"See you at HQ, right, Carl? Nine o'clock tomorrow morning?" Assad's voice echoed in the receiver.

"Tomorrow's Saturday, Assad. Haven't you ever heard of days off?"

There was noise on the line as Rose handed the phone to Assad.

"Listen, Carl. If Rose and I can work on the rest day, you can drive to Fyn on a Saturday, can't you?"

It wasn't a question.

25

September 1987

Rita looked out across Peblinge Lake, outwardly relaxed, yet tense and expectant, her body craving nicotine. Two cigarettes and she would head for the gray brick building, press the entry-phone button, push open the front door, and climb the stairway that would return her to her past. And then life would begin again.

She smiled to herself, and to the young man who was jogging by and who cast a flirtatious glance in return. Though she'd been up at the crack of dawn, she was in high spirits. She felt invincible.

With a cigarette between her lips she noted how the jogger stopped twenty meters on and began doing stretches, his gaze trained on her open coat and ample breasts.

Another day, perhaps, her eyes signaled as she lit her cigarette.

The only thing that mattered at the moment was Nete. Seeing Nete was more urgent than a kid with his brains dangling between his legs.

She had been turning the question over in her mind from the day she opened the letter until this morning, when she'd climbed into her car and headed for the capital. Why did Nete want to see her? Hadn't they agreed years ago never to meet up again? Hadn't Nete made that abundantly clear last time they saw each other?

"It was your fault I ended up on that bloody island. You're the one who dragged me into it that day," Rita mouthed, mimicking her former friend between drags on her ciggie, the young jogger still trying to gauge his chances.

Rita laughed. Those had been pretty unhealthy times, back in the solemn rigor of the asylum in 1955.

The day Nete arrived at the institution in Brejning in eastern Jutland, four of the less-retarded patients had got themselves into a fight. The high-ceilinged halls echoed with shouts and cries. It sounded like bedlam.

Rita loved days like that, when something happened. She'd always enjoyed watching a good punch-up, and the staff excelled at meting out punishment in kind.

She was standing by the entrance as the two police officers led Nete in. A brief glimpse was all she needed to realize that here was a girl much like herself. Keen eyes, shocked by the ugliness of what she was seeing. Not only that, there was a fury about her. Nete was a survivor, the same as herself.

Rita set store by anger. It was what kept her going. Stealing, relieving gullible fools of their wallets, pushing those aside who stood in her way. Of course, she knew anger would never be a solution, but somehow the emotion was enough in itself. With a rage inside her, she felt capable of anything.

The new girl was given a room two doors from her own. Rita decided to approach her that evening. They would be friends, allies, no matter what. She would cultivate her.

She took the girl to be a couple of years younger than herself. Essentially naive, poorly broken in. Most certainly intelligent, but without yet having learned enough about life and human nature to understand everything worked like a game. Rita would teach her.

When the girl tired of darning socks all day long, and her first clashes

with the staff knocked her out of synch, she would come to Rita for comfort. And Rita would provide. Before the beech tree came into leaf, the
two of them would abscond, Rita promised herself. They would cross the
Jutland peninsula to the west coast, where they would board a fishing
boat in Hvide Sande that would take them to England. There would always be fishermen ready to help two pretty girls on the run. Who in his
right mind would pass up the chance of rocking the boat with the two of
them belowdecks?

When they reached England, they would learn English and get jobs,
and when they were ready they would move on to America.

Rita had the plan. All she needed was someone to carry it out with.

Less than three days passed before this new girl's problems began. She
asked too many questions, it was that straightforward. The way she stood
out from all the other deranged and simpleminded souls, her questions
would never be taken as anything but criticism, an assault upon the
system.

"Keep your head down," Rita told her in the corridor. "Don't let them
know how clever you are. It won't do you any good. Do as they say, and
do it in silence."

And then she pulled Nete toward her and drew her tight. "You'll get
away, I promise, but first there's something I need to know. Is anyone
likely to come and visit you here?"

Nete shook her head.

"So there's no one to go home to if they ever let you out?"

The question clearly shocked her. "What do you mean, if they ever let
me out?"

"You don't think anyone ever just gets out of here, do you? I know the
buildings look nice, but it's still a prison. We might be able to look out
on fields and the fjord, but all around us there's invisible barbed wire

growing up out of the ground. You'll never scale that fence without me, so you'd better fucking get used to the idea."

Nete giggled unexpectedly.

"Hey, we're not supposed to swear in here," she admonished quietly, digging a playful elbow into Rita's side.

She was all right.

After Rita had smoked her two cigarettes she looked at her watch. It was 10:58. Time to put her head into the jaws of the lion. Time to break its teeth.

The jogger was now leaning against a tree. She almost called out to him, to tell him to wait until she came back, but then she thought of Nete's luscious hair, her curves, and thought better of it. There'd always be cocks available. All she had to do was snap her fingers. Anywhere. Anytime.

Nete's voice seemed unfamiliar over the entry phone, but she didn't let this bother her.

"Nete! How lovely to hear your voice again," she said into the mike, pushing open the front door at the buzzer. Maybe Nete really *was* ill. It sounded like it.

A moment's unexpected apprehension vanished when Nete opened the door of the apartment and stood looking at her as if the twenty-six years that had passed had been but a gust of wind, and all the bad blood between them was gone.

"Come in, Rita, you look marvelous. And thanks for being on time," Nete said.

She led her to the living room and invited her to sit down. Still the same white teeth, the full lips. And the same blue eyes that could shift from frost to fire like no one else Rita had ever met.

Fifty years old, and quite as beautiful after all these years, Rita thought to herself as Nete stood with her back to her, pouring the tea. Those fine slender legs of hers in neatly pressed slacks. A tight blouse that clung to the curve of her hips, her bum as firm as ever.

"You've kept well, darling. I can't believe that whatever's wrong with you can be anything serious. Tell me it's not true. That it was just a wheeze to get me here."

Nete turned to face her with the teacups in her hands and warmth in her eyes. But she said nothing. The quiet one, as ever.

"I was sure you never wanted to see me again, Nete," Rita went on, looking around the room. It wasn't opulent. Not for a woman Rita's inquiries told her was good for millions. "Even so, I've thought about you a lot, as I'm sure you can imagine," she added, now looking at the tea Nete placed in front of her.

She smiled. Two cups, not three.

She turned and peered out of the window. No lawyer. This was looking cozy.

Rita and Nete made a good team. The staff realized as much instantly. "We're short of hands in the children's ward," they said, and equipped them with spoons.

For a couple of days they fed children who stood tethered to radiators because they were mentally incapable of sitting at the table. It was horrible, messy work that took place slightly removed from the others in order to spare them the sad spectacle. When the girls proved worthy of this new responsibility and able to keep their charges presentably clean, they were rewarded with the additional task of keeping the other end of the digestive system equally unsoiled.

Rita puked. Where she came from, the only foreign excrement that encroached upon her life was what the sewers occasionally spewed up when the heavens opened in sudden, torrential downpours. Nete, on the other hand, could wipe bums and wring dirty nappies like she'd never done anything else.

"Shit's just shit," she stated. "It's what I was brought up in."

She told of cowpats and pig shit and horse dung, of days so long that being at the asylum must have seemed like a holiday in comparison.

But Nete knew it was no vacation. That much was plain from the dark blotches under her eyes, and her cursing the doctor who had duped her with his outrageous IQ test.

"None of the doctors here know what it's like getting up at four in the morning to milk cows in winter, or even in summer for that matter," she would snarl when a besmocked physician made a rare appearance. "Would he recognize the smell of the shed when a cow has an infection in the womb that won't go away? Never in a million years. So why call *me* stupid, just because I don't know who's king of Norway?"

When they'd been wiping mouths and arses for two weeks and found they could come and go on the children's ward as they pleased, Rita began her crusade.

"Have you been to see the consultant yet, Nete?" she would ask in the mornings. "Or any of the other doctors? Have they written that recommendation to the parish council yet? Have they even noticed you're here?" She rattled the questions off like a machine gun

And after a week had passed, Nete had heard enough.

When lunch was over that day, she looked around her at the vacant faces, the crooked frames, the short legs and shifty eyes. It was beginning to dawn on her.

"I want to speak to the consultant," she said to one of the nurses, who passed her by with a shake of her head. And after she'd repeated her request a couple more times with no response, she stood in the middle of the room and screamed it as loud as she was able.

Now Rita's experience stood her in good stead.

"You'll certainly see him if you keep *that* up. Only before you get there you'll have been strapped to a bed for days on end and given injections to shut you up. I'm not joking."

Nete leaned her head back to scream out her shrill appeal with renewed force, but Rita stopped her.

"The only way girls like you and me can get out of here is either by doing a runner or getting sterilized. Do you realize how fast they can sort who's to be sterilized from who isn't? I know for a fact the consultant and the psychologist picked out fifteen girls in ten minutes last week. How many do you think got off? No, once the cases have been through the board in the Ministry of Social Affairs, you can be sure most of them are packed off to Vejle General Hospital before they know what's happening.

"So I'll ask you again, Nete. Is there anyone outside this place you're going to miss? Because if there isn't, then do a bunk with me after we've given the kids their dinner."

The events of the two weeks that followed were easy to sum up.

They stole a pair of white blouses and matching skirts the same day and walked out through the gates like anyone else on the staff. They hid in bushes, walked for hours, and left the asylum far behind. The next morning they broke the window of a farmhouse while everyone was at work in the sheds and stables, stole a few items of clothing and some money, and were gone.

They got to Silkeborg in the sidecar of a Nimbus and were spotted by police as they stood hitching on the main road to Viborg. There was a dash through woodland before they were safe again. Then three days spent in a hunting cabin, living on tinned sardines.

Rita tried it on with Nete at night, snuggling up to her winter-white skin and laying her arm across her breast, only for Nete to push her away, muttering something about there being two kinds of human beings for a reason and how it wasn't natural for a person to lie with their own kind.

On the third day, with cold rain lashing, their rations ran out. For three hours they stood at the roadside before a truck driver took pity on the two drowned mice and let them dry themselves in the cab with some rags. He stared a lot, but made sure they got to Hvide Sande.

There they found a fisherman with a gleam in his eye, just as Rita had predicted, a man who jumped at the chance of taking them out to the fishing grounds. And if they were nice enough, he would gladly pass them on at sea to one of the English boats whose crews were quite as short on female company. At least that's what he told them.

He asked them to make themselves ready, so he could sample the goods, but Nete shook her head and he had to make do with Rita alone. And when he'd had his way with her for a couple of hours, he called up his brother, a policeman in Nørre Snede.

They didn't realize what had happened until two brick shithouses from the Ringkøbing Police snapped the cuffs on them and led them over to a patrol car.

When they arrived back at the Keller Institution at Brejning, both Nete and Rita finally found audience with the consultant physician.

"You are a despicable delinquent, Rita Nielsen," he said. "Not only have you abused the trust of staff members, you have also served your own interests poorly. You are of execrable character. You're stupid, mendacious, and sexually deviant. If I were to allow an antisocial individual like yourself to go about freely, you'd be indulging in sexual relations with most anyone who happened to cross your path, and before long society would have to deal with your subhuman offspring. For that reason, I have attested in writing that you are unfit to receive any treatment other than that which I have now made compulsory, and which will be of such duration as to teach you a lesson you're unlikely to ignore."

Later that day Rita and Nete sat together on the backseat of a black

Citroën with locked doors. On the front seat lay the consultant's attestations. They were being dispatched to Sprogø. The island of outcast women.

"I should never have listened to you," Nete sobbed as they drove across Fyn. "It's all your fault."

"This is rather bitter, Nete," she said after the first sip of tea. "Perhaps you've got coffee instead?"

Nete's face instantly took on an odd expression, as though Rita had handed her a gift, only to snatch it back again just as she reached out to accept it. It was more than disappointment. It was something deeper.

"No, I haven't, I'm afraid," Nete replied, her voice subdued, as though the world were about to collapse around her.

Now she'll offer to make another cup instead, Rita thought to herself, amused by how seriously Nete seemed to be taking the role of hostess.

But no such proposal was forthcoming. Nete said nothing, but sat there as though everything had begun moving in slow motion.

Rita shook her head.

"Not to worry. A drop of milk would be nice, though. I'm sure that'll do the trick," she said, puzzled now at the visible signs of relief that spread across Nete's face.

"Of course," Nete said, almost leaping to her feet. "Be with you in a jiffy!" she called out from the kitchen.

Rita glanced over at the sideboard on which Nete had placed the teapot. Why hadn't she put it on the table? Maybe it wasn't the done thing for a proper hostess. But then, what did she know?

For a second she thought about asking for a glass of that liqueur, or whatever it was, in the decanter next to the tea, but then Nete came scuttling back with the milk, doing the honors with a smile that seemed more strained than the situation called for.

"Sugar?" Nete asked.

Rita shook her head. Nete was so hectic all of a sudden, as if she were in a hurry. It made Rita curious. Was this just a ritual, something to be completed as quickly as possible before Nete finally extended her hand toward her and declared how glad she was that she had accepted her invitation? Or was it something else altogether?

"So, where's the lawyer you said would be here, Nete?" Rita asked, a wry smile on her lips. A smile that remained unreturned, but then she hadn't been expecting one either.

As if she hadn't already got Nete sussed. There *was* no lawyer, there *was* no ten million, and Nete wasn't ill at all.

But she would play her cards right all the same, so the journey wouldn't be a complete waste.

Keep your wits about you, she's up to something, Rita told herself, nodding when Nete replied that the lawyer was running late, but would be along any minute.

It was a farce. So beautiful, so wealthy, and yet so transparent.

"Bottoms up," Nete chuckled without warning, raising her teacup.

Talk about manic, Rita thought to herself in puzzlement, images of the past milling suddenly in her mind.

Did Nete really still remember their ritual? The one the girls performed when on rare occasions they were left unsupervised during dinner with no one to shush them? There in the dining room they would pretend to be free, imagining themselves at the Dyrehavsbakken amusement park, beer glasses held aloft and doing exactly as they pleased.

"Bottoms up!" Rita would always urge at some point, whereupon they would all guzzle down their tap water. And everyone would laugh, apart from Nete, who sat in her corner, staring out of the window.

Did she really remember?

Rita smiled at her, sensing the day might turn out nice after all as she put the teacup to her lips and downed its contents in one.

"Bottoms up!" they chorused, laughing now as Nete went to the sideboard to pour another cup.

"Not for me, thanks," said Rita, still chuckling. "Imagine you remembering that," she continued, repeating the cry once more for good measure. "We had a laugh, didn't we?"

More reminiscences were shared about the pranks she and a couple of the other girls had always been up to out there on the island.

She nodded to herself. It was odd, the way the atmosphere in Nete's apartment suddenly provoked so many memories. Strange, too, that they should be so pleasant.

Nete put her cup down on the table and laughed again, differently than before, as though there was more to their amusement than seemed apparent. But before Rita had time to digest the thought, Nete spoke to her calmly, her eyes piercing and intense:

"To be frank, Rita, if it hadn't been for you I'm sure I could have led a completely normal life. If only you'd left me alone I'd never have ended up there on Sprogø. I'd have learned how to behave in those institutions so the doctors would see I was normal and let me go. If you hadn't ruined everything, the doctors would have realized I wasn't antisocial at all, that it was just my background. They'd have known I was no threat to anyone. Why couldn't you have just left me alone?"

So that was it. Nete needed to confront her past. In which case she'd come to the wrong person. And before she headed back for Kolding, Rita would give this silly little cow what for. She could pay for her trip tenfold, and have her arse walloped into the bargain.

Rita cleared her throat. She was going to say the tea was abysmal, that Nete would never have got away from Sprogø or Brejning without being sterilized, and that she was a little tart who ought to take responsibility for her own actions. But all of a sudden her mouth was so dry.

She clutched at her throat. It felt funny, like the kind of allergic reaction she got from eating shellfish or if she'd been stung by a wasp. A searing sensation passed over her skin as though it had been rubbed with nettles. The light stabbed her eyes.

"What the hell did you put in the tea?" she groaned, her eyes darting about the room in confusion. Now her esophagus was burning. Something was dreadfully wrong.

The figure before her rose and came closer. The voice was gentler now, though strangely hollow.

"Are you all right, Rita?" it said. "Lean back in the chair, otherwise I'm afraid you'll fall. I'm going to call a doctor, all right? You may be having a stroke. Your pupils look all funny."

Rita gasped for breath. The copperware on the shelves started dancing before her eyes as her heart at first began to pound and then gradually subsided.

She reached out a leaden arm toward the figure in front of her. For a brief second it resembled a beast rearing up on its hind legs, claws extended.

Then her arm fell back, and her heart was almost still.

And when the figure before her vanished, the light vanished, too.

26

November 2010

She woke him up with beams of sunlight and dimples in her cheeks so deep he could have curled up in them.

"Rise and shine, Carl! You're off to Fyn today with Assad, remember?"

She kissed him and drew up the blinds. Her body seemed almost ethereal now, after the night's antics. Not a word about the four times he'd had to race to the loo, not one bashful look on account of the numerous boundaries they may have breached during their lovemaking. Mona was her own woman, and yet she had clearly demonstrated that she was his, too.

"Here," she said, putting down a tray on the bed next to him. A delight of aromas, and in the middle of it all was a key.

"It's for you," she said, pouring his coffee. "Use it wisely."

He picked it up and weighed it in his hand. Two and a half grams. Not much for an entry into paradise, he found himself thinking.

He turned the little plastic tag it was attached to and read what was written on the back in block letters: LOVER'S KEY, it read.

He wasn't sure he liked it.

It looked used.

Four times they had called Mie Nørvig. Four times in vain.

"We'll just have to chance it and see if they're in," Carl said, as they approached Halsskov with the Storebælt Bridge beyond.

They found the house looking like a caravan put away for winter.

Windows shuttered, carport empty. Even the water had been turned off, Carl noted, twisting the outside tap for the garden hose.

"Nothing to see here either," said Assad, his nose stuck between two shutters round the back of the house.

"Bollocks," Carl snapped. They'd done a bunk.

"We could break in," Assad suggested, producing his pocketknife.

Did his assistant have no inhibitions?

"For fuck's sake, Assad, put it away. We'll come back later, maybe they'll have turned up."

He didn't even believe it himself.

"That's Sprogø over there," said Carl, pointing toward the island visible between the great pylons of the bridge.

"It looks pleasant now, not like it was before," Assad mused, his knees wedged against the glove compartment. Couldn't he ever sit properly in a car?

"This must be it here," Carl noted, as they approached the island and the works exit halfway across the strait. He turned off and came to a barrier that seemed unreasonably closed. "Looks like we'll have to park here." He sighed.

"But what do we do after? Reverse back along the motorway over the bridge? Has your mind been lost, Carl?"

"Tell you what, I'll put the hazard lights on, soon as I knock her into reverse. No one'll run into us then," Carl replied with a gleam in his eye. "Come on, Assad, the day'll be gone if we start mucking about calling up for authorization."

Less than two minutes passed before something happened. A woman with short hair came striding toward them in high-heeled shoes and a hi-vis vest with fluorescent chevrons all over it. A striking combination, to say the least.

"You can't stop here, this is a no-access area! We'll open the barrier for you, then you either carry on to Fyn or follow the track under the viaduct here and turn back to Sjælland without delay. That means *now*!"

"Carl Mørck, Department Q," Carl rejoined drily, holding up his badge. "This is my assistant, and we're investigating a murder. You got keys to this place?"

It had some effect, but the woman was clearly not without authority of her own. She withdrew a couple of steps and put a walkie-talkie to her ear. Words were exchanged, after which she turned toward them with the full clout of officialdom behind her.

"Here," she said, handing him the radio.

"Carl Mørck, Department Q, Copenhagen Police. Who's this?"

The man at the other end presented himself. Some officious exec from the offices of the agency that ran the bridge link in Korsør. "You can't just access Sprogø without prior clearance. Surely you can understand that?" the bloke barked.

"Course I do. Same as I can't pull my pistol on a crazed gunman if I'm not a trained policeman on duty. More than our job's worth, isn't it? Thing is, we've got a job on here. We're dead busy investigating some very nasty stuff that seems to be linked to what went on here on Sprogø."

"Like what?"

"Can't say, I'm afraid. But feel free to call the police commissioner in Copenhagen. That'll get you your clearance before you get your breath back." It was a slight overstatement. Sometimes it could take a quarter of an hour just to get through to the commissioner's front desk. They were run off their feet these days.

"In that case I'll do so right away."

"How kind of you. Thank you, indeed. You've been a great help," Carl said, shutting off the walkie-talkie and handing it back.

"He gave us twenty minutes," he told the woman in the hi-vis vestments. "Is that enough time for you to show us round? We want you to tell us everything you know about when this place was a women's home, OK?"

There was hardly anything left of the original layout, the place having been rebuilt at various stages since, their guide explained.

"Down at the far end of the island was a small building they called the Retreat, where the women could be on their own for a week in the daytime. It was like their holiday. Back in the old days it was actually a quarantine station for plague-stricken sailors. It's all gone now, though," she told them, leading them into a closed courtyard where a tree towered above cobbles.

Carl looked around at the four buildings that surrounded the yard.

"Where were the girls' quarters?" he asked.

The woman pointed. "Top floor, those little windows in the roof. It's all been rebuilt now. Today it's used for seminars and courses, that sort of thing."

"What did the girls actually do while they were here? Did they have any say?"

She gave a shrug. "I doubt it. They grew vegetables, tended the fields, looked after the animals. In there they had a sewing room," she said, indicating the east wing. "Apparently the mentally challenged were good at using their hands."

"So the girls were actually mentally challenged?"

"Well, that's what they say. They probably weren't, though. Not all of them. Do you want to see the punishment cell? It's still there."

Carl nodded. He certainly did.

They passed through a dining room with high wooden paneling and a fine view of the strait.

Their guide swept her arm around the room. "This is where the girls had their meals. The staff dined in the room next door. They made sure to keep things separate. The other end of this building here was where the matron and her deputy lived, but again it's all been done up since then. Follow me."

She led them up a steep flight of stairs to more humble surroundings. A long washing trough of terrazzo ran along one wall of the narrow corridor. On the other side were a number of doors.

"It must have been rather cramped, sharing two to a room," she said, showing them a low-ceilinged room with sloping walls.

Then she opened a door that led into an oblong attic containing musty furniture, shelves, and numbered coat hooks.

"The girls could keep things here they didn't have space for in their rooms," she explained.

Their hi-vis hostess led them out to the corridor again and indicated a little door equipped with two heavy bolts.

"This is the punishment cell. They threw the girls in here if they didn't behave."

Carl stepped up and went inside through the low, heavy wooden door to find himself in a space so small there was barely room enough to lie outstretched.

"They could be holed up in here for days at a time or even longer. Sometimes they'd be put in restraints, and if they were too hard to handle they'd be sedated. It was no party."

An understatement if ever there was one, Carl thought. He turned to Assad, who had a frown on his face and looked clearly out of sorts.

"You OK, Assad?"

He nodded slowly. "It's just that I have seen marks like this before."

He pointed to the inside of the door where a recent paint job had been unable to conceal a number of irregular grooves in the wood.

"These marks are from people clawing at the wood, Carl. Believe me."
He reeled out of the room and leaned against the wall for a moment.
Maybe one day he'd tell him what it was all about.

There was a beep from their guide's walkie-talkie.

"Yes?" she said, her expression changing in seconds. "I see. OK, I'll pass it on." She put the device back in her belt and gave them a look of disappointment.

"I'm to say from my boss that he wasn't able to get hold of the police commissioner and that some of my colleagues have seen us going about on their monitors. He wants you out of here immediately. Which means *now*, in case it hasn't sunk in."

"Sorry about that. Tell them I tricked you into it. But thanks, we've seen enough."

"You all right, Assad?" he asked after a long period of silence crossing Fyn.

"Yes, no need to worry, Carl." Assad straightened up in his seat. "Leave the motorway by exit 55," he said, indicating the GPS.

Carl was sure the little contraption would let them know itself before long.

"In six hundred meters, turn right," came the tinny voice.

"No need to tell me, Assad. The GPS is looking after us."

"And here we pick up route 329 to Hindevad," his human assistant went on, unabashed. "Then about ten kilometers to Brenderup."

Carl sighed. Right now it sounded like ten K too far.

Assad's commentary continued at intervals of about twenty seconds before finally he indicated their destination.

"This is the house Tage lived in," he said, two seconds ahead of the GPS.

"House" seemed to be stretching things a bit. More like a wooden barracks stained black and stuck on a heap of surplus materials ranging from breeze blocks to sheets of corrugated iron. Its various stages of development were visible like growth rings, from the foundation to the weathered tin roof. Not much of a recommendation for the area, Carl thought, getting out of the car and hitching up his trousers.

"You're quite sure she's expecting us?" he asked, after ringing the doorbell for the fifth time.

Assad nodded. "Oh, yes. A most charming lady on the phone," he said. "She has a stutter, but the appointment is good, Carl."

Carl nodded back. A most charming lady. He was beginning to sound like a phrase book.

They heard the coughing fit before the footsteps, but at least there was life.

It was a cough nourished by a blend of smoking-induced emphysema, cat hairs, and concentrated alcohol fumes, but despite such obvious handicaps and the utterly unsuitable nature of the dwelling with respect to human habitation, this aged individual by the name of Mette Schmall nevertheless managed to negotiate her way through the establishment with the kind of elegance that more properly belonged to a lady of the manor.

"Tage and I were n-n-never married, but the l-l-lawyer knew that if I m-m-made an offer for the house, it'd be most f-f-fitting if I g-g-got it." She lit a smoke. It wasn't the day's first, not by a long chalk.

"T-t-t-ten thousand k-k-kroner. Lot of m-m-money in those days. N-nineteen n-n-ninety-four, by the time it all got s-s-sorted."

Carl looked around the place. As far as he remembered, ten grand was about what a camcorder cost back then, which might have been a lot of money for a camcorder, but definitely not for a house. On the other hand, who wouldn't rather have a camcorder than this heap of rubble?

"This was Tage's h-h-hideaway," she said, gently nudging aside a pair of cats whose tails were raised like flagpoles. "N-n-never come in here myself. It's like s-s-somehow it'd be wrong."

She pushed open a door papered with old adverts for various engine lubricants and they stepped into a pong far more malodorous than the one they'd just left.

It was Assad who found a passage into the open air, and then the source of the acrid stench. Five wine bottles in a corner behind the bed, each containing stale urine. Judging by the state of them, they'd all been filled to the brim, for the glass was now completely opaque with what-ever it was that was left behind when piss evaporated.

"They should have been ch-ch-chucked out ages ago," the woman said, tossing them into the weeds outside the house.

The room they were standing in was a combined bicycle and moped workshop. A jumble of tools and old junk, and in the midst of it all a bed whose covers were approximately the same color as the oily floor.

"Didn't Tage ever tell you what he was doing when he went off that day?"

"No. Very s-s-secretive he was, all of a s-s-sudden."

"OK. Mind if we have a look round?"

She made a gesture, indicating the place was theirs.

"There's been n-n-no one here since the l-l-local officers were here b-b-back at the t-t-time," she said, absently smoothing the bedcovers. A fat lot of good it would do.

"Nice ladies," said Assad, nodding toward the pin-ups.

"Yeah, from the days before silicone knockers, tattoos, and the lady shaver," Carl grunted, grabbing a stack of assorted papers balanced pre-cariously on top of an egg carton full of ball bearings.

It really was hard to believe any of these piles of junk would tell them anything at all about the fate that had befallen Tage Hermansen.

"Did Tage ever talk about a man called Curt Wad?" Assad asked.

The woman shook her head.

"Who *did* he talk about? Anyone you can remember?"

Negative again. "No one, really. M-m-mostly he went on about K-k-kreidler Floretts and P-p-puchs and SCOs."

Assad was lost.

"Mopeds, Assad. You know, vroom, vroom," Carl explained, twisting a pair of imaginary throttles.

"Did Tage leave any money?" he went on.

"Not a p-p-penny, no."

"Might he have had any enemies?"

She laughed, sending her headlong into a coughing fit. When she had finished and dried her eyes, she looked at Carl with a telling expression.

"What do *y-you* think?" She threw out an arm. "Not exactly the kind of p-p-place that makes a person f-f-friends, is it?"

"OK, so the neighbors might have wanted him to tidy the place up, but I'm probably right in saying it all looks pretty much the same now as it did then, so that's not likely to be the reason for his disappearing like that, is it? Do you have any thoughts as to what might have happened to him, Ms. Schmall?"

"N–n-none w-w-whatsoever."

He sensed Assad rummaging through the girlie mags. Was he thinking of taking some home with him, or what?

He turned round to find himself facing an envelope Assad was holding up in front of his nose.

"It was stuck up over there."

He pointed to a drawing pin stuck into a sheet of particleboard above one of Tage's pin-up girls.

"You can see the hole. The envelope was attached with two drawing pins. See for yourself."

Carl peered at the board. If Assad said so, he was probably right.

"The second drawing pin must have fallen out so the envelope slipped down behind the poster, still hanging from the first one."

"So what about it?" Carl asked, taking the envelope from Assad.

"It's empty, but read what it says on the back."

Carl read: *Nete Hermansen, Peblinge Dossering 32, 2200 Copenhagen N.*

"Yes, Carl. Now turn it over and look at the postmark."

He did so. It was rather obliterated, though still legible.

28-08-1987. Just a week before Tage disappeared.

Not that it had to be significant. Things would always be turning up that bore some relation to the time leading up to their owner's disappearance. Few people had a thorough tidy-up just before going missing. Not without a good reason. Like knowing you weren't coming back.

Carl looked at Assad. The man's mind was churning, that much was obvious.

"I'll give Rose a ring," he mumbled, dialing her number. "She must hear about this envelope. It's down her street, I feel it."

Carl scanned the workshop. If there was an envelope, there must have been a letter as well. Maybe it, too, had got stuck behind Tage's pin-up girl. Maybe it was under the bed or in the wastepaper basket. They needed to sift through.

"Do you know who this Nete Hermansen is, Ms. Schmall?" he asked.

"N-no idea. F-f-family, though, I should th-think. If the n-n-name's anything to g-g-go by."

After an hour rummaging in vain through Tage's stuff, followed by three-quarters of an hour in the car, they once more approached the colossal bridge linking the islands of Fyn and Sjælland, its towering pylons striving upward into the cloud.

"Our cursed island again," Assad said, pointing to Sprogø as it appeared out of the mist ahead.

He stared in silence for a while, then turned to Carl. "What if this Herbert Sønderskov and Mie Nørvig are still not in, Carl?"

Carl glanced across the island as they drove past. It looked peaceful, its man-made extremity cradling the motorway in the transition from the low-level western section of the bridge to the high-level suspension bridge in the east, the lighthouse white on its hill of green, pleasant yellow buildings sheltering from the wind, wide-open meadows and wild vegetation.

Hell on earth, Rose had called the place, and at once Carl sensed the malice of old breaching the crash barriers of the motorway, ghosts of the past appearing before him, souls torn asunder, barren wombs forever scarred. Had Denmark really allowed, even encouraged, such violations to be perpetrated by its well-trained doctors and those supposed to provide care? He found the idea hard to swallow. And yet. Discrimination was always rampant, even today, even if much of it failed to cause scandal.

He shook his head and put his foot down on the accelerator. "What was that you said, Assad?"

"I asked what we should do if Herbert Sønderskov and Mie Nørvig have not returned."

Carl turned his head to look at him. "Well, you've still got your pocket-knife, haven't you?"

Assad nodded. So that was settled. They were going to have a good nose in that bloody archive and see what this Hermansen case Mie Nørvig had mentioned was all about. Warrant or no. They'd never get one anyway, even if they applied.

Carl's mobile chimed. He switched on the speaker. "Yeah, Rose, what is it?" he said.

"I went into HQ when Assad called. Better option than gawping out of the window in Stenløse. Anyway, I've delved into things a bit." She sounded excited. "I might as well tell you straight off, I got a shock, I did. Would you believe there's still a Nete Hermansen registered at that address in Nørrebro? Brilliant, eh?"

Assad stuck his thumbs in the air.

"OK, but she'll be getting on a bit now, won't she?"

"Yeah, I haven't checked her out yet, but I can see she's been living in the same place in the name of Nete Rosen. Nice name, don't you think? Maybe I ought to be called that. Rose Rosen. It's all right that, isn't it? Maybe she could even adopt me. Can't be any worse than the mother I've got."

Assad chuckled, while Carl refrained from comment. Officially he knew nothing about Rose's private life. If it got out that he'd been poking around and had spoken to her real sister Yrsa, all hell would be let loose.

"Nice work, Rose. We'll have a look at that later. In the meantime I want you to check up on whatever else we've got on her, OK? We're on our way to Halsskov now to have a look at Nørvig's files. Anything else we should know?"

"Well, I've got more of a handle on Curt Wad's escapades now. Been in touch with a journalist, name of Søren Brandt. He's collated a whole lot of stuff about the party Wad's behind."

"The Purity Party?"

"Yeah. Doesn't look like Wad's private life's been that pure, though. Not a nice man at all, it seems. He's been reported loads of time over the years, with charges preferred, but never been convicted of anything, amazingly enough."

"How do you mean?"

"He's been up to all sorts, but I've not got that far yet. This Søren Brandt's going to send me more info, but right now I'm trawling through old case documents, and you can safely assume it's not what I'd prefer to be doing, not by a long sodding chalk."

Carl nodded. He wouldn't be best pleased either.

"There's an old rape charge from 1955—no details, only that Wad got off. Then there's three different cases of proceedings brought by Legal

Aid. In 1967, 1974, and most recently in 1996. He's been reported for racist remarks on several occasions, for inciting hatred, invasion of private property, slander. None of it's ever stuck, though according to Søren Brandt most of it ought to have. Lack of evidence, mostly."

"Nothing for manslaughter or anything like that?"

"Not exactly, but sort of. Charged with performing forced abortions more than once. I'd call that killing, wouldn't you?"

"Er, I don't know, really. Maybe. Certainly aggravating circumstances if the women hadn't given their consent."

"OK, but we're still dealing with a man who has rigidly differentiated between so-called inferior types and worthy citizens. A very able physician when decent people came to him seeking help to have children, and the exact opposite when the *Untermenschen* came after getting knocked up."

"What happened then?" Carl had his own inklings from what Mie Nørvig had alluded to. Maybe they were about to be substantiated.

"Well, like I said, he's never been convicted of anything, but the health authorities have been on to his practice more than once, investigating claims of him performing abortions without the consent or sometimes even knowledge of the women involved."

Carl sensed Assad shifting in his seat. He wondered if he'd ever had anyone call him an inferior human being.

"OK, thanks, Rose. We'll talk about this when we get back."

"Wait a sec, Carl. One more thing. One of the Purity Party's supporters, a Hans Christian Dyrmand from Sønderborg, just committed suicide. That's how I got in touch with this Søren Brandt, the journalist. He wrote on his blog that there could well be a link between what Curt Wad had been up to in the past and what Dyrmand did to himself."

"A bastard, this man," Assad exclaimed suddenly. Strong words indeed, coming from him.

———

They found the house in Halsskov as empty as they had left it that morning. Assad reached into his pocket and was already on his way round the back when Carl stopped him.

"Hang on a minute, Assad. Get back in the car," he said, then steered toward the bungalow on the other side of the quiet residential street.

He flashed his badge and the neighbor standing in front of her house stared at it aghast. It worked like that sometimes, if people didn't spit on it.

"No, I've no idea at all where Herbert and Mic might be," she said right away when he asked.

"Do you happen to know them personally?"

She thawed slightly. "Yes, we're good friends, we get along very well together. Bridge once every two weeks, that sort of thing."

"And you've no idea where they might be now? Holiday home, visiting the children, weekend cabin by the sea?"

"No, none whatsoever. They do go on holiday once in a while, of course. Me and my husband water the plants for them if their daughter's not staying. Mutual favors, you know. We've got plants that need tending, too, when we're away."

"The place is shuttered. That'd mean they'd be away for more than a couple of days, I suppose?"

She scratched her neck. "Well, yes, we've been worried about that. You don't think there's anything untoward going on, do you?"

He shook his head and thanked her for her help. The woman would be beside herself with curiosity now and would certainly be keeping an eye on what they were doing on the other side of the road.

He went back to the car, only to find that Assad wasn't there. Moments later, he noted that the living-room shutters at the back of the house were open and the window behind them ajar. Not a mark or a scratch. Obviously, Assad had done this sort of thing before. More than once.

"Go to the door in the basement, Carl," his assistant instructed from within.

Thankfully, the filing cabinets were still there, which meant maybe the disappearance of those who lived there hadn't anything to do with their visit the day before.

"Hermansen, that's the first name we need to check," Carl said to Assad.

It took twenty seconds before Assad stood with a suspension file in his hand.

"Under H, where else? But the Hermansen here is not Tage Hermansen."

He handed the file to Carl. CURT WAD VS. NETE HERMANSEN, it read on the front, and inside were the proceedings of the court case from 1955, listed in chronological order. The documents bore the stamp of the district court as well as Philip Nørvig's company logo.

A quick scan of the contents revealed such wordings as "charge of rape" and "claim re. having paid for termination of pregnancy," all of which inclined toward the burden of proof lying solely on this Nete Hermansen. The case had been concluded with Wad being acquitted, so much was apparent from the records, but what subsequently happened to Nete Hermansen remained a mystery.

Carl's mobile chimed.

"It's not a good time right now, Rose," he said.

"I think it is, Carl. Listen to this: Nete Hermansen was one of the girls from Sprogø. She was kept there from 1955 to 1959. What do you say about that?"

"I say it doesn't surprise me," he replied, weighing the file in his hand.

It was as light as a feather.

———

Fifteen minutes later they were finished chucking folders into the car.

As they were closing the boot, a green van came up the hill toward them. It wasn't so much the van itself that caught Carl's attention, more the way it suddenly slowed down.

He straightened up and fixed his gaze on it. The driver seemed to hesitate, unsure as to whether to pull up or pull away.

What he did was glance toward the house as he drove past. Maybe he was searching for a number, but in a neat residential area like this the house numbers were all clearly visible, so what was the problem?

The driver turned his head away as he drove by. Carl saw only a glimpse of white, wavy hair.

27

September 1987

He felt like a king, watching Sjælland roll by through the windows of the train. It was a journey to paradise, he thought to himself, and gave a boy in the compartment a coin.

A regal day, a coronation. The day his wildest dreams would come true.

He imagined Nete adjusting her hair and demurely inviting him in. He could feel the deed of transfer in his hand already. The instrument that would transfer to him ten million kroner, to the unequivocal satisfaction of the tax authorities and his own eternal joy.

But when eventually he found himself standing at Copenhagen's Central Station, realizing he had less than half an hour to find Nete's address, he was overcome by sudden anxiety.

He tore open the door of a taxi and asked the driver how much it would cost. And when he found the suggested tariff to be more than a couple of kroner on the wrong side of what his means allowed, he asked to be taken as far as possible for what he had in his pockets. He dumped his coins in the driver's hand, to be driven seven hundred meters and put down on Vesterbros Torv, with directions that would lead him through Teaterpassagen and along the City Lakes. He needed to get a move on.

Tage wasn't used to walking. The bag across his shoulder slapped heavily against his hip as perspiration seeped through his new clothes, darkening his jacket at the armpits.

You're going to be late, you're going to be late, he told himself, the words pounding inside him for every hastening step along the path, joggers of all ages briskly passing him by.

Every cigarette he'd ever smoked wheezed in his lungs, every bottle of beer, every shot of whisky strained on the muscles of his legs.

He unbuttoned his jacket and prayed to God that he would get there on time, and when eventually he arrived it was 12:35. Five minutes late.

For that reason tears of gratitude welled in his eyes when Nete let him in and he handed her the invitation as the letter had instructed.

He felt pitiful in such a fine abode, standing there in front of his life's best companion, now a grown woman bidding him welcome with open arms. He could have cried when she asked him if he was well and whether he'd like a cup of tea, offering him another a few minutes later.

And he would have had so much to say to her, if he hadn't suddenly felt so dreadfully unwell. He would have told her he had always loved her. That the shame of having abandoned her had almost destroyed him. He would have got down on his knees and begged her forgiveness, if only nausea had not surged so violently inside him that he unwittingly began to disgorge bile all down his nice new jacket.

She asked if he was ill, and whether he would like a glass of water or some more tea.

"It's hot in here," he groaned, struggling to draw in breath, only to find his lungs would not obey. And while she was out fetching him water, he clutched at his heart and realized he was about to die.

Nete considered the figure slumped on the chair in front of her in such an awful suit. There was a lot more of him than she had imagined. The weight of his upper body alone almost brought her to her knees as she tipped him toward her in order to get a grip under his arms.

"Oh, Lord," she groaned, glancing at the swinging pendulum of the grandfather clock. This was going to take too long.

She released the body, allowing it to fall forward. There was an unpleasant thud as Tage's nose and forehead struck the floor. She only hoped her downstairs neighbor would not be alarmed.

Then she got down on all fours and manhandled Tage's body onto its side in the middle of her Bokhara rug, using all her strength to drag it over to the door leading into the hallway, where she paused despairingly. Why hadn't she thought about this before? Coir matting ran the length of the corridor. She'd never be able to drag the body over it, even on the rug. There'd be too much friction.

She heaved the corpse with all her might, bundling it around the door before reluctantly abandoning her plan.

She chewed on her lip. Rita had been trouble enough, albeit nowhere near as heavy. Her body had seemed almost jointless, as though limbs extended from between her every rib. Time and again, she'd been forced to stop to lay the woman's arms across her stomach, and eventually she'd had to tie them together to finish the task.

She looked at Tage with disgust. What a difference between the boy with whom she had cavorted and this bloated, sweaty face, these flabby arms.

She shoved him into a sitting position, his head and torso flopping forward like a fat acrobat about to perform a tumbling routine. It gained her perhaps half a meter.

She looked down the hallway. At this rate it would take at least ten minutes to get him into the sealed room, but she couldn't stop now.

She pressed his head to the floor, rolling him forward over his shoulder and repeating the procedure in a series of slow-motion somersaults, finding that all that was required was the strength to ensure the continued momentum.

But now she flagged. Her bad leg, her hip, and her spine throbbed with pain, her whole nervous system in a state of alarm.

When finally she bundled him into the room, to the dining table, and the seven chairs, she gave up on seating him next to Rita's corpse, which she had positioned before its place card, head resting on its shoulder, torso secured to the back of the chair with twine.

She looked down at Tage, who lay with eyes open wide, fingers hooked and clutching. This was deplorable. She would have to get him into place before the day was done.

Then something caught her attention. The breast pocket of Tage's revolting shiny suit was torn, with a small strip of cloth missing. Surely it hadn't been like that all the time? She needed to be certain.

It was now twenty to two. Viggo would be arriving in five minutes.

She closed the door of the room and scanned the hallway without seeing the scrap of material anywhere. Perhaps it really had been missing all along. Perhaps she just hadn't noticed. She hadn't taken her eyes off Tage's face for a second once he'd sat down in the chair.

She took a deep breath and went out to the bathroom to tidy herself up. She considered her perspiring face in the mirror with satisfaction. She was doing well, in spite of all the hurdles. The henbane extract worked like it was supposed to and everything was going according to plan. Of course, it would be only natural if she felt a reaction that evening when it was all over. Perhaps she might suddenly look upon these people in a new light. Perhaps, though she would do her utmost to avoid it, she would even ponder on the thought that they, too, had once lived in the midst of family and friends who had loved them and wished them only the best in life.

But this was something she couldn't afford to think about now.

She adjusted her hair and thought of those still to arrive. Was Viggo now as corpulent as Tage had become? If he was, then it was imperative he arrive on time. She didn't dare contemplate the consequences if he didn't.

It was at that moment she thought of Curt Wad's towering frame and what it might weigh. And then she noticed Rita's coat still hanging on the hook in the hallway.

She grabbed it and tossed it onto the bed where Rita's handbag lay. Her cigarettes fell out of the pocket.

She stared at them for a moment.

Damned things, she thought to herself. How costly Rita's filthy habit had been.

28

November 2010

"**Just to let you** know, the maintenance supervisor says you gents aren't allowed to use the men's room in the corridor until Wednesday, when he's got time to come and fix it," Rose informed them, hands on hips. "*Someone* used so much paper yesterday, they blocked it up. Which one of you was it?"

She turned from Assad and glared at Carl, eyebrows raised to the vicinity of her jet-black hairline.

Carl threw up his hands in self-defense. In international body language it translated as "How should I know?" In his own personal lingo it meant "What fucking business is it of yours?" He wasn't about to share his toilet habits and gastric maladies with an underling of the opposite sex. No way.

"So when you use the ladies," make sure you either sit down when you're having a pee, or else lift the seat and put it down again when you're finished. You with me?"

Carl frowned. This was getting a bit personal for his liking.

"Check everything we've got on Nete Hermansen and put it down for me in a list. But first you can give me the number of this journalist of yours, Søren Brandt," was his riposte. If she wanted to wind him up, she could do it any other time but on a weekend. There was a fucking limit, surely.

"I have actually just spoken to this Brandt, Carl," Assad said, putting a steaming cup of sickly smelling, caramel-like substance to his lips.

Carl looked at him askew. Amazing.

"You just spoke to him?" He frowned again. "You didn't tell him we'd nicked all those files, did you?"

Now it was Assad's turn to put his hands on his hips. "Do you think a camel dips its toes in the lake from which it drinks?"

"You did, didn't you?"

Assad sagged visibly. "Perhaps only slightly. I told him we had something on Curt Wad."

"And what else?"

"A little bit about this Lønberg from the Purity Party."

"What have we got on him?"

"It was filed under L. Nørvig, who conducted some cases for him."

"OK, we'll get back to that. What did Søren Brandt have to say?"

"He said he had heard about The Cause. He had actually spoken to Nørvig's first wife and she told him nurses and doctors had for years referred pregnant women with unsuitable backgrounds for gynecological examination by members of the organization. The women did not know what was happening, and very often it ended in abortion. Søren Brandt has information and is willing to exchange it for copies of what we have ourselves."

"Christ Almighty, Assad! Do you realize what you're playing at? We'll be out of here on our arses if it gets out we've been burgling for evidence! Give me his number."

Carl dialed with trepidation.

"Yeah, I just spoke to your colleague," Søren Brandt said, after introductions. He sounded young and keen. They were always the worst.

"I believe you and Assad discussed some kind of trade-off."

"We did, and I'd be grateful indeed. I'm still looking for links between members of the Purity Party and The Cause. Imagine if we can put a clamp on these lunatics before they gain real influence."

"Well, I'm sorry to disappoint you, but I'm afraid Assad has promised more than he can deliver. We'll be passing our material on to a state prosecutor."

The journalist snorted. "Fat lot of good that'll do, but I can understand you wanting to look after number one. It's not as if jobs hang on trees these days, is it? You can breathe easy, though. Wild horses wouldn't make me give you away."

It was almost like listening to himself.

"Listen, Mørck, Wad's people are militants. They kill unborn children without batting an eyelid. They've got a system, fine tuned, to cover up all traces. Millions of kroner from funds and foundations. Gorillas on the payroll, the kind of people you don't want to get on the wrong side of. Do you think I'm living at my registered address these days? No way. I look out for myself, because these guys will stop at nothing if anyone casts aspersions on their depraved view of humanity and the politics they pursue, believe me. Look at that doctor, Hans Christian Dyrmand. He didn't OD on sedatives voluntarily, if you ask me. So I keep my mouth shut, you understand?"

"Until you go public, is that it?"

"Until then, yeah. And I'm prepared to go to prison to protect my sources, don't you doubt it for a minute. As long as I bring down Wad and that lowlife mob of his."

"OK. In that case, let me tell you we're investigating a series of disappearances that look like they're linked to women from that home that used to be on Sprogø. Would it be reasonable to assume that Curt Wad might have been involved somewhere along the line? Goes back fifty years, but maybe you know something anyway?"

He listened to the man's breathing for a moment before all went quiet.

"You still there?"

"Yeah, I'm here," Brandt replied. "Just needed to get myself together for a sec. My mother's aunt was a Sprogø girl. Told the most hair-raising stories. Not about Curt Wad specifically, but others like him. I don't know how he might be involved in that shit, but it wouldn't surprise me in the slightest if he was."

"OK. I spoke to another journalist, bloke called Louis Petterson. He did some critical articles on Curt Wad at one point. Do you know him?"

"I know his name. And I've read his stuff, of course. He's the kind of guy proper journalists don't like. Worked freelance and seemed like he was actually on to something, but then it looks like Wad turned him round by getting him involved in Benefice, that tendentious little news agency of his. Most likely they pay him a bundle. Anyway, the critical stuff dried up overnight."

"Anyone ever make you an offer like that?"

Søren Brandt laughed. "Not yet, but you never know with those hyenas. I did piss Curt Wad and Lønberg off at the Purity Party congress yesterday, though."

"This Lønberg, what've you got on him?"

"Wilfrid Lønberg. Wad's right-hand, his little pet. Father of Benefice's puppet chairman, cofounder of the Purity Party, and highly active in The Cause. So, yeah, I'd give him some bother, if I were you. Put Lønberg and Wad together and you've got Josef Mengele reincarnated."

They saw the glow of the bonfire long before they reached the house. On a dark November afternoon, it was hard to miss.

"A well-to-do neighborhood," Assad observed, nodding at the posh houses.

Lønberg's wasn't that different from the others that lined the quiet road, white and imposing, with large casement windows and a roof of black glazed tiles. It was set slightly farther back than its neighbors', and the walk up the crunching gravel path was sufficient to announce their arrival.

"What are you doing on my property?" a voice demanded.

They rounded a hedge and saw an elderly man wearing a brown apron and heavy-duty gardening gloves.

"What's your business?" he barked angrily, stepping in front of the flaming oil drum he was in the process of feeding with sheets of paper from the wheelbarrow at his side.

"I ought to inform you that burning rubbish like that in the open is against the law," Carl said, squinting to see if he could determine its more specific nature. Files and documents, most likely, relating to all the shit Lønberg and his ilk stood for.

"Really? And what law would that be, then? There's not exactly a drought on, is there?"

"We'd be happy to go to the trouble of calling the Gentofte Fire Department in order to clarify the local authority's regulations." He turned to Assad. "Would you like to take care of that, Assad?"

The man tossed his head. "Oh, come on, it's only paper. How can that bother anyone?"

Carl produced his badge. "I imagine it would bother quite a few people, actually, if it turns out what you're destroying here is evidence that could answer a lot of questions relating to your and Curt Wad's activities."

What happened in the seconds that followed was something not even Carl in his wildest imagination would have believed a man of Lønberg's age and skeletal stature could effectuate so quickly and with such resolve.

In one seamless movement he lifted the entire heap of documents from the wheelbarrow and deposited them in the oil drum, grabbed a plastic bottle of paraffin at his feet, removed the top, and tossed the whole thing onto the pyre.

The effect was astonishing and immediate. Carl and Assad leaped back as a column of flame exploded into the air, almost reaching the crown of the tall copper beech that stood majestically in the middle of the garden.

"There," said the man. "*Now* you can call the fire brigade. What'll it cost me? Five thousand? Ten? See if I care."

He was about to turn and go back up to the house when Carl stopped him with a hand on his shoulder.

"Does your daughter, Liselotte, know what sort of nauseating enterprises she's lending her name to, Lønberg?"

"Liselotte? Nauseating enterprises? If you're thinking of her chairmanship of Benefice, then I can tell you she has reason only to be proud."

"Oh, you think so, do you? Is she proud of The Cause and all its illegal abortions, or haven't you told her about that? Does she share your sick views on humanity? Does she sympathize with your murdering innocent children? Is she proud of that, or have you just been keeping her in the dark?"

Lønberg glared. His eyes were ice that no flame could melt.

"I have no idea what you're talking about. If you've anything at all of substance that you wish to discuss, I suggest you call my lawyer first thing Monday morning. His office opens at eight thirty. Caspersen's the name. He's in the book."

"Ah, yes, Caspersen," said Assad, in the background. "We know this man from the television. One of the people from the Purity Party, yes? We would very much like to have his number. Thank you very much, indeed."

Assad's breeziness seemed momentarily to take the wind out of Lønberg's arrogance.

Carl leaned into the man's face and almost whispered his parting shot:

"Thanks a lot, Lønberg. I think we've got enough now to be getting on with. Say hello to Curt Wad and tell him we're off to see one of his old acquaintances in Nørrebro. The Hermansen case, wasn't that what they called it back then?"

Nørrebro was a war zone. Concrete tenements knocked up overnight had provided ideal conditions for a complex of social problems, spawning crime, violence, and hatred. Not like the old days, when social work in the district had been all about helping hard-grafting workers keep a grip on a decent life. Only when you came strolling into the neighborhood along the City Lakes did the grandness of former times become visible in all its glory.

"The Lakes are still the best place in the city," Antonsen out in Rødovre always claimed. It was true. Standing there, looking at the rows of magnificent buildings nestling behind chestnut trees with their views across the gentle water, swans gliding over the surfaces, the thought seemed absurd that only a few hundred meters away the immigrant gangs and the bikers ruled the roost, and a person would do well to keep a watchful eye out when passing through after dark.

"I think she is in, Carl," said Assad, pointing up at the windows on the top floor.

Carl nodded. Like all the others in the gray apartment building, they were lit up.

"Nete Hermansen? It's the police," he said into the entry phone. "I'd like to ask you some questions. Would you be kind enough to let me in?"

"What sort of questions?" came the reply.

"Nothing out of the ordinary. Routine, that's all."

"Is it to do with the shooting incident on Blågårdsgade the other night? I did hear something going on, yes. If you'd be so good as to step back and hold up your badge so I can see it. One has to be careful."

Carl gave a sign to Assad to stay by the door, then stepped backward into the space between the ground floor's tiny flower beds so the light illuminated his features.

A moment passed before a window opened at the top and a head appeared.

Carl held his badge as high as he could.

Thirty seconds later the entry phone buzzed.

After a seemingly endless and increasingly breathless ascent to the fourth floor, they found the door of the apartment already wide open, so she obviously wasn't *that* careful.

"Oh!" she exclaimed, startled as Carl stepped into the slightly musty hallway with Assad lurking behind his shoulder. The ongoing menace of Nørrebro's immigrant gangs had left its mark here, too.

"Ah, I'm sorry, but you've no need to be alarmed by my assistant. Salt of the earth, he is," Carl lied.

Assad extended a hand in greeting. "How do you do, Ms. Hermansen." He bowed like a schoolboy of old asking for a dance at the end-of-term ball. "Hafez el-Assad, but you can call me Assad. A pleasure to meet you."

She hesitated a moment before accepting the gesture.

"Would you care for a cup of tea?" she asked, seemingly oblivious to Carl vigorously shaking his head.

The living room was like most others belonging to a lady of her age and standing. A vibrant jumble of heavy furniture and reminders of a long life. Only the absence of framed family photos seemed conspicuous. Carl recalled Rose's brief outline of Nete Hermansen's life. There were reasons enough for such portraits to be missing.

She came in with the tea on a tray, limping slightly, but good-looking for all her seventy-three years. Blonde hair, presumably dyed, and rather elegantly cut. It was obvious that money had rubbed off well in spite of the misfortunes that had befallen her. Money generally did.

"What a lovely dress," said Assad.

She said nothing, but poured his tea first.

"This is about the shooting on Blågårdsgade last week, isn't it?" she asked, sitting down between them and nudging a small plate of cookies in Carl's direction.

Carl declined and shifted in his armchair.

"Actually, no, it's about something else. In 1987 a number of people disappeared and never turned up again. Our hope is that you, Nete . . ." He paused. "May I call you Nete?"

She nodded. A tad reluctantly perhaps, though it was hard to tell.

"Our hope is that you might be able to help us find out what happened to them."

A pair of fine wrinkles rose on her brow. "Well, if I can be of any use."

"I've got a summary here outlining a certain period of your life, Nete. I can see that you endured some considerable hardship. I want you to know that those of us conducting these investigations are outraged by the abuse you and women like you were subjected to."

She raised an eyebrow. Was this too uncomfortable for her? Most likely it was.

"I'm sorry to have to open old wounds, but the fact is that several of these missing persons were linked to the women's home on Sprogø. I'll get back to that in a minute." He took a sip of his tea. Rather bitter for his liking, but a vast improvement on Assad's wallpaper paste. "Our main reason for being here is because we're investigating your cousin Tage Hermansen's disappearance in September 1987."

She looked at him askew. "Cousin Tage? Disappeared? I've not heard from him in years, but still I'm sorry to hear it. I had no idea."

"I see. We were at his workshop in Brenderup earlier on today. We found this envelope there."

He removed it from its plastic sheath and showed it to her.

"Yes, I remember. I wrote and invited Tage to come over and see me. Now I understand why he never replied."

"I don't suppose you'd have a copy of that letter? A carbon copy, or a printout, perhaps?"

She smiled. "I'm afraid not. It was a handwritten letter."

Carl nodded.

"You were at the women's home at the same time as a nurse by the name of Gitte Charles. Do you remember her?"

The wrinkles on her forehead appeared again. "Yes, I most certainly do. I'll never forget anyone from Sprogø."

"Gitte Charles disappeared, too, around the same time as your cousin."

"How strange."

"And Rita Nielsen."

This seemed to catch Nete slightly unaware. Her brow smoothed, and she drew back her shoulders.

"Rita? When was this?"

"The last thing we know is that she bought a pack of cigarettes in a kiosk just up the road from here on Nørrebrogade on the fourth of September 1987, at ten past ten in the morning. Besides that, her Mercedes was found on Kapelvej. Not far from here either, is it?"

Her lips tightened. "But that's awful. Rita came to see me that day. The fourth of September, you say? I remember it was late summer, though not the exact date. I'd reached a point in my life where I felt the need to confront my past. I'd lost my husband a couple of years before and found myself unable to move on. That's why I invited Rita and Tage."

"So Rita Nielsen visited you?"

"She did, yes." She gestured toward the table. "We sat there and had tea. The same cups we're using now. She was here for a couple of hours. I clearly remember that seeing her again was strange, and yet salubrious at the same time. We sorted things out, you understand. We hadn't always been the best of friends in the women's home."

"There were appeals for information following her disappearance. A lot of attention in the media. Why didn't you go to the police, Nete?"

"Oh, this is dreadful. What on earth can have happened to her?"

She stared into space for a moment. If she didn't answer Carl's question, it was because something was wrong.

"Why didn't I go to the police?" she repeated eventually. "Well, I couldn't, you see. I went to Mallorca the day after she was here, to buy a house there. I don't think I saw a Danish newspaper for six months or more. The house is in Son Vida. I go there for the winter. The only reason I'm not there now is that I've been having some bother with kidney stones, and I prefer to have them treated here."

"I assume you've got the deeds to this property."

"Of course. But now I get the feeling you're interrogating me. If you suspect me of anything, then I would ask you to be frank about it."

"That's not the case at all, Nete. But we do need to account for certain things, one of which being why you didn't react to the missing persons bulletins that were out on Rita Nielsen. May we have a look at those deeds?"

"Well, it's a good thing they're not still in Mallorca, isn't it?" she said, slightly offended. "They were, actually, until last year when there was a spate of break-ins in the area. One has to take precautions."

She knew exactly where the documents were, placing them in front of Carl and indicating the date of purchase. "I bought the place on the thirtieth of September 1987, but by that time I'd been looking for somewhere suitable and negotiating for three weeks. The owner was trying to pull a fast one on me. He failed, of course."

"But . . ."

"Yes, it's some time after the fourth, I realize that, but that's how it happened. If you're lucky, I might still have the plane tickets somewhere. In which case you'll see that I wasn't at home. But it'll take me rather longer to find them."

"A stamp in your passport or some other form of documentation will do just as well," Carl said. "I'm assuming you've kept your old passports, and there's bound to be some sort of stamp to prove it, don't you think?"

"I'm sure I have, but you'll need to come back another day, I'm afraid. I shall have to look for them."

Carl nodded. She was almost certainly telling the truth. "What was the nature of your relationship to Gitte Charles, Nete? Can you tell me about that?"

"What business would it be of yours?"

"I'm sorry, you're right. I ought to have worded that differently. The fact is we have very little to go on in Gitte's case. Hardly anyone who knew her then is alive today, so it's hard for us to get a picture of the kind of person she was and why she might have disappeared. How would you describe her?"

It was obvious this was traumatic for her. Why should the prisoner speak well of her guard? Clearly, it was something of a dilemma.

"Was she unkind to you? Is that why you cannot answer so easily?" Assad piped up.

Nete Hermansen nodded. "I do find it rather difficult, I must admit."

"Because Sprogø was a bad place, was it not? And she was one of the ones who kept you there, yes?" Assad went on, his eyes fixed on the plate of cookies.

She nodded again. "I haven't thought about her for years, to be honest. Or about Sprogø, for that matter. What went on there doesn't bear thinking about. They kept us isolated from the rest of the country and they made us infertile. They said we were retarded. I've no idea why. And while Gitte Charles wasn't the worst by any means, she never helped me in terms of getting away from the place."

"You have had no contact with her since?"

"None, thank goodness."

"Then there is a Philip Nørvig. You remember him, yes?"

She nodded faintly.

"He disappeared that day, too." It was Carl's turn again. "We know from his widow he'd received an invitation to Copenhagen. You've told us you had come to a point in your life where you needed to confront your past. In a way, Philip Nørvig was to blame for your unhappy plight, was he not? It was thanks to him that you lost the case against Curt Wad, isn't that right? So wasn't he one of the people you needed to confront, Nete? Did the invitation he received come from you?"

"No, it most certainly did not. I invited only Tage and Rita, no one else." She shook her head. "I don't understand. So many all at once, and me knowing them all. What on earth can have happened?"

"That's why Department Q has been brought in. Unsolved cases, cases requiring special scrutiny, that's what we deal in. So many disappearances all at once, and all linked, indicates to us that we're dealing with something out of the ordinary, as you suggest."

"We have been looking into this doctor, Curt Wad," Assad chirped. Rather earlier than Carl had intended, but what else was new?

"There are many things about this man that seem to connect him to our missing persons," Assad continued. "Nørvig, in particular."

"Curt Wad!" She raised her head like a cat discovering a bird in reach of its claws.

"Yes, we realize he's most likely where your misfortunes began," said Carl. "We've been through Nørvig's files and read about the way he rebuffed your charges against him and turned them back on you. I'm sorry to have to bring it up again, but if you can in any way provide us with some kind of plausible connection between Curt Wad and these persons going missing, we'd be grateful indeed."

She nodded. "I'll give it some thought, certainly."

"Your own case was probably the first of many in which Curt Wad succeeded in making a mockery of the truth and turning matters to his own advantage with scant regard for the injustice he thereby occasioned.

If charges were to be brought against Curt Wad, it'd be highly likely you'd be called as a witness. How would you feel about that?"

"About taking the stand against Curt Wad? Oh, no, I wouldn't care for that at all. All that's water under the bridge for me now. Justice will catch up with him without my involvement. Beelzebub is most likely rubbing his hands with glee as we speak."

"We quite understand, Nete," said Assad, leaning forward and looking as though he was about to pour himself another cup.

Carl stopped him with a movement of his hand.

"Perhaps we'll speak again soon, Nete. Thanks for the tea and hospitality," he said, informing Assad with a nod that the audience was over. If they got a move on he might just be able to nip home for a change of clothes before seeing if his new key to Mona's chambers worked like it was supposed to.

Assad offered his thanks, swiping another cookie in the process, the quality of which he praised before suddenly raising a finger into the air.

"Just a minute, Carl. There was one more person we did not ask about." He turned to face Nete Hermansen. "A fisherman from Lundeborg went missing, too. His name was Viggo Mogensen. Would that by any chance be anyone you ever ran into? From Lundeborg to Sprogø is not far in a boat."

She smiled. "No, I'm afraid I've never heard of him."

"You look tensive, Carl. What is going on inside your head?"

"*Pensive*, Assad. There's no such word as *tensive*. But apart from that, there's a lot to think about, wouldn't you say?"

"I would say so, yes. I cannot get my head around this either, Carl. Apart from this Viggo Mogensen, it's like there are two cases in one: Rita and Gitte and Curt Wad and Nørvig and Nete on the one side. Here, the cousin, Tage, seems not to fit in, not having anything to do with Sprogø as far as we know. But then on the other side there is Tage and Nete. This means she is the only one who has something to do with all of them."

"Yeah, maybe you're right, Assad, though we've no way of knowing for sure. Maybe Curt Wad ties it all together in some way. That's what we need to delve into now. The idea of some collective suicide, or a coincidence of inexplicable, simultaneous accidents somehow isn't on my agenda anymore."

"Say again, Carl. Agenda, and *what* kind of accidents?"

"Forget it, Assad. We'll talk about it later."

29

SPROGØ, 1955 / COPENHAGEN, September 1987

A flock of women stood on the jetty, waving as though Nete and Rita were long-awaited friends. They seemed like children, boisterous and giggling, spick and span. And Nete didn't understand.

What did they have to smile about? The boat from Nyborg was no lifeboat come to save them. It wasn't a Noah's Ark to sail them off to sanctuary. Quite the opposite, from what she'd heard. The boat was a curse.

Nete looked out over the railing at the lighthouse on its hill, and then beyond, at the cluster of red-roofed buildings with yellow walls, their windows like eyes watching over the island landscape and the poor souls upon it. A pair of French doors in the middle building swung open and a small, erect figure appeared on the step, one hand firmly placed on the handrail. An admiral to welcome the fleet, or rather Sprogø's queen monitoring her realm. She who reigned supreme.

"Have you brought cigarettes?" was the first thing the girls shouted out to them. One even clambered out and took up position on the wooden pilings with arms outstretched. If they had, she'd be first in line.

The girls milled around the new arrivals like a chorus of cackling geese. Names resounded in the air, hands sought contact.

Nete glanced at Rita with concern, but Rita was in her element. Rita had cigarettes, and cigarettes were the pathway to the top of the hierarchy. She lifted the packets above her head to show them off, then returned them just as quickly to her pocket. No wonder she was the one with all the attention.

Nete was given a room up under the sloping roof. A single skylight was her window on the world. The place was chilly, the wind worming its way through the rickety window frame. There were two beds and the little suitcase belonging to her roommate. Had it not been for a crucifix and two small photographs of film stars she didn't recognize, it would have seemed like a prison cell.

The room was one in a row of many, and outside the door was a terrazzo trough in which they washed.

Throughout her childhood Nete had toiled mucking out the stalls, but she had never been less than thorough with her hygiene, scrubbing her arms and hands with a stiff brush and the rest of her body with the sponge.

"You must be the cleanest kid in the world," Tage always used to say.

But here ablutions took place at the trough amid a tumult of activity that made it difficult to wash properly. The girls stood there all at once, stripped to the waist, washing frenziedly with only five minutes allocated. The same soap flakes as at Brejning that made their hair stiff like helmets and quite as undecorative. Moreover, they made a person smell worse than before they washed.

The rest of the day was marked out by the ringing of the bell, a set timetable, discipline. Nete hated the place and kept to herself as much as possible, the same way she'd done in her foster home. The advantage was that she could grieve over her fate in peace, and yet one all-consuming shadow prevailed: Sprogø was an island from which escape seemed inconceivable. Perhaps some friendly soul among the staff or a good friend among the girls might have made her time there more tolerable, but the women who watched over them were bossy and obnoxious, and Rita had enough on her own to keep her busy, wheeling and dealing and hustling her way up the ladder, eventually to rule the roost over her simple underlings like a regent upon a throne.

The bed opposite Nete's belonged to a feeble-minded girl who blathered on about little children. Jesus had given her a doll, and if she looked after it well enough she would one day be rewarded with a child of her own, she kept insisting. She was beyond all reason, but many of the other girls were bright enough. One of them wanted dearly to be able to read, but the staff poked fun at her, dismissing her wish as a "luxury" and packing her off to work.

Nete worked, too. She had asked to be in the stables, but her request was declined. While Rita spent her days in the washhouse, boiling clothes and larking about with the other girls, Nete was in the kitchen, peeling vegetables and scrubbing pots. When she tired and began to work more slowly, to pause and gaze out of the window, she became an easy target. The wardens and the other girls would pick on her. And when one girl threatened her with a knife and shoved her to the floor, Nete returned the provocation by hurling a scalding hot lid in her face and kicking a dent in a saucepan. And thus she was summoned to the matron's office for the first time.

The matron and her office were as one body. She aloof, the room cold and impersonal, its contents ordered systematically. Shelves of binders to one side, filing cabinets to the other. In these archives, human destinies were neatly arranged, ready to be taken out, assessed, and dismissed.

"They say you're causing trouble in the kitchen," the matron said, wagging a finger of admonishment.

"Then send me to the stables. I'll behave myself there," Nete replied, watching the flutter of the woman's hands on the desk. These hands were a window. Through them a person could read the matron's thoughts, said Rita. And she ought to know, from all the times she'd been called in herself.

Piercing eyes glared at her. "There's one thing you should know, Nete. We are not in the business of handing out privileges to make life easier. In spite of your wicked characters and feeble minds, our aim is to teach you that even such things as provide no pleasure in life may nonetheless be endured to great benefit. You are here in order that you may learn to get on as human beings and not as the animals you have hitherto emulated. Is that understood?"

Nete shook her head almost imperceptibly, barely registering the movement herself. But the matron was alert, and suddenly the fluttering hands were still.

"I might choose to interpret this reaction as impertinence, Nete, but for the moment I shall take it to be a sign that you are merely a dimwit, simple and empty-headed." She straightened up in her chair. Her upper body was plump. Most certainly not an object of desire for the majority of men.

"I shall place you in needlework instead. Some months earlier than is right and proper, but the kitchen doesn't want you any longer."

"Yes, Matron," said Nete, eyes fastened to the floor.

The sewing room could hardly be worse, she thought, but she was wrong.

The work itself was OK, though she was somewhat inept at lacemaking and hemming sheets. The worst part was being with the other girls. Stuck in a room with all their chatter and nonsense. One minute they could be the best of friends, the next they were at one another's throats.

Nete was aware that there were many things in life of which she was ignorant. Places and history, general knowledge. Having such a poor grasp of letters and numbers meant she was compelled to pay particular heed to whatever information came to her by word of mouth, and Nete had been around few people in her life who'd been able to capture her attention in this way.

She had become skilled in the art of not listening, but in the sewing room this was no longer an option. The inconsequential chatter that filled the room drove her up the wall. Ten hours, every day.

"Grethe, be a good girl and hand me the reel, would you?" one of them might say, only for Grethe to spit back: "What do you think I am, you brainless nitwit? Your housekeeper?"

And so it was that the mood could change from one moment to the next. And all but Nete and the girl on the receiving end would fall about laughing as invective flew through the air, until just as suddenly they made friends again and the chatter resumed, the same stories over and over.

But apart from the paucity of cigarettes, rumors of handsome men in boats, and terrifying tales of the surgeon and his scalpel over in Korsør, there was little to talk about.

"I'm going out of my mind here," she whispered to Rita in the court-yard one day before lunch.

Rita looked her up and down as though she were an item on a grocer's shelf. "I'll see to it we get a room together. Then I can cheer you up a bit."

That same evening Nete's roommate was injured in an accident and had to be sailed over to the hospital in Korsør. They said she'd got too close to the cauldron in the washhouse and it was her own fault. She was stupid and clumsy, and her head was empty save for silliness and her little doll-child.

They heard her screams all the way over in the sewing room. Nete didn't know what to think.

Rita moved into Nete's room, and laughter returned to her life, for a short time at least. Funny stories were even funnier when Rita told them, and she was good at collecting them. But Rita's company had its price, and Nete discovered what it was on the very first night.

She protested, but Rita was strong and forced her. And when Nete gasped with delight, she resigned herself to the situation.

"You keep your mouth shut, Nete. If this gets out, you're done for, understand?" Rita hissed. And Nete understood.

Rita was not only strong of body, but of mind as well, much more so than Nete. Though Rita loathed being on the island, she never seemed to doubt that some brighter future lay ahead. She was convinced that one day she would find a way to escape, and until she did, she knew better than anyone how to make her life comfortable.

She wangled the best jobs and was always first served at table. She smoked cigarettes behind the washhouse, cavorted with Nete by night, and was regent in the day.

"Where do you get those cigarettes from, anyway?" Nete asked once in a while, never receiving an answer until the night in spring when she caught Rita climbing out of bed, putting on her clothes, and unlatching the door, quiet as a mouse.

The alarms will go off any minute, Nete thought to herself. In all the doors was a little pin that popped out when the door was opened, activating a bell and summoning enraged staff to mete out frenzied blows and enforce a cooling-off in one of the contemplation rooms, as they called the punishment cells. But the bell did not ring, for Rita had jammed the mechanism.

When Rita disappeared along the corridor, Nete got up to see what she had done, discovering a piece of wire, ingeniously bent, that could be twisted into the pinhole when opening the door. It was simple as that.

It took Nete less than ten seconds to pull on her dress and sneak off down the corridor after her roommate, heart pounding in her chest. One creak of a floorboard, one squeak of an unoiled hinge and all hell would break loose. But Rita had shown the way.

Reaching the outer door, she found it unlocked, Rita again having circumvented security.

From a distance she saw the figure slip past the henhouse and down through the meadow, as though she knew every stone, every pool of mud in the darkness.

There was no doubt Rita was on her way to "the Retreat," as the girls called the little house farthest away, facing west. It was where the most well-behaved girls were allowed to spend their daytime hours in what was referred to as holiday week. In olden days it had been "The Plague House," a place where sailors with contagious diseases were sent into quarantine. As Nete discovered that night, it was a plague house still.

Several small boats with nets and fish crates were drawn up onto the shore and inside the Retreat flickered the faint light of a pair of paraffin lamps.

Nete crept forward with caution and peered in through the window. The sight that met her eyes astonished her. On one end of the little dining table were several cartons of cigarettes, and bent forward over the other end, hands flat against the surface, was Rita, her naked sex thrust back to allow the man at her rear to enter her with ease.

Behind him stood two other men, awaiting their turn. Their faces were flushed, wide eyes fixed on the sight before them. Three fishermen. And Nete knew the one on the right only too well.

It was Viggo Mogensen.

She recognized Viggo's voice on the entry phone immediately. This time her heart was beating fast as she listened to the footsteps echoing up the stairwell. When she opened the door, she knew right away it would be harder this time.

He greeted her in a deep, warm voice, stepping past her into the hall-way as though he were a familiar guest. He was still handsome, a man who could awaken feelings in a woman, just as he had done that day at the fair. His skin, once so weathered, now seemed finer, his hair gray and distinguished, softer-looking than before.

So soft, she thought she might run her fingers through it after she killed him.

30

November 2010

Carl awoke in a state of bewilderment, with no idea what day it was or why the bedroom reminded him of the bazaar in some concrete immigrant ghetto. Was that the waft of Assad's syrupy hot beverages and leftover shawarmas that drifted into his nostrils, along with a repugnant hint of doctor's surgeries?

He reached for his watch and discovered it was twenty-five past nine.

"Bollocks!" he spluttered, flinging back the duvet. Why hadn't anyone got him up? Now Jesper would be late. Him, too, for that matter.

It took him less than five minutes to remove the grime of the day before and don some reasonably clean clothes. "Get a move on, Jesper!" he hollered, pounding his stepson's door for the second time. "You're late, and it's your own fault."

"What's up, Carl? You off to church? Service isn't until ten," Morten ventured cautiously. He was standing at the stove in his pajamas and his favorite apron, looking like something out of a comic.

"Morning, Carl," came a voice from the front room. "Nice lie-in, eh?"

A breezy Mika clad in white from head to toe beamed a smile. In front of him, Hardy lay on his bed in the altogether, and on the cart at his side were two steaming bowls containing a liquid Mika was applying to the big man's limp body with facecloths.

"Just getting Hardy freshened up. He said he thought he smelled a bit off, so now we're giving him a combined camphor and menthol wash. That'll get you all fragrant again, eh, Hardy?"

"Morning, Carl," said the head at the end of the pale, gaunt frame.

Carl frowned, and at the same moment as Jesper roared from upstairs to the effect that Carl was the biggest idiot on earth, the realities of the Gregorian calendar dawned on him.

"It's Sunday, you bloody idiot!" he reprimanded himself, burying his head in his hands. "What's going on here, anyway? You opening a diner, Morten?" he inquired, with reference to the cooking smells that filled the house.

He closed his eyes and tried not to recall the downward-spiraling conversation he'd had with Mona the night before.

No, she was afraid he couldn't come over to hers, because she was going over to see Mathilde, she'd said.

"Mathilde?" he'd asked. "Who's Mathilde when she's at home?" And could have punched himself on the nose for asking such a moronic question.

"Mathilde? Mathilde happens to be my eldest daughter," she'd answered him with an iciness that had him writhing in his bed until daybreak. Bollocks. Had she ever actually told him her other daughter was called Mathilde? On the other hand, had he ever asked? Of course he hadn't. And now the damage was done.

He heard Morten twittering in the background but was oblivious to what he might actually be telling him. "Say that again?" he said after a moment.

"I said breakfast's ready, Carl," his lodger replied. "A big hearty meal for hungry tummies and a pair of boys madly in love." His eyelashes fluttered berserkly at the mere mention.

The lad was head over heels, Carl thought to himself. About time and all.

Morten arranged his culinary creations on the kitchen table. "There you go. Fried garlic on slices of smoked lamb sausage and goat's milk cheese. Vegetable juice and rose-hip tea with honey."

"Christ on a bike," Carl muttered under his breath, and thought about going back to bed.

"We're kicking off Hardy's exercise program today," Mika announced from the front room. "And we want it to hurt at some point, don't we, Hardy?"

"It'd be marvelous if it did," Hardy replied.

"Without building up any expectations, of course."

"I don't expect a thing; all I do is hope."

Carl turned toward him and gave him a thumbs-up. How could he stand here feeling sorry for himself with Hardy bearing up like that?

"You're to ring Vigga, Carl," said Morten.

OK. There was his answer.

Carl sat grumbling over his sausage, ignoring the sulking Jesper. This business with Vigga was no good. He'd actually given up thinking about it when the solution suddenly appeared to him in all its logical simplicity, a revelation that induced him to politely thank Morten for the meal, though he had seldom, if ever, tasted anything quite as disgusting in his life.

"I'm glad you rang," said Vigga. For once, she sounded tense. This was a woman who tended to proceed from the assumption that the world adapted itself to her needs rather than the other way round. But it wasn't his fault she was arranging to get married before she'd even got divorced.

"Have you spoken to the bank yet, Carl?" she asked, straight to the point.

"And a very good morning to you, too, Vigga. No, I haven't. Didn't need to, did I?"

"I see. So now you're going to tell me you can raise six hundred and fifty thousand without a bank loan, is that it? Hardy's going to help you out, is he?"

Carl laughed. The sarcasm would fizzle out in a minute.

"The figure you're asking's fine by me, Vigga. Half the equity in the house is yours."

"Well, Carl, I must say . . ." She was speechless.

Carl chuckled to himself. He wasn't finished yet.

"But apart from that, there are some accounts outstanding. I've added them up."

"Outstanding accounts?"

"Indeed, darling. You may still be living in the hippie era, but I'm afraid the rest of us no longer reside in a world of flowers and free love. This is the age of the ego, and these days everything's marked up in kroner and øre."

He savored the silence that ensued. To think she could be so quiet. It was like having two days off for Christmas.

"OK, listen. First there's the five or six years Jesper's been living on his own with me. Three years at upper secondary haven't been cheap, regardless of whether he got through or not. His college is costing, too. But let's just say we split the expense, eighty thousand a year. The court would find that reasonable."

"Wait a minute," she interjected. Now it sounded like the fight had started. "I've been paying for Jesper all along. Two thousand kroner a month."

Now it was Carl's turn to be taken aback.

"You *what*? I hope you've got receipts, because I've never seen a penny of it."

It was a killer return. She fell silent again.

"OK, Vigga. Looks like we're thinking the same thing. Your little cherub's been lining his pockets."

"The little sod," she hissed.

"All right, Vigga, listen. There's not much we can do about that now. We need to move on. You want to get hitched to this Gherkin bloke in Currystan, yeah? So what happens is I give you the six hundred and fifty grand, and you give me six times forty grand for Jesper's final year at comprehensive, his three years in upper secondary, and the two years he's got ahead of him at his prep college. If you don't pay for the college, then you just give me a hundred and fifty thousand and have him stay with you until he's ready for university or whatever. It's up to you."

The silence spoke volumes. So Gherkin and Jesper weren't the best of mates.

"And then there's your own assets. I've checked on the web and it says that shack of yours is valued at five hundred thousand, meaning two hundred and fifty would be mine. So all in all, I give you six hundred and fifty thousand, less two hundred and forty thousand, less two hundred and fifty thousand, which leaves one hundred and sixty thousand kroner, plus half the household effects, of course. You can come over and pick out what you want."

He glanced around at the furniture and almost had to stifle a laugh.

"Are you sure you've got your sums right?" she asked eventually.

"I'll pop a calculator in the post for you if Gherkin can't get his head around figures that big," he proffered. "On the upside, you won't have to pay the two thousand a month for Jesper. He's had all he's getting already. And I'll do my utmost to make sure he gets through his prep college. How does that sound?"

There was a pause so protracted he could almost hear the phone company rubbing its hands with glee.

"Not good," she said after a while. "The answer's no."

Carl shook his head. Of course it was.

"Do you remember that nice lawyer in Lyngby, the one who sorted out the paperwork when we bought the house?"

Vigga grunted.

"She's moved up the ladder since then, lawyer to the Supreme Court now. Send your claims to her. And remember, Vigga: Jesper's not my flesh and blood. So any trouble and he's yours, warts and all. The sums remain the same."

Again, money poured into the phone company's coffers. She'd put her hand over the receiver. He could hear voices, more wooly than usual.

"OK, Carl. Gurkamal says yes, and so do I."

God bless her little Sikh, and all strength to his beard.

"But we need to get one thing straight," she went on in a prickly tone. "Our arrangement regarding my mother. We agreed you were to visit her at least once a week, and you haven't. I want it in writing this time. If you don't go and see her fifty-two times a year, it'll cost you a grand every time you miss. Are you with me?"

Carl pictured his mother-in-law. Others suffering from dementia probably had few long-term prospects to speak of, but with Karla Alsing you never knew. This could turn into a crippling compromise.

"I'll need twelve weeks holiday in there," he ventured.

"*Twelve weeks?* You're not a member of parliament, you know. No one ordinary has twelve weeks holiday. You can have five like everyone else!"

"Ten," he rejoined.

"No way. Seven, and not a day longer."

"Eight, or it'll be that lawyer in Lyngby."

Another pause.

"OK, eight," Vigga eventually responded. "But at least an hour at a time, starting today. And as for household effects, I don't want any of your junk, thank you very much. Who'd want a Bang and Olufsen radio from 1982 when Gurkamal's got a Samsung surround-sound with six speakers? So no, you can forget about that."

———

This was brilliant. Hard to believe, almost. He'd sorted it all so he could get divorced from Vigga for a paltry one hundred and sixty thousand kroner. He wouldn't even have to borrow.

He looked at his watch and realized he could probably call Mona now, regardless of how late she'd been at Mathilde's.

She didn't sound like it was OK when eventually she answered.

"Did I wake you?" he asked.

"No, not me. You woke Rolf, though."

Who the fuck was Rolf? He felt like a whole year of Sunday depressions had suddenly been rolled into one. An instant nosedive, and now he was going down in a spin.

"Rolf?" he squeaked, a sense of dread looming. "Who's Rolf?"

"Don't worry yourself, Carl. We'll talk about it some other time."

Oh, they would, would they?

"What're you calling for, anyway? To say sorry for not knowing my daughter's name?"

Straight to the jugular. He may well have been given the lover's key, but who was to say she couldn't let someone else in with her own? Some bloke called Rolf, for instance. The glad tidings he'd intended to bring seemed not to matter all of a sudden.

Rolf. Bloody stupid name, he thought, endeavoring to suppress the image of a trim male body cavorting about on his turf.

"Actually, no. I just thought I'd let you know that Vigga and I have reached an agreement regarding the divorce. I called to tell you I'll soon be a free man."

"You don't say," she replied with little enthusiasm. "I'm happy for you, Carl."

Eventually, he ended the conversation and was left sitting on the edge of the bed, the mobile idle in his hand.

Talk about falling from a great height.

"What are you all miserable about, Carlo?" Jesper asked from the landing.

Of all the moronic questions the anemic teenager could have asked him, that was probably the worst.

"Your mother and I are getting divorced," he replied.

"Yeah, so what?"

"What do you mean, so what? Doesn't it mean anything to you, Jesper?"

"No, what the fuck's it got to do with me?"

"I'll tell you what it's got to do with you, young man. It means the two grand you've been lining your pockets with every month these past couple of years is history from this very second. *That's* what!"

Carl clapped his hands together so the lad could see the money box snap shut for himself.

Oddly enough, the otherwise so inventive adolescent found himself unable to come up with a single item of invective by which to return Carl's body blow, and had to resort to slamming every door in the house in his wake.

In his miserable state of discontent Carl reckoned he might as well get his chore out of the way and pay a visit on the woman he happily would soon be able to refer to as his former mother-in-law.

He noticed a young man in a gray-blue suit leaning against a car door in the parking lot, but apart from the guy turning his head away when Carl walked past, he seemed like any other young hopeful waiting for the concrete dwellings to release their fair maidens into the world for a bit of Sunday shenanigans. But Carl didn't give a shit about anything after he'd woken up Rolf, and Mona had actually had the nerve to have a go at him about it. How low could she get?

He drove the fifteen kilometers to the Bakkegården nursing home in

Bagsværd in a state of oblivion, totally unaware of the traffic. And when a caregiver let him in, he hardly even glanced at her.

"I'm here to see Karla Alsing," he said to another staff member in the dementia section.

"She's asleep," came the prompt reply. It suited him fine. "I'm afraid she's rather a strain at the moment," the prickly woman went on. "She smokes in her room, though she knows perfectly well it's not allowed. There's no smoking anywhere here. We don't know where she gets them from. Perhaps *you* might know?"

Carl pleaded his innocence. He hadn't been there for months.

"Well, anyway, we've just had to confiscate a pack of cigarillos. It really is a problem for us. Perhaps you could encourage her to take her nicotine pills when she gets the urge to smoke? The only damage *they* can do is to her purse."

"I'll tell her," said Carl, though he'd barely been listening.

"Hello, Karla," he said, without expecting a response. This former waitress through two ages of Copenhagen nightlife lay on her sofa with her eyes closed, skinny thighs bare for all to behold, in a kimono Carl had seen before, though never quite as open.

"Oh, darling," she replied to his surprise, opening her eyes and fluttering her eyelashes in a manner that would make Bambi seem fiendish.

"Erm, it's Carl, your son-in-law."

"My gorgeous, strapping policeman. Have you come to see me? How delightful!"

He was going to say something about coming to visit her more frequently, but as usual it was hard to get a word in edgeways in the company of the woman who'd taught Vigga to express herself in sentences so long, it was a wonder she didn't pass out from lack of oxygen.

"Would you like a cigarillo, Carl?" she asked, producing a pack of Advokat and a disposable lighter from behind a cushion.

She opened the pack with exaggerated professionalism and offered him one.

"You're not supposed to smoke in here, Karla. Where did you get them from?"

She leaned toward him, her kimono falling open to expose the rest of her former delights. Carl didn't know where to put himself.

"I provide services to the gardener," she said, digging an elbow into his side. "Of a personal nature, you know." And then the elbow again.

It was hard to know whether to make the sign of the cross or kneel down in unmitigated admiration of geriatric libido.

"No need to tell me to take my nicotine pills either. I know all about it."

She took out a pack of them and put one in her mouth.

"They started out giving me the chewing gum, but it didn't work. All it did was get stuck in my dentures so they kept falling out. Now I get the tablets instead."

She tapped a cigarillo from the pack and lit up. "And do you know what, Carl? They're nice to chew on while you're having a smoke."

31

September 1987

"**No, thanks. I don't** care for tea," said Viggo. Nete stood at the sideboard, about to pour.

She turned in consternation. What now?

"A cup of coffee wouldn't be amiss, though. Nothing like a couple of hours traveling to make a man drowsy and in need of a pick-me-up."

Nete looked at the clock. Damn it, this was the second time someone hadn't liked tea. Why on earth hadn't she foreseen it might happen? She'd just assumed everyone drank tea these days; it seemed to be the fad. Rose-hip tea, herbal tea, peppermint tea, there was no end to the varieties people consumed, which was a good thing indeed, because tea was ideal for masking the taste of the henbane. But then again, coffee was equally suited. Why hadn't she brought some Nescafé home from the supermarket while she was there?

She put her hand to her mouth so he wouldn't hear how deeply she was breathing. What to do now? There was no time to pop down to Nørrebrogade and pick up coffee beans, boil water, prepare the brew, and add the extract.

"A drop of milk would be nice, too," Viggo added from his chair. "Stomach's not what it has been," he said, and laughed the way he had done all those years ago, the way that had made Nete yield to him.

"Just a minute, then," Nete said, and scuttled out into the kitchen to put the kettle on.

She went to the pantry and realized she was right. She was completely out of coffee. She looked down at the toolbox, opened the lid, and stared at the hammer.

If she was going to use it, she'd have to strike hard. There would be blood. Perhaps even a lot. It didn't seem like an option.

For that reason, she picked up her purse resolutely from the counter, opened the front door of the apartment, and stepped across the landing to her neighbor's.

She pressed the bell firmly and waited impatiently, hearing only the little Lhasa apso growl behind the door. Of course, she could wrap a tea towel round the hammer and deliver a blow to the nape of his neck. It would almost certainly knock him unconscious, and then she could pour the henbane extract down his throat at leisure.

Nete nodded to herself. She didn't care for the thought of it, but it was what she would have to do. However, as she turned to go back inside and get it over with, the door opened behind her.

Nete had never really taken notice of her neighbor. Yet now, as they stood facing each other, she recognized the weary features and distrustful gaze behind the thick lenses of the woman's glasses.

It took a moment for Nete to realize the woman had no idea who she was. It was understandable. They'd only ever acknowledged each other once or twice while passing on the stairs, and the old biddy was seemingly blind as a bat.

"I do apologize. I'm your neighbor, Nete Hermansen," Nete ventured, her eyes on the dog that was growling at the woman's heel. "I'm afraid I've run out of coffee and I've a visitor who's only here briefly, so I was wondering if perhaps . . ."

"My neighbor's name is Nete Rosen," the woman interrupted, full of mistrust. "It says so on the door."

Nete took a deep breath. "Yes, I am sorry. Hermansen is my maiden name, you see. It's the name I've reverted to. And that's what's on the door now."

As the woman bent forward to peer at the evidence, Nete raised her eyebrows, brightening her countenance, endeavoring to appear trustworthy, as a proper neighbor should. But inside, desperation was tearing her apart.

"I'll pay, of course," she proffered, controlling her breathing and opening her purse to produce a twenty-kroner note.

"I'm sorry, but I haven't any coffee beans," the woman replied.

Nete forced a smile, thanked her, and turned back to her apartment. It would have to be the hammer.

"I do have some instant, though," came the voice from behind.

"Be with you in a sec," Nete called from the kitchen, as she poured milk into a little jug.

"Lovely place you've got here, Nete," said Viggo from the doorway.

Nete almost dropped the coffee cup as he reached out to take it. He wasn't supposed to have it yet. Not before she'd put the henbane in.

She held on to the cup and stepped past him.

"No, let me. Come in and sit down," she said. "We've a lot to do before the lawyer gets here."

She heard him lumber along behind her and pause in the doorway of the living room.

She glanced back at him and felt herself jump as he bent down toward the door's bottom hinge to investigate something that seemed to be stuck there. She saw right away what it was. So that was where Tage's jacket had been torn.

"What might that be?" he inquired with a smile, holding up the shred of cloth.

Nete shook her head slightly, then put the milk jug down on the sideboard next to the decanter of henbane extract. A couple of seconds later the coffee was spiked. The milk could come afterward.

"Would you like sugar?" she asked, turning to face him with the cup in her hand.

He was only a pace away. "Hope you didn't tear a skirt or something?"

She stepped toward him, trying to look puzzled.

Then she laughed softly. "Goodness, no. Whoever would go about in something like that?"

He frowned, much to her concern.

Then he stepped into the light of the windows and considered the strip of material for a moment. Rather too long, rather too intensely.

The cup in her hand began to tinkle on its saucer.

He turned to face her, pinpointing the source of the sound.

"You seem nervous, Nete," he said, noticing her trembling hand. "Anything the matter?"

"No, not at all. Why should there be?"

She put the cup down on the little table next to the armchair. "Sit down, Viggo. We need to talk about why I've asked you to come here today, and I'm afraid time is rather short. Drink your coffee and I'll tell you what's going to happen."

Would he ever stop pondering that piece of cloth?

He looked at her. "It seems to me you're out of sorts, Nete. Am I right?" he asked, tipping his head to one side inquiringly as Nete gestured for him to take a seat.

Was it really that obvious? She would have to take better control of herself.

"Yes, well," she replied. "I'm not in the best of health, as you know."

"I'm sorry to hear it," he said without feeling, handing her the scrap of material. "I'd say that was a piece of someone's breast pocket. How on earth would a piece of cloth from a breast pocket get stuck on the bottom hinge of a door?"

She took it in her hand and examined it more closely. What was she supposed to say?

"I think I do have an idea where it might be from, though it puzzles me, too."

She looked up at him anxiously. What's going on? How much does he know? she wondered.

Viggo frowned. "You seemed a bit surprised for a moment there, Nete."

He took back the fragment of cloth and seemed almost to be gauging its weight in his hand, fixing his eyes on her as the furrows in his brow deepened. "I came half an hour early today, Nete. Stood under the chestnuts and had a couple of smokes while I waited. And do you know what I saw?"

She shook her head, but the lines on his forehead remained.

"I saw a fat man come waddling along in the cheapest-looking suit I've ever seen. And do you know what? I'd say it was the exact same material as this. Rather a coincidence, don't you think? What's more, he rang your entry phone. A man dressed in this very same cloth." He held up the scrap in his hand. "Don't you think that's odd, Nete?"

He nodded as if to confirm his own suspicion. And then his expression changed. She realized his next question could be fatal.

"We were told to arrive on the dot today. Because of other appointments, your letter said. I took that to mean you were expecting other visitors. Was the man in this ugly suit one of them, by any chance? And if so, how come I didn't see him leave again? He wouldn't still be here, would he?"

It was clear to her that the slightest untoward reaction would provide him with the answer to his question, so all she did was smile, calmly getting to her feet and going out into the kitchen, where she opened the pantry, bent down to the toolbox, and took out the hammer.

She had no time to wrap it in a tea towel before he appeared behind her and repeated his question.

It was her signal. Seamlessly, she spun round and brought the hammer down hard against his temple with a loud crunch.

He sank to the floor, out cold. There wasn't much blood. When she realized he was still breathing, she went back into the living room and fetched his coffee.

He spluttered slightly as she opened his mouth and poured the warm liquid inside him. But that was all.

For a moment she sat and looked at him. If only Viggo had never existed, everything would have been different.

But now he existed no more.

The shame and disgust at what she had witnessed that night at the Retreat weighed so heavily upon her that eventually Nete was unable to conceal it any longer.

Rita asked her a few times what was wrong, but Nete merely recoiled. Only in the darkness underneath her duvet when Nete was drifting away into sleep was there any contact between them. The kind of contact Rita demanded in return for her friendship.

As if Nete needed it any longer.

A single glance during the slaughtering was what gave her away.

Some of the field girls in overalls had brought one of the pigs up to the courtyard to be butchered, and Rita came out of the washhouse to see what was going on. Nete, too, appeared from inside to get some fresh air into her lungs. Rita noticed her presence and turned her head toward her, their eyes meeting across the yard amid the squeals of the distressed animal.

It was one of those days the sewing room had got Nete in the dumps. All she could do was sob, and her longing for a better life made her bitter and angry. Therefore the look she sent Rita was unguarded, and the look Rita gave in return was alert and full of mistrust.

"So, you are going to tell me what's wrong," Rita demanded in their room that night.

"You fuck men for cigarettes, I've seen it with my own eyes. And I know what you use this for." She plunged her hand under Rita's mattress and pulled out the piece of wire Rita used to silence the alarm bell.

If Rita was at all capable of being shocked, she was now. "If I hear you've told anyone about this, you'll pay." She jabbed an index finger at her. "If you ever betray me or drop me in the shit, I'll make sure you regret it for the rest of your life, understand?" she warned, eyes flashing with rage.

And so it came to be.

Rita made good on her threat, and the consequences proved immense for them both. Now, more than a quarter of a century later, Nete had finally exacted her revenge and Rita and Viggo sat dead in the airtight room of her apartment.

Twine around their waists and their sparkling eyes now sightless.

32

November 2010

Curt Wad was worried. Ever since the police had been to see Herbert Sønderskov, Mie Nørvig, and Louis Petterson, everything seemed to be going wrong. The safety net they had meticulously established over a number of years was being unraveled faster than he had ever thought possible.

Curt had always been keenly aware that his activities demanded the utmost care and discretion, and for that reason he had felt convinced that as soon as any threat arose it would be a small matter for his people to nip it in the bud. What he had not envisaged was that events from a distant past would return to haunt him.

But what were these two policemen after? Something to do with a missing person, Herbert Sønderskov had said. Why on earth had he not questioned Herbert sufficiently on the matter while he had the chance? Was it a first sign of dementia? He certainly hoped not.

And now Herbert and Mie seemed to have vanished from the face of the earth. Herbert had not sent a single photo of where they were, as Curt had instructed him to, and his failure to comply could mean only one thing.

When it all boiled down, Curt ought to have seen it coming. He should have known that the officious little pen-pusher wouldn't have the guts to do what was necessary when the time came.

He arrested his train of thought and shook his head. There he went again, letting his mind run away with him. He never used to succumb like that. He would have to keep himself in check. For who was to say Herbert hadn't had the courage to do away with Mie? After all, there were so many other ways to end the problem for good, besides the method he had demanded. Perhaps one day the decomposed remains of Herbert and Mie would be found, hand in hand in a ditch by the side of a road. Was suicide not the best option in their case? The idea was by no means foreign to Curt himself, certainly not if this chaos should escalate and begin to approach closer to home. If it should come to that, he knew plenty of painless ways a person could shuffle off the coil.

What would it matter? He was an old man, and Beate was ill. His sons were well established and could look after themselves. Wasn't the most important thing the Purity Party? Defeating debauchery and the degeneration that threatened Danish society? Was this not his life's work? The party, and The Cause?

It was his moral obligation to continue safeguarding these values in the short time that was left to him. To see his work come to nothing would be almost like never having existed. Like leaving the world without progeny or having made his mark. All the ideas and visions would have been to no avail. All the risks and honorable ambitions would be in vain. It was a thought he found unbearable, and it readied him for battle. No means would be shunned to prevent these police investigations from blocking the path of the Purity Party into parliament. None.

That was why he now took precautions and set off the chain of text messages that compelled members of The Cause to follow up on the decision of the meeting after the national congress. Everything was to be burned! Files, referrals, correspondence, the lot! The documentation of fifty years of work was to go up in smoke that very day.

He had no cause for concern as regards his own archives. His files were safe in the strong room in the outbuilding. In the event of his death, there were instructions to Mikael as to what to do with them. He had taken care of it.

Elsewhere, he had set the incineration in motion, and a good thing, too, he told himself later that same Saturday afternoon as his landline phone rang.

It was Caspersen.

"I've spoken to our contact at Station City. He's given us some details about the two detectives who were poking around at Nørvig's place. Not encouraging, I'm afraid."

He explained that Carl Mørck and his assistant, Hafez el-Assad, were attached to what was called Department Q at Police Headquarters. El-Assad was apparently not trained with the police, but was gifted with remarkable intuition, talked about in police districts throughout the capital region.

Curt shook his head. An Arab! How he despised the thought of a wog nosing about in his affairs. The very idea!

"According to our contact, Carl Mørck's Department Q, or the Department for Cases Requiring Special Scrutiny, to use its more unsettling official title, may prove to be something of a threat. They specialize in cold cases and, though our contact was loath to admit it, the unit appears to be more efficient than most. The bright spot, however, is that they seem to work mostly on their own, so other departments are likely to be in the dark as to what they're up to at any given time."

The information threw Wad into a state of alert, not least the fact that the unit's specialty was apparently digging around in dirt from the past.

Caspersen went on, explaining that he had inquired into how vulnerable these two men might be and had been told by the man from City that while Carl Mørck had the shadow of a somewhat nasty case hanging over him, a case that in its worst scenario could end up costing him a suspension, it now appeared to be in competent hands at Police HQ and for that reason would be difficult to manipulate from outside. Even if it were possible, it would take at least a week to effect a suspension, which was time they probably didn't have. Alternatively, they might delve into

Hafez el-Assad's terms of employment and find something useful to them there, but that, too, would take time. Again, it was time they didn't have.

Caspersen was right. If they were to act, they would have to do so now.

"Ask our man at City to e-mail me a couple of photos of them both," Wad said, and then hung up.

The e-mail arrived within the hour. He opened it and studied the faces. Two men smirking as if the photographer had just cracked a stupid joke, but it could also have been arrogance. They were as different as night and day. Both of somewhat indeterminable age, though Carl Mørck was probably older than his assistant. He found it hard to tell with Arabs.

"You clowns are not going to stop us," he said out loud, slapping the palm of his hand against the screen just as his secure mobile began to chime.

It was their driver.

"Yes, Mikael, what is it? Did you get hold of Nørvig's archive?"

"I'm afraid not, Mr. Wad."

Curt frowned. "What's that supposed to mean?"

"Two men in a dark blue Peugeot 607 got there first. Police, I reckon. You can spot them a mile off."

Curt shook his head. This couldn't be happening. "Was one of them an Arab?" he asked, already sure of the answer.

"Looked like it, yeah."

"Describe them to me."

He scrutinized the features on the computer screen as Mikael reeled them off. He had a keen eye, Mikael. It all matched. It was a disaster.

"How much did they take away with them?"

"Well, I can't say for sure. But the four filing cabinets you told me about were empty."

More bad news.

"OK, Mikael. We'll need to get it all back somehow. And if we can't, we shall have to make sure our two friends meet with an accident. Understood?"

"I'll tell the lads, make sure they're ready."

"Good. Find out where our two friends live and keep them under surveillance round the clock so we can go in at the first opportunity. Call me for the go-ahead when the time comes."

Caspersen appeared at Curt Wad's home a couple of hours later. Wad had never seen him so unnerved. This unscrupulous lawyer who wouldn't hesitate to take the last fifty kroner from an impoverished single mother of five and hand it over to her violent ex-husband.

"I'm afraid that as long as Mie Nørvig and Herbert Sønderskov aren't here to personally file a complaint with the police, our chances of recovering the stolen archives are rather slim, Curt. I don't suppose Mikael took pictures of the offense as it was being committed?"

"No, he got there too late for that. Otherwise he'd have given them to me, don't you think?"

"What about the neighbor? Could she give us anything to go on?"

"Only that it was two officers from Copenhagen. But she'll be able to identify them, of course, if needs be. They don't exactly blend in, as far as I can make out."

"Quite. But before we get as far as retrieving these documents, the whole lot will have vanished into the depths of Police HQ, we can be sure of that. We've no direct evidence of these two being responsible for the break-in."

"Fingerprints?"

"Out of the question," came Caspersen's reply. "They were at Nørvig's house the day before on legitimate business. As far as I'm aware, science hasn't proceeded as far as to be able to pinpoint fingerprints in time."

"Well, it looks like our way out of this will need to be rather more dramatic than would be ideal. I've already set the wheels in motion. All I need now is to give the signal."

"Are you talking about killing people, Curt? If that's the case, I'm afraid I can no longer be part of this conversation."

"Calm down, Caspersen. I'll keep you out of it, don't worry. But you should be aware that things may become rather violent for a time and that you should prepare yourself to take over the helm."

"What on earth do you mean?"

"Just as I say. If this all ends the way it looks like it might, then you will have a political party on your hands, as well as an estate to administer here on Brøndbyøstervej. No traces will be left, and in the nature of things I shall be unable to take the stand in any court of law, if it should come to that. *Alea iacta est.*"

"God forbid, Curt. Let's just concentrate on recovering Nørvig's archives first, yes?" Caspersen replied, following the golden rule of all lawyers: what was never discussed had never occurred. "I'll contact our man at Station City. I think we can assume the files are at Police Headquarters as we speak. Department Q is in the basement, so I've been informed. There's no one down there at night, so I'm sure it wouldn't be too hard for another officer to remove Nørvig's archive material."

Curt looked at him with a sense of relief. If Caspersen was right, they'd pretty much be back in business.

It was a positive state of mind from which he was almost immediately wrenched when the phone rang and an incensed Wilfrid Lønberg informed him that the two policemen had appeared at his property.

Curt turned the speaker on so Caspersen could hear what was being said. He had almost as much at stake here as Wad himself.

"They just turned up, completely without warning. And there I was, burning documents. If I hadn't been quick and chucked the whole lot on the fire, we'd have been in a terrible pickle. Watch out for them, Curt.

Before you know it, they'll be on your doorstep, or at someone else's in the front line. You must issue a warning so people are prepared."

"What did they want?"

"I've no idea. I think they were just trying to put the wind up me. Which worked rather well, I can tell you. Now they *know* something's going on."

"I'll set off a new text-message chain right away," said Caspersen, withdrawing slightly.

"They're thorough, Curt. I get the feeling it's you they're after primarily, but believe me, they know more than is good for us about other things besides. Not that they were specific about anything, but they did mention Benefice and someone called Nete Hermansen. Does that ring a bell? I understood they were on their way to Nørrebro to have a word with her. They may be there by now."

Curt rubbed his brow. The room felt stuffy all of a sudden.

"Yes, I know who Nete Hermansen is, though I must say I'm rather surprised she's still alive. Nevertheless, that can be remedied. Let's wait and see what happens during the next twenty-four hours. I think you may be right in that they're mostly interested in me. I don't know why, but then I don't need to either."

"How do you mean? Surely you need to know that?"

"What I mean is simply that everything might all be over before we know it. You look after the Purity Party and let me take care of the rest."

After Caspersen had left, clearly weighed down by the latest developments, Curt called Mikael again and told him that if they got a move on they might just be able to intercept the two police officers at Peblinge Dossering and tail them from there.

An hour and a half later Mikael called him back to inform him that they'd been too late, but now they had a man posted in the parking lot outside Carl Mørck's address, and Mørck had just arrived home.

Hafez el-Assad, however, had given them the slip. At any rate, the flat on Heimdalsgade that was registered as his home address was completely empty.

Early on Sunday morning Curt called the doctor. Beate's heavy sighs and irregular breathing next to him in bed seemed to have grown so much more pronounced during the last couple of hours.

"Well, Curt," said the doctor, whom Curt knew to be an excellent GP from Hvidovre. "As your own professional opinion already suggests, from what you were telling me on the phone, I fear your wife doesn't have much time left. Her heart's worn out, it's as simple as that. My guess is we're talking days, perhaps even hours now. You're quite sure you don't want me to call an ambulance?"

He shrugged. "What good would it do?" he said. "No, I think I prefer to be alone with her to the end. But thanks, all the same."

When he'd gone and they were alone together he lay down on the bed beside her and reached for her hand. This little hand that had caressed his cheek so many times. This dear little hand.

He looked out across the balcony at the dawn and wished for a moment that he believed in a god. He would say a quiet prayer for his beloved in her final hours. Three days earlier he had felt prepared for this inevitable development, ready to live on in its aftermath. Now everything had changed.

He glanced at the bottle of sleeping pills. Potent and easy to swallow. It would take twenty seconds at most. He smiled to himself. And a minute to fetch a glass of water, of course.

"Do you think it would be best for me to take them now, my love?" he whispered, and gave her hand a squeeze. If only she had been able to answer him. He felt so alone.

He stroked her thin hair gently. How often he had admired her hair when she sat brushing it in front of the mirror, the light giving it a sheen. So quickly life had passed.

"Oh, Beate. I loved you with all my heart. You were the light of my life. If I could live it over again with you, I would. Every second. If only you could wake up for just a moment so that I might tell you, my dearest."

Then he turned toward her and snuggled up to the faintly breathing, irrevocably expiring, and most delightful body he had ever known.

It was almost twelve when he woke up to the ringing of a phone that suddenly stopped.

He lifted his head slightly and saw without relief that Beate was still breathing. Couldn't she just die without him having to watch?

He shook his head at the thought.

"Pull yourself together, Curt," he told himself. Beate wasn't going to die alone, no matter what. He refused to let it happen.

He looked through the French window that led out onto the balcony. The sky was November gray and the wind whistled in the bare branches of the cherry plum trees.

Not a good day, he thought, reaching for both his mobile phones.

There were no new messages on either, but then he pressed the display of the landline and saw a number he didn't recognize.

He activated the call-back function, only to sense immediately that he shouldn't have.

"Søren Brandt," said a voice he had no wish to hear.

"We two have nothing to discuss," Wad said brusquely.

"I wouldn't be so sure if I were you. Can I ask if you've read my blog about Hans Christian Dyrmand's suicide."

The man at the other end waited a moment to see if any answer would be forthcoming. It wasn't.

Bloody swine. Bloody Internet.

"I've spoken to Dyrmand's widow," the bastard of a journalist went on. "She's most perplexed by what happened. Would you have any comment on that?"

"None whatsoever. I hardly knew the man. And you listen to me now. I'm in grief at the moment. My wife is on her deathbed. So if you'd be decent enough to leave me in peace, we can speak another day."

"I'm sorry to hear it. I was going to tell you that information has come my way about you being in the police spotlight in connection with a missing persons case. But I have a feeling you're not going to comment, is that right?"

"What missing persons case?" He had absolutely no idea what it was about, and this was the second time it had been brought to his attention.

"That'd be a matter between you and the police, wouldn't it? But as far as I understand it, they're rather eager to exchange information with me about The Cause and its obviously criminal activities. So my last question for now is whether you and Wilfrid Lønberg intend to make similar activities, such as forced abortions, part of the Purity Party's official platform?"

"Enough slander! I'll sort the matter out with the police, make no mistake. And if you publish so much as a word without documentation, I promise you I shall make sure you end up paying dearly."

"OK. Documentation's not a problem, actually, but thanks for your comments. It's always nice to have a couple of quotes."

And then he hung up. *He* hung up. Curt Wad was fuming.

What kind of documentation was he referring to? Had knowledge of Nørvig's archives really reached that far already? This was going to be Brandt's downfall. Bloody lowlife.

He picked up the secure mobile and dialed Caspersen's number.

"What's the status on our foray into Police HQ, Caspersen?"

"Not good, I'm afraid. Our man got in, no problem, but as soon as he went down to the basement he ran into Hafez el-Assad. It seems he sleeps down there."

"Damn it! He's guarding Nørvig's archive, is that it?"

"It looks like it, yes."

"Why didn't you call and inform me?"

"I did, Curt. I called you several times this morning. Not this number, the other one."

"I'm not using my iPhone at the moment. For security reasons."

"But I called your landline, too."

Curt reached out and pressed the display. He was right. There were several unanswered calls before Søren Brandt's. Caspersen had been calling every twenty minutes since eight o'clock.

Had he really slept so soundly next to Beate? Would it be the last time in their lives together?

He hung up and looked at Beate as he thought about what to do.

All three had to be eliminated, there was no other way. The Arab, Mørck, and Brandt. He would decide about Nete Hermansen later. She wasn't nearly as dangerous as the others.

He dialed Mikael's number on the secure mobile.

"Can we trace Søren Brandt?"

"I should think so. He's staying at a weekend cabin in Høve at the moment."

"How do we know?"

"Because we've been keeping an eye on him ever since he kicked up a fuss at the national congress."

Curt smiled. It was the first time that day.

"All right, Mikael, well done. What about this Carl Mørck? Do we know what he's up to?"

"We do, yeah. Right now he's on his way across the parking lot where he lives. Our man's on his tail. If anyone knows what he's doing, he does.

Former Police Intelligence guy. We still don't know where the Arab is, though."

"In that case I can enlighten you. He's in the basement of Police Head-quarters. You can put a man outside the mail terminal over the road so we know when he leaves. And Mikael?"

"Yeah?"

"When everyone's asleep at Carl Mørck's place tonight, an accident will happen. Are you with me?"

"A fire?"

"Yes. Starting in the kitchen. Make it explosive. A blaze with lots of smoke. Tell our people to make sure they get out of there without being seen."

"That'll be me, I reckon."

"Good. Cover your back and get out quickly."

"Will do. What about Søren Brandt?"

"Put your dogs on him, and do it now."

33

November 2010

Carl was woken by someone shaking him hard.

He opened his eyes and hazily registered a figure bent over him. He tried to get up, only to feel dizzy and suddenly and inexplicably find himself on the floor by the side of his bed. Something was wrong, drastically wrong.

To his bewilderment he felt the rush of wind from an open window and smelled gas.

"I've got Jesper awake now," someone shouted from the landing. "He's vomiting. What should I do?"

"Turn him onto his side. Have you opened the window?" the dark figure at Carl's side shouted back.

He felt a hard slap against his cheek, then another. "Carl, look at me. Focus. Are you OK?"

He nodded, but wasn't sure.

"We need to get you downstairs, Carl. There's still too much gas up here. Can you manage to walk?"

He got up slowly, staggered onto the landing, and descended the stairs unsteadily. It felt like he was falling into a hole. Not until he was sitting on a chair in front of his garden door did the blur of outlines become more distinct, enough to start making sense.

He peered up at Morten's boyfriend, who was standing beside him.

"What the fuck?" he mumbled. "You still here? Have you moved in?"

"If he has, we should all be very grateful," came the dry comment from Hardy's bed.

Carl turned his head, still woozy. "What happened?"

There was a commotion as Morten lugged Jesper down the stairs. Carl's stepson was looking even worse than he'd done the time he came home from two weeks' partying in Kos.

Mika gestured toward the kitchen. "Someone's been in the house. Whoever it was doesn't like us."

Carl got to his feet with difficulty and went to see.

He saw the gas cylinder immediately, one of the new ones made of hard plastic. It was a kind he knew he didn't have. He used the old yellow ones for the gas barbecue; there was nothing wrong with them. And what was it doing there, anyway, with a length of rubber tubing attached to the regulator?

"Where'd that come from?" he asked, still too befuddled to remember the name of the man standing next to him.

"It wasn't here at two this morning when I looked in on Hardy," the guy answered.

"Hardy?"

"Yeah, he had a reaction to his treatment yesterday. Hot flushes, headaches. It's a good sign he responds so strongly to the stimuli. Plus it almost certainly saved our lives."

"No, you did that, Mika," Hardy called out from his bed.

That was it, yeah. Mika.

"Explain," Carl commanded, policeman's instinct kicking in.

"I've been looking in on Hardy every two hours since yesterday evening. I'll keep on over the next couple of days so I can observe exactly how he's reacting. Anyway, half an hour ago my alarm went off and I woke up to a smell of gas. It was very strong in the basement and almost knocked me out when I came up here to the ground floor. I turned off the flow from the cylinder and opened all the windows, and then I noticed there was a little saucepan on the stove with smoke coming off it. When I looked closer I could see it was almost dry, apart from a little bit of olive oil in the bottom and a scorched piece of paper towel. That was where the smoke was coming from."

He gestured toward the kitchen window. "I chucked it out as quick as I could. A moment later and the paper would have caught fire."

Carl nodded to his colleague from Fire Investigation, Erling Holm. Strictly speaking this wasn't his patch, but Carl didn't want to get the Hillerød police involved, and Erling lived only five kilometers away in Lynge.

"Very nasty, this, Carl. Twenty, thirty seconds more and that paper towel would have burst into flame and ignited the gas. And as far as I can gauge from the weight of the cylinder, a lot had already seeped out. With that regulator and the wide-bore tubing on the nozzle it'd have taken about twenty minutes at most, I reckon." He shook his head. "That's why whoever did this didn't turn the stove up full whack. He wanted the house full of gas before it all went off."

"And we needn't hazard a guess at the outcome, eh, Erling?"

"Put it this way. Department Q would have been advertising for a new boss."

"Big explosion, then?"

"Yes and no. But effective, certainly. All your rooms and everything in them would have gone up in flames at once."

"But Jesper and Hardy and I would have died from the gas before then, right?"

"Hardly. It's not poisonous like that. Might have given you a headache, though." He laughed. Funny buggers, these fire investigators. "You'd have burned to death in an instant, and those in the basement wouldn't have been able to get out. The most fiendish bit is it's by no means certain our boys would've been able to determine any crime had taken place. We'd most likely have localized the source of the blaze as the gas cylinder and the saucepan on the stove, but it could easily have looked like an accident. Lack of due care and attention. We see it all the time these days, now everyone's got a barbecue. To be honest, I could imagine whoever it was getting off scot-free."

"He bloody won't, not if I can help it."

"Any idea who might have done it, Carl?"

"Yeah. Someone with a pick gun. There's a lot of little marks on the front-door lock. Apart from that, I've no idea."

"Suspicions?"

"My life's full of them."

Carl gave his thanks and assured Erling that everyone in the house was OK before doing a quick round of the neighbors to find out if anyone had seen anything. Most of them were annoyed. Who wouldn't be at five in the morning? But all in all, the majority seemed genuinely shocked, though no one was able to identify any suspects.

It took less than an hour for Vigga to turn up, her hair all over the place and a reluctant Gurkamal at her side with his turban, big white teeth, and extravagant beard.

"Oh, my God," she gasped. "Tell me Jesper's all right."

"He's fine. Puked on the sofa and all over Hardy's bed, but apart from that he's right as rain. First time in ages I've heard him say he wanted his mum, though."

"Oh, goodness, the little dear." Not a word as to how Carl was doing. The difference between soon-to-be ex-husband and son was obvious indeed.

He heard her fussing over her offspring in the background when the doorbell rang.

"If that's him back with another gas cylinder, tell him we've still got some left in the first one," Hardy called out from his bed. "He can come back next week instead."

What on earth's Mika been doing to the bloke? Carl mused, opening the door.

The girl standing in front of him was pale from lack of sleep. She had dark shadows under her eyes, a ring through her lip, and was sixteen years old at most.

"Hi," she said. She jerked a thumb over her shoulder toward his neighbor Kenn's house, and the way she was squirming with embarrassment she seemed almost in danger of dislocating something.

"I'm going out with Peter from over there and we'd been at a party at the youth club. I was sleeping at his house because I live in Blovstrød and there's no buses at that time of night. We got back a few hours ago and Kenn came down to look in on us in the basement after you'd been over to ask if anyone had noticed anything strange going on around your house last night. He told us what had happened and we said we'd seen something when we got home, so Kenn wanted me to come over and tell you about it."

Carl raised an eyebrow. Clearly, she wasn't as dozy as she looked, with all those words coming out of her.

"OK. What did you see, then?"

"There was a man at your door when we walked past. I asked Peter if he knew him, but his mind was on other things." She giggled.

Carl went on. "What was he like, this man? Did you get a look at him?"

"Yeah, he was standing in the light by the door. It looked like he was messing with the lock, but he didn't turn round so I didn't see him from the front."

Carl felt his shoulders droop at least a couple of degrees.

"He was pretty tall, quite well built as far as I could make out, and his clothes were all dark. He was wearing a coat or a big anorak, something like that. And a black knitted beanie like Peter's. I noticed his hair, though. Very fair hair, it was, almost white. And there was like a gas bottle of some sort on the ground at his side."

Almost white. The information on its own was nearly enough. If Carl was right, Curt Wad's flaxen-haired gorilla, the man they'd seen in Halsskov, was skilled at more than just driving a van.

"Thanks," he said. "You're very observant, and you've been a great help indeed. You did right, coming over."

She squirmed with embarrassment again.

"Did you notice if he was wearing gloves, by any chance?"

"Oh, I forgot about that," she said, momentarily suspending her physical contortions. "He was, yeah. The kind with holes at the knuckles."

Carl nodded. In that case he needn't bother getting the lock cylinder checked for prints. The issue was whether they could trace the rather special-looking regulator, but he doubted very much it would lead them anywhere, for there was bound to be loads of them knocking about.

"Right, if everything's OK here, I'll be off to HQ then," he announced to the assembled household a moment later, only for Vigga to grab hold of his sleeve.

"Sign this before you go. There's one copy for you, one for the regional state administration, and one for me," she informed him, laying all three out on the kitchen counter. *Agreement on Division of Property*, it read at the top.

He read through it quickly. It was exactly as they had agreed the day before. Saved him doing it himself.

"That's fine, Vigga. It's all in there, I can see that. Right down to the bit about visiting your mother. I'm sure the authorities will be pleased to know you've given me eight weeks' holiday in that respect. Very generous." He laughed sarcastically and signed his name next to her own spidery hand.

"Then there's the divorce petition," she said, shoving another document in front of him. He signed it without hesitation.

"Thanks, lover." She almost sniffled.

It was nice of her, but the word only made him think of Mona's Rolf, which wasn't the most desirable association. He was a long way off coming to terms with the hurt. Mona wasn't just anybody. It would take an age for him to get over it.

He snorted. *Lover.* A bit over the top for a parting salute, he thought, considering how stormy their marriage had turned out.

He gave the documents to a smiling Gurkamal, who bowed before extending his hand.

"Thank you for your wife," he said in what Carl presumed was a Sikh accent. It was a deal.

Vigga beamed. "Now that all the formalities have been dealt with, I can tell you I'm moving in with Gurkamal above his shop next week."

"Hope it's warmer than the last place," Carl rejoined.

"Oh, now you mention it, I sold it yesterday for six hundred thousand. That's a hundred thousand more than we reckoned it was worth in our agreement. I thought I might keep the change, if that's all right with you."

Carl was lost for words. That Gherkin of hers had certainly taught her a thing or two about business. He was quicker than a camel could shite, as Assad most likely would have put it.

"Good thing I bumped into you, Carl," said Laursen, on the stairs of the rotunda back at HQ. "Come upstairs a minute, eh?"

"Actually, I was on my way up to see Marcus Jacobsen."

"I've just taken him his lunch. He's in a meeting. Everything all right?"

"Fine," Carl replied. "Apart from the fact that it's Monday, I just got fleeced by my soon-to-be ex, my girlfriend's shagging someone else, we all got poisoned with gas last night, and the house nearly blew up. Add to that the trouble and strife this place is giving me, and I couldn't be better. Even got rid of that diarrhea."

"That's all right, then," said Laursen, three steps ahead of him. He'd heard fuck all.

"Listen," he said eventually as they sat in the back room behind the kitchen, surrounded by fridges and stocks of vegetables. "There's been a development in the nail-gun case. That photo of you and Anker together with the bloke who got done in. They've had various labs analyze it, and I can put your mind at rest and tell you most of them reckon it's a digital composite, put together from various sources.

"Of course it is, that's what I've been saying all along. It's a setup. Maybe someone I wound up the wrong way once. You know how vengeful some of these bastards can be. They can sit around in prison for years, working out how to get their own back one day. Stands to reason it has to happen once in a while. But I can tell you this much: I never knew this Pete Boswell they're trying to get me mixed up with."

Laursen nodded. "The photo's got no halftone dots. It's like all the tiniest elements are all merged together. I've never seen anything like it."

"What does that mean?"

"It means you can't see the join, basically. It may be several photos edited together and then photographed incrementally using a Polaroid camera, for instance, with the Polaroid image eventually being photographed with an analog camera with regular film in it and then developed. Or it might have been blurred in a digital-image editing application before being printed. They don't know for sure. The paper itself doesn't tell us anything either."

"Sounds like gibberish to me."

"Yeah, but the possibilities are endless these days. Or, more precisely, two years ago when Pete Boswell was still among the living."

"All right, so everything's turning out for the better, is that what you're saying?"

"Well, that's what I wanted to talk to you about." Laursen handed Carl a beer, which he declined. "They've not reached any conclusion yet, and the fact of the matter is that not *everyone* out there at the labs thinks it's a fake. At the end of the day, what I just told you proves nothing, only that it's all a bit suspect. But from what I've heard, most of them reckon someone's done their best to make it look genuine."

"So where does that leave me? Are they still wanting to hang me out to dry? Are you telling me there's a suspension on its way?"

"No, it's not that. What I'm trying to say is that all this is going to take time. But I think Terje's the one to fill you in on it." He gestured toward the dining area.

"Terje Ploug's here?"

"Yeah, he comes in every day at the same time, if he's not out and about. One of my most faithful customers, he is, so be nice to him."

He found Ploug sitting in the far corner.

"Playing hide-and-seek, Terje?" he quipped, sitting down and planting his elbows on the table in the close vicinity of Ploug's painfully PC plate of vegetables.

"Good to see you, Carl. You're a hard man to find these days. Laursen tell you about the photo?"

"He did, yeah. Seems I'm not out of the woods yet."

"Out of the woods? No one's accusing you of anything as far as I know. Or are they?"

Carl tossed his head back. "Not officially, no."

"Well, then. Anyway, here's where we're at. We're all going to get our heads together. Meaning me, those we've got investigating the murders at the repair shop in Sorø, and the Dutch lot working on the killings in Schiedam in the Netherlands. In a few weeks, a couple of months, maybe, we're going to collate everything we've got on these nail-gun cases. Facts, evidence, background material, the lot."

"And now you're going to tell me I'll be called in as a witness."

"No, just the opposite. You won't."

"Why not, because I'm under suspicion?"

"Take it easy, Carl. Someone wants to drag you through the mud, we realize that. So no, you're not under suspicion. But once we get as far as drawing up a joint report, we'd like you to assess it."

"I see. And that's despite my prints being on the coins, the dodgy photo, and Hardy reckoning Anker was mixed up with our colored friend, and that maybe I knew Georg Madsen?"

"Despite that, yeah. As I see it, you're the one who's got most to gain by this case being investigated as thoroughly as possible."

He gave the back of Carl's hand a gentle pat. It was quite touching really.

"It's a good, honest policeman's best shot at doing things properly, and I think we should respect Terje for that, Carl," said the chief. Jacobsen's corner office was still reeking of Laursen's "Dish of the Day." Had Ms. Sørensen gone that soft as to allow dirty plates and cutlery lying around for more than five minutes?

"Yeah, if you look at it like that." Carl nodded. "But I'm still riled. That case is getting on my nerves."

Marcus nodded back. "I've spoken to Erling from Fire Investigation. I hear you had visitors last night."

"No harm done."

"No, and thank Christ for that! But why did it happen, Carl?"

"Because someone wants me the fuck out of it. And I don't think it's one of my stepson's jilted girlfriends either." He tried to smile.

"Who, then?"

"Most likely one of Curt Wad's people. The Purity Party guy."

Jacobsen nodded again.

"We're bothering him. That's why I'm here. I want to put a tap on his phone. Likewise a gent by the name of Wilfrid Lønberg and a journalist called Louis Petterson."

"I'm afraid I can't authorize that, Carl."

Carl probed into why not, annoyed to begin with, then turned sulky before eventually submitting with an exasperated shrug. The only thing he was coming away with was a warning to take care, and strict instructions to report back if anything unusual occurred.

Unusual. Fucking odd word to bandy about the place. *Everything* in their line of work was unusual, and just as well for that.

Carl got to his feet. Unusual? He wondered what his boss would say if he knew about the stack of files piled up in the dimly lit offices of Department Q, the archive material they'd procured in a manner which even by their standards was more than unusually dodgy.

For once, both secretaries waved cheerily to him from the front desk as he came out.

"Hi, Carl," said Lis, sweet as sugar, Ms. Sørensen chirping an identical greeting a second later. Same words, same tone, same inviting smile.

A turnabout if ever there was one.

"Erm . . . Cata!" he stuttered, directly addressing the woman whose mere presence had formerly been sufficient to prompt teams of hardened investigators, among them Carl himself, into making long detours just to avoid having to walk past her.

"Do you fancy letting me in on what this NLP course you've been on is all about? It wouldn't be contagious, would it?"

She drew her shoulders up, a flourish of body language possibly intended to display delight at having been asked, then beamed a smile at Lis before stepping intimidatingly close to Carl.

"Neurolinguistic programming, it stands for," she said, her voice suddenly full of mystery, as though she were about to seduce an Arab sheik. "It's rather hard to explain fully, but let me give you an example."

The shoulders came up again, like a little foretaste of what lay in store.

She picked up her handbag and fished around in it, eventually producing a piece of chalk. An odd item for a woman to be carrying around. Wasn't chalk meant for the trouser pockets of cheeky schoolboys? Was it gender equality again?

She bent down and drew two circles on the floor, which in itself would have been enough to make her faint only a few weeks earlier. Others, too, for that matter. Then she drew a minus sign in one and a plus sign in the other.

"There you go, Carl. A positive circle and a negative circle. Now I want you to stand first in one, then the other, and say exactly the same sentence. In the negative circle you pretend you're speaking to someone you dislike, and in the positive circle, to someone you're fond of."

"I see. This was the upshot of it, was it? Because I can do that already."

"Come on, let's hear it, then," Lis urged, folding her arms under her scrumptious bosom and stepping closer. Who could say no?

"Choose something simple, like: 'I see you've had your hair done.' Say it nicely first, then not so nicely."

"I don't get it," he lied, scrutinizing both women's short-cut hair. This was going to be too easy. Ms. Sørensen's thatch didn't have quite the same appeal as Lis's, if he was to say so.

"All right, let me demonstrate the positive," said Lis. "Then Cata can do the negative."

Hang on, that ought to be the other way round, Carl thought to himself, distractedly tracing a little circle with his foot.

"I see you've had your *hair* done!" Lis was all smiles as she spoke. "That's how you talk to a person you like. Now it's your turn, Cata."

Ms. Sørensen laughed, then collected herself. "I see *you've* had your hair done!" she spat with envy. She looked truly gruesome. Just like the good old days.

Both women fell about, spluttering with laughter. This was getting girlish.

"Was that it? Not exactly an earth-shattering difference, was it? What am I supposed to get out of that?"

Ms. Sørensen pulled herself together. "The point is that exercises like this teach you to understand how subtle little changes of tone can impact on your surroundings in different ways. It gives you an insight into the effects of what you say and the kind of signals you send. And not least, as an extra plus, how it all rubs off on your own self."

"Isn't that just the same as saying what goes around, comes around?"

"You could call it that. Do you know how you impact on *your* surroundings, Carl? That's what the course can teach you."

I learned that when I was seven, he thought to himself.

"Sometimes the things you say can seem rather harsh, Carl," Ms. Sørensen went on.

Thanks for the compliment. Rather choice coming from you, he mused. "Well, thank you both for making me aware in such a considerate fashion," was what he eventually said, now eager to be on his way. "I'll be certain to give it some thought."

"Try the exercise first, Carl. Step into one of the circles," urged Ms. Sørensen aka Cata. She gestured to indicate which one he should start with, only to discover he'd succeeded in erasing most of it with the toe of his shoe while they'd been playing charades.

"Oops," he said. "I *truly* am sorry, *indeed*." He withdrew from their aura. "Afternoon, ladies. Stay cheerful, eh?"

34

September 1987

As she stood there gazing out of the window, part of her hatred had gone. It was as though the blow to Viggo's temple and his final intakes of breath after she had given him the henbane had drawn a splinter from her mind.

Her eyes passed along Peblinge Dossering and the swarms of people enjoying the last of summer. Ordinary people, each with their own lives and destinies, and most probably their secrets and skeletons, too.

Her lips began to quiver. All of a sudden she felt overwhelmed by emotion. Even Tage, Rita, and Viggo were human in the eyes of the Lord, and now they were dead by her hand.

She closed her eyes and pictured it all. Viggo's face had expressed such warmth when she opened the door. Tage had been so grateful. And now it was Nørvig's turn. The lawyer who wouldn't listen when she'd desperately needed help. The man who had guarded Curt Wad's reputation so fiercely and with such scant regard for her life.

But was she entitled to do unto him as he had done unto her? To take his life away?

The doubt remained inside her when she spotted his wiry figure by the lakeside in front of her building.

Although more than thirty years had passed, she recognized him immediately. Still fond of his tweed jacket with its leather buttons. Still the brown attaché case under his arm. A man who seemingly had not changed, yet she could sense from his body language that perhaps not everything was the same as before.

He wandered a few steps back and forth beneath the chestnut trees, glancing out over the lake. He took a handkerchief from his pocket and dabbed at his face as though wiping away perspiration or perhaps tears.

And then she noticed his jacket was too big for him, his polyester slacks, too, sagging at the shoulders and knees, respectively. An outfit bought in better times, for a frame of greater substance.

For a second she felt sorry for the man, who at this moment stood oblivious, soon to enter the grave.

What if he had children who loved him? Grandchildren?

The very thought made her clench her fists. Her eyelids twitched uncontrollably. Had *she* ever had children to love her? And whose fault was that?

No. She needed to look out for herself and stay focused. Tomorrow at ternoon she would leave this life behind her. But first she had to complete what she had now begun. She had promised this man who was a lawyer by profession that he would receive ten million kroner. She had done so in writing, and a man like him would never allow her to rescind her word.

Not Philip Nørvig.

He stood there, not quite as tall as she remembered him, staring at her like a repentant puppy dog, eyebrows aloft. As though this meeting with her was of immeasurable importance to him and the first impression he gave was crucial.

His eyes had been considerably colder the time he'd lied in court and coerced her into uttering foolish words. Not once had he blinked or allowed himself to be moved by her emotional outbursts. Her sobs had only made him deaf, just as her tears made him blind.

Were these really the same uncompromising eyes, now lowered so humbly as she let him in? The same implacable voice, now thanking her?

She asked if he would like some tea, and he accepted the offer gratefully, still struggling to lift his gaze from the floor and look her in the eye.

She handed him the cup and watched as he drank it down. A momentary frown appeared on his brow.

Perhaps he didn't care for the taste, she thought to herself, but then he held out his cup and asked for more.

"I'm afraid I'm in need of sustenance, Miss Hermansen. There are so many things I have to say to you."

Finally, he lifted his head and looked up at her. And words that should have remained unsaid began to pour from his lips. But the occasion for it had long since passed.

"When I received your letter, Nete . . ." He paused. "I'm sorry, may I address you informally?"

She nodded almost imperceptibly. It hadn't bothered him then, so why should it now? "When I received your letter, I found myself suddenly confronted by something that has been eating away at me for a very long time. Something I would like to make up for, if indeed that were possible. I have to confess that I have come to Copenhagen today with the intention of rescuing both my own life and that of my family. The money is not without significance, I must admit, but I have also come to apologize." He cleared his throat and took another gulp of his tea.

"In recent years I've often thought back upon the desperate girl who sought justice in the courts only to be committed to the asylum at Brejning. And I've wondered what could have possessed me to thwart the accusations you leveled against Curt Wad. I knew, of course, that what you were saying might be true. All that fabrication about how feeble-minded and dangerous you were was so obviously inapplicable to the girl who sat before me on the stand, fighting for her life."

He bowed his head for a moment. When he looked up again his pale skin seemed even more colorless than before.

"I forced you from my mind when the case was over. And there you remained, banished from memory until the day I read about you in the magazines. About you having married Andreas Rosen. Such an intelligent, beautiful woman." He nodded as if in acknowledgment. "I recognized your face immediately. It all came back to me, and I was ashamed."

He sipped his tea again and Nete glanced at the clock. Any moment now, the poison would kick in. Only she didn't want it to, not just yet. If only time could stand still. This was her moment of redress. How could she allow him to go on drinking? He was repentant, it was so obvious.

She looked away as he continued speaking. The evil she was perpetrating became even more evident when she looked into his trusting eyes. She had never imagined such feelings could be wakened inside her. Not for a second.

"At the time, I'd been working for Curt Wad for a number of years. I was beguiled, I admit. I have to concede I'm not nearly as strong as him in nature." He shook his head and put the cup to his lips again. "But when I saw you on the front of that magazine I resolved to reassess the deeds I had committed, and do you know what became clear to me?"

He didn't wait for her reply and failed to notice as she slowly turned to look at him once more, shaking her head.

"I realized I'd been exploited and misled, and there were so many things that occurred in that period that I have since come to regret. It was hard for me to acknowledge my mistakes. I want you to know that. But looking back through my files I could see how Curt Wad tricked me time and again with his lies and distortions, his suppressions of the truth. I saw that he had taken advantage of me quite systematically."

He reached out his cup for more tea, prompting her to wonder for a moment if she might have forgotten to add the extract.

She poured him some more, then noticed that he had now begun to perspire, his breathing growing heavy and labored. Seemingly, he wasn't aware of it himself. He had too much on his mind.

"Curt Wad's mission in life was—and is—to ruin those he believes are unfit to share this country with him and other so-called normal, upstanding individuals. To my shame, I can now say that this has resulted in his personally having performed more than five hundred abortions on pregnant women, often without their knowledge and nearly always against their will, and I believe him to have willfully caused irreparable sterility by surgical means in just as many instances." He looked at her as though he had wielded the scalpel himself.

"Dear God, this is so dreadful. Nonetheless, I'm compelled to confess." Nørvig's words were accompanied by a sigh that had been years in the making. "Through his work with an organization calling itself The Cause, whose affairs I administered for some years, Wad established contact with scores of doctors who shared his convictions and determination. You can hardly begin to imagine the scope of it all."

Nete tried, and found little difficulty.

Nørvig pressed his lips together, struggling now to hold back the tears that welled in his eyes.

"I have aided in the killing of thousands of unborn children, Nete." He emitted a single gasp, then went on in a trembling voice. "Destroying the lives of just as many innocent women. Grief and misery are what my life has spawned, Nete. That is what I have created." His voice quavered so violently that he was forced to stop.

He turned his eyes toward her, seeking forgiveness. It was so obvious, and Nete no longer knew what to say or do. Behind her calm exterior she was breaking down. Was what she was doing to this man truly just? Was it?

For a moment she almost took his hand. To offer absolution and ease his burden as he drifted away into unconsciousness. But she couldn't. Perhaps it was because she, too, felt shame. Perhaps her hand simply had a will of its own.

"A couple of years ago I decided to come forward with what I knew. The pressure of it had become too great for me, but Curt Wad intervened and took away everything I had. My law practice, my honor, my self-respect. I had a business partner by the name of Herbert Sønderskov. Curt talked him into divulging information about me that would ruin me for good. I argued with them both and threatened to blow the whistle on The Cause. They tipped off the police anonymously, claiming I'd embezzled funds from my clients' accounts. And though it wasn't true, they made it look like it was. They had access to all the documents, they had the contacts, and not least the means to do as they found fit."

Nørvig lowered his head. His eyes began to flicker. "Herbert, that swine. He was always after my wife. He said to me that if I didn't keep my mouth shut for good, they'd make sure I went to prison." He shook his head. "I had a daughter who never would have coped with the humiliation. There was nothing I could do. Wad was dangerous, and he still is. Nete . . . Do you hear me? You must stay away from that man."

And then he slumped forward, still speaking, though his words were muddled. Something about Wad's father, who thought he was God. About deluded, self-righteous, cynical human beings. Psycopaths.

"My wife forgave me going bankrupt," he said with sudden clarity of voice. "I thank God for showing"—he searched momentarily for the words, spluttering and trying to swallow—"for showing grace and allowing me to see you today, Nete. And I promise God to remain with Him from this day on. With your money, Nete, my family and I might . . ."

And with that he fell to the floor, his elbow striking the armrest of the chair. For a moment he looked like he was going to be sick, his stomach convulsing, his eyes wide with bewilderment. And then he abruptly sat up.

"Why are there so many people here all of a sudden, Nete?" He seemed afraid now.

She tried to say something, but found no words to utter.

"Why are they all looking at me?" Nørvig mumbled, his eyes seeking light from the window.

He began to weep, reaching out his hands to probe the air.

Nete wept with him.

35

November 2010

Never had Assad and Rose resembled each other so strikingly. Dark, somber expressions and a total absence of anything even touching upon a smile.

"Lunatics," Rose exclaimed. "They should be lined up and forced to breathe in that gas of theirs until they lift off into the sky and vanish for good. How despicable can you get, trying to burn five people to death just to shut you up, Carl? I can't stand that sort of thing, me."

"They have shut only exactly this much of your mouth now, Carl." Assad formed a zero with his index finger and thumb. "Now we know we are on the right track. These swine have much dirt under their carpets, we know this now." He thumped his fist into the palm of his hand. It would have hurt like hell if anyone had got in the way.

"We will get them for this, Carl," he went on. "We shall work day and night, and then we will close this bloody Purity Party down and stop The Cause and everything else Curt Wad is involved in."

"Cheers, Assad. But I'm afraid it's not going to be that easy, and definitely not without danger. I reckon it's a good idea for you two to stay put and carry on here for the next couple of days." He smiled. "I suppose you were going to anyway."

"At least we were lucky I was here on Saturday night," Assad added. "There was someone snooping around. He was in a police uniform, but when I came out of my office I gave him a fright."

Who wouldn't have got a fright being confronted with Assad's bleary eyes at that time of night? Carl mused. "What was he after?" he asked. "And where was he from? Did you find out?"

"He told me rubbish, Carl. Something about the key to the archive room and a lot of nonsense. He was looking for something of ours, I'm sure of it. He was on his way into your office, Carl."

"Looks like we're dealing with a pretty extensive organization," said Carl. He turned to Rose. "What have you done with Nørvig's files, Rose?"

"They're in the gents' room. Which reminds me. If you do have to stand up for a widdle in the ladies', remember to put the sodding seat down again when you're finished, all right?"

"What for?" said Assad. So he was the culprit.

"If you knew how many times I've had this discussion, Assad, you'd rather be sitting twiddling your thumbs at scout camp on Langeland right now, I can assure you."

It was plain from Assad's expression that he had no idea what she meant. Neither did Carl, for that matter.

"OK, then listen up. You forget to put the seat down after you've had a wee, right?" She raised a finger in the air. "*One*. All toilet seats are yucky underneath with one thing or another. Sometimes yucky isn't quite the word. *Two*. When women need to go and the seat's up, their fingers are in contact with it before they sit down. *Three*. Touching the seat means we've got all sorts of nasty germs on our fingers when we wipe ourselves, which isn't hygienic at all. But maybe you've never heard of urinary infections? *Four*. Why should we have to wash our hands twice, just because you couldn't be arsed to do something simple like putting the seat down? Is that reasonable? No, it's not!" She planted her fists on her hips. "If you lot learned to put the seat down after your widdle, we wouldn't catch germs and neither would you, because you'd be washing your hands afterward anyway. At least, I bloody well hope you would."

Assad stood for a moment in contemplation. "Do you think it would be better for me to lift the seat before I widdle? Because then *I* will have germs and must wash my hands even before I begin."

Rose raised her digit again. "First of all, that's exactly why you men should sit down when you're having a wee. Second, if you think your-selves too masculine to sit down, just remember that men with normal colons have to sit down once in a while *anyway* to do their jobs, in which case you *have to* put the seat down. Assuming, that is, you don't do your number twos standing up as well."

"But we don't need to put the seat down if a lady has been there be-fore us, because then it will be down already," Assad rejoined. "And do you know what, Rose? I think now I will find my nice, green rubber gloves and fix the gentleman's toilet with these two fine helpers of mine." He stuck his hands in the air. "They will take hold of toilet seats and reach into U bends. Fortunately, some of us do not mind getting our hands dirty, my squeamish friend."

Carl saw that Rose's rapidly reddening cheeks were about to spark a gigantic bollocking. Instinctively, he stepped between the quarreling parties. End of discussion. Thank Christ his own upbringing had been reasonably sensible in that respect. What else, in a home where the toilet lid had a fluffy orange cover on it?

"OK, you two, let's get back to matters at hand," Carl intervened. "There's been an attempted arson attack on my home and we've got a bloke sneaking around the basement here, looking to nab our evidence. Anyone can access the toilet where you've stashed Nørvig's files, Rose, so do you reckon it's a good idea to keep them there? I don't think an *Out of Order* sign is going to deter a burglar, do you?"

She took a key out of her pocket. "No, but this might. And now you mention security, I'm not thinking of hanging around HQ more than necessary. I mean, it's not *that* cozy here, is it? I've got things in my handbag to defend myself with if it comes to that, but still."

Carl found himself thinking of pepper sprays and stun guns, nasty stuff Rose was by no means authorized to use.

"OK, but be careful anyway, Rose."

She twisted her face at him. It was almost a weapon in itself.

"I've been through all Nørvig's files now and entered the names of all defendants in my database." She placed several sheets of paper, stapled together, on the desk in front of him. "Here's the list. Note that some of the reports bear the signature of a notary named Albert Caspersen. For the benefit of anyone unfamiliar with the name, I can tell you he's now a leading figure in the Purity Party, and everyone seems to think he'll end up its leader after Wad."

"So he worked for Nørvig's firm?"

"Nørvig and Sønderskov, yeah. Then, when they split up the partnership, Caspersen moved on to another law firm in Copenhagen."

Carl scanned the pages. Rose had made four columns for each case. One with the name of the client the firm was defending, one with the name of the plaintiff, the two others for the date and the nature of the case.

The fourth column contained an unusual number of complaints concerning abuse of intelligence testing, general medical carelessness, and most paramount, cases involving "unsuccessful" or unnecessary gynecological intervention. The column headed "Name" comprised common Danish surnames as well as a number that appeared more foreign.

"I've picked some of the cases out and gone through them quite meticulously," said Rose. "To my mind, what we're dealing with here is some of the most systematic abuse I've ever seen. Pure discrimination, a contemptible *Übermensch* mentality. If this is just the tip of the iceberg, then these men are guilty of no end of crimes against women and unborn children."

She indicated the five names that recurred most often. Curt Wad, Wilfrid Lønberg, and three others.

"If you check out the Purity Party's Web site, four of these names appear as influential members, the fifth now being deceased. What do you think of that, *meine Herren*?"

"If this scum gets to have any say in Denmark, Carl, it will be war, I promise you this," Assad growled, ignoring the infernal racket of the phone on his desk. It was the umpteenth time it had assailed their eardrums already that morning.

Carl looked at Assad with wary eyes. This case was affecting him more than any other they had worked on together. The same was true of Rose, for that matter. It was as if it cut them to the quick. Hardly surprising, for these two people he'd sent into the breach were each scarred in their own way. And yet Carl still found it odd that Assad should become so deeply involved in the case that it fazed him like it did.

"If a person can get away with deporting women to an island," Assad went on, his dark eyebrows knitted, "taking the lives of so many unborn children and making so many women sterile, then I should think he could get away with most anything at all, Carl. And this is not good if that person happens to become a member of his country's parliament."

"Listen, both of you. What we're primarily investigating is the disappearance of five people, right? Rita Nielsen, Gitte Charles, Philip Nørvig, Viggo Mogensen, and Tage Hermansen. All of them go missing at pretty much the same time and none of them ever turns up again. That on its own gives rise to the suspicion that a crime was committed. On the one hand we've established the common denominators of Nete Hermansen and the women's home on Sprogø. On the other hand there's a lot of stuff revolving around Curt Wad and his activities that definitely seems worthy of our attention. Maybe Wad and his work is what we should be targeting, and maybe not. Under any circumstances, our first objective should be clearing up these missing persons cases. The rest we should probably turn over to the security authorities at PET or the National Investigation Center. It's out of our league, too big for three people on their own to handle, and potentially explosive to boot."

Assad was clearly dissatisfied. "You saw for yourself those marks gouged in the door of the punishment cell on Sprogø, Carl. With your own ears you have heard what Mie Nørvig had to say about Curt Wad, and you can read this list with your own eyes. We must get out there and question this old swine about all these despicable crimes he has committed. That is all I will say."

Carl raised his hand. The chiming of his mobile came as a welcome interruption to their disagreement. At least, that's what he thought until he saw it was Mona.

"Yes, Mona, what is it?" he said, in a rather more detached tone than he'd intended.

The warmth of her voice, however, was just as he might have hoped. "It's been so long since I've heard from you, Carl. Have you lost your key?"

He stepped into the corridor. "No, it's just that I didn't really fancy butting in. Thought maybe Rolf might still be having a lie-in."

The ensuing silence wasn't that uncomfortable, but it brought him down nonetheless. There were so many ways to tell the woman you were mad about that you didn't want to share her with anyone else. And the upshot was almost always a breakup.

He counted the seconds and was on the verge of hanging up out of sheer frustration when peals of laughter of Olympic proportions almost blew his eardrum into his skull.

"Oh, God, you're so sweet, Carl. You're jealous of a dog, darling! Mathilde talked me into looking after her Cairn terrier puppy while she's off taking a course."

"A dog?" Carl felt himself promptly deflate like a balloon. "Then why the hell did you have to go and say a thing like, 'Don't worry yourself, we'll talk about it some other time' when I called you? I've been at my wits' end here."

"Listen, silly. Maybe it'll teach you that some women might not be in the mood for early-morning small talk with their boyfriends until they've had a chance to spend half an hour in front of the mirror."

"Sounds like you're telling me it was a test."

She laughed. "You *are* a good policeman, aren't you? Another mystery solved."

"Did I pass?"

"We'll talk about it tonight. That is, if you don't mind Rolf being here, too?"

They turned off Roskildevej onto Brøndbyøstervej, clusters of tower blocks rising up on both sides of the road.

"I know Brøndby Nord quite well," said Assad. "Do you, Carl?"

He nodded. How many times had he been out on patrol here? They said Brøndbyøster had once been a lively community with three bustling squares, a place that had everything going for it. Good neighborhoods, people with purchasing power. And then the shopping centers came, one after another: Rødovre Centrum, Glostrup Centret, Hvidovre Centret, the Bilka hypermarkets in Ishøj and Hundige. The place never stood a chance. Shops closed down like it was an epidemic. Decent, well-run shops, and now there was next to sod all left. Brøndby looked like the most neglected town center in the country. Where was the pedestrian street, where were the boutiques and stores, the cinema, the community facilities? Now the only people who lived here were those mobile enough to shop elsewhere or whose requirements were few.

It was all glaringly obvious on the squares of Brøndbyøster Torv and Nygårds Plads. Apart from its football team, Brøndby had little to be proud of. It was a dead end, and its northernmost area, Brøndby Nord, was a case in point.

"Yeah, I know it pretty well, Assad. Why do you ask?"

"I'm certain not many pregnant women in Brøndby Nord would slip through the mesh of Curt Wad's net. It makes me think of the doctors from the concentration camps standing at the train wagons, sorting the Jews," he said.

Maybe that was putting it a bit strongly, but Carl nodded nevertheless as he stared ahead past the bridge that led over the S-train tracks. A little farther down the road the old village came into view. An oasis in the asphalt jungle. Quaint old cottages with thatched roofs and proper fruit trees, the kind that hadn't been cultivated through continuous grafting. There was room enough here for people to breathe.

"We need to go along Vestre Gade," said Assad, checking the GPS. "Brøndbyøstervej is a one-way street, so you'll have to go all the way down to Park Allé and back."

Carl looked at the signposting. It seemed right enough. And then, just as they entered the village, he saw the shadow of a truck hurtling toward them from a side road. Before he could react, the vehicle smashed into the back end of the Peugeot with such force that the car was sent careering off the road and onto the pavement, where its path was halted by a thick privet hedge. The seconds that passed as though they were minutes were a mayhem of shattering glass, crunching metal, and the smack of airbags deploying into their faces. And then it was over. They heard the hiss of the engine and a clamor of approaching voices. That was all.

They looked at each other, shaken but relieved, as the airbags deflated.

"Look what you've done to my hedge!" an elderly man exclaimed, as they tumbled out of the car. Not a word of concern as to their state of health. Luckily, they were all right.

Carl gave a shrug. "Get on to your insurance company. Environmental restoration desk." He glanced around at the nearest bystanders. "Anyone see what happened?"

"It was a truck going like a bat out of hell the wrong way down a one-way street and then back onto Brøndbyøstervej. He carried on up to Højstens Boulevard, I think," said one.

"It came down from Brøndbytoften. They'd been parked up there a while. I can't tell you what make it was, though, other than it was blue," said another.

"No it wasn't, it was gray," a third chipped in.

"I don't suppose anyone managed to get the number down?" said Carl, assessing the damage. He might as well call in to the motor pool right away and get it over with. Knowing them, he and Assad would be catching the S-train back.

And if his gut feeling was right, it wouldn't be much good asking around the industrial estate at Brøndbytoften if anyone knew anything about that truck.

It was a brazen attempt to do away with them. Certainly no accident.

"Would you credit it? Curt Wad's house is right opposite the police academy. Can't think of a better cover for dodgy goings-on than that, can you, Assad? Who'd ever think of looking here?"

Assad pointed at a brass nameplate fixed to the yellow-brick wall next to the front door.

"That is not his name on the sign, Carl. It says 'Karl-Johan Henriksen, MD, Consultant Gynecologist.'"

"I know, Wad sold his practice. Look, there's two doorbells, Assad. Let's try the top one, eh?"

They heard a muffled version of Big Ben somewhere from within. When no one appeared after repeated tries at both doorbells, they went through between the gable-end of the house and a yellow-washed former stables with a tiled roof that looked like it was from the days of King Cnut.

The garden was a small oblong, crowned by snowberry bushes and surrounded by a wooden fence. There were a couple of flower beds that seemed reasonably well cared for, and a rickety-looking shed.

They ventured into the middle of the lawn to discover the face of an old man staring out of the window at them from what appeared to be the living room. It was Curt Wad, no doubt about it.

He shook his head at them. Carl held his badge up to the pane, which only made Wad repeat his dismissive gesture. He clearly had no intention of letting them in.

Then Assad went up the step and rattled the back door. It opened.

"Curt Wad," he said in the doorway. "May we come in?"

Carl watched Wad through the window. His reply was an angry tirade, though Carl was unable to hear what was said.

"Thank you very much, indeed," said Assad, and slipped inside.

Cheeky bugger, Carl thought to himself, and went in after him.

"You're trespassing on private property. I must ask you to leave immediately," Wad protested. "My wife happens to be on her deathbed upstairs and I'm not in any mood for visitors."

"We are in a bad mood, too, as it happens," Assad rejoined.

Carl took hold of his sleeve. "We're sorry to hear that, Mr. Wad. We'll make it brief, I promise."

He sat down uninvited on a rustic settle with oak panels, though the owner of the house remained standing.

"We've an idea you know why we're here, judging by the games you've been playing with us this morning. But let me sum up."

Carl paused in order to note Wad's reaction to his suggestion of two attempts on his life, but none was forthcoming. The man's body language, however, told him they were unwelcome and would do well to leave, the sooner the better.

"Apart from our having delved a bit into your activities in various organizations and political parties, we're here because we'd like to know if your name can be linked to the disappearance of a number of individuals at the beginning of September 1987. But before I ask you specific questions, would there be anything you'd like to tell us in that respect?"

"Yes. I'm telling you to leave."

"I don't understand," said Assad. "I could have sworn you just invited us in."

It was an Assad quite without the usual gleam in his eye. Tenacious, bordering on the aggressive. Carl could see he'd have to keep him on a short leash.

The old man was about to protest, but Carl held up his hand. "Like I said, just a few short questions. And you keep quiet for a minute, Assad."

Carl glanced around. There was a door leading out into the garden, another into what looked like a dining room, and then a set of double doors that were closed. All were of teak-veneered plywood. A typical sixties revamp.

"I assume that'd be Karl-Johan Henriksen's surgery through there? Is it closed now?"

Curt Wad nodded. Carl could see the man was on the alert and keeping himself in check, but his rage was bound to emerge once the questioning became more forceful.

"So anyone entering the front door would have three ways to go. Up the stairs to the first floor where your wife is, left into the surgery, and right, through the dining room and presumably on into the kitchen area. Is that correct?"

Wad nodded again, most likely puzzled by where Carl might be headed, but nevertheless electing to remain silent.

Carl checked the doors again. If they were going to be attacked it would probably come from the double doors of the surgery, he thought to himself. He kept an eye on them, and one hand in the region of his pistol.

"What disappearances are you referring to?" the old man eventually asked.

"A Philip Nørvig. We know he worked for you."

"I see. I haven't seen him in twenty-five years. But there were others, you say? Which others?"

OK, he seemed to be calming down a bit.

"People connected to Sprogø in one way or another," Carl replied.

"Well, I can't help you there, I'm afraid. I'm from Fyn," Wad said with a smirk.

"But your professional assessments did result in a great many women being sent to the island. Moreover, you were in charge of a diligent and very smoothly run organization that had women placed in the home there during the years 1955 to 1961. At the same time, this organization seems to have been involved in a remarkable number of cases of forced abortion and unlawful sterilization."

Wad's smile broadened. "And did any convictions ever ensue? None whatsoever. It was stuff and nonsense, the lot of it. Is this really about retards from Sprogø? I can't see what that would have to do with the cases you're investigating. Perhaps you should be talking to Nørvig instead."

"Nørvig disappeared in 1987."

"So you say, yes. But perhaps he had good reason to. Perhaps he was at the bottom of whatever it is you're interested in. Have you looked for him?"

The arrogance of the man was astounding.

"I won't listen to this, Carl." Assad turned to face Wad directly. "You knew we were on our way, yes? You didn't even come to the door to see who was there. You knew the truck you had waiting had failed to stop us. And now you are in the shit."

Assad stepped up close to the man. Things were taking a turn, and fast. They still had no end of details they needed to get out of Wad. The way this was going, he'd shut up like a clam.

"No, wait, Carl," said Assad, when he realized his superior was about to intervene. And then he put his arms around the waist of the old man, who was head and shoulders taller than him, picked him up, and then put him down forcibly in an armchair by the fireplace. "So now you are more under control. Last night you tried to kill Carl and his friends by burning down his house. The night before, you tried to steal evidence from Police Headquarters. Documents have been incinerated. All dirty work done by your people. Do you think I will be nicer to you than you have been to us? Because if you do, you are much mistaken!"

Wad sat smiling at Assad, calm and collected. The man was almost asking for it.

Carl took over in the same aggressive tone as Assad. "Perhaps you'll tell us where Louis Petterson might have got to, Wad?"

"Who?"

"Don't mess me about. You know perfectly well who you've got on the payroll at Benefice."

"Benefice? What might that be?"

"OK, so tell me how come Louis Petterson rang you up immediately after we questioned him about you at a bar in Holbæk."

The smile stiffened slightly. Carl saw that Assad noticed, too. The first mention of anything concrete that could be pinned on him personally, and Wad reacted. Touché!

"And why did Herbert Sønderskov call you up before that? According to our information, that would have been just after we'd been to see him and Mie Nørvig in Halsskov. Any comments?"

"None." Curt Wad placed his hands demonstratively on the armrests, a signal to them that he would now remain silent.

"Tell me about The Cause," Carl went on. "An interesting little phenomenon, that. It'll be all over the papers soon. Out in the open. How does that make you feel? After all, you're the founder, aren't you?"

No reply. Just hands that tightened around the armrests.

"Are you prepared to admit to your part in Philip Nørvig's disappearance? Because if you are, we might just be able to concentrate our efforts on that, instead of all your other funny business with political parties and secret organizations."

Wad's reaction now was crucial. All Carl's experience told him so. For no matter how minuscule the response, it would be his guideline as to what strategy to employ in dealing with this fossilized felon. Would he grasp the opportunity to come clean and save the party, or would he try to save himself? Carl was most inclined to believe the latter.

But Wad didn't react at all.

Carl looked at Assad. Was he thinking the same thing? That in Curt Wad's eyes, doing a deal in the Nørvig case was no exchange for The Cause. He wasn't going to cop it for the lesser crime, regardless that it might save him going down for the greater one. Hardened criminals wouldn't have hesitated for a moment, but Wad wasn't buying. Maybe he didn't have anything to do with their missing persons at all? The possibility couldn't be ruled out. Or was he so much shrewder than Carl realized?

For the moment, they were no further.

"Caspersen still works for you, doesn't he? Just like he did when you and Lønberg and others in the Purity Party destroyed the lives of all those innocent people?"

Wad didn't flinch. Assad, on the other hand, was about to blow.

"You realize of course that purity means being pure, especially in moral behavior? You stupid old man!" he seethed.

Carl noted that no matter how innocent Assad's charge, it seemed to hit home. The comment appeared to have the old man riled more than all the others put together. Being lectured in semantics by this pushy little foreigner was an unspeakable provocation, that much was plain.

"What's the name of your driver, the one with the white hair who left that gas cylinder at my place?" Carl continued, piling on the pressure. And then, finally: "Do you remember Nete Hermansen?"

Wad sat up. "I must ask you to leave at once." So now he was getting formal again. "My wife is dying and I must ask you to leave now and respect the fact that these are our last hours together."

"The way you respected Nete when you had her shipped out to the island? The way you respected the women who couldn't meet your sick, degenerate standards, whose children you murdered before they were even born?" Carl spat out the words with the same smirk on his face as Wad had used.

"How dare you even try to compare such things?" Wad got to his feet. "I've had enough of this hypocrisy." He stepped toward Assad. "And you imagine you can bring your foul Arab urchins into the world and call them Danes? You worthless, ugly little raghead!"

"Ah, so there we have it." Assad smiled. "The beast within. The ugly underside of Curt Wad."

"Get out of here, you bloody camel fucker! Back to your own country where you belong!"

He turned to Carl. "Yes, I played a part in sending antisocial, feeble-minded girls with deviant sexual tendencies to Sprogø. Yes, they were sterilized. And you would do well to thank me for not having to contend with their offspring running around the streets like rats, for I can assure you the police would be at a loss as to what to do about their feral behavior. To hell with the both of you! If I'd been a younger man, I swear . . ."

He raised his fists toward them. Assad was clearly willing to let him have a go. Wad looked considerably frailer now than on TV. The sight of him was almost comical. This old man, squaring his shoulders for fisti-cuffs in a living room displaying a lifetime's clutter of furnishing styles. But Carl knew better. Appearances deceived, and the man's frailty ex-tended only to his body. Wad's weapon was his brain, and his brain was intact. The man was ruthless and driven by malice.

So Carl took his assistant by the collar and led him out through the back door.

"They'll get him sooner or later, Assad, don't you worry," he assured him, as they trudged along Brøndbyøstervej toward the S-train station.

But Assad was having none of it.

"*They?*" he spluttered. "You say *they* and not *we*? Who are *they* who will stop him? Curt Wad is eighty-eight years old, Carl. No one will get him before Allah himself, unless we do."

They didn't say much on the way back. Each was lost in thought.

"Did you notice the arrogance of this bastard? The house did not even have a burglar alarm," said Assad at one point. "A person could break in there in a jiffy. What is more, somebody ought to before Wad destroys important evidence. I think he will do this for certain, Carl."

He didn't specify who that somebody might be.

"Don't even think about it, Assad," Carl replied. "One break-in a week is more than enough." There seemed little reason to elaborate, so he left it at that.

They had only been back at HQ for five minutes when Rose came into Carl's office with a sheet of paper in her hand.

"This was in the fax machine. It's for Assad," she said. "From Lithuania, as far as I can make out. Pretty gruesome photo, don't you think? Any idea why they might have sent it to us?"

Carl glanced at the image and felt his blood run cold.

"Assad, get in here!" he hollered.

It took a bit longer than usual. It had been a hard day.

"Yes, what is it?" he asked, when he eventually slunk in.

Carl pointed to the fax.

"Recognize the tattoo, Assad?"

Assad studied the dragon that had been divided in two by the near severance of Linas Verslovas's head. The face of the man whose acid attack had disfigured Børge Bak's sister was captured in an expression of simultaneous fear and astonishment.

Assad's was rather more composed.

"This is unfortunate," he said. "But I have nothing to do with it, Carl."

"So you don't think this might be your doing in some way, directly or indirectly?" Carl asked, slapping the fax down on the desk. His nerves were frayed, too. It was hardly surprising.

"A person can never know about indirectly. But this is not something I did on purpose."

Carl fumbled around for his cigarettes. He needed a smoke and he needed one now. "No, I don't believe you did either, Assad. But why the hell would the Lithuanian police, or whoever the fuck it was who sent this, think you ought to be informed? And where's my fucking lighter, have you seen it anywhere?"

"I don't know why I should be informed, Carl. Perhaps I should call them and ask?" It was a question delivered in a tone more sarcastic than the situation warranted.

"Do you know what, Assad? I reckon it can wait. For the time being I think you should get off home, or wherever it is you go to when you're not here, and concentrate on trying to clear your head. Because as far as I can see, you're heading for a blow-out any time now."

"In which case it is only strange that *you* are not, Carl. But if you insist, then I shall go." He didn't show it, but he was angrier than Carl had ever seen him.

And then he turned round and left, with Carl's lighter sticking demonstratively out of his back pocket.

This did not bode well.

36

September 1987

When Nørvig's head flopped down onto his chest, Nete's world was consumed by silence. Death itself had appeared before her, beckoning her unto the flames of hell. But now she was alone.

Never before had she felt it to be as close. Not even when her mother died. Not even when she lay in her hospital bed and was told her husband had been killed in the car accident.

She kneeled down in front of the chair where Philip Nørvig sat slumped, open eyes still red from weeping, no longer breathing.

Then she reached out her trembling hands to touch his clenched fingers, searching for words that could not be found. Perhaps she wanted only to say "sorry," but somehow it didn't seem enough.

He has a daughter, she thought, and felt a queasiness spread from her stomach to the rest of her body.

He had a daughter. These lifeless hands had a cheek they would never again caress.

"*Stop it*, Nete!" she shouted abruptly, sensing where she was leading herself. "Bastard!" she snarled at Nørvig's corpse. Who was he to come here, repentant, and think her life would be made better on that account? Was he now to rob her of her vengeance, too? First her liberty, her fertility and motherhood, and now her triumph?

"Come here," she mumbled, putting her arms round his torso, imme-

diately registering the smell that filled her nostrils. He had emptied his
bowels at the moment of death. More work to do. And time was short.

She looked at the clock: 4 P.M. In fifteen minutes it would be Curt
Wad's turn. Although Gitte came after him, Curt would be her crowning
achievement.

She pulled Nørvig from the chair and saw the malodorous brown
stain of excrement on the upholstery.

Nørvig had left his final mark on her life.

After she had wrapped his nether regions in a bath towel and dragged
him into the sealed room, she knelt at the armchair, scrubbing frantically with all the windows in the living room and kitchen thrown wide.
Neither the stain nor the smell would go away, and now, at fourteen
minutes past four, everything in the room, down to the minutest piece of
bric-a-brac, seemed to announce to her that something in the apartment
was terribly amiss.

Two minutes later, the armchair had been pushed away into the corner of the sealed room, its usual place now glaringly vacant. For a moment she thought about substituting a dining chair, only then to decide
against it. She had nothing else that would do.

Curt Wad will have to sit on the sofa by the sideboard while I mix the
tea and the extract, she thought. I'll just have to stand in between so he
won't see.

Time passed and Nete stood anxiously at the window. But Curt Wad
didn't come.

After Nete had spent more than eighteen tormented months on the island,
a man stood one day in a corner of the courtyard, photographing the

view down to the sea. A gaggle of Sprogø girls were gathered around him, whispering and giggling, eyeing him up as though he were fair game. But the man was big and stout, and the occasional hand that ventured to brush against him was firmly dismissed.

He seemed to be a good sort, as her father would have said. Ruddy as a farmer and hair that shone with life and spoke of something other than crude soap flakes.

Four of the female wardens came out to waylay him, and when things seemed to be getting out of hand they shooed the girls away, back to their chores. In the meantime, Nete drew back behind the tall tree in the middle of the courtyard, waiting to see what would happen.

The man looked around, taking in the surroundings, producing a notebook and jotting down his impressions.

"Would it be possible to speak to one of the girls?" she heard him inquire. One of the women laughed and told him that if he held his virtue dear, it would be better he left the girls alone and spoke to *them* instead.

"*I'll* behave myself," said Nete, stepping forward wearing the smile her father always called her "twinkle."

Right away she saw in the eyes of the staff the punishment that now awaited her.

"Go back to work," said the one they called Weasel, the smallest of the four women, the matron's assistant. She tried to keep it civil, but Nete knew better. Weasel was an aggrieved woman, much like her colleagues, a person who seemed to have nothing left in life but harsh words and embitterment. "A woman no man in his right mind would ever want," Rita always said. "The kind who takes pleasure in the calamity of others."

"No, wait," said the man. "I'd like to speak to her. She seems harmless enough."

Weasel snorted but said nothing.

He stepped closer. "I'm from a magazine called *Photo Report*. Do you mind if we talk?"

Nete shook her head eagerly, despite the four pairs of eyes she felt glaring at her.

The man turned back to the wardens. "Ten minutes, that's all. Down by the jetty. Just some questions and a couple of photos. If you want, you can be on hand to intervene if it turns out I'm unable to defend myself," he added with a chuckle.

As the women withdrew, one of them made off for the matron's office after a nod from Weasel.

You've only a moment, Nete thought to herself, walking on ahead of the journalist through the passage between the buildings and down to the water.

The light seemed unusually bright that day, and at the jetty the motor-boat that had sailed the reporter out to the island lay moored. She'd seen the boatman before on some occasion. He smiled and waved.

She would have given years of her life to be sailed away in that boat.

"I'm not retarded or abnormal in any way," she explained hurriedly to the journalist, turning to face him. "I was sent here because I was raped. By a doctor called Curt Wad. You can look him up in the phone book."

The man was immediately alert.

"Raped, you say?"

"Yes."

"By a doctor? A Curt Wad?"

"Yes. You can check the court records. I lost the case."

He nodded deliberately, though without making notes. Why wasn't he putting this down?

"And your name is?"

"Nete Hermansen."

This he jotted in his notebook. "You say you're quite normal, and yet I happen to know for a fact that everyone here has been given a diagnosis. What might yours be?"

"Diagnosis?" She didn't know what it meant.

He smiled. "Nete, can you tell me the name of the third largest town in Denmark?"

She turned her eyes toward the hillock and its fruit trees, knowing full well where things were heading. Three more questions and she would be pigeonholed.

"I know it's not Odense, because that's the second biggest," she answered.

He nodded. "Sounds like you're from Fyn yourself."

"I am. I was born not far from Assens."

"Then perhaps you can tell me about Hans Christian Andersen's childhood home in Odense. What color is it?"

Nete shook her head. "Won't you take me away from here? I'll tell you such a lot of things you'll never find out otherwise. Things no one knows."

"Such as?"

"About the wardens. If any of them are nice to us, they're sent back to the mainland. And if we're disobedient, they beat us and lock us up in the contemplation rooms."

"Contemplation rooms?"

"Yes, punishment cells. Just a room with a bed, and nothing else."

"But this isn't supposed to be a holiday, is it?"

She was desolate. He didn't understand. "The only way we can get away from here is if they cut us open and sterilize us."

The man nodded. "Yes, I'm aware of that. It's so that you won't put children into the world that you can't look after. Don't you find that humane?"

"Humane?"

"Yes, kind."

"Why shouldn't I be allowed to have children? Are my children worth less than others?"

He looked past Nete at the three wardens who had followed on behind, doing their utmost to listen in on what was said.

"Which of these women beats you?" he asked.

Nete turned. "They all do, but the smallest one's the worst. She hits us on the neck and it hurts for days."

"I see. Look, the matron's coming now, so one more question, that's all. Tell me something you're not allowed to do here."

"The staff keep the herbs and spices for themselves. All we're allowed is salt and pepper and vinegar."

He smiled. "Well, if that's the worst you can think of, I'd say you were doing quite nicely. The food's decent enough. I've tasted it myself."

"The worst thing is that they hate us. They don't care about us and they treat us like we're all the same. They never listen to anything we say."

He laughed. "You should meet my editor. I think you've just described him."

She heard the wardens disperse behind her, noticing just before the matron gripped her arm and marched her off that the man in the boat had lit a cigarillo and was in the process of trimming his nets.

She had not been heard, at least not properly. Her prayers had been in vain. She was no more worthy of attention than a tuft of grass.

To begin with, she lay in the punishment cell and wept. And when it didn't help, she screamed at the top of her lungs for them to let her out, kicking and clawing at the door. Eventually, when they tired of her commotion, two of them came in, twisted her arms into the straitjacket, and strapped her to the bed.

For hours she was distraught, sobbing uncontrollably and imploring the grimy wall to fall away and reveal her pathway to freedom. Eventually, the door opened and the matron stepped inside, followed by her zealous little weasel of an assistant.

"I have spoken to Mr. William from *Photo Report*, and you can thank your lucky stars he won't be publishing any of the cock-and-bull stories you've been telling him."

"I didn't tell him stories and I never tell a lie."

Nete failed to see the hand that swiped through the air and struck her on the mouth, but she was prepared when Weasel drew back her arm a second time.

"All right, Miss Jespersen, I think that will suffice," said the matron.

She looked down at Nete again. Of all the staff, the matron may have had the kindest eyes, but right now they were as cold as ice.

"I've telephoned Dr. Wad and informed him that you continue to put forward these outrageous and wholly insubstantial lies about him. I was interested to hear what he thought we should do about you. His opinion was that in view of your intransigent and mendacious character, no period of confinement would ever suffice as punishment." She patted Nete on the head. "The decision is not his to make, but nonetheless I have decided to follow his advice. You can remain here for a week to begin with, and we shall see how you get on. If you behave and refrain from making such a racket we shall remove the straitjacket tomorrow. What do you say, Nete? Do we have an agreement?"

Nete twisted slightly under the belt.

A silent protest.

Where on earth's he got to? Nete wondered. Had Curt Wad really decided not to come? Was he really so arrogant that not even the prospect of ten million kroner could lure him from his lair? It was a situation she hadn't anticipated.

She shook her head despairingly. This was the last thing she needed. Though she closed her eyes, the body of the scrawny lawyer still stared pitifully at her, but Nørvig had been little more than Wad's errand boy, and if she wouldn't spare him, she certainly would not be kind to Curt Wad.

She bit her lip and looked over at the grandfather clock, its pendulum swinging relentlessly.

Would she be able to go to Mallorca with her job incomplete? She wouldn't, she was certain of it. Curt Wad was the most important of her intended victims.

"Come on, come on, come on, you swine!" she spat in frustration, gathering up her knitting and frenziedly picking up stitches. And with every click of the needles her gaze out of the open windows and down the path along the lake grew more intense.

Was that him? That tall figure by the bunker? Or what about the man behind him? But that wasn't him either.

What to do now?

And then the doorbell chimed. Not the entry phone downstairs, but her own front door. She gave a start and felt a chill go through her body.

She dropped her knitting and glanced around, satisfying herself that everything was ready.

There was the extract. The cozy was on the teapot. The documents bearing the fabricated letterhead of her fictitious lawyer were laid out on the lace cloth on the coffee table in front of the sofa. She sniffed the air. As far as she could tell, the stench of Nørvig's passing was gone.

Then she went to the door, wishing she'd had one of those little spyholes fitted. She took a deep breath and lifted her head, ready to look Curt Wad in the eye when she opened up.

"I discovered I did have some coffee all along. It took a while with these foolish eyes of mine," said a voice from about half a meter lower down than she'd been anticipating.

Her neighbor held out a pack of Irma's own brand and craned her neck to peer down the hallway of Nete's apartment. What could be more exciting than a peek into the unknown world of one's neighbor?

But Nete refrained to invite her in.

"Thank you so much," she said, accepting the coffee. "The instant was all right, but this is better, of course. Can I pay you for it right away? I'm afraid I shan't be able to return in kind for the next couple of weeks. I'm going away, you see."

The woman nodded and Nete hurried into the living room and took her purse from her bag. It was 4:35 now and Curt Wad still hadn't arrived. It was imperative the neighbor be gone if the entry phone rang. Imagine if a missing persons bulletin went out to the newspapers or television. Women like Nete's neighbor sat staring at the box all day long. Nete could even hear it droning when the rush-hour traffic died away.

"You've done the place out nicely," said the woman behind her.

Nete swiveled round like a top. The woman had followed her in and was now standing in the living room, looking about inquisitively. The open windows and the documents on the coffee table were an immediate source of interest.

"Yes, I like it," Nete replied, handing her a ten-kroner note. "Thanks for helping me out, it was very kind of you."

"What have you done with your visitor?" she asked.

"Oh, some errands to do in town."

"Perhaps we could have a cup while you wait?" the woman suggested.

Nete shook her head. "I'm afraid I can't. Another time, certainly. I have some paperwork I need to sort out."

She gave the woman a friendly nod, noting her look of disappointment before taking her by the arm and leading her back out to the landing.

"Thank you for being so kind," she said by way of conclusion, and closed the door behind her.

She stood for thirty seconds or more, waiting until satisfied her neighbor had returned to her own apartment.

What would she do if the woman turned up again while Curt Wad or Gitte Charles was there? Would she have to do away with her, too?

Nete shook her head at the thought of police milling about the place and all the questions they would ask. It was too close to home.

Please God, don't let her come back, she prayed silently.

Not that she believed He would come to her aid. Her prayers would never be enough.

She knew that from experience.

The fourth day of rye bread and water was a trial. Nete's world had diminished, with no room anymore for tears or the prayers she had offered to the Lord day and night. Night, especially.

Instead, she screamed for air and liberty. And most of all for her mother.

"Come and help me, Mother! Hug me, and stay with me forever," she wailed incessantly. Oh, if only she could sit with her mother now in the little garden of their smallholding, shelling peas. If only she could . . .

She stopped when they began to pound their fists against the door, shouting at her to shut up. It wasn't the wardens, but some of the girls from down the corridor. And the bell in the hall rang because they had left their rooms, and screams and shouts and general tumult made way for the matron's stern warnings and a rattling of the bolt in the door of her cell.

Seconds later, Nete was forced backward through the cramped space. She threw back her head and howled as the long needle was jabbed into her flesh, and then the room began to spin before her eyes.

When she came round with her arms fastened by a strap, she no longer had the strength to cry out.

And thus she lay all through the day without uttering a word. When they tried to feed her she turned away and thought of her sanctuary outside, beyond the hillock with the plum trees, sparkling beams of sunlight filtering through the leaves. And she thought back on the impression left in the hay by her lovemaking wth Tage in the barn.

Her thoughts were concentrated and intense, for if she wasn't careful Curt Wad's smug face would appear in her mind's eye instead. It was the last thing she wanted.

She did not wish to think about Curt Wad. That detestable man had destroyed her life and she would never leave the island as the person she had once been. She knew that now. Life had passed her by, and every time her lungs filled with air she wished her breathing would stop.

Her last meal was already digested, she told herself. Curt Wad, the Devil, and all his dark deeds made it impossible for her to imagine a life after this.

When several days went by without her eating and there was nothing left inside her bowels to be emptied, they called for a doctor from the mainland.

He was meant to be her savior, calling himself her friend in need, but his aid was a hypodermic in her arm and a trip across the strait to the hospital in Korsør.

Here they kept her under observation and turned away when she began to plead with them to show her the mercy of believing that she was a girl like any other, stricken by terrible misfortune.

Only once did anyone come who might have listened to her, but Nete was so sedated she dozed nearly all day long.

The person was a man in his mid-twenties visiting a little girl with hearing difficulties who had been brought in that morning and who now lay behind curtains in a bed opposite Nete's. Nete overheard that she was suffering from leukemia, and though she was unaware of what it was, she realized the girl was dying. In her hazy state she saw it in the eyes of the parents when they came away. Nete was in so many ways envious of that little girl. Liberated from the miseries of the world and yet surrounded by people who loved her. How benevolent a fate. And this man, who came to ease her final time by reading for her, or allowing her to read for him.

And Nete closed her eyes and listened to how his soothing voice helped the child shape the syllables, words, and sentences until they made sense, and slowly enough for Nete in her languid state to follow along.

He smiled warmly to her as he passed by her bed.

It was a smile that gripped her heart and prompted her to swallow just a tiny morsel of food that same evening.

Two days later the child was dead and Nete was on her way back to Sprogø, more silent and introverted than before. Even Rita left her alone in the night, but she had trouble of her own to contend with now. They all had.

For the same boat that took Nete back to the island brought with it Gitte Charles.

37

November 2010

As Curt lay on his side in the double bed, gazing at his beloved's almost transparent eyelids, which had not opened on life for three days and nights, he had all the time in the world to curse the events of the past couple of days.

Everything was falling apart. His security apparatus, set up specifically to remove all obstacles, had made fatal errors, and people who once were silent were now sounding off.

It was as though, amid all the recent triumphs of his Purity Party, disasters were now queuing up to happen, snapping at him and his life's foundation like rabid dogs.

Why had they been unable to stop those two policemen? It was imperative it be done. Mikael, Lønberg, and Caspersen had all promised to do their utmost, and yet they had failed.

Beate's face twitched almost imperceptibly yet sufficiently to make him jump.

He looked at his bony hand as he stroked her cheek and felt strangely at odds with himself. It seemed almost to merge with her skin, so slight was the difference between her aging and his. But in a few hours she would be dead and he still alive. That was the issue he had to address, if indeed he wanted to live at all. And at this moment he did not. But he had to. There were jobs to be taken care of, but when they were done he would find a headstone, and the mason would carve not one name, but two.

A sudden, urgent noise came from his bedside table. It was his iPhone, not the secure connection he mostly used now. He turned over, picked it up, and opened the text message that had come in.

It was a link from Herbert Sønderskov.

So he had done as he was told, Curt thought to himself, pleased by the prospect. One person less to go shooting their mouth off.

He tapped the link and waited a moment until an image appeared. When it did, he sat up abruptly in a state of alarm.

The photo showed a beaming Herbert and Mie, waving to him amid lush, luxuriant surroundings. Above the image was a brief caption: *You'll never find us.*

Once he'd transferred the file to his laptop he opened it again and enlarged the photo until it filled the screen. It had been taken only ten minutes before, and the sky above the smiling couple was burning red in the last throes of sunset. Behind them were palm trees and, farther back, dark faces and an expanse of blue ocean.

He opened the "Planets" app on his iPhone and tapped "Globe" for an exact specification of the sun's present position. He studied the data and saw that the only tropical location where the sun had set ten minutes ago was the southern tip of Madagascar. The other areas within its axis were open sea, Middle Eastern desert, and temperate regions of the former USSR.

Since they were standing with their backs to the sunset, they had to be on the western side of the island. Madagascar was large, certainly, but not big enough to conceal them forever. If he sent Mikael down there to ask around for two elderly, gray-haired Scandinavians, he would find them in no time. A bribe here and there always worked wonders, and there would be plenty of sharks in those waters to erase all traces.

It was the first good news of the day.

He smiled and felt his strength return. "Nothing wears a man down like faintheartedness," his father always said. A wise man indeed.

He leaned his stiff frame backward and peered out at the police cadets engaged in their role-playing beneath the trees of the academy grounds on the opposite side of the road. To his disgust he noted that several of the young people in uniform were dark-skinned, and then the Nokia rang on the table.

"It's Mikael. I'm with one of our people. No need for you to know the name. Seven minutes ago we observed Hafez el-Assad leaving Police HQ. He's now on his way down the stairs from Tietgens Bridge to the platforms at Central Station. What do you want us to do?"

What should they do? Surely it was obvious.

"Follow him. If you get the chance to do so unseen, grab him and take him away. Keep the line open so I can listen in. And make sure he doesn't see you."

"Like I said, there's two of us. We're keeping our distance, no need to worry."

Curt smiled. Second piece of good news. Maybe this was a turn-around.

He lay down again next to his dying spouse, his ear pressed to the Nokia on the pillow. Life and death, juxtaposed.

When he had lain there listening for some minutes and sensed that Beate's breathing had all but ceased, a whisper sounded in the receiver at his ear.

"We're on the S-train now, heading for Tåstrup. He might be leading us to his proper address. We're at each end of the carriage by the doors, so he's not going to give us the slip, you can be sure of it."

Curt commended him and turned to Beate. He placed his fingertips against her neck. There was still a pulse, but it was weak and unpredictable as death itself.

He closed his eyes for a moment and his mind filled with memories of rosy cheeks and laughter that chased away all concerns. How could we ever have been so young? he wondered.

"RIGHT!" Curt awoke with a start at the sudden exclamation from the mobile. "He's off the train at Brøndbyøster. I reckon he's on his way to your place, Curt."

Had he nodded off? He shook away his bewilderment and sat up in bed with the mobile to his ear. "Keep your distance. I'll be ready when he gets here. But be discreet. The cadets from the police academy over the road are running around like cowboys and Indians."

Curt smiled. He would give this Assad a warm welcome.

He would have to leave Beate for just a few minutes. He turned to ask her for her patience, only to see that her eyes were wide open, her head thrust back.

He held his breath for a few seconds, then gasped as he looked into her glazed, lifeless gaze. She seemed to be staring at where he had lain, as though in her final moment she had sought contact. And he had been asleep. He was mortified. He had not been there for her when she needed him the most.

He felt his abdomen tighten into a knot, then a pounding sensation delivered into his chest, causing him to convulse, a guttural sound rattling in his throat. His face contorted, and then a long, almost inaudible howl penetrated his sobbing.

Thus he remained for some minutes, holding her hand in his, until finally he closed her eyes and got to his feet without looking back.

In the room next to the dining room he found the bat with which his sons had hammered the daylights out of countless tennis balls. He weighed it in his hand, finding it suitably heavy, and then went out into the yard to lie in wait behind the gable end of the outbuilding.

He listened to the boisterous sound of voices from over the road, where the police cadets were acting out their youthful ideals, separating good from bad. It was exactly what Curt was about to do now. He would deliver a crippling blow to the nape of Hafez el-Assad's neck, then drag him quickly away to the safety of the outbuilding. When the others arrived they would help him get the body into the strong room.

His mobile thrummed in his pocket.

"Yes?" he whispered. "Where are you now?"

"We're standing at the junction of Vestre Gade and Brøndbyøstervej. He's given us the slip."

Curt frowned. "What?"

"He ducked into a housing development and all of a sudden he was gone."

"Split up and get after him immediately."

He snapped the mobile shut and looked around. He felt quite safe here in the corner of the yard, a high wall behind him facing Tværgaden. An intruder could come from only one direction, which was up the driveway, parallel to the outbuilding at whose far end he stood concealed. He was prepared.

Only a few minutes passed before he heard the sound of footsteps. Cautious, tentative footsteps in the driveway, moving closer, meter by meter.

Curt tightened his grip on the bat and crept forward to the corner of the building. He took a deep breath and held it until he saw a head appear.

In the split-second before he hammered the weapon home, the head was withdrawn.

"It's me, Curt!" said a voice, quite unlike the Arab's.

A figure came forward, one of their own. A man Mikael used once in a while at some of their larger events.

"You blithering idiot!" Curt hissed. "Get out of here, you'll frighten him off. Back to the road, and make sure he doesn't see you."

He stood for a while, his heart thumping in his chest as he cursed the fools in his midst. Come on, you little wog, he urged as the sounds of the police training exercises dwindled. Let's get this over with.

Hardly had the thought of the impending encounter flashed through his mind before a dull thud came from behind him. He glanced back in time to see a pair of hands appear on top of the wall, and as he turned the man landed like a cat, crouched on all fours in front of him, glaring at him with eyes that had fixed their prey.

"We need to talk, Curt," the Arab uttered immediately, but Wad raised the bat and brought it down with all his might.

In one swift movement, the short, thick-bodied man spun aside, propelling himself upright with a powerful thrust. And as the bat struck the ground with a heavy thump, he leaped forward and grabbed Curt firmly with both arms around his torso.

"We're going inside now, understand?" he whispered. "You have too many hyenas running loose out here."

He squeezed hard until Curt felt his breath fail. He wanted to scream for help but was unable to fill his lungs with air.

The Arab hauled him quickly across the yard onto the lawn by the back door. A couple of seconds more and they would have been inside. But then came the sound of footsteps running up the driveway and the figure of Mikael appeared, stopping suddenly and staring at them in surprise. Curt's assailant squeezed harder, until the old man almost passed out. And then he released him.

Curt lay for a moment facedown in the grass. He heard the tumult behind him. Blows exchanged, the invective of two languages.

He got to his feet with difficulty and staggered over to the outbuilding where the bat still lay on the ground.

When he picked it up, the Arab was standing in front of him.

Curt glanced instinctively toward the lawn, where Mikael lay unconscious. Who was this man?

"Let go of that," said Hafez el-Assad, in a tone that excluded defiance.

The sound of the wooden bat as it fell to the flagstones was like the feeling Curt had in his stomach.

"What do you want with me?" he asked.

"I know people like you better than you think, and you will not go free," the Arab replied. "I want to know all about your activities, and I'm certain everything we need to incriminate you is inside this house. You are a murderer, Curt Wad."

He gripped Curt's wrist firmly and dragged him along behind him.

They reached the back door when something flew through the air, impacting on the Arab's skull with a sickening crack. He crumpled to the ground.

"There!" said a voice from behind. It was Mikael's man. "That's as far as he gets."

Not long after Curt had called his protégé in the surgery he heard the key rattle in the lock downstairs.

"Thanks for coming so quickly, Karl-Johan," he said, as he led him to the bedroom.

Karl-Johan Henriksen did as required, then removed his stethoscope and looked at Curt with a grave expression. "I'm very sorry, Curt," he said. "But she's at peace now."

He filled in the death certificate with trembling hands and seemed to be even more affected by the situation than Curt himself.

"What are you going to do now, Curt?"

"I've made arrangements with one of our supporters, an excellent undertaker in Karlslunde. I've just been on the phone to him and I'll be seeing him this evening. Tomorrow I'll call the pastor. Beate will be laid to rest in the old cemetery here at Brøndbyøster church."

Carl took the document and accepted Karl-Johan Henriksen's condolences. They shook hands.

And with that, a long and seemingly everlasting chapter had come to an end.

It had been a truly strenuous day.

He sat for a while with his wife and noted that her body was already cold. How fleeting life was.

Then he made her up and tidied the bedroom. He took his car keys, went over to the outbuilding, opened the strong room, and saw there was still life in the dark figure that lay on the concrete floor.

"Sleep well, my foolish little Arab. And if you have not departed this world when I get back from the undertaker, I shall be only too happy to help you off on the final journey."

38

September 1987

The closer Gitte got to Copenhagen, the more her plan took shape.

Ten million was a lot of money, but Nete had more, plenty more. Gitte was only fifty-three, and ten million kroner was hardly going to last a lifetime. Not the way she spent money, not with all the dreams inside her head. If she looked after herself and cut back on her drinking, she might easily have another thirty or forty years ahead of her. In that case, it didn't take an accountant to work out that ten million was on the short side.

The plan, therefore, was for Gitte to assume control of everything Nete owned. As yet, she was unsure as to how. It would depend on the way things panned out. The best thing would be if Nete was still as malleable as before. But if she really was as ill as she made out, Gitte would just have to make herself indispensable until her time was up. Nete's will and the signatures that would be needed were an obstacle she felt confident of surmounting.

And if Nete wasn't cooperative, more drastic means were always an option. It wasn't what she wanted, but at the same time she was certainly not ruling it out. She'd done it before, sending terminally ill patients on to the afterlife quicker than fate had intended.

It had been Rita Nielsen who first discovered Gitte's weakness for women. With her soft lips and damp hair hanging in front of her eyes she could make Gitte weak at the knees. It was forbidden, of course, but when Rita's blouse clung tightly in the steam of the washhouse, and Gitte at the same time was invested with the authority to order her down to the meadows at will, Gitte was the one who took the lead.

And Rita Nielsen was more than willing. Her soft, warm body craved pleasure, and Gitte delivered.

Their liaison continued for as long as Rita was obliging, but when she got up one night and pulled her blouse back down over her breasts, it all came to an end.

"I want away from here and you're going to help me," she announced. "You're to tell the matron I'm rehabilitated and that you recommend they let me out of the system. Do you understand?"

It wasn't the way Gitte was used to being spoken to by the girls of Sprogø, and she wasn't prepared to accept it. The girls scattered at Gitte's command, and that was how she intended it to continue. They looked up to her and feared her for the tyrant she could be when the occasion suited her.

No one sent as many to the contemplation rooms as Gitte. No one made such a noise if a girl should be disrespectful. The other members of the staff found her actions laudable and admired her, for she was a qualified nurse and good-looking to boot.

Gitte thought about cutting Rita for her impudence, but hesitated a moment too long, and instead found herself on the receiving end of a slap in the face that almost took her breath away and caused her to stumble backward to the ground. How dare this simple girl raise a hand to her?

"You know full well I can destroy you. I can describe your body in every detail, and I will, in front of the matron, unless you help me," Rita calmly stated, standing over her. "And when I tell her how you force me to please you, my descriptions alone will be enough for her to realize I'm telling the truth. So you're going to send me back to the mainland. I know it's the doctors who decide, but you'll sort it."

Gitte's eyes followed a flock of geese passing across the sky. And then she nodded faintly.

Rita would return to the mainland, but not until it suited Gitte. Not a moment before.

The next morning, Gitte pinched herself hard on the cheeks before knocking firmly on the matron's door and stepping inside to be met by a look of immediate horror from her superior behind the desk.

"Good gracious, Gitte! What on earth has happened?"

Gitte held her breath and turned slightly so the matron could see not only that her white smock had been torn, but also that she was not wearing underclothes.

She described briefly how the mentally deranged, sexually deviant psychopath Rita Nielsen had torn the clothes off her behind the washhouse, wrestling her to the ground and parting her legs.

She forced her voice into a trembling stutter and stared in shame at the floor as she told of the assault and her futile attempts to defend herself.

"I recommend Rita Nielsen be put into the punishment cell for ten days and furthermore that she be stripped of all privileges," she said, concluding from the matron's fluttering hands and shocked expression that her request would be granted.

"Moreover, I think we ought to consider sterilization and then send her away from here. The girl is sexually obsessed and in my view she'll become an intolerable burden on society if we fail to act."

The matron's fists clenched as she stared stiffly at the marks on Gitte's throat.

"Of course," she said, and got to her feet.

———

Rita kicked up a fuss, but her charges against Gitte were all dismissed. She was clearly astounded that her scheme had not only failed but also had been turned against her. Gitte reveled in it.

"Of course you can tell me what Gitte's body looks like," said the matron. "You assaulted her yourself. Callous and malicious as you are, I am in no doubt that you will endeavor to twist any situation to your advantage, but I'm afraid you can't pull the wool over my eyes, young lady. What else can be expected of a feeble-minded girl with such a despicable history as your own?"

News of these events spread like wildfire, and before the day was over gossip had long since reached the stables, the fields, the henhouses, and every conceivable nook and cranny within the institution's walls. Rita yelled and screamed from her cell, and sedatives were administered. Many of Gitte's colleagues, and even a number of the girls, gloated.

Her release turned out to be but a brief respite, for Rita was as tough as nails and found it hard to keep a civil tongue in her head. Only a week later she was again confined to the cell, restrained to the bed, shouting like a woman possessed.

"Nete Hermansen is a good girl. She shouldn't be sharing with a monster," Gitte said to the matron. And so they moved all of Rita's things out and let Nete have the room for herself.

All of this made Nete see Gitte in a different light, a fact Gitte sensed immediately.

It was Nete who took the initiative. Naive, full of hope, and so utterly desirable.

They had been put to work unloading sacks of coal from the boat, and one of the girls twisted her ankle and fell, yelping like a dog in distress. Everyone gathered round, though the wardens shouted and lashed out, and in the middle of all this commotion Nete and Gitte found themselves standing next to each other, in close proximity.

"I've been sent here by mistake," Nete whispered, her eyes bright and clear. "I'm not stupid, and I know there are others here who aren't, but I'm not a slut either, like they say I am. Can't they review my case?"

She was gorgeous. Full lips and a body as firm and alluring as no other on the island. Gitte wanted her and had known as much for a long time. Now was her chance.

They stood for a moment as blows were meted out and cries filled the air. It was enough for Nete to begin to weep. But then Gitte took her hand and led her away. The effect was electrifying. A tingle ran through the girl's body, as though Gitte's touch and attention were the key to everything she desired. And Gitte brushed away Nete's tears, drawing her down toward the marsh and nodding considerately in all the right places as the girl let out her troubles.

It was all quite innocent. Within ten minutes Gitte had won her full confidence.

"I'll do what I can, though I can't promise you anything," Gitte told her.

She had never seen a smile as big in all her life.

Things didn't go quite as easily as Gitte had thought they might. Though they talked freely on their walks down to the marsh, Nete seemed unwilling to surrender herself.

In a roundabout way it was the lighthouse keeper's cat that came to Gitte's aid.

Intense rivalry between two cockerels in the lighthouse keeper's henhouse had wreaked havoc on the man's sleep for several nights in succession, and the culprits had hitherto resisted all efforts to be seized. Accordingly, the lighthouse keeper's assistant was dispatched into the meadows to gather dried-up henbane so they could anesthetize the entire population of the henhouse with the smoke from the burning plant, thereby facilitating the capture and subsequent throttling of one of the offending fowl.

A few of these plants were tossed aside in a puddle, where they remained fermenting for some time until the cat, whose name was Mickey, found himself attracted by the smell, cautiously lapping at the stagnant water by way of investigation.

A short time later, the bemused lighthouse keeper and his assistant observed the feline tearing up and down a number of trees for an hour or so before eventually lying down outside the pantry, where it rotated a couple of times on its own axis and then expired.

Everyone but the lighthouse keeper's wife found the story hysterically amusing, and so it was that Gitte learned of the rare plant that grew wild on Sprogø and whose properties had the most peculiar effects on those who ingested it.

She ordered books on the subject from the mainland and was soon knowledgeable enough to be able to conduct her own experiments.

Gitte became fascinated by the notion of possessing power over life. It was a fascination that was to prove near-fatal for one girl in particular, whom the wardens found to be especially insolent. Gitte dipped a cigarette into an extract of the plant and allowed it to dry. And when the time came, she planted it in the pocket of the girl's tartan dress.

They heard how she began to wail and cry out the strangest utterances down by the Cairn, the pile of stones that marked the midpoint between Sjælland and Fyn, where the girl would often go for a smoke on her own. And yet they were not unduly alarmed when suddenly she fell silent.

The girl survived, though she was never the same obstreperous delinquent as before. Fear of death had gripped her forever.

Gitte was pleased, for now she possessed a means by which to make Nete comply.

Her threats to make her insane or even end her life for good, coupled with the knowledge of what Gitte really wanted from her, shocked Nete to such an extent that she was unable even to cry. It was as though all the malice in the world had taken up residence in her savior, and now all the dreams she harbored of returning to a normal life were at once extinguished.

Gitte understood her reaction, and it suited her well. She tricked her with assurances that as long as Nete was willing to please her, Gitte would do all she could to convince the matron to review her case. Thus Nete acquiesced, and though Gitte was reluctant to admit it, she found herself growing dependent on their relationship. It made tolerable her isolated life among these embittered, vengeful, and unsavory women so different from herself. Indeed, it made her believe that she wanted nothing to change.

With Nete lying at her side in the tall grass, she could shut everything else out and breathe freely in her island prison.

Unsurprisingly, it was Rita who drove a wedge between them, although Gitte didn't learn this until later.

By the time Rita was finally released from the contemplation room, the matron had begun to waver.

"In matters of sterilization I'm obliged to consult the head physician," she declared. "He's coming to the island soon, so let's wait for his opinion."

But the intervals between the physician's visits were long, and Rita made use of the time to plot revenge, opening Nete's eyes and convincing her that Gitte Charles could on no account be trusted, and that the only way out was for the two of them to escape.

From then on it was mayhem.

39

November 2010

"I've called him a dozen times now, Carl, and there's still no answer. I'm sure he's switched off his mobile. But why would he do that? He's never done it before." Rose seemed genuinely concerned. "It's all your fault, you big oaf. Just before he went he said you'd accused him of murdering that Lithuanian, Verslovas."

Carl shook his head. "No, I didn't, Rose. But that fax raised a number of questions. None of us is beyond suspicion when it comes to matters like that."

She stood in front of him, fists planted firmly on her hips. "Now you listen to me. We're having none of that here, thank you very much. If Assad says he had nothing to do with that sicko Linas Verslovas getting snuffed, it means he's telling the truth, right? The problem here is that you're pressuring us, Carl, without a thought for anyone's feelings. That's what's wrong with you."

It was a rant and a half. The girl had managed to turn everything on its head, which was definitely one of her strong points in an ongoing investigation, but a major drawback when it came to personal relations. At any rate, these were allegations he could well do without.

"OK, Rose, keep your hair on. As far as I can see, you and Assad take care of all the emotional stuff quite nicely on your own. And if you'll excuse me, I haven't really got time for Love Thy Neighbor at the moment. I've got an appointment for a bollocking from Marcus Jacobsen."

———

"You mean it's a write-off? And you want a new car?" The chief gawped at him in disbelief. "It's November, Carl. Haven't you ever heard of a thing called a budget?"

"Funny you should mention that, Marcus. I'm quite up on the subject, as it happens. Department Q was allocated eight million this year, yeah? Where the hell's it all gone?"

Marcus Jacobsen's shoulders drooped. "Are we really going to have that shouting match again, Carl? You know perfectly well those funds are divided between our two departments."

"*My* department's funds, Marcus, and I get about a fifth. Isn't that right? Pretty cheap setup the nation's got going down there in the basement, wouldn't you say?"

"That's as may be. But there'll be no new car, I can tell you that much. The money's not there, it's as simple as that. You've no idea the cases we've got swallowing resources at the moment."

Carl said nothing. He knew it was true, even if it was beside the point.

Marcus extracted another piece of nicotine gum from his pack. His mouth was almost full now. Good for him, packing in the smokes, but the copious amounts of their substitute that he'd been chewing had been making him hyper after his cold had gone away.

"I think there's another Peugeot 607 in the motor pool," he said eventually. "You'll have to share it, but I'm afraid I can't see any other way out until the new financial year, Carl."

"Think again."

Jacobsen let out a weary sigh. "All right, give me the whole story. You've got five minutes."

"Five minutes isn't enough."

"Try anyway."

A quarter of an hour later Marcus almost hit the roof. "First you break in to Nørvig's place and steal his archives. Then you force your way into the home of a well-known politician while his wife's on her deathbed. Not to mention at least a hundred other breaches."

"We don't actually know if his wife's dying or not. Haven't you ever used that one yourself? Your nonexistent auntie's funeral when you felt like a day off?"

Marcus almost choked on his lump of gum. "Certainly not, and I hope to God you haven't either, at least not on my watch. But listen to me, Carl. I want Nørvig's archives up here sharpish. And as soon as Assad gets back you're going to explain to him that he can be out of HQ on his arse as quickly as he got in. Moreover, you're dropping that case as of now! Otherwise you're going to end up in the kind of trouble I haven't got time to get you out of again."

"Oh, really? Well think about this for a second: if we kick this case into touch, you're going to be six-point-eight million down on next year's budget."

"Meaning?"

"Meaning what's the point of having a Department Q if we're to leave well alone?"

"Carl, all I'm trying to say is that you're on thin ice, and that's putting it mildly. So unless from the relative safety of your desk you can come up with some hard evidence of Curt Wad and other leading members of the Purity Party having committed criminal acts, you stay away. No further close encounters with him. Understood?"

Carl nodded reluctantly. So that was it. Did everything in this world come down to politics?

"We were talking about a car," he said, changing tack.

"Yes, all right, I'll see what I can do. In the meantime, get downstairs and fetch those files up."

Carl kicked every baseboard in sight all the way to the front desk. Bollocks.

"Miffed, are we, Carl," said Lis, as she handed a pile of documents over the counter to a dark-skinned guy with black curly hair in one of the force's standard-issue winter jackets.

He turned toward Carl and nodded. He knew the face.

"Samir," Carl blurted. Assad's best mate in person. "Business slow in Rødovre, is it?" he quipped. "Did Antonsen finally retire and take everything home with him?"

He laughed at his own one-liner, and laughed alone.

"We've plenty to be getting on with, but thanks for asking all the same. Just some paperwork we need to exchange," Samir replied, weighing the stack in his hand.

"Quick word, Samir, now you're here, yeah? What's all this with you and Assad? And don't tell me there's nothing wrong. I just want to know the score, that's all. You'll be helping me out."

"The only thing that'll help you out is realizing how dysfunctional he is."

"Dysfunctional? What are you talking about? Assad's not dysfunctional. What makes you say that?"

"Ask him yourself, I'm staying well out of it. He's off his head, and I've told him so. It's the truth, and he can't hack it."

Carl took him by the arm. "Listen, Samir. I've no idea what Assad might or might not be able to hack, but I've a strong feeling you *do*, OK? And if you—or Assad, for that matter—don't spill the beans of your own accord, I might have to force it out of you when the time comes. Do you get my drift?"

"Fine by me, Mørck. Give it a try."

He wrenched himself free and marched off down the corridor.

Lis gave Carl a look of equal parts sympathy and concern. "Don't worry about your car, Carl. Soon have it sorted for you," she said.

Word spread like the clap with its arse on fire here.

"Still nothing from Assad?"

Rose shook her head. She definitely looked worried now.

"How come you're so bothered about him all of a sudden, anyway?"

"Because I've seen him rattled a couple of times recently. Never seen that before."

Carl knew what she meant. She didn't miss a trick.

"We've been told to get Nørvig's archives up to the third floor."

"Better get a move on, then, hadn't you?"

Carl dropped his head slightly so his circulation didn't grind to a halt. "What are you so pissed off about, Rose?"

"Don't worry yourself," she replied. "You haven't got time for all that"—finger quotes—"'Love Thy Neighbor' stuff. You said so yourself."

He struggled to hold back his temper, then calmly managed to inform her that if she didn't get her backside into gear and start lugging those fucking files, he'd tell her to go home and send for Yrsa instead.

And he meant it, too.

Rose frowned. "Do you know what, Carl? I don't think you're right in the head."

He heard her making a racket as he called Assad's number several times in succession, legs jiggling with tension underneath the desk. Assad had half-inched his lighter, and if he didn't have a smoke in a minute his calf muscles were going to cramp up.

"Be seeing you," came the shrill sound of Rose's voice from the corridor. Carl turned to the doorway just in time to see her stride past with her overcoat on and her pink bag slung over her shoulder.

So that was that.

Bollocks! Was she really sodding off? He almost burst into tears at the thought of the consequences. She'd be sending her alter ego, Yrsa, in the morning. At best.

His mobile thrummed and twirled on the desk. It was Lis.

"OK, I've got your car sorted. If you go to the parking lot over by the National Investigation Center, I'll send someone along with the keys."

Carl nodded. About fucking time. All he had to do now was find
Assad. Rose had got him worked up about it now.

Two minutes later he was standing in the parking lot, looking around
in vain. No car, no minion with a key. He frowned and was just about to
call Lis when a pair of headlights blinked at him at the far end of the lot.

He went over and discovered Rose with her fluorescent bag on her lap,
seated in the passenger seat of a car smaller than his trouser pocket. He
swallowed hard as he tried to digest his horror. The color of the vehicle
was enough on its own. It reminded him of the hunk of Danish Blue he'd
put in the fridge a couple of months back and forgotten all about.

"What the fuck's this, and what are you doing in it, Rose?" he spluttered as he opened the door on the driver's side.

"It's a Ford Ka and you're on your way to find Assad, right?"

He nodded. You had to hand it to the gangly goth. Her intuition was
spot-on.

"Well, I'm going with you. And this is the car Marcus Jacobsen's
leased for you for the rest of the year." She managed to stifle a giggle,
then became serious again. "Come on, Carl. It'll be dark soon."

They got down on their knees, one after the other, and peered through
the letter box of the flat on Heimdalsgade, and as Carl expected they saw
neither furniture nor any sign of Assad.

The last time Carl had been here he'd been confronted by a pair of
painstakingly tattooed brothers with foreign names and biceps as big as
coconuts. This time he had to make do with the general clamor of domestic disputes in languages that might just as easily have been Serbo-Croat
as Somali. It was what they called a lively neighborhood.

"He's been living in a house out on Kongevejen for quite a while now.
Don't ask me to explain," said Carl, as he climbed back into their mobile
hatbox.

They drove for fifteen minutes without a word, until eventually they stood before a whitewashed cottage that seemed almost to have merged into the woods where the road to Bistrup opened out onto Kongevejen.

"Doesn't look like he's here either, Carl," said Rose. "Are you sure this is the right address?"

"It's the one he gave me, anyway."

They stared at the nameplate. On it were two archetypal Danish women's names. Maybe they'd sublet the place to Assad. With the property market bottomed out, everyone knew someone these days who'd suddenly found themselves stuck with two homes on their hands and a pressing need for cash. The heady days of finance ministers using their bollocks for brains and banks lining their pockets at ordinary people's expense weren't over yet by a long chalk.

A few moments later the ebullient dark-haired woman who had opened the door was assuring him that if this Assad chap he knew happened to be homeless, he would be welcome to stop on their sofa for a couple of nights for a modest sum. But apart from that, she and her partner had never heard of him.

So there they were.

"Don't you know where your own workers live?" Rose asked scathingly as they got back in the car. "I thought you ran Assad home every now and then, knowing how nosy you are and all."

Carl considered the affront for a moment before hitting back. "OK, little Miss Know-It-All. What do *you* know about Assad's domestic life?"

She gazed through the windshield, eyes unfocused. "Not a lot. He used to mention his wife and his two daughters occasionally, but that's a while back now. To be quite honest, I don't think he lives with them anymore."

Carl nodded pensively. The thought had occurred to him, too. "What about friends? Has he ever mentioned any? Maybe he's holed up with one of them."

She shook her head. "You probably think I'm daft now, but something tells me Assad hasn't got a home."

"What makes you think that?"

"I've this feeling he's been sleeping at work for a while. I think he might even go out for a couple of hours at night just to make it look right. But it's not like we clock in or anything, is it? So it's hard to know for sure."

"What about his clothes? He's not in the same gear every day, is he? So he must have a base somewhere."

"I suppose we could check his cupboards and drawers at HQ. Perhaps he keeps all his stuff there. He can get his laundry done in town. Come to think of it, he does come in toting plastic bags every now and then. I always just thought it was all those funny snacks he gets in from the immigrant stores."

Carl sighed. Whatever Assad's plastic bags contained, it was no help to them now.

"He's probably just gone off on his own to let off steam. You'll see, he's more than likely back at the office now. Give him a call, will you, Rose?"

She raised her eyebrows. The usual why-don't-you-do-it-yourself. But then she got her phone out and did it anyway.

"Did you know he has voicemail on that new phone of his, Carl?" she asked, ear pressed to her mobile. "He's got a greeting set up and everything."

He shook his head. "What's it say?"

"It says he's out of the office on police business, but he'll be back by six."

"And what time is it now?"

"Almost seven."

Carl picked up his own phone and called the duty desk at HQ.

They'd seen neither hide nor hair of him.

"Police business," Assad's message had said. It was odd.

Rose hung up and stroked her chin for a moment.

"Are you thinking what I'm thinking, Carl? I wouldn't put it past him, the mood he was in."

Carl sat a while, squinting at the headlights flashing by on the busy road.

"I'm afraid you might be right."

They left the dwarfmobile on Tværgaden, across from the police academy. Curt Wad's house was twenty-five meters farther along, at the end of what was a rather pleasant street. As far as they could see from a distance, the house was dark behind the high wooden fence.

"Not exactly promising," said Carl.

"We don't know yet," Rose replied. "I'm just glad we've got weapons with us, because my intuition's got all its alarms going off here."

Carl patted his service pistol. "Well, *I* feel equipped. What have *you* got in your bag?"

He gestured toward the voluminous pink monstrosity Rose had almost certainly nicked off her real sister Yrsa.

She said nothing. Instead, she swung the bag once above her head, bringing it down with an almighty whack against the green garbage bin one of the residents had put out on the pavement.

When they saw the extent of the damage to the bin, which now lay halfway up the man's driveway with a train of rubbish scattered in its wake, they immediately turned and legged it. Before the light came on at the front door they were already out of sight.

"What the fuck have you got in there, Rose? Boulders?" Carl spluttered breathlessly as they stopped in front of Curt Wad's driveway on Brøndbyøstervej.

"The collected works of Shakespeare. Bound in leather."

———

A minute later Carl stood in Wad's garden for the second time that day, peering in at the living-room window, this time with Rose stationed at an appropriate distance, eyes scanning the dark.

It had been a long time since she'd been with them in the field, and she seemed jumpy in the pitch-blackness. Even the stars in the sky looked like they'd jacked it in for the night.

Carl went over and tried the back door. It was locked, but the frame didn't look in the best of shape. He wondered what Assad would have done now, then heaved at the door with such force that the frame gave way audibly.

He gripped the stainless-steel doorknob more firmly, took a couple of deep breaths to muster strength, and placed one foot against the brickwork before yanking so hard he immediately felt something give in his shoulder. He tumbled backward over the doorstep, ending up on his backside in the grass with the doorknob in his hand and a pain down one side.

"Nice work," said Rose, noting that while the door and the lock had remained intact, the pane had cracked, one long fracture running lengthwise and what looked like a thousand little tributaries.

She lifted a foot and pressed the sole of her boot gently against the glass.

There was a clatter as the pane dislodged into the room inside. Carl counted the seconds, hoping Assad had been right in his observation about the place not being alarmed. He certainly didn't fancy trying to explain to a pair of security guards that the sirens had gone off when the door suddenly fell apart on its own.

"How come there's no alarm?" Rose whispered. "There's a doctor's surgery on the premises."

"There will be in that part of the house, believe me," Carl whispered back.

What they were doing seemed ridiculous. Why break into a house when Assad so obviously wasn't there? Was this his female intuition trying to kick in? Or was he now driven by his desire to give this degenerate old man a taste of his own bitter medicine?

"What now, Carl?" Rose whispered.

"I want to see what's upstairs. I've got a feeling we'll find something there, maybe something that can confirm his involvement in what happened at my place. Wad tried to tell us his wife was on her deathbed. But wouldn't he be here now if he were telling the truth? I mean, who's going to leave their dying wife all alone in an empty house? No, I reckon he's hiding something up there. Gut feeling."

Carl switched on his flashlight, illuminating their way through the dining room and the hallway, where a floral blind pulled down over the window by the front door prevented anyone from looking in. He tried the door of the surgery. It was solid, just as he'd thought, probably reinforced with steel and protected by all manner of alarms that would go off the second it was opened by anyone unauthorized.

He looked up the stairway, with its corner cupboard on the landing, rounded teak banisters, and gray carpeting. He was upstairs in an instant.

The first floor wasn't quite as presentable as below. A long, dark corridor with built-in cupboards and rooms that seemed like they'd only recently been vacated by the children who had lived there: ancient Idol posters on the sloping walls and cheap floral-patterned sofa beds.

And then he saw a dim light seeping from under a door at the far end. He turned off the flashlight and took hold of Rose's arm.

"Curt Wad may be in there, though he probably isn't," he whispered, so close to Rose's ear that his lips touched it. "If he was, he'd have come down as soon as we smashed the window, but you never know. Maybe he's the kind who prefers to lie in wait with a shotgun. That'd be more his style, come to think of it. Get behind me and be ready to hit the deck."

"If he's there, and he's not armed, how are you going to explain what we're doing here?"

"I'll say we got an emergency call," Carl whispered back, hoping he wouldn't have to repeat the excuse to Marcus Jacobsen at some later point.

He stepped up to the teak-veneered door and held his breath for a second, his hand sliding toward his pistol.

He counted to three in his head, then kicked open the door with one foot, spinning back to safety behind the wall on the other.

"Police, Wad. We received an emergency call . . . ," he began, keeping his voice as subdued as possible, then noticing the light flicker as though it came from a candle.

He leaned forward with caution and peeped into the room, sensing immediately how stupid a move it was, only to discover a small female figure laid out on the bedspread. The head was exposed, a white sheet covering the body and a withered bouquet of flowers placed between the folded hands. She was illuminated only by the candle her devoted husband had placed by the bed.

Rose stepped inside. Everything was silent. Such was death.

They stood staring at the deceased for a moment, and then Rose let out a faint sigh. "I'd say that was her bridal bouquet, Carl," she said.

Carl swallowed twice.

"Come on, let's get out of here, Rose. What we just did was the height of stupidity," said Carl as they came back out into the garden and stood for a second at the wrecked door. He picked up the metal doorknob from where he'd dropped it on the lawn, wiping it thoroughly with his handkerchief before tossing it back onto the ground. "I hope you haven't had your fingers all over the place in there," he said.

"Of course I haven't. I was too busy thinking about getting a good swing in with my bag if you got shot to pieces," she replied. How considerate of her.

"Give me the flashlight," she commanded. "I hate tagging along behind. Can't see a thing."

She waved it about like an excited schoolboy engaged in nocturnal antics, so nobody for miles around would be in the slightest doubt that a break-in might be going on. Carl hoped the bloke with the garbage bin wasn't still on the prowl.

"Keep the beam on the ground, Rose," he instructed.

She did as she was told.

And then she stopped in her tracks.

The spot of blood in the grass wasn't big, but it was there. She shone the flashlight around the area, finding a second patch in the driveway. And then a trail of drips, almost unnoticeable, leading to the outbuilding.

Carl's gut feeling returned at full force. An unpleasant knot in his stomach.

If only they'd seen this before they broke in, he would have called for assistance. Now things weren't quite as straightforward.

He pondered for a second.

Maybe they'd get away with it anyway. They had seen enough on the premises to indicate something suspicious might be going on. Surely that would be to their advantage? And who was to say *they* were responsible for breaking in? *They* certainly didn't have to tell anyone.

"I'm going to call this in to Glostrup," he said. "We could do with making it more official."

"Didn't you say Marcus Jacobsen told you to stay away from Curt Wad?" Rose asked, the beam of her flashlight sweeping between the three doors of the outbuilding.

"That's true."

"So what are you doing here at his house?"

"You're right, but I'm going to call Glostrup anyway," he replied, pull-ing his mobile out of his pocket. The Glostrup lads would be able to tell him what car Curt Wad owned and could put out an alert right away. Maybe Wad's car was out there somewhere with an injured person in the boot, and that person might be Assad. Carl's imagination was running riot.

"Wait," said Rose suddenly. "Look!"

She shone the flashlight on the padlock that hung from the middle door of the old stables. A regular padlock of the sort you could get for ten kroner in Netto. Only this one, if examined closely, had two marks on it that could only be fingerprints.

She rubbed some spit on them, then sucked her finger.

It tasted of blood.

Carl looked closer at the lock, then took his pistol from its holster. The easiest course would have been to blow it to pieces, but Carl opted for the less dramatic solution, hammering the butt of his weapon down on the padlock until his fingers throbbed with pain.

Rose gave him a rare pat of approval when finally it gave way.

"It won't make much difference now," she said, feeling around for a light switch inside the door.

They blinked a couple of times as the flickering fluorescent light re-vealed a room that could have belonged to almost any outhouse in the town where Carl grew up. Shelves along one wall, with flower pots on them, discarded pans and receptacles, and wizened flower bulbs that hadn't seen soil for years. Against the other wall was a humming deep freezer, in front of it a steel ladder leading up through a trapdoor to a loft where Carl could see a dimly illuminating naked lightbulb, 25 watts at most.

He climbed up and looked around a room cluttered to the gills with framed pictures, old mattresses, and heaps of black bin liners from which old clothes spilled.

He shone the flashlight over the sloping, hessian-clad walls and found himself thinking the place must have made a great den for the youngsters who had grown up here.

"Oh, God! Carl!" Rose suddenly exclaimed from below.

She was standing at the deep freezer with the lid raised and her head drawn back. Carl's heart began to pound.

"This is gross!" she said, twisting her face in disgust.

OK, Carl thought to himself. If it was Assad she'd found in there, she'd have said something else.

He climbed down and peered into the freezer. It contained a number of transparent plastic bags, inside which were human fetuses. He counted eight. Eight small lives that never were. He wouldn't have called it gross. The sight that confronted him gave rise to quite different emotions.

"We don't know the circumstances here, Rose."

She shook her head and tightened her lips. It was obvious she was deeply affected.

"The blood you saw out there could be from one of these bags. Maybe the new doctor dropped one in the driveway, maybe it dripped onto the flagstones. That could explain the fingerprints as well."

Again she shook her head. "No, the blood out there is fresh, and these fetuses are frozen stiff." She gestured toward the contents of the freezer. "Do you see a hole in any of these bags?"

It was an excellent observation. He seemed to be lagging behind at the moment.

"Listen, we're not going get this sorted without help," he said. "As I see it, there are three options. Either we get out of here while we've still got time, or we call Glostrup and inform them of our suspicions, which I reckon is what we should do. The third thing is we ought to try Assad's office phone again," he added. "He might be back now, for all we know." He nodded as if to convince himself. "Maybe he's finally got his mobile charged."

He took out his phone. Rose shook her head. "Can you smell something burning?" she asked.

Carl couldn't. In the meantime he got Assad's voicemail at HQ again.

"Look," said Rose. "There." She pointed toward the ceiling.

He glanced up as he dialed Assad's mobile. Was that smoke up there or just dust swirling in the dim light?

He watched as Rose's swaying backside disappeared up the ladder while a phone company message informed him the subscriber was unavailable.

"There *is* something smoldering," she called down to him. "But it's coming from where you are."

She was down the ladder in no time. "That loft extends farther than the space down here. There must be another room behind there," she said, pointing to the end wall. "And right now there's smoke coming from somewhere inside it."

Carl saw right away that the wall seemed to consist of two large sheets of plasterboard.

If there's a room behind that wall, there's no way in from here, he thought, then saw the first wisps of smoke begin to seep out.

Rose leaped forward and started thumping her fist exploratively against the wall elements. "Listen! That one's solid enough, but this one sounds hollow," she said excitedly. "Like it's metal or something. There's a sliding door here, Carl, I know there is."

He nodded and glanced around. Unless the door was activated by remote control, somewhere in the room there had to be the means to open it.

"What are we looking for?" Rose asked.

"A switch, wiring, anything on the wall that looks out of place," he replied with a rising sense of panic.

"What about over there?" she said, pointing at the wall above the freezer.

Carl's eyes scanned the surface until he saw what she meant. She was right. There was a line, a crack that seemed to indicate a repair of some kind.

His eyes followed its path to an old brass fitting above the freezer that looked like it had once belonged on a ship or to some large machine.

He lifted it from the nail on which it hung and behind it discovered a small metal flap, which he opened.

"Shit," he blurted, as the smoke leaking out between the plaster-boards thickened. Instead of a switch, the little panel behind the flap contained a display and a keypad with letters and numbers on it. Finding the combination that would activate the mechanism and open the sliding door seemed out of the question.

"People use all sorts of things for codes: the names of their kids, civil registration numbers, the wife's birthday, lucky numbers. What the hell are we supposed to do?" Carl ranted, as he began to look around for something that might break down the wall.

In the meantime, Rose's contrastingly calm systematic logic kicked in.

"We begin with what we can remember, Carl," she said, stepping up to the keypad.

"Which is sod all in my case. The man's name is Curt Wad and he's eighty-eight years old. That's all I can remember."

"All right, no need to get your knickers in a twist. I get your drift," Rose rejoined.

She typed in some characters: P-U-R-I-T-Y-P-A-R-T-Y. Nothing. T-H-E-C-A-U-S-E. Nothing.

One by one she tried names and figures from the records and cuttings on Curt Wad that she'd been poring over during the past days. Even his wife's birthday had stuck in her memory.

Then she paused for a moment and pondered, while Carl's attention was divided between the smoke coming out of the wall and the passing headlights that occasionally swept over the building.

All of a sudden she lifted her head toward him, indicating that behind the emo eyeliner and Gothic demeanor resided the germ of an idea that seemed both logical and plausible.

He watched her fingers as they typed.

H-E-R-M-A-N-S-E-N

There was a click. The wall elements slid open and revealed a hidden room filled with smoke that now billowed forth toward them. At the same moment the abrupt infusion of oxygen sent a flame leaping into the air.

"Shit!" Carl yelped. He snatched the flashlight from Rose's hand and plunged into the room.

He saw another freezer and shelving that looked like it housed an archive. But it was the limp figure that lay outstretched on the floor that focused his gaze and all of his senses.

The fire licked at Assad's trouser legs. Carl dragged him out, yelling for Rose to throw her coat over their colleague and suffocate the flames.

"Oh God, oh God, oh God, he's hardly breathing," she stuttered in a frenzy, Carl glancing back into the room only to note that the fire had taken hold to the extent that the idea of retrieving anything at all from inside was futile.

The last thing he noticed before they dragged Assad outside were the words daubed in blood on almost every available surface of the cramped little room, "ASSAD WAS HERE!" And then, on the floor by the deep freezer, the melting remains of a lighter that looked remarkably like the one Carl had left on his desk only hours before.

The paramedics arrived first and attended to Assad. They put him on a stretcher, an oxygen mask pumping life back into his lungs.

Rose was silent as the grave. The way she looked, she was liable to break down any minute.

"He's going to be all right, yeah?" Carl asked the ambulance crew, struggling to contain a turmoil of emotions he hardly knew he possessed. He raised his eyebrows in a feeble attempt to stem the tears, but they came anyway. "For fuck's sake, Assad. Come on, mate!"

"He's still alive," one of the men replied. "But a case of smoke inhalation like this is often going to be fatal. There can be thermal damage, burns to the respiratory system, poisoning. You should be prepared for the worst. The blow to the back of his head looks nasty, too. There may well be a fracture of the skull and internal hemorrhaging. Do you know him well?"

Carl gave a slow nod. This was hard on him, but nothing compared to how Rose was taking it.

"There's always a hope," said the paramedic, as firemen shouted instructions to one another and began rolling out hoses.

Carl put his arm around Rose and felt her trembling.

"It's going to be OK, Rose. He'll pull through, I know he will," he told her, realizing how empty the words sounded.

When the medic arrived in a response vehicle a moment later, he proceeded to tear open Assad's shirt to gain a quick impression of his heart rate and breathing, but something seemed to get in the way. He tore some more, and removed a handful of papers from Assad's clothing, tossing them aside onto the ground.

Carl picked them up.

There were two distinct sets. One consisted of a number of sheets stapled together. On the front was written THE CAUSE: MEMBERSHIP LIST.

The second was a thin folder: FILE NO. 64.

40

September 1987

It was twenty past five and Nete had knitted row upon row.

Beneath the wide-open windows, people of all shapes, sizes, and ages had passed by, some even pausing momentarily in front of the building. But there had been no sign of Curt Wad.

Nete tried to recall her last conversation with him. The exact moment she had put the phone down. Hadn't she been left feeling that he had swum into her net? And yet she had been mistaken. Or had she?

Perhaps he was standing down there behind the trees, keeping watch. Could he have seen Philip Nørvig enter and fail to come out again? Was that it?

She rubbed the back of her head pensively. Without Curt Wad there would be no triumph, no peace of mind, and now she felt nervous tension building into a headache. If she didn't take her medicine straightaway, the migraine would set in and she had neither the time nor the energy to contend with it. At this moment she needed more than ever to think clearly and be at the ready.

She went into the bathroom, her head beginning to pound, took her pills from the medicine cabinet, and realized there was only one left.

No matter, there's another bottle in the cupboard with the table linen, she thought. She stepped back out into the hallway and looked along its length at the closed door of the dining room. She would have to go in there again, to the sight of the silver cutlery, the decanter, the crystal glasses, and the corpses that had now consumed their last supper.

Resolved, she opened the door of the airtight room as swiftly as she was able, closing it behind her in the same manner. Even now, the smell was pungent in the air, mostly on account of Philip Nørvig.

She stared at his corpse with disdain. She would have a job on her hands with him once the bodies were to be made ready. Perhaps even with all of them, she thought to herself as she found her extra tablets.

She sat down at the head of the table and studied her victims one by one.

Apart from Tage, who still lay on the floor like a beached walrus, they all sat nicely in a row. Rita, Viggo, and Philip.

She poured herself a glass of water, put three pills into her mouth, aware that two would suffice, then raised her crystal glass to the dull eyes and hanging heads.

"*Skål*, ladies and gentlemen," she said, and swallowed her pills.

She chuckled at her toast and thought of all the formalin she would soon be forcing down the throats of her silent guests. It would stem the worst of their decomposition.

"Patience, now. You'll have your drinks soon enough. And in a short while you'll be receiving company. One or two of you know her already. Gitte Charles is her name. That's right. That nasty blonde woman who made life miserable for some of us on that infernal island. She was a decent sort once, so we must hope she has retained some of the same quality. We don't want her bringing down our standards, do we?"

She laughed heartily until her headache told her enough was enough. Then she got to her feet, curtsied to her guests, and hurried back out.

She didn't want Gitte Charles to wait.

———

After breakfast Rita Nielsen drew her aside. "Listen, Nete. When Gitte gets tired of you she'll dump you, and that's when your problems will start. You saw what happened to me."

She thrust out her arm and showed Nete the needle marks. Five in all, Nete counted. Four more than she had received herself.

"My life's sheer hell here now," Rita went on, glancing around warily. "Those bastard wardens are always shushing me and slapping me about if I don't watch out. They've got me cleaning the toilets, washing menstrual rags, and running slops to the compost heap. The worst jobs, with the worst idiots, all day long. They're always on at me, 'Don't do this, don't do that' and 'We've already told you once.' It's like it's all right for them to be getting at me all the time now. And it's Gitte's fault. Have a look at this."

Rita turned her back, loosened the straps of her overalls, pulled them all the way down, and displayed a bloom of blue-red bruises across the back of her thighs, just below her buttocks. "Do you think they just appeared on their own?"

She turned back to face Nete, index finger raised in the air. "And I just *know* that next time the doctor comes they'll talk him into having me sterilized. That's why I've got to get away now, and you're coming with me, do you hear? I need you."

Nete nodded. Gitte Charles's threats to poison her with henbane were one thing, but her ice-cold demeanor toward the other girls was quite another. The way she howled with laughter when describing how she did with them as the fancy took her, recommending them for sterilization as she saw fit, no matter their willingness to please.

Nete, too, had become afraid of Gitte's whims.

"How are we going to cross the strait?" Nete asked.

"Leave that to me."

"Then what do you need me for?"

"To get us money."

"Money? How?"

"You're going to steal Gitte's savings. She boasted about them when I was her little pet. I know where she keeps them."

"Where?"

"In her room, silly."

"Why don't you do it yourself?"

Rita smiled and indicated her clothing. "Do you think they let us girls in overalls wander about the corridors in there?" Her face grew serious again. "It's got to be done in the daytime, while Gitte's bossing us about outside. You know where she keeps her key. You said so yourself."

"You want me to do it in the daytime? But I can't."

Rita clenched her fist and pressed it hard against Nete's chin. She was white in the face, her cheek muscles tensed.

"You can, and you will, if you know what's good for you, understand? What's more, you're going to do it now. We can get away tonight."

Gitte's room was on the floor above the sewing room. Nete sat for most of the morning with beads of perspiration on her upper lip, waiting for a suitable moment to nip out unseen for a few minutes. But the moment wouldn't come. The work that day was easy and the warden sat quietly at the window with her embroidery. There was an unusual calm about the place. A day without tumult, and no errands to run.

Nete looked around. There would have to be a commotion of some sort. The question was where and how.

And then she had an idea.

In front of her sat two girls who had been living as prostitutes, working the old Pisserenden area of inner Copenhagen. They went by the names of Bette and Betty on account of their always going on about Bette Davis and Betty Grable, whom they admired and did everything they could to model themselves on. Nete had no idea who these two Hollywood stars were, for she had never been to a cinema in her life, and the girls' incessant chatter about them had long been getting on her nerves.

And then there was another tart, Pia from Århus, who sat behind Nete with her weaving. Pia was less talkative than most, perhaps because she was rather slow-witted, one of the older prostitutes who had been on the game for a long time and done just about everything that could be done with a man. She and Bette and Betty had plenty of stories to exchange about their profession, but could do so only in brief moments when the warden was not present. These were stories of crabs and the clap, of process charged for various sexual services, of malodorous men and how surprisingly effective a well-aimed kick in the gonads could be when it came to prompting a recalcitrant punter into paying up.

Nete looked over her shoulder. The girl from Århus looked up and smiled at her. She had three pregnancies behind her and all three children had been forcibly removed for adoption immediately after birth. Her history indicated that she would more than likely soon be on her way to be sterilized at the hospital in Korsør. Nete knew all too well what happened there, and talk was always rampant among the girls. Upon request of the head physicians of the mental asylums, the Ministry of Social Affairs referred many girls for sterilization without their knowledge. It was a time bomb in their lives that could go off at any minute. All of them knew it, including Pia from Århus. For that reason, she kept her head down and immersed herself in daydreams. Everyone on the island had their dreams, and most of them were about family and children.

Pia's and Nete's, too.

Nete turned toward her and put her hand up to cover her mouth as she whispered. "I'm sorry to have to tell you, Pia, but Bette and Betty have been blabbing. I heard them say to the warden that you'd told them you could make a hundred kroner in one morning by sucking men off, and that you'd be doing it again if you ever got out of here. Just so you're warned. I think Gitte Charles might already know. I'm really sorry to have to tell you, but that's how it is."

The sound of the loom stopped and Pia put her hands in her lap. She needed to sit for a moment and digest what Nete had said. To grasp the consequences, and Bette and Betty's unspeakable treachery.

"They said you were going to stick a pair of scissors in Gitte Charles, too," Nete whispered. "Is it true?"

And then something snapped inside the girl, and seconds later she got to her feet and showed them just how hard a streetwalker from Århus could get stuck in.

Nete backed away and out of the room as the warden called for help and the ruckus between the three prostitutes spread to the other girls.

They came running from the kitchen and the stores, and someone rang the bell that hung outside the matron's office. In no time at all, an otherwise uneventful day became a deluge of yells and screams, the air filled with words decent girls ought never to utter.

She was up the stairs and into Gitte's room in seconds, finding the key on the ledge above the door.

Nete had never been inside before, but now she saw how tidy the place was, with fine drawings on the walls and the bed neatly made. Gitte had only a small number of possessions in a small chest of drawers, and a pair of sturdy walking shoes Nete had never seen her wear.

Inside them she found almost five hundred kroner and a ring with an inscription: *Alistair Charles to Oline Jensen, Tórshavn, August 7, 1929.*

She left the ring where it was.

That evening, both the punishment cell in the basement and the one upstairs were occupied by the sewing-room combatants.

It was one of those days when not a word was exchanged during dinner. None of the girls felt inclined to draw attention to themselves as long as several of their guardians still wore the bruises of the brawl earlier in the day. Tension crackled in the air.

Rita stared at Nete and shook her head. Stirring up this kind of trouble was not what she'd had in mind.

She raised all ten digits in the air, then two on their own. It meant they'd be leaving at midnight, though how on earth Rita thought they were going to get out of this seething place Nete had no idea.

She wouldn't in a million years have guessed that Rita would set her roommate's bed on fire. Of course, matches were an item the wardens were extremely careful about, but Rita was Rita, and all she needed was a single safety match and a scrap of the striking surface of a matchbox stolen from the kitchen. It had been well hidden under her bosom most of the day, waiting to be put to use when her imbecilic roommate had fallen asleep.

The roommate it was who raised the alarm when she awoke to find her blanket alight and the room filled with smoke. Everyone was up and out in no time, for it had happened before. The stables had been ablaze on several occasions, and a number of years ago the whole institution had gone up in flames. The lighthouse keeper and his assistant appeared, too, almost within seconds, shirts hanging out and braces dangling at their hips as they organized pumps and buckets and instructed water-carriers.

Rita and Nete met up behind the herb garden and looked back at the fire that made the skylight of Rita's room suddenly burst with a bang, sending smoke spiraling into the clear night sky.

It wouldn't be long before Rita was suspected and a search initiated, so time was short.

As Nete had guessed, boatmen awaited them in the glow of the Retreat's paraffin lamp. What she had not expected was that Viggo would be among them and that he would fail to recognize her.

He eyed her up with the same lustful grin on his face as when Nete had seen him and his mate look on as a third man took Rita from behind. The kind of look a woman might want from her lover, but not from a stranger, and a stranger was what he was now.

When she told him she was the girl from the fair, he couldn't even remember the episode. He laughed and said if they'd already rolled in the hay once, they might as well do it again.

Nete felt her heart being wrenched in two.

Another of the men had counted the money, and now he declared that it wasn't enough. They'd have to lie down on the table and spread their legs to make up the difference.

This clearly wasn't part of the agreement. Rita began to kick up a fuss, lunging at the man in anger. It soon turned out it was the wrong thing to do.

"Right, you can stay behind on the island," the man said, then slapped her in the face. "Get lost."

Nete glanced at Viggo, hoping he would protest, but he remained passive. It told her he wasn't in charge and was content with his inferior status.

Rita changed her mind. She pulled up her dress, but the men were no longer interested. Why bother with an insolent harpy they'd shagged before on countless occasions, when they could have someone new? That was how they put it.

"Come on, Nete, let's go. Give us our money back," Rita demanded. It only made the men laugh even louder as they divided the cash between them.

Nete was horrified. Gitte Charles would know that Nete had stolen her savings. How could she possibly go back to the home tonight? It would be hell on earth.

"You can d-do it with me," she stammered, climbing onto the table as the men bundled Rita out of the shed.

She heard Rita cursing outside, but then all was still, apart from the grunting of the stranger inside her.

When he had finished and it was Viggo's turn, the thought came to her that she would never again be able to cry, and that life as it ought to have become had now been irrevocably snatched from her hands. She had never imagined so much betrayal to be possible, so much malice.

And while Viggo satisfied himself, her eyes wandered around the small space as though she were saying farewell not only to Sprogø, but also to the girl she once had been.

At the same moment as Viggo's body tensed toward climax, his friend grinning in the corner, the door was flung open and she was confronted by Rita's accusing finger and the piercing glare of Gitte Charles.

The men were gone in an instant, leaving Nete as though fixed to the table, her sex laid bare.

From that moment Nete's hatred of both women, and of Viggo, who called himself a man but was little better than a pig, knew no bounds.

41

November 2010

Rounding the bend by Brøndbyøster Church, Curt was surprised to see such hectic activity, clusters of onlookers huddled in the cold.

A shiver ran down his spine when he realized they were standing outside his house. Flashing blue lights, shouts and cries, and the drone of fire-engine pumps. It was everyone's nightmare.

"I'm the owner. What's happened?" he barked, defense mechanisms primed and ready.

"Ask the police. They were here until a few minutes ago," a fireman shouted back, as he doused down the last glowing embers inside the outbuilding. "What was his name, that detective who was here? Can you remember?" he asked a colleague who was busy rolling hoses.

"Mørck, wasn't that it?" He shook his head, apparently unsure, but the answer was sufficient.

Curt had already heard enough. This wasn't good.

"You've been lucky, sir, I can tell you," the second fireman continued. "A few more minutes and the outbuilding would have been gone and most likely that thatched place on the other side of Tværgaden, too. There was a badly injured person inside, I'm afraid. Looked like a gypsy. Maybe some derelict who'd found himself a place to kip down. We reckon he's probably the cause of the blaze, though we don't know for sure yet. He burned some paper in there, probably to keep warm I shouldn't wonder, but it's still only guesswork at the moment. I suggest you keep in touch with the police."

Curt didn't respond. Nothing could be further from his intentions.

He shone his flashlight into the outbuilding and saw that the sliding door of the strong room was open, the floor beyond a slush of ash. It was a sight that shocked him.

He waited until the firemen had gone, then waded through the sopping wreckage into the archive only to realize that nothing, absolutely nothing was left.

What there was, however, was writing on the walls.

ASSAD WAS HERE!

He almost collapsed.

"It's all gone," he said to Lønberg on the secure line. "Everything. Files, cuttings, documents of constitution, membership lists, patient records. The blaze took it all!"

"I hope you're right," said Lønberg. "It's dreadful, of course, but we must hope everything was indeed lost. You say this Hafez el-Assad was still alive when you left him, but do we know how the police found him? Did his mobile phone lead them perhaps?"

"No, we took that and switched it off. Mikael and the others are going through its memory to see if it might give us something to go on. But the phone itself has been turned off since it's been in our possession. So no, I've absolutely no idea how Mørck could have found him."

"All right, give me ten minutes to check with the hospitals. I'll call you back."

Curt trembled with anger and grief. If only he'd put off going to see the undertaker until tomorrow, if only he hadn't known the man from his sterling work in the party, none of this would have happened.

He shook his head in frustration. Why did they have to have that second cup of coffee? And why had the undertaker's wife spent so much time offering her condolences? But what the hell use were all these questions now? What good was "if only"? It had happened, and that was it.

What they had to do now was follow the plan. It was simple enough. Once they had eliminated the Arab they would go straight for his colleague. And when he was out of the way, which could be as early as the following day, they could send their man from Station City into the basement of Police HQ to remove Nørvig's files.

As such, the most immediate threat to the party would soon be averted. This was their primary task.

The fact remained, however, that there was a female assistant in the department, too. She wasn't that bright, their informant had told them, so that hurdle would be easily surmounted. And if their man was wrong, they'd soon find a way to compromise her and have her out of the system in no time. That much he could promise.

Søren Brandt was no longer a problem either, as far as Curt was informed. And Mikael would soon be dispatched to Madagascar to take care of Mie Nørvig and Herbert Sønderskov.

After that, only one potential threat would remain. Nete Hermansen.

It was imperative her death appear natural. A death certificate and a quick funeral, and that would be the end of it.

Forever, he hoped.

Now Curt's archive had succumbed to fire, just as his comrades in The Cause had destroyed their own records, and with Carl Mørck and Hafez el-Assad's imminent demise the police investigation would most likely cease to be a threat if, as Curt had been told, Department Q preferred to keep their investigations to themselves. The party would soon be left in peace to establish itself, and his life's work would thus bear fruit.

Curt nodded to himself. Now he'd thought things through, he felt certain no damage had been done. On the contrary.

All he had to do was wait for Lønberg's report from the hospital where the Arab had been admitted.

He went upstairs and lay down for a while beside his beloved. Her skin looked like snow and felt colder already.

"Let me warm you, dearest Beate," he said, drawing her body toward him. It was no longer yielding. Rigor mortis had set in while he had been having coffee with people who meant nothing to him. What had he been thinking?

His mobile rang.

"Yes, Lønberg. Have you found him?"

"He's been taken to Hvidovre, condition critical. He's not doing well at all, apparently."

Curt heaved a sigh of relief.

"Who's with him?"

"Carl Mørck."

"I see. Do you know if he retrieved anything from the strong room?"

"I doubt it. Can't be much, if he did, anyway. Our contact at the hospital is sitting in the waiting room opposite Mørck as we speak. I'll ask her on the other phone if she knows anything. Just a sec."

He heard Lønberg's voice in the background, and then the rustle in his ear as he returned.

"It seems it's hard to tell. She can't get that close to see. Mørck's got something that looks like a list, but it might be just the hospital's information sheet for patients' friends and next of kin."

"A list, you say?"

"Yes, but take it easy, Curt, it's probably nothing. The worst is over, my friend. From the historical perspective it's a shame, obviously, that we've lost all our documentation regarding the founding of The Cause and the Purity Party. But just as we consigned our patient records to the bonfires, it could well turn out for the best that your archives have gone up in smoke, too. How are you anyway, Curt? Bearing up all right?"

"No." He took a deep breath. "Beate's dead."

A long silence ensued. Curt knew how Lønberg and a number of the older members of the organization felt about Beate. Not only as an excellent organizer, a person who made them gel, but also as a woman. Beate had been quite unique.

"May God bless her," was all Lønberg could say.

The agreement with the undertaker was that he and his assistant were to come and collect Beate's body at ten o'clock the next morning. The procedure should not be postponed further, they informed him. The timing was unfortunate, to say the least.

Curt gazed with sadness upon her. He had decided he would follow her that night. When the undertakers arrived, they would discover they would have to make two trips.

But events had now dictated otherwise.

First he needed to know for certain that Carl Mørck and Hafez el-Assad were out of the way, and that the list the investigator at this moment sat reading in the antiseptic waiting room was not what Curt feared it to be.

He dialed Mikael's number.

"Unfortunately, Hafez el-Assad survived the blow to his head and managed to set fire to the archive," Wad reported. "But it seems likely he won't survive the effects of his injuries. We're trying to keep abreast of the situation with the assistance of a good and loyal contact at the hospital. A nurse who has come to our aid several times in the past and who will not hesitate to help us again. All in all, I don't think we need to worry too much about the Arab. Our problem is Carl Mørck."

"OK," came the reply at the other end.

"This time you're not to let him out of your sight for a second, Mikael. You'll find him at Hvidovre Hospital. I want him closely monitored wherever he goes, do you understand? I want him eliminated at the first available opportunity. Run him over, whatever you need to do. But do it, and do it without delay."

42

The way Rose stood staring at Assad's deathly pale face, her nerves all on edge as they took him out of the ambulance in front of the emergency entrance, Carl reckoned a long night's waiting around for bulletins on Assad's condition would be too much for her.

"You all right to drive home on your own?" he asked her, in the reflection of flashing blue lights. He handed her the car key, only to remember what a truly awful driver she was, but by then it was too late.

"Thanks," she said, hugging him for a brief, transcendent moment before sending a pitiful little wave in the direction of Assad's stretcher and wandering off back to the Ka.

At least there's not much traffic on the roads at this time, Carl thought to himself. If anything should happen to Rose as well, he'd be packing in his job first thing.

Maybe he would, anyway.

They toiled with Assad in surgery until finally a doleful-looking doctor appeared before Carl in the waiting room and informed him that his assistant's lungs thankfully seemed to be all right, but the fracture he'd sustained to his skull and the subsequent accumulations of blood were such that they couldn't promise anything. In fact, Assad's condition was so serious, they would be transferring him to the Rigshospital, where the trauma center was already preparing for his arrival. He would be given a thorough examination and most likely sent into surgery again before being admitted to intensive care.

Carl nodded, anger and grief tussling inside him. He wouldn't be passing this on to Rose just yet, he sensed.

He clutched one of the sheets of paper that Assad had hidden under his shirt to his chest. Curt Wad was going to pay for this. And if they couldn't nail him lawfully, there were other ways of going about it. He didn't give a shit now.

"I've only just heard," a familiar voice said from the corridor, and Marcus Jacobsen bounded toward him.

So fucking sad and touching all at once that Carl had to dry his eyes.

"We might as well get back to HQ, Marcus," said Carl. "I can't face going home, and there's a lot needs getting on with first."

Marcus Jacobsen looked up into the rearview mirror and adjusted it slightly.

"Funny, how long that car's been on our tail," he said, then looked at Carl. "Yeah, I understand. But you'll be no good to anyone without sleep and sustenance."

"OK, you can start by pouring me a Gammel Dansk as soon as we get back. The sleep bit can wait."

He briefed Marcus on what had happened during the day. He didn't see how he could get out of it.

"I ordered the two of you to stay well away from Curt Wad, Carl. You disobeyed me, and now look where it's got us."

Carl nodded. Fair enough. It had to come.

"That said, it's a good thing you persisted," he added.

Carl turned his head to look at him. "Thanks, Marcus."

His boss hesitated for a moment before dropping his bombshell.

"There are people I need to consult before I can let you go on with all this, Carl."

"I'm sure. But the way things are, I can't wait for that."

"In which case I'll have no option but to suspend you."

"If you do, these bastards are going to get away with it."

"Get away with what, Carl? Attempting to burn your house down? Assaulting Assad? Or with all their crimes of old and what they've built that party into?"

"The lot!"

"Let me tell you something, Carl. If you don't lay off until this has been upstairs, Curt Wad and his people are going to end up getting away with murder. There's no sense in letting that happen. So let's just agree that for the time being you're staying put until I say the word, OK?"

Carl gave a shrug, deciding it was better to be noncommittal.

They left the car in the parking lot, then stood for a moment outside the grim concrete structure, staring across at Police HQ, mulling over the events of the day.

"You wouldn't have a ciggie, would you, Carl?" Marcus asked all of a sudden.

Carl smiled at his chief's wavering willpower. "I would, as a matter of fact. Just haven't got a light, that's all."

"Wait a minute," Marcus replied. "I've got a lighter in the glove compartment."

He turned and had taken only a few steps when a dark-colored car that had been waiting with its lights off outside HQ on the opposite side of the road suddenly accelerated toward them.

It flew into the air at an angle as it hit the curb, and the piercing sound of scraping metal tore in Carl's ears as he threw himself aside and rolled away on the pavement. The car screeched to a halt, the driver flung it into reverse, gearbox grinding, and the pungent smell of burning rubber filled the air as the tires spun to get a grip.

They heard the shot but had no idea where it came from. The only thing they registered in the milliseconds that followed was the altered path of the vehicle that was now clearly out of control, hurtling over the road and smashing into a parked police car.

Only then did they see the motorcycle officer come running from HQ with his pistol raised, and only then did Carl become aware of how much invective his chief was able to spew out in one breath.

While Marcus Jacobsen and the press officer kept the reporters and TV crews occupied, Carl checked their assailant's data. To be sure, the guy didn't exactly have ID on him, but all it took was a quick round of his HQ colleagues before a photo of the dead man, slumped in the car with a hole in his throat, gave a result. The guys of Criminal Investigation's Department C were no slouches, he'd give them that.

"That's Ole Christian Schmidt," one of them said without hesitation. It was all Carl needed to know. Formerly a highly vociferous right-wing activist who'd recently been released after a two-and-a-half-year sentence for grievous bodily harm against a female executive committee member from the Socialist Party and a young immigrant lad who just happened to be walking along the street, minding his own business. Not much of a record, perhaps, but certainly enough to cause concern as to the man's future career opportunities.

Carl glanced up at TV2's news channel, which had been droning away on the flatscreen since he'd sat down.

The briefing on the shooting incident appeared to have gone well. Not a word about an ongoing investigation, not a hint as to the motive. All they got was that the incident was considered a one-off, the work of a disturbed individual, and that providence and a keen-eyed motorcycle officer were to be thanked for having saved the lives of two investigators.

Carl nodded. What had happened clearly demonstrated that Curt Wad was a desperate man, and that he more than likely wasn't finished yet. Once Marcus was back in his office they'd have to discuss how best to make some quick arrests.

Then the image on the screen cut away and the studio anchor gave a brief summary of Marcus Jacobsen's merits, apologizing that the names of the dead man and the officer who had shot him had not yet been made public.

The producer cut to another camera, but the expression on the anchor's face on the split screen remained the same.

"The body of a man was discovered off Sejerø this morning by a yachtsman crossing over to the island from Havnsø. TV2 News understands the identity of the man, presumed to be the victim of a drowning accident, to be Søren Brandt, a thirty-one-year-old journalist. Police say next of kin have been notified."

Carl put his coffee cup down and stared blankly as the image of a smiling Søren Brandt filled the screen.

Was there no end to this?

"You know Madvig from the old days, don't you, Carl?" said Marcus, gesturing for his guests to be seated.

Carl nodded and shook the man's hand. Karl Madvig, one of the hard knocks from PET. Carl knew him better than most.

"Long time no see, Mørck," said Madvig.

It was an understatement. Their paths hadn't crossed since the two of them had been in the same class at the police academy, but then Madvig had been far too busy lighting up the night sky of intelligence with his dazzling career. He used to be a decent bloke, but rumor had it that over the years he'd lost most of his natural charm. Maybe it was the dark suit he always wore, or maybe self-importance had got the better of him. Whatever, Carl wasn't bothered.

"All right, Jellyfish?" he said, savoring the obvious displeasure of the man on hearing his old nickname suddenly materialize from the mists of oblivion. "So now we've got security in on the case. Not that it comes as any surprise," he added, sending a telling glance in the direction of Marcus.

The chief rummaged in his pocket for his nicotine gum. "Carl, Madvig's in charge of PET's investigation of the Purity Party and all those in its inner circle, including Curt Wad. They've been keeping an eye on them for four years, so I'm sure you'll agree . . ."

"I get the picture," said Carl, turning to Madvig. "I'm all yours, Jelly. Fire away!"

Madvig nodded and offered his condolences for what had happened to Carl's assistant. Carl hoped to God it was the wrong word.

He was briefed on what PET had on the case. Madvig was forthright and in many ways passionate in his presentation. It was obvious this was a case that was dear to his heart. He, too, had been down in the murky depths and discovered what these seemingly respectable people were capable of.

"We've had influential members of the Purity Party, as well as a number of those involved in The Cause, under systematic surveillance, at least as systematic as conditions have allowed, and we're already well up on a lot of the things you've informed Marcus Jacobsen about. Naturally we've got witness statements and documents to corroborate our findings. We can get back to that if and when it proves necessary. But those files you and your assistant 'found'"—he made air quotes around the word— "at Nørvig's place haven't turned up anything we didn't know already. All those old court cases against members of The Cause are freely available in the archives of the police districts in question. What's new to us, however, are the very current indications of Curt Wad's stormtroopers being employed in outright criminal activities, which, in a way, is a good thing. With that information there can be little doubt that our task in making the powers that be understand the necessity of stopping these people once and for all will be that much easier."

"Indeed," the chief intervened. "You've every right to feel indignation at my not having informed you of PET's investigations before now, Carl, but it was imperative we keep a lid on. Imagine the outcry if the press got wind of a new and ostensibly democratic party being kept under surveillance, perhaps even infiltrated, and so massively as has been the case. Can you see the headlines?" He swept an imaginary pen through the air. " 'Police State, *Berufsverbot*, Fascism.' Accusations that could never reasonably be leveled at our methods, and quite beyond the mark in terms of what these investigations are actually about."

Carl nodded. "Thanks for your confidence. I'm sure we could have kept our mouths shut, though. Still, never mind. Have you heard they've had Søren Brandt bumped off now?"

Marcus and Madvig exchanged glances.

"OK, so you didn't know. Søren Brandt was one of my informants. They found him this morning floating around Sejerø Bay. I'm assuming you know who he is?"

Madvig and the chief looked at him with identical lusterless expressions. OK, so they knew who Brandt was.

"It was murder, believe me. Brandt feared for his life. He'd holed himself up somewhere, wouldn't even tell me where. Didn't help him much in the end, though."

Madvig gazed out of the window. "OK, so they killed a journalist," he mused, pondering the consequences. "In that case the press are going to be on our side. No one here's going to tolerate echoes of journalist killings in Ukraine and Russia. We can go public with this soon," he said, turning back to face them with the rudiments of a smile on his face. If the subject matter hadn't been so tragic, he'd probably have been slapping his thighs.

Carl studied the two of them for a second before playing his trump card.

"I've got something I'd like to pass on to the two of you, but in return I want a free hand to conclude the case we've been working on downstairs. In my estimation, wrapping it up is going to add substantially to the charges against Curt Wad, because there's a good chance he's responsible for a number of people going missing back in the eighties. Is that a deal?"

"That depends on what you're offering, doesn't it? Besides, we can't have your efforts to nail Wad putting your own and other people's lives in jeopardy," Jacobsen responded, sending him a look that said, *No way!*

Carl produced a number of sheets fastened with staples. "Here," he said. "This is a list of all the members of The Cause."

Madvig's eyes nearly popped out of their sockets. This was what he hadn't dared imagine existed, not even in his wildest dreams.

"Interesting stuff, I can tell you. Lot of well known doctors, a number of policemen, including one over at Station City, nurses, social workers. You name it. And not only that, there's detailed information here on all of them. Not least the people Wad sends out into the field to do his dirty work. They've got a whole column to themselves."

He ran his fingers down the list. With Germanic attention to detail, Curt Wad had not only entered private addresses, names of spouses, employers, e-mail addresses, civil registration numbers, telephone and fax numbers, but also the function each individual had within the organization. Information, Referrals, Research, Intervention, Cremation, Legal Support, were just some of the numerous designations. And then, finally: Field Work. It didn't take a detective to realize what that meant.

It was nothing to do with digging up spuds, at any rate.

"Under Field Work we've got Ole Christian Schmidt, just to take an example," he said, prodding a finger at the list. "No need to look baffled, Marcus. He's the guy who almost snuffed us out this morning."

Madvig could hardly contain himself. Carl could picture him already, storming back to his unit and proclaiming the crucial breakthrough. But Carl was unable to share the man's obvious delight, the procurement of the information having cost so dearly.

Assad was fighting for his life at the Rigshospital.

"Going by the civil registration numbers of those under Field Work, we can see they're all in a different age group than those who perform the abortions, for instance," he went on. "None of those working in the field is a day over thirty. What I suggest now is that we from HQ get out there and carry out preventive arrests on the lot of them, and then put the screws on as to their whereabouts and activities the last few days. That way there'll be no more killings, no more attempts on anyone's lives for the time being, we can be sure of that. In the meantime, you lot from intelligence can take care of the paperwork."

He drew the list of members toward him. "Getting hold of the information here may have cost my good friend and colleague his life, so I won't be handing them over to anyone unless you tell me we've got an agreement. That's how it is."

A moment passed as Madvig and the chief again exchanged glances.

"I should tell you Assad briefly regained consciousness, Rose," Carl said into the phone.

There was a silence at the other end. The information was hardly enough to put her at ease, he realized that.

"The doctors said he opened his eyes and looked around. And then he smiled and said: 'They found me. Very good indeed!' After that he drifted off again."

"Oh, God," Rose stammered. "Do you think he's going to recover, Carl?"

"I've no idea. We'll just have to wait and see. I'll get on with the case in the meantime. You can take a week off, Rose; it's about time you did anyway. It'll do you the world of good. It's all been rather hard going these past few days."

He heard her breathing become heavier. "That's as may be, but listen. I've discovered something that doesn't add up, Carl."

"Yeah? What?"

"The folder Assad took out of Curt Wad's archive was still in the car when I got home. I've been having a look at it this morning. File 64, you know."

"What about it?"

"Now I know why Assad thought it was so important he tucked it away inside his shirt before he set fire to the place. He must have been through the whole archive, seeing as how he picked this one out specially, as well as that membership list you've been looking at. Good thing he nicked that lighter off you, otherwise he wouldn't have been able to see a thing in there."

"What about the file, Rose?"

"It's Curt Wad's case records of Nete Hermansen's two abortions."

"Two?"

"Yeah, she was fifteen the first time. They called the doctor because she'd started bleeding after falling into a stream. According to the record it was a miscarriage. And do you know who the doctor was? Curt Wad's dad."

"Poor girl. At that age, and all. Must have been a very shameful thing in those days."

"Maybe, but the case that interests me is the one we already know from Nørvig's files. When Nete Hermansen accused Curt Wad of raping her and receiving money for performing an illegal abortion on her."

"There won't be much about that in his file."

"True, but there's something else that's even more interesting."

"Like what, Rose? Come on!"

"There's the name of the bloke who got her pregnant."

"Who was it?"

"Viggo Mogensen. The one you said she'd never heard of when you went round to see her the other day."

43

September 1987

Nete spotted Gitte Charles when her silhouette appeared in the distance on
the path coming from the direction of the Pavilion. That characteristic
gait, the sway of her arms that gave Nete the creeps. For more than thirty
years she had been spared the sight that now made her clench her fists
and glance around the living room to make sure everything was ready so
the killing could be done with a minimum of fuss. She needed this one to
go smoothly, her migraine continuing unabated, like a razor blade slicing
through her cerebral cortex, so sickening she felt she could throw up.

She silently cursed the affliction, hoping it would ease when finally
she escaped from all the things that reminded her of this life that had
been torn into pieces.

All she needed was to get away for a few months and everything
would be different. Perhaps she might even come to terms with Curt
Wad's continued presence in the world.

The way he was carrying on at the moment, his past would no doubt
catch up with him anyway and destroy him at some point, she mused.

The thought was imperative. Otherwise she would never find the
strength to kill Gitte Charles.

Four days after the arson and their failed escape, a pair of uniformed
police officers came and collected Rita and Nete. Not a word about what

was going to happen, yet they were in little doubt. "Feeble-minded, degenerate fire-starter" was hardly the kind of designation to bring anyone into the good books on Sprogø, and Gitte Charles's revenge had been precise and purposeful. Thus, Rita and Nete were sailed over the strait and taken by ambulance to the hospital in Korsør, all the while restrained by leather straps as though they were prisoners being led to the gallows. It was a feeling reinforced by the sight of burly hospital staff coming toward them with determined strides, prompting Nete and Rita to scream and kick out at them as they were bundled through the corridors and into the ward. Here they were strapped to the beds where they lay side by side, whimpering and praying for their unborn children. The staff seemed not to care. They had seen too many of these "morally deficient" individuals to be moved by Nete's tears and cries for help.

Eventually Rita, too, began to yell and shout. At first she demanded to see the consultant, then the police, and finally the mayor of Korsør himself, but none of it helped.

Nete went into shock.

Two doctors and two nurses came in without a word and stood by their beds as they prepared the hypodermics. They tried to put them at ease, telling them it was for their own good and that afterward they would be able to lead a normal existence. But Nete's heart pounded for the tiny lives she now would never bring into the world. And when they jabbed the needle into her vein, her heart seemed almost to stop entirely, causing her to let go of herself and abandon every dream.

When she awoke some hours later, only the pain in her abdomen remained. Everything else had been taken away from her.

For two days, Nete didn't say a word. Nor did she speak when she and Rita were taken back to Sprogø. Grief and despair were all she had left.

"The dimwit's lost her tongue. Perhaps she's learned her lesson now," the wardens would say. She heard them, and knew it to be true. For a month she refused to utter a sound. What good would it do her anyway?

And then she was discharged.

Rita remained behind. There was a limit to who could be let out into society again, they told her.

Nete stood in the boat facing aft and watched the island disappear behind the waves, the lighthouse gradually sinking into the horizon. And all the while she thought she might just as well have stayed there, because now her life was over.

The first family she came to was a blacksmith and his wife and their three sons, who were motor mechanics, all of them living from hand to mouth on odd jobs or on the fiddle. No family had greater need of some-one to yell at and toil for them all day long. It was a need abundantly fulfilled after Nete moved in. They had her doing everything, from tidy-ing up the yard that was littered with rusting scrap metal to waiting on a callous, unfeeling mother whose only pleasure seemed to be bullying everyone in sight, especially Nete.

"Little slag," the woman would spit. "Stupid whore." Not a single opportunity missed to deride or denigrate.

"Imbecile. Can't you read, you simpleton?" the woman berated her one day, indicating the back of a packet of washing powder. And when Nete admitted that she could not, her humiliation was compounded by a stinging blow to the back of her neck.

"Don't you understand Danish, you cretin?" became her litany, and Nete all but faded away.

The sons fondled her breasts at will and the husband threatened to go even further. When she washed herself they would come, one after an-other, sniffing her out like dogs, hanging around outside the door, shame-lessly howling their lust.

"Let us in, Nete. We'll make you squeal like the pig you are," they snorted. Thus passed the days, but the nights were worse. She closed the

door of her room tight, wedging the bentwood chair under the handle
and bedding down on the floor at the foot of the bed. Should one of them
succeed in getting in, she would make sure he received an unpleasant
surprise. For the bed would be empty and the iron bar she'd found in the
yard was more than heavy. If it came to that, she didn't care if she beat
whoever it was senseless or even killed them. What could befall her now
that could be worse than this?

Now and then she thought about spiking the family's evening coffee
with some of the henbane she'd brought with her from the island. But
each time her courage failed, and nothing came of it.

But then came the day the wife dealt her husband one stinging slap
in the face too many, whereupon he went out and fetched the shotgun and blew apart not only her skull but also the family's means of
subsistence.

Nete sat for hours all on her own in the kitchen, rocking restlessly
back and forth while forensics officers picked lead shot and brain matter
from the walls.

Not until evening did her future destiny become clear.

A straight-backed young man, perhaps no more than six or seven
years her senior, stood with his hands outstretched toward her and presented himself: "I'm Erik Hanstholm, and my wife, Marianne, and I have
been asked to look after you."

The words "look after you" sounded so alien to her. Like the faint
sound of music from a long forgotten age. And yet also they were a warning signal. Such words had given her hope to cling to so many times
before, hope that had proven futile. But here in this dreadful home,
where the echo of the fatal shot still lingered, they had never before
sounded so genuine.

She looked up at the man and studied his face. He seemed kind, but
she dismissed the thought immediately. How many times had she been
taken in by men she thought to be kind?

"If you want," she said with a shrug, for what else was there to say? She had no choice in the matter.

"Marianne and I have taken on an appointment teaching the deaf in Bredebro. In 'darkest Jutland.'" He chuckled at the expression. "We hope you might like to accompany us."

Only then did she look into his eyes. Had anyone ever suggested before that she might have a choice as to her own future? As far as she recalled, it had never happened. And how many times had anyone said they hoped she "might like to"? None since her mother died, of that she was certain.

"We've seen each other before, albeit many months ago," the man said. "I read a book out loud for a girl who was hard of hearing and very ill with leukemia. It was at the hospital in Korsør and you were in the bed opposite. Do you remember?"

He nodded when he saw her bewilderment, the way she blinked quickly in succession as though to shield herself from his searching gaze.

Was it really him?

"Don't you think I noticed you listening to us then? Well, I most certainly did. How could a person forget such lovely blue eyes as yours?"

And then he extended his hand cautiously without taking hers, simply waiting, his hand held out toward her.

Until she reached out and accepted.

Everything in Nete's world was turned on its head only days later in the house that came with the couple's job in Bredebro.

She had been lying on her bed since arrival, waiting for the slavery to commence. Waiting for the harsh words and betrayal that seemed to follow her like a shadow.

It was Erik Hanstholm's young wife, Marianne, who fetched her from her room and took her down into the study, where she gestured toward an alphabet board.

"I want you to concentrate, Nete. I'm going to ask you some questions. Take all the time you need before answering. Will you do that for me?"

Nete looked at the letters. In a short while her world would collapse, for she knew all too well what this was about. The alphabet had been her curse ever since she attended the village school. The swish of the cane across her buttocks, the snap of the ruler against her knuckles would remain with her forever. And when this woman now standing before her discovered that Nete could at best recognize fewer than a quarter of the letters of the alphabet, and moreover was incapable of joining them together in any meaningful way, she would once again be condemned to the mire where everyone told her she belonged.

Nete tightened her lips. "I'd like to, Mrs. Hanstholm. But I can't."

They looked at each other for a moment in silence, Nete wondering when the blow would fall, but Marianne Hanstholm simply smiled.

"Trust me, dear. You *can* do it, only not that well yet. Would you like to tell me which of these letters you know? That would please me a lot."

Nete frowned. And when nothing happened other than the lady opposite her smiling encouragingly, she reluctantly got to her feet and stepped up to the board.

"I know this one," she said. "It's an N for Nete."

Mrs. Hanstholm clapped her hands and laughed. "Well, that's a start, wouldn't you say?" she exclaimed, jumping to her feet and giving Nete a hug. "We'll show them, just you wait and see."

Enveloped by these warm arms, Nete began to tremble, but Marianne Hanstholm kept tight hold of her and whispered in her ear that everything was going to be better now. Nete could hardly believe what was happening. She continued to tremble and then began to cry.

At that moment Erik Hanstholm came in, drawn by the excitement, and was at once visibly moved by the tears in Nete's eyes and the way she clung to his young wife.

"That's right, Nete. You have a good cry. Let it all out, because as from today you'll never have to suffer that pain again," he told her. Then he softly whispered the words that from that moment on banished from her life all the malice she had ever known.

"You're good enough, Nete. Remember it always: you're good enough."

Nete ran into Rita outside the chemist's in Bredebro one day in the autumn of 1961. The news came blurting out before Nete even managed to react to the coincidence of their meeting again.

"They've shut down the home on Sprogø," Rita announced, laughing at Nete's sudden bewilderment.

Then all at once she was serious again.

"Most of us were put into service, working for board and lodgings, so as far as that goes, nothing's changed. Grafting from dawn to dusk and not a penny to show for it. A girl can get tired of that, Nete."

Nete nodded. She knew all about it. And then she tried to look into Rita's eyes. It was hard. She never thought she would ever see them again.

"What are you doing here?" she eventually asked, uncertain of whether she wanted to know.

"I work at a dairy twenty kilometers away. Pia, that old slag from Århus, is there, too. We slog our guts out from five in the morning until late. It's misery. So now I've done a bunk and come to ask if you'll come with me."

The idea was completely alien. Nete didn't even want to hear it. Everything inside her balked at the sight of Rita. How dare she come here after what she'd done? Had it not been for Rita's jealousy and selfishness, everything would have turned out differently.

Nete would have got away from the island and still been able to have children.

"Come on, girl. Let's take off, you and me. Sod everything. Remember the plans we made? First England, then America. A place where no one knows us."

Nete looked away. "How did you know where I was?"

Rita let out a dry, gutteral laugh that told of years of smoking. "Don't you think Gitte Charles has been keeping tabs on you, you silly sod? The cow tormented me day in and day out, taunting me about where you were and how your life had turned out on the outside."

Gitte Charles! Nete clenched her fists at the mention of the name. "Charles! Where is she now?"

"If I knew that, she'd have something coming to her," came Rita's retort.

Nete studied her for a moment. She had seen what Rita was capable of. Seen her take the wooden laundry tongs to the girls who wouldn't pay up for cigarettes, thrashing the daylights out of them and making sure the bruises were visible only when the girls removed their clothes.

"I want you to go now, Rita," she said, in a measured voice. "I never wish to see you ever again, do you understand?"

Rita lifted her chin and looked down her nose. "So I'm not good enough for you anymore, is that it? You little scrubber!"

Nete nodded deliberately. Life had taught her to stick to two universal truths. The first was her brother's observation about the two kinds of beings: male and female. The other was that a person's life is an eternal balancing act, a tightrope walk across a void of temptation, and that the consequences of failing to proceed along the straight and narrow were immeasurable.

At that moment, Nete was tempted to use her fist to wipe the smirk off Rita's face, but it was a temptation she resisted. If anyone should fall into the void it wasn't going to be her.

"Look after yourself, Rita," she said, turning away. But Rita wasn't finished yet.

"Just you wait a minute," she spat, grabbing her arm and then glaring at two startled housewives who happened to be passing with their shopping bags.

"Here are two tarts from Sprogø who'll shag the arses off your husbands for ten kroner, and this one here's the worst," she yelled, grasping Nete roughly by the cheeks and forcing her to face the two astonished women. "Have a good look at this one. Don't you think your husbands would rather bonk her than a pair of dogs like you? She lives here in town, so I'd watch out if I were you!"

Rita turned back to Nete, her eyes narrow. "So, are you coming with me or not? Because if you're not, I'm going to stand here and scream my head off until the police arrive. And that's not exactly going to make life easy for you here, is it?"

Later there was a knock on the door of her room where she sat crying. Her foster father ventured in.

His face was grave, and he said nothing for a long time.

Now he's going to tell me to leave, she thought to herself. And I'll be sent on to a family who can keep me away from normal people. A family who won't be ashamed. A family who don't even know what shame is.

Erik Hanstholm placed his hand cautiously on hers. "Nete, I want you to know that the only thing people are talking about in town is how you managed to retain your dignity. You clenched your fists, they saw that. But you didn't strike out. You fought back with words instead, and for that you deserve praise indeed."

"But now everyone knows," said Nete.

"Knows what? The only thing they know is that you stood your ground and told her: 'You're calling *me* a tart? Do you know what, Rita? Next time you mistake me for your twin sister, I think these people here will be happy to show you the way to the nearest optician. Go away, and don't come back, otherwise I'll call the police. Do you understand me?'" He nodded. "*That's* what they know, Nete. And it reflects well."

He looked at her and smiled until she smiled, too.

"One more thing, Nete. I've got something for you."

He reached behind his back.

"Here," he said, and handed her a diploma written in big letters. She read her way through it slowly, word by word.

No one who can read this can be called illiterate, it read.

He gave her arm a squeeze. "Hang it on your wall, Nete. When you've read all the books in our bookcase and done all the maths we do with the deaf, we'll send you to grammar school."

It was all in the past before she even noticed. Grammar school, the technical college, her training as a laboratory technician, being taken on by Interlab, her marriage to Andreas Rosen. A wonderful past that Nete thought of as her second life. The time before Andreas was killed, long before she sat here in her apartment with four killings on her conscience.

Once Gitte's out of the way, my third life will begin, she thought to herself.

And at that moment the entry phone buzzed.

When Nete opened the door, she found Gitte standing before her, a marble pillar ravaged by time yet beautiful still and elegant as ever.

"Thanks for inviting me, Nete," she said without pause, slipping inside as a serpent into a rat hole.

Gitte glanced around as she stood in the hallway, handed her coat to Nete, and proceeded into the living room. Each silver spoon was registered, each painting on the wall assessed by Gitte's keen eye.

Eventually she turned to face her hostess. "I'm so awfully sorry to hear how poorly you are, Nete. Is it cancer?"

Nete nodded.

"And there's no more they can do?"

Nete nodded again, ready to offer Gitte a seat, though wholly unprepared for what her guest had in store.

"No, you take the weight off your feet, Nete. I'll take care of things. I see you've made tea. Let me pour you a cup."

She steered Nete backward onto the sofa and turned to the sideboard.

"Do you take sugar?" she asked.

"Not for me, thanks," Nete replied, standing up again. "I'll make a fresh pot; that'll be cold by now. I made it for my previous guest."

"Your previous guest? You mean there have been others?" Gitte looked at her inquiringly, then began to pour despite Nete's protests.

Nete felt unsure of herself all of a sudden. Was Gitte burrowing? Did she suspect something wasn't right? Nete had seen her coming from the direction of the Pavilion, so the risk of her having bumped into one of the others had to be rather small.

"Yes, there's been a couple before you. You're the last."

"I see." She handed Nete her tea and poured a cup for herself. "Are we all being favored in the same way?"

"No, not everyone. The lawyer's just popped out, by the way. Some errands before the shops close, so you'll have to be patient, I'm afraid. Are you in a hurry?"

The question prompted an odd outburst of laughter. As though being in a hurry was the last thing in the world Gitte could imagine.

Keep the conversation going until she lets me pour, Nete told herself. But how? She racked her brains amid the stabbing pain of her migraine. It felt like a helmet lined with spikes had been clamped on her skull.

"It's so hard to understand that you should be ill, Nete. The years seem to have been so kind to you," Gitte commented, stirring her tea.

Nete shook her head. As far as she could see, they resembled each other in many ways, and the word "kind" didn't quite seem appropriate in describing how the years had treated them. Wrinkles, pasty skin, and gray hair had long since become a part of their appearance. No, it was obvious that life had not been without its trials for either of them.

Nete tried to think back to their time together on the island. It all felt so strange now that she knew their roles had switched.

They chatted about nothing for a while, then Nete got to her feet, picked up her own and Gitte's cups, and went over to the sideboard, where she stood with her back to her guest just as she had done four times before. "More tea?" she asked.

"No, thanks, not for me," Gitte replied. "But don't let me stop you."

Nete ignored her and poured anyway, adding several drops of the extract. How many times had she been bossed about by Gitte Charles on that dreadful island? She put the cup down on the table in front of Gitte without refreshing her own, the throb of migraine pulsing in her ears. Even the smell of the tea made her queasy.

"Do you mind if we swap places, Gitte?" she said, nausea welling in her throat. "I've a terrible headache and I'm afraid I can't bear to sit facing the window."

"Headache, too? Oh, you poor thing," Gitte consoled, standing up as Nete moved her cup across the table.

"I can't really talk right now, to be honest," Nete added. "I need to close my eyes for a while."

They swapped places and Nete closed her eyes, trying her utmost to think. If her former tormentor didn't drink her tea, she'd be compelled to use the hammer again. She would offer her coffee, fetch the hammer, bring it down hard against the nape of her neck, then sit and wait for the worst of her headache to pass. There would be blood, of course, but what did it matter with Gitte being the last? She could always wash the carpets after she'd dragged the body into the room where the others were.

She heard her guest approach yet was surprised to feel Gitte's hands on her neck and shoulders.

"Sit still, Nete. I'm good at this, but you're sitting rather awkwardly. It'd be much better if you were in the chair," came the voice from behind and above, her fingers pinching and kneading the muscles of Nete's neck.

She heard the voice babbling away, but the words faded. She'd felt this touch before under quite different circumstances. It was stimulating, delectably sensual, and she hated it.

"I think you should stop," she said, pulling away. "Otherwise I may be sick. Let me sit for a while. I've taken a tablet and I'll be all right soon. Drink your tea, Gitte. Then we'll talk about it all once the lawyer gets back."

She opened her eyes a crack and felt Gitte's fingers withdraw as though they'd touched something electric. She sensed her walk around the table before sitting down gently on the sofa next to her. After a moment or two came the quiet clink of a teacup on its saucer.

Nete leaned her head back slightly and squinted through her eyelashes as Gitte raised the cup to her lips. She appeared tense and ill at ease, nostrils flaring as she sniffed at the tea before taking a sip. Then suddenly her eyes grew wide with suspicion, all systems seemingly on the alert. She sent Nete a brief, piercing look and sniffed at her tea once more.

When she put down the cup, Nete slowly opened her eyes.

"Ahh," she said, trying to assess what was going on in Gitte's mind. "I feel a bit better already. That was a lovely massage, Gitte. You're very good."

Get up now, she commanded herself. Fetch the hammer and get it done. After that, pour the formalin down her throat, and then you can go and lie down.

"I think I need a glass of water," she said, standing up gingerly. "The pills make my mouth so dry."

"Why don't you have a sip of tea?" Gitte rejoined, holding out her cup.

"No, I don't like it unless it's hot. I'll put the kettle on and make us some more. I'm sure the lawyer will be here any minute."

She went out into the kitchen and opened the cupboard, and as she bent down to pick up the hammer she was startled by Gitte's voice behind her.

"If you ask me, Nete, I don't think there *is* a lawyer."

44

November 2010

Police HQ was a mechanism in which even the smallest movement of the tiniest cog at the remotest extremity was registered. It was an anthill where signals crackled round the building so swiftly as to defy explanation. Whenever a person under arrest tried to bolt, whenever evidence disappeared, whenever a colleague became seriously ill, or the commissioner was in hot water with the politicians, the news reached every ear.

It was that kind of day. The place was electric. Visitors at the duty desk, the commissioner's floor a whirr of energy, advisers, and high-ranking staff from the public prosecutor's office swarming.

And Carl knew why.

The issue of The Cause and those behind it was explosive, and explosives are liable to go off unless doused with water in copious amounts. So upstairs was sopping wet.

They reckoned on the region of forty people would be charged before the day was over, and each case entailed a scramble to find evidence that would stick. The ball was rolling, and the police officers whose names appeared on Curt Wad's membership list had already been brought in for questioning. If anything leaked before they were ready, all hell would break loose.

Carl knew the various departments all had the right people for the job.

That much had been demonstrated so often before. But at the same time, he felt just as certain that even in this finely meshed net of concrete and circumstantial evidence, there would be holes through which a man could pass. All it took was power, and the people they were after now had plenty. Sod the petty hooligans. Sod Curt Wad's stormtroopers. Sod the foot soldiers. They wouldn't be going anywhere; experience told him that. It was the strategists, the tacticians they were after. Ahead of them lay hour upon hour of patient police work interrogating the minnows who would lead them to the big fish if only the investigators made sure to do their job properly.

The only thing was that Carl was more impatient than most, especially now. Reports on Assad's condition were the same as before: they would be lucky if he survived.

Who could stay patient in a situation like that?

He sat for a while, wondering how best to proceed. The way he looked at it, there were two issues here that might or might not be linked. On the one hand were the disappearances in 1987. On the other were the injustices committed against a large number of women and the attacks on Assad and himself.

Rose had got him confused. Until her report, all their efforts had been focused on Curt Wad, whereas Nete Hermansen had seemed only to be a victim, a puzzling yet innocuous link between missing persons. But after what Rose had come up with, warning lamps were coming on everywhere.

Why the hell had Nete Hermansen lied to him and Assad? Why had she conceded to connections with all their missing individuals except Viggo Mogensen, when the fact of the matter was that he appeared to be responsible for starting the whole unhappy chain of events that had so marked her life: unwanted pregnancy, abortion, rape, unjust confinement to mental asylums, and compulsory sterilization.

Carl was at a loss.

"Tell Marcus Jacobsen he can reach me on the mobile," he barked at the duty officer when eventually he decided to move into action.

His feet were taking him in the direction of the motor pool, but his head realized their mistake. Bollocks, he'd given the fucking car to Rose.

He glanced toward the rail terminal, nodding to a couple of plainclothesmen who were making off somewhere on foot. Why not walk? He could do that. What was two kilometers for a man in the prime of life?

He made it to Central Station a few hundred meters up the road before he found himself flagging and decided to sod it and grab a taxi.

"Bottom of Korsgade, by the Lakes," he told the driver, the city crowds bustling. Carl looked back over his shoulder but couldn't tell if anyone was following him.

He felt for his pistol. He wasn't going to be caught with his pants down this time.

The elderly lady sounded surprised over the entry phone but recognized his voice and asked him to come up and wait a moment outside her door.

He stood there for a few minutes until eventually it opened and Nete Hermansen bid him welcome in a pleated skirt, hair neatly brushed.

"I hope you'll forgive me," he said, his nostrils registering a smell that indicated even more than last time he'd been here that she was a woman who perhaps wasn't quite as inclined to air her rooms as often as she ought to.

He looked down the hallway. The matting by the bookcase at the far end had been scuffed up into a bump that had come loose from the carpet tacks.

He turned toward the living room. It was a signal that he wasn't intending to leave just for the minute.

"I'm sorry to come bothering you like this without prior warning, Ms. Hermansen, only I've got a couple of issues I'd very much like to talk to you about."

She nodded and showed him in, reacting to a sudden click from the kitchen, a sound that in Carl's home meant the kettle was boiled.

"I'll make us a nice cup of tea," she said. "It's about that time anyway."

Carl lifted his head. "I'd prefer coffee, if it's no trouble," he said, recalling Assad's molten tar, which for once he would have accepted gladly. The thought that it might never be offered again was devastating.

Two minutes later she was standing behind him at the sideboard in the living room, pouring him Nescafé.

She handed him the cup with a smile, poured herself some tea, then sat down facing him, hands folded in her lap.

"So, how can I help you?" she asked.

"Do you remember last time I was here we talked about those missing persons and I mentioned a Viggo Mogensen?"

"I do indeed." She smiled. "I may be seventy-three, but I've not lost my marbles yet."

Carl smiled back. "You said you didn't know him. Might you have been mistaken?"

She gave a shrug. What was he getting at?

"You knew all the others, which was hardly surprising, given the circumstances. Nørvig, the lawyer who defended Curt Wad against the charges you brought. Your cousin Tage. Gitte Charles, the nurse who worked in the home on Sprogø. Rita Nielsen, who was there at the same time as yourself. Obviously it wouldn't have done you any good to deny that."

"No, of course not. Why should I? Though, granted, it does seem to be a lot of coincidences all at once."

"And yet one of those missing persons was someone you didn't know at all. That's what you told me, and I assume in doing so you supposed we might turn our attentions elsewhere."

There was no reaction.

"When we came to see you last Saturday, I told you we were investigating Curt Wad. For that reason, I think you probably thought you were in the clear. But do you know what, Nete? We now know that you were lying to us. You *did* know Viggo Mogensen, rather well, in fact. He was the cause of all your misery. You had a relationship with him and he got you pregnant, which sent you straight into the arms of Curt Wad, who performed an illegal abortion. We can see that from Curt Wad's own records, which I can inform you are now in our possession."

At this point he'd expected her to tense up, perhaps even break down and cry. But on that count he was mistaken. Instead, she leaned back slightly in her chair, sipped her tea, and shook her head slowly.

"Well, what am I supposed to say?" she replied. "I'm sorry I didn't tell you the whole truth. What you say is correct, of course. I did know Viggo Mogensen. What's more, you're right in assuming I had no choice but to claim that I did not."

She looked at him with eyes that had lost their luster.

"The fact of the matter is I have nothing whatsoever to do with any of it, and, as you suggest, I felt that everything nonetheless seemed to be pointing toward me. What else could I do but seek to ward off your attentions? I can assure you I am guilty of nothing and have absolutely no idea what happened to all these unfortunate people."

She expelled a sigh of indignation, as though for emphasis, then gestured toward Carl's cup. "Drink your coffee and explain it to me again. And by all means take your time."

Carl frowned. Nete Hermansen was unusually confident for a woman her age. With hardly a pause for thought, she seemed in little doubt.

Well-formed sentences, and never a question posed. It was all so matter-of-fact: *Explain it to me again.*

Why should that be necessary? And why should he take his time? Was she trying to stall him? Was that it? Why had she made him stand outside the door all that time? Had she called someone? Someone who might help her out of a jam?

Carl couldn't work it out. Had she joined forces with her archenemy, Curt Wad?

It seemed like he had nothing but questions. He just wasn't sure what they were.

He scratched his chin. "Would you mind if we searched your apartment, Nete?"

This time there was a slight darting of her eyes. A tiny, almost imperceptible dissociation from the here and now. He'd seen it before, hundreds of times, and it told him more than as many words.

Now she would say no.

"Well, if you must, I'm sure there'd be no harm in your looking around. Just as long as you don't make a mess."

She tried to look coy but failed.

Carl leaned forward. "In that case, I think I will. But I must inform you that you have hereby granted me permission to search the entire property as I find relevant to our investigations. We'll be thorough, and it may take some time. As long as you know."

She smiled. "Drink your coffee. It sounds like you'll be needing the energy. It's not a small apartment, by any means, as I'm sure you realize."

He swallowed a mouthful. It tasted horrendous and he put the cup down again.

"Let me just call my superior and then I'll ask you to confirm to him what we've just agreed, OK?"

She nodded her consent, got to her feet, and went out into the kitchen. Maybe she needed to collect herself after all.

Carl was sure of it now. Something here wasn't right.

"Yeah, hi, Lis," he said when his call was finally taken. "I want you to get hold of Marcus . . ."

He sensed the shadow behind him. Startled, he turned his head.

And saw that the hammer aimed at the back of his neck was about to hit him full-on.

45

November 2010

He had held the hand of his beloved all through the night and into the morning. Squeezing, kissing, and caressing it until the funeral director arrived.

Curt trembled with emotion when they asked him to come into the living room and he saw her laid out in the coffin in snow-white silk, hands folded around her bridal bouquet. For months he had known this day would come, and yet it was practically unbearable. The light of his life, the mother of his children. There she lay. Departed from the world, departed from him.

"Allow me a moment alone with her," he instructed, his eyes following the besuited undertaker and his assistant as they left the room and closed the door behind them.

He bent forward and stroked her hair one last time.

"Oh, my dearest," he murmured, barely able to find voice. He dried his eyes, but the tears had a will of their own. He cleared his throat but choked still on his sorrow.

Then he made the sign of the cross above her face and softly kissed her frigid brow.

The shoulder bag on the floor beside him contained everything he needed. Twelve 20 ml ampoules of Propofol, the contents of three already drawn into hypodermic syringes. Enough anesthetic to end the lives of five or six human beings. But there was flumazenil, too, to counter its effect should the situation so demand. He was well prepared.

"We shall be reunited tonight, my love," he whispered, before straightening up. The way he'd planned it, two more would die before his own turn came.

He was waiting only for the word.

Where was Carl Mørck?

He was met by his informant two buildings away from Nete's apartment on Peblinge Dossering. The man who had taken out Hafez el-Assad.

"I thought he was going to walk the whole way, so I just tagged along on his tail. I was right behind him until we got to the Central Station," he said with an apologetic shrug. "It's a good place to shove someone under a bus, but all of a sudden he was in a taxi. I took the next in line and followed him from a distance, but he was already on his way into the building when I came round the corner."

Curt nodded. Another idiot incapable of doing a proper job.

"How long is it since he went in?"

The man glanced at his watch. "An hour and a quarter now."

Curt looked up at the windows of the apartment. Apparently she had lived here ever since she sent him her invitation all those years ago. And who could blame her? It was an imposing building with a commanding view, centrally situated amid the vibrant hum of city life.

"Have you got that pick gun for me?" he asked.

"Yeah, but there's a knack. Let me show you."

Curt nodded and followed him to the front door. He was familiar with the basics.

"The lock here's a six-pin tumbler and looks pretty tricky, but it's not," his man explained. "We can assume she's got the same kind in her apartment door. I'd say they probably changed the whole lot when they installed the entry phone."

He produced a small leather case and glanced about. Apart from a young couple idly strolling arm in arm along the path, there was no one around.

"First there's the torque wrench here," he explained, inserting it into the lock. "Don't touch it until you squeeze your trigger. Place the gun all the way into the keyway right under the pins. You can actually feel them. Keep your needle at a slight angle like this, then squeeze and apply pressure to the wrench, OK?"

He squeezed the trigger a couple of times, tweaking the wrench simultaneously. The door opened almost immediately.

He nodded and handed Curt the tools. "Now you're in. Are you going to be OK, or do you want me to come up with you?"

Curt shook his head. "No, I'll be fine. You can go home now."

From now on he preferred to handle things on his own.

The stairs were empty. Apart from the faint sound of a television, there was no indication that anyone else in the building was at home.

Curt put his ear to Nete's door, expecting to hear voices inside but heard none.

He stuck his hand into his shoulder bag, producing two hypodermics. He made sure the needles were in place, then put them in his coat pocket.

His first attempt with the pick gun failed. He recalled his instructions and tried again.

Despite its age, the lock was rather stiff, but after angling the needle and squeezing the trigger again he eventually felt the cylinder turn. Cautiously, he pressed down on the door handle with his elbow, and the door opened.

An odd, musty smell filled his nostrils. Like moldy books or cupboards that hadn't been opened for years. Old clothes and mothballs. A secondhand shop with no customers.

In front of him was a long hallway with doors leading off. It was dark at the end, but light seeped from the two rooms that were nearest. Judging by the cold flicker, the room on his right was a kitchen illuminated by fluorescent lighting, while the warm glow to his left most likely came from a number of incandescent lightbulbs of the kind the EU had now all but criminalized.

He took a step into the hallway, putting his bag down on the floor and reaching for a hypodermic in his coat pocket.

If they were both in there, he would need to go for Carl Mørck first. A quick jab into a vein in the neck and he would be out in a moment. If it came to a struggle, he would have to thrust the needle directly into Mørck's heart, though this was a solution to which he felt less inclined. The dead were rather unforthcoming, and Curt wanted information. Errant information that could cause irreparable damage to his Purity Party and end up destroying the vital work carried out by The Cause.

Nete had been plotting some kind of vengeance against him, of that he was in little doubt. It all matched up. Her peculiar invitation all those years ago, and now Carl Mørck. It was imperative now to find out once and for all if there was anything in this apartment that might jeopardize his life's work. Once he'd got the two of them under control, they would talk. And the information they gave him could then be acted upon by others within the organization.

He heard a sound in the room to the left. Light, rather shuffling footsteps that certainly did not belong to a man of Mørck's stature.

He stepped forward and glanced over the startled woman's shoulder as he appeared in front of her, quickly surveying the living room and finding it empty.

"Good evening, Nete," he said, turning his gaze and looking straight into her face. Her eyes were duller than he recalled, gray and lackluster. So less sprightly she had become, her features not nearly as fine and angular as before, her proportions transitioned by time. It was only to be expected.

"Sorry to barge in on you like this, but the door was open and I took the liberty. I'm sure you don't mind. I did knock, of course, but you mustn't have heard."

She shook her head slowly.

"We're old friends, you and I, aren't we, Nete? Curt Wad will always be welcome in your home, isn't that right?"

He smiled as she stared at him in bewilderment, then scanned the room more closely. Nothing out of the ordinary here, it seemed, apart from the two cups on the table and Carl Mørck being nowhere in sight. He fixed his eyes on the cups. One was almost full. Black coffee, nearly to the brim. The other was half empty.

Curt stepped closer to the table, making sure that Nete stayed put. He reached out and put his hand to the first cup. The coffee was lukewarm rather than hot.

"Where is Carl Mørck?" he asked.

She seemed frightened. As though Mørck was concealed in some corner, watching them. He looked around the room again.

"Where is he?" he repeated.

"He left a short time ago."

"No, he didn't, Nete. We would have seen him leave the building. So I'll ask you again: Where is he? You would be advised to answer me."

"He went down the back stairs. I don't know why."

Curt stood still for a moment. Had Mørck spotted his shadow? Had he been one step ahead of them all along?

"Show me the back door," he commanded, indicating for her to lead the way.

She put her hand to her breast and stepped hesitantly past him into the kitchen.

"There," she said, gesturing toward the door in the corner, clearly ill at ease. Curt could understand her feeling out of sorts.

"So he went this way, did he? Meaning he moved all these bottles aside, the vegetable basket, and the rubbish bag, then put them all back again before he left? I'm sorry, Nete, but I'm afraid I don't believe you."

He placed his hands on her shoulders and twisted her abruptly toward him. Her gaze fell to the floor, and no wonder. The simple little bitch was a born liar. Always had been.

"Where is Carl Mørck?" he repeated, taking a hypodermic from his pocket, removing the safety cap, and placing the needle to her throat.

"He went down the back stairs," she said again, a whisper.

And then he jabbed the needle into her neck and pressed the plunger halfway down.

Seconds later she began to sway, then collapsed like a rag doll.

"So, now I have you, Nete Hermansen. If there's anything you wish to confide, I assure you it'll remain between the two of us. Do you understand me?"

He left her in a heap on the floor and went back into the hallway, where he stood still for a moment, listening for the faintest sound, anything that might give cause for alarm. The sound of breathing, the creak of a floorboard, muffled movements. But there was nothing. He returned to the living room. Once it had been two rooms, now knocked into one. It was easy to see, looking up at the stucco that bordered the ceiling. Formerly there would have been a door over in the corner of the far room leading out to the hallway, but it was gone now.

All in all it was a home befitting a woman of Nete's age and standing. Neither too old-fashioned nor too modern. A grandfather clock with a ticking pendulum next to a CD player. Some classical music but also one or two more popular albums that Curt's own taste would have excluded.

He stared again at the cups on the table and then sat down. He tried to assess what might have become of Carl Mørck and what they would have to do to find him again, and as he did so he picked up the first cup and drank. The coffee tasted bitter, and he put it down with revulsion.

He reached into his trouser pocket for his secure mobile. Perhaps he should send a man out to Police HQ to see if Mørck had turned up there by some strange and inexplicable means. He looked at his watch. Or maybe he should get someone out to Mørck's house in Allerød. It was getting late.

Curt's head dropped for a second. He felt drained. Age was catching up to him. And then he noticed a tiny spot in the pattern of red and gold at his feet. It looked fresh. Strange, he thought, and dabbed his index finger to see if it was dry.

It wasn't.

He stared in bemusement at his fingertip, trying to grasp what was going on.

Why would there be fresh blood on Nete Hermansen's carpet? What could have happened? Was Mørck still here?

Abruptly, he stood up, went out to the kitchen, and stared at Nete lying there on the floor. He felt a dryness in his mouth and then sudden nausea. He rubbed his cheeks, drank water directly from the tap, moistening his brow while supporting himself against the counter. It was little wonder that the dreadful hours he had been through this last day and night should now take their toll.

He collected himself and reached for the next hypodermic with its contents of Propofol, making sure it was ready before putting it back in his pocket. If necessary, he could stab it into an assailant within seconds.

With caution he went out into the hallway, slowly proceeding along its length and gingerly opening the first door to find only an unmade bed and untidy piles of shoes and underwear.

He carried on to the second door, here to be confronted with a verita-

ble trove of remains from a previous life: robes, handbags, coats. Everything a lady of society could once have desired, put away on shelves and
hangers and hooks.

Nothing here, he decided, closing the door behind him, then sensing
once more the same sickly sweet smell that had been there when he first
entered the apartment, only now it was stronger. Much stronger.

He paused, sniffing the air. His senses led him toward the bookcase at
the far end of the hallway. Strangly it was almost empty. A few ancient
copies of *Reader's Digest* and some old weeklies, otherwise nothing.
Hardly the source of such an odor.

Curt stepped closer and breathed in deeply. It was difficult to pinpoint, a thin veil in the air, like the lingering smell of fish or curry from
yesterday's dinner.

It was probably a dead mouse behind the baseboard somewhere. What
else could it be?

As he turned back to further investigate the living room, he stumbled
and nearly fell.

Looking down to find the cause, he discovered a fold in the mat. The
angle of it puzzled him. As if a door had been opened and had dragged
the floor-covering up with it. And there in the middle was blood. Not
old, coagulated blood but dark red and fresh.

He turned to the bookcase and looked again at the mat.

Then he took hold of one side of the bookcase and pulled it away from
the wall.

It wasn't heavy. He found himself staring at the door it had concealed.
A paneled door with a bolt.

His heart began to pound. He felt strangely excited. As though this
door represented the sum of all the illicit, clandestine activities that had
shaped his entire adult life. His secrets of children never born and lives
made to fail. Deeds of which he was proud. Some would be offended by

such gratification, but it was what he felt. In front of this hidden door he somehow felt at ease, though his mouth remained dry and his head spun.

He dismissed it all as fatigue and drew back the bolt. It slid easily, the door releasing from the frame with the sound of suction. A rank smell began to fill his nostrils. His eyes passed along the frame, finding it lined with weather strips of strong rubber. He pushed against the door. It felt heavy, quite unlike the others in the apartment, and did not seem to have remained unused for any great length of time.

Curt's senses were suddenly on alert. He pulled out the hypodermic.

"Mørck?" he ventured quietly, without expecting an answer.

Then he opened the door wide, and the sight that met him almost caused his legs to buckle.

Here was the source of the smell, its cause so immediately apparent.

His eyes swept over the bizarre scene before him. Carl Mørck's motionless body on the floor, the grotesquely mummified heads with their dusty, brittle hair, retracted lips, and blackened teeth. Shrunken, fusty corpses clad in fine clothes, faces frozen, awaiting the last supper. He had never seen anything like it. Gaping sockets stared emptily upon crystal and silver. Transparent skin encased protruding bones and thick tendons. Crooked fingers with yellow nails on the table's edge. Hands that would never reach out again.

He swallowed hard and stepped into the room. The smell was pungent, though in no way foul as rotting flesh, and now he recognized it, recalling how he had once opened a glass cabinet containing stuffed birds. Death and eternity all at once.

Five mummies and two empty chairs. Curt looked down at the first unoccupied place and saw the name NETE HERMANSEN printed neatly on the place card. It wasn't hard to imagine who the second place was reserved for. The name on the card was almost certainly his own.

How fiendish she was.

He bent down to examine Mørck's motionless frame. The hair at his temple and the back of his skull was matted with blood that still trickled from the wound. Probably he was still alive. He put two fingers to the policeman's carotid artery and nodded with satisfaction, partly because Nete had secured his arms and legs so effectively with duct tape, and partly because the pulse was normal. He hadn't lost that much blood either. It was a nasty blow, certainly, but hardly more than would give a slight concussion.

Curt looked again at the empty place intended to be his own. How fortunate that he had ignored her invitation all those years ago. He tried to work out exactly how long it had been but found himself floundering in time. It must have been twenty years at least. No wonder the guests looked tired.

He chuckled at his own black humor as he returned down the hallway and into the kitchen, where he took his unconscious hostess firmly under the armpits.

"Come on, Nete, up you get. Time for your party at long last."

He dragged her back to the sealed-off room and heaved her onto the chair at the head of the table, the place she had reserved for herself.

Again he felt unwell and stood for a moment breathing deeply before collecting himself and retrieving his shoulder bag by the front door. Then he went back to the room and closed the door behind him. With the physician's nonchalance he tossed the bag onto the table and produced from it an unused hypodermic and an ampoule of Flumazenil. A modest shot of the antidote and Nete would be returned to the here and now.

She trembled slightly as he pressed home the plunger, hesitantly opening her eyes as though even now she realized that reality would be overpowering.

Curt smiled at her and patted her cheek. In a couple of minutes she would be lucid enough to talk.

"And what are we to do about this Carl Mørck?" he mused out loud, glancing about the room. "Ah," he noted. "An extra chair." He nodded politely to the ghastly assembly as he drew the chair from the corner. There were dark stains on the upholstery.

"Ladies and gentlemen, I'm delighted to announce we've a new guest in our midst. Do make him feel welcome, won't you?" he said theatrically, lifting the chair with a flourish and placing it next to Nete's at the head of the table.

Then he bent down and took hold of the rugged investigator who had caused him so much consternation, and manhandled his dead weight into position.

"Excuse me," he said, reaching across the table and nodding an apology to the figure of what had once been a man. "Our guest seems to be in need of refreshment."

He raised the decanter above Carl's head, removed the stopper, and doused his bloodied scalp with twenty-year-old water that drew colorful deltas on his pallid face.

46

November 2010

Carl came round within seconds and yet in stages. First the water in his face, then the pain that seared through his skull, the ache in his elbow and lower arm, which he had used to parry the blow. His head lolled forward, eyes still closed. He drifted away, then became conscious again, aware of a more general discomfort of a kind he couldn't remember ever having felt before. His throat was dry, images flashed in his mind, swirling light and waves of color. He felt dreadful, spinning with nausea, a thousand small voices warning him that if he opened his eyes things would only be worse.

And then a voice more distinct than the rest.

"Come on, Mørck, pull yourself together."

A voice that did not belong in the place he believed himself to be.

Slowly he opened his eyes and saw the blur of a figure gradually coming together, until suddenly he found himself staring at a mummified human corpse, its jaw agape in a strangled scream.

It brought him to alertness with a gasp, his eyes still struggling to focus as they shifted from one shriveled cadaver to the next.

"Fine company, wouldn't you say, Inspector?" said the voice above him.

Carl tried to move his head, testing the muscles of his neck, but the pain stopped him. What the hell was this? Bared teeth and dead flesh everywhere. Where was he?

"Allow me," said the voice, and he felt a hand grab him by the hair and force his head back with a vicious jolt. It felt as though all his nerve endings screamed at once.

The old man into whose face he now peered didn't seem that much different from the corpses at the table. His skin parched and wizened, the blush of his cheeks gone forever, eyes, once so keen, now wreathed by death. Only a day had passed and yet Curt Wad was changed.

Questions accumulated in his mind. About what he was doing there, and whether Wad and Nete were acting in collusion after all. But he was unable to muster a word.

And why should he bother? Curt Wad's presence was answer enough.

"Welcome to the party," the old man said, snapping Carl's head to the side.

"As you see, Carl, you're in the company of our hostess. She's even still breathing, so I'm sure we're going to have a wonderful time."

Carl stared into Nete Hermansen's face. She sat slumped, features limp, jaw hanging open.

His eyes passed over her figure. She was restrained like himself, torso strapped to the chair with duct tape, legs and feet likewise bound.

"You're not sitting comfortably, Nete," Curt Wad said, producing the roll of tape. A series of short ripping sounds ensued as he fastened her arms to the armrests. "A good thing you kept the best chair for yourself." He laughed, seating himself on the only one that remained empty.

"Ladies and gentlemen, allow me to bid you all welcome. Dinner is served. Bon appétit!"

He raised his empty glass and acknowledged the assembled company in turn.

"Perhaps you'd care to introduce me to your guests, Nete?" he suggested, with a nod in the direction of the rawboned carcass in the dusty, moth-eaten tweed who had been placed at the opposite end of the table.

"I know Philip there, of course." He raised his glass. "*Skål*, my old friend. Never a worry as long as Nørvig is at the head of the conference table, isn't that what we used to say?"

He broke into deranged laughter. Carl felt like throwing up.

Curt Wad turned to face their hostess. "Oh dear, Nete, are we feeling out of sorts? A little more Flumazenil, perhaps? You do seem rather peaky. I've certainly seen you in better fettle, I must say."

She whispered something in reply that Carl didn't quite catch. It sounded like, "That's what you think."

Wad didn't seem to hear it either, but his expression changed.

"Enough mirth. I see you've had plans for us all, Nete, and in view of what you were intending, I'm all the more pleased to be here today on my own terms. What's going to happen now is that the two of you will inform me briefly of how much information you have passed on to outsiders about my work. On that basis I shall be able to assess the extent of the damage and consider how my people might best restore order and renew faith in our misson."

Carl glared at him blearily, still struggling to regain his senses. He tried to breathe as comfortably as possible, but only when he began to inhale through the corner of his mouth did he feel any kind of improvement, more control over the odd sensations coursing through his body. He became more aware of his swallowing movements, the numbness in his neck and palate dissipating. He could breathe deeper now.

"You're full of shit," he spat.

Wad heard him but merely smiled.

"Ah, he speaks. What a wonderful development. We're in no hurry, but let's begin with you, shall we, Carl?" He peered into his bag on the table. "I shall make no bones about it. This night will be your last. Needless to say, that goes for the both of you. However, I can promise you that if you cooperate with me, death will be both painless and swift. If not . . ."

He reached into the bag and produced a scalpel. "Need I say more? I'm sure you're aware that the instrument here is far from unfamiliar to my hand."

Again Nete tried to speak but was seemingly still too confused.

Carl focused on the scalpel and tried to gather himself. He twisted his wrists against the duct tape, but there was no strength in him. He struggled to shift his weight in the chair, but his body seemed loath to even react. He didn't know whether to laugh or cry.

What the fuck's the matter with me? he asked himself. Was this how a concussion felt? Was that what it was?

He looked across at Curt Wad. Did he see perspiration running down the bridge of the old man's nose? Was it fatigue that made his hands tremble?

"Tell me how you found each other. Did you get in touch with the police, Nete?" Wad wiped his brow and laughed. "No, I don't suppose you did. After all, you've rather a lot to hide here, haven't you?" He swept out a hand, indicating the macabre scene. "And who might the rest of these unfortunate people be, these sorry individuals with whom you intended I should end my days? That one over there, for instance. What kind of worm was he, I wonder?"

He jabbed a finger toward the corpse directly opposite. Like the others, it was taped tightly to the chair, though no longer entirely upright. A shapeless individual whose former corpulence remained readily discernible despite the passage of time.

Curt Wad smiled, only then to clutch his throat in an abrupt reflex, as though he were about to spew bile or had suddenly become unable to breathe. Carl would have done the same if he could have got his hands free.

Wad cleared his throat a couple of times and wiped his brow again. "Tell me what documents you obtained, Mørck. Did you find anything of interest in my archive?" He raised the scalpel and slashed open the tablecloth. The instrument was hideously sharp.

Carl closed his eyes. He had no intention of shuffling off the coil yet, and definitely not like that. But if his number was up, he was prepared to go out with a flourish. Wad wasn't getting a peep out of him other than what he decided to tell him himself.

"So you choose to remain silent. Very well. When I've finished with you both, I shall call my people and instruct them to remove your bodies, although . . ." Wad stared blankly into the air in front of him and took a couple of deep breaths. He wasn't feeling well at all. He undid the top button of his shirt. "Although it seems a shame to spoil such a pleasant get-together," he concluded.

Carl wasn't listening. He was concentrating on trying to breathe. Inhaling through the corner of his mouth, exhaling through his nose. It stopped the room from spinning so fast. He felt shit, and was painfully aware of it.

Then Nete Hermansen came to life. A sudden, unexpected utterance.

"You drank the coffee!" she said, hoarsely and yet almost without sound, glaring coldly at her tormentor.

The old man stiffened for a moment, then gulped down some water and drew in air to the bottom of his lungs. He seemed addled and unsteady, and Carl knew exactly how he felt.

Nete expelled a couple of sounds that could have passed for laughter. "I see it still works. I was in doubt."

The old man lowered his head and stared at her with piercing eyes that expressed anything but weakness. "What was in the coffee, Nete?" he asked.

Her response was more laughter. "Let me go and I'll tell you. But I'm not sure it'll help."

Curt Wad put his hand in his pocket, produced a mobile phone, and pressed a number, his eyes still fixed on Nete. "You tell me what was in that coffee, Nete, or else I shall be forced to make an incision. Do you understand me? In a very short while, one of my people will be here and will administer an antidote. Tell me, and I shall let you go. Then we'll be quits."

He sat for a moment, waiting for his call to be answered, then snapped the phone shut and dialed once more. And when again there was no reply he became frantic and pressed another number. Still nothing.

Carl felt his diaphragm tighten. He drew in breath sharply, as deeply as he could. The pain was excruciating, but as he exhaled again the torturous cramp in his tongue and the muscles of his throat seemed to ease and he felt relief.

"If you're calling your pet gorillas, you'll have a long wait," he spat, looking Wad straight in the face. It was obvious the man had no idea what he was talking about.

Carl smiled. It was hard not to. "They're all in custody. We found the membership list of The Cause in that strong room of yours."

A shadow passed over Wad's face and he winced. He swallowed twice, his eyes darting feverishly about the room, his air of supremacy suddenly vanished from the features of his face. He coughed a couple of times, then raised his head and glared at Carl, aflame with hatred.

"I'm afraid I must eliminate one of your guests, Nete," he snarled. "And when it's done, you're going to tell me what you've poisoned me with. Understood?"

He straightened his long, bony frame and pushed back his chair. The scalpel lay firmly in his hand, his knuckles showing white. Carl lowered his gaze, unwilling to allow his butcher the pleasure of looking into his eyes when he began to cut.

"How dare you call me by my first name?" came the sound of Nete's rasping voice at his side. "I resent the familiarity, Curt Wad. You don't know me. You don't know me at all." Her breathing was irregular, but her voice was clear now. "Before you get up, I think you should present yourself properly to the lady at your side, the way a gentleman ought."

The old man stared at her with empty eyes, then turned and inspected the place card. He shook his head. "Gitte Charles. The name's unfamiliar, I'm afraid."

"In that case, I think perhaps you ought to have a closer look. *Look* at her, you beast."

Carl raised his head and saw Wad turn his face toward the corpse as if in slow motion, leaning forward and twisting over the table to get a better look at the woman's features. His crooked hands took hold of the mummy's head and drew it toward him. There was a dry, crackling sound.

And then he let go.

Slowly, he fell back in his chair, mouth agape, eyes out of focus.

"But . . . it's Nete," he stammered, clutching suddenly at his chest.

And with that he seemed to lose all control of his facial muscles. His expression changed abruptly, his face becoming almost deformed. His shoulders sagged, and what remained of Curt Wad's status and poise seemed thereby to collapse.

His head lolled as he gasped for breath. And then he slumped forward.

They sat in silence and watched the spasms subside. He was still breathing, but it wouldn't be for long.

"I'm Gitte Charles," the woman said, turning to look at Carl. "The only person I've killed at this table is Nete Hermansen. It was her or me, and it wasn't murder. A single blow with the hammer she'd intended to slay me with."

Carl nodded, realizing he had never spoken to Nete at all. It seemed to explain a lot.

They sat for a while in silence, staring blankly at Curt Wad's forlornly blinking eyes, the heaving of his chest as he struggled to draw in oxygen.

"I think I know who all these people are," Carl said eventually. "But which of them did you know?" he asked.

"Besides Nete, only Rita." Her eyes indicated the shrunken corpse at Carl's side. "It was only when you came and questioned me that I understood the connection between the names on the place cards and the actual people who had crossed Nete's path. I was just one of them."

"If we get out of here I'll have to arrest you. You tried to kill me with that hammer, and that's not all, I reckon," Carl told her. "I don't know what you put in that coffee, but you may have done away with me yet." He nodded toward Wad, whose barely flickering eyelids revealed that the life inside him was now all but extinguished. The cocktail of poison, age, and shock would soon prove lethal.

Time's running out, Carl thought, and what could matter less? Curt Wad's life for Assad's. Justice of a kind.

The woman next to him shook her head. "You hardly drank at all. I'm quite sure it won't kill you. The mixture was old."

Carl studied her, perplexed.

"Gitte, you've been living Nete's life for twenty-three years. How did you pull it off?"

She tried to laugh. "There was always a certain resemblance. I was older, of course, by a few years, and rather jaded by the time it happened. But I soon got myself sorted out again. A few months in Mallorca and I'd slotted into place, as it were. Bleached my hair, nice clothes for my wardrobe. It all suited me well. Nete's life was so much more preferable to my own. I was afraid of being found out going through passport control, naturally. And in the bank, and a lot more places besides. But do you know what? I discovered that no one in Copenhagen knew Nete at all. As long as I remembered to limp a bit, that seemed to be the only thing people noticed. And my guests here weren't going to tell. I found a stock of formalin in the kitchen, so it wasn't hard to work out what Nete had been planning to do. Down their throats with it to stop them rotting, and here you see the result. All sitting nicely, exactly where they were put. What else could I do? Chop them up and throw them in the rubbish and risk being discovered by chance? I decided Nete had got it all worked out. And now we're here with her and unable to leave."

She began to laugh hysterically. It was easy to see why. She'd carried it off, a double life for more than two decades. But what good was it now? Here she was, bound tight in a room sealed off from the rest of the world. It didn't matter how much they yelled, no one was going to hear them. So who was going to find them? And when? Rose was the only person who knew he might be here, but he'd just given her a week off. What were the odds?

He looked over at Curt Wad, who suddenly stared at them, eyes wide open. A tremor ran through his body as though he was trying to muster what little remained of his strength. Then he rolled over and thrust his hand toward Gitte Charles in a final, agonizing convulsion.

Carl heard Curt Wad die. A brief, listless rattle. A tiny expulsion of air. And then the man was still, eyes staring emptily at the ceiling. Eyes that had looked upon humanity and divided his fellow human beings into those who were worthy and those who were not.

Carl inhaled deeply. Perhaps in relief, or maybe despondency. He couldn't tell. He turned his head to the woman at his side. The scalpel was embedded in her throat. Not a sound had she made.

Silence was all there was.

For two nights he was entombed with these seven corpses. And at every moment his thoughts were elsewhere. With people he now knew he held more dear than he had ever thought possible. Assad, Mona, and Hardy. Even Rose.

When the third night descended upon the lifeless figures in his midst, he let go and drifted away. It wasn't hard. To sleep, and sleep forever.

He awoke to loud cries and people shaking him. He didn't know who they were, but they said they were from PET. One of them put his fingers to his neck and felt for a pulse, having seen immediately how weak he was.

Only when they gave him water to drink did he sense the sublime relief of survival.

"How?" he uttered, with the greatest effort, as they removed the tape from his legs.

"You mean how did we find you? We've been making arrests all over the place. The guy who tailed you here and tipped off Curt Wad suddenly started talking," a voice replied.

Tailed me? Carl repeated to himself. Had he allowed someone to follow him?

He was getting too old for this lark.

EPILOGUE

December 2010

It was the kind of day Carl detested most. December slush in the streets and Christmas lights in everyone's eyes. Why the sudden glee over water turning white and the department stores' unscrupulous abuse of the world's dwindling energy resources?

It was bollocks, all of it, and his mood was long since ruined.

"You've got visitors," Rose announced from the doorway.

He swiveled round, ready to spit out his annoyance. What was the matter with people? Couldn't they phone first?

It was an emotion compounded by the appearance of Børge Bak.

"What the fuck do you want? Found a new dagger to stab me in the back with? How did you even get through . . ."

"I've brought Esther with me," Bak said. "She'd like to say thanks."

Carl stopped short and looked up at the woman as she stepped forward.

She wore a jazzy scarf around her head and throat, and only little by little did she allow him to see her face. First the side that was only slightly discolored and swollen, then the side the plastic surgeons had worked on so intensely and that was still a blackened surface of scabs, partially covered by hospital gauze. She looked at him with one sparkling eye. The other was closed. She opened it slowly, as though not to startle him. It was milky white and dead, its luster gone. And yet he sensed a smile.

"Børge told me how you made sure Linas Verslovas disappeared. I want to thank you. I'd never have felt safe anywhere again if he was still around."

She stood with a bunch of flowers in her hand. Carl reached out to accept them, suitably humble, when she asked if she might meet Assad.

Carl nodded to Rose, and while she went to get him they waited in silence.

So much for thanks.

Assad appeared and didn't utter a word as the woman introduced herself and explained why she had come.

"Thank you so much, Assad," she said, holding out the flowers.

A moment passed before Assad extended his left arm, and another before he was able to properly grasp the bouquet.

"This makes me very happy indeed," he said. His head still trembled slightly when he spoke, but he was improving. He smiled awkwardly and tried to raise his right hand in acknowledgment but was unable.

"Let me put those in some water for you, Assad," Rose said obligingly, as Esther Bak gave him a hug and nodded good-bye to them both.

"Be seeing you soon. I'm starting back on the first of January, in stolen goods storage. Still a whiff of police work, I suppose, registering burglars' loot," were Bak's parting words.

Christ. Børge Bak in Carl's basement.

"Here's your mail, Carl. Even got a postcard for you today. You'll like the picture, I'm sure. And once you've spelled your way through it we can get going, OK?"

Rose handed him the card. The motif was mainly a pair of gigantic suntanned tits discreetly covered by a caption proclaiming *Happy Days in Thailand*. The rest was a miscellany of beaches, palm trees, and colored lanterns.

Carl turned it over with trepidation.

All right, Carl!

Your old cousin here, saying hello from Pattaya to tell you I'm now done writing down my (our) story about the old man's death. All I need now is a book contract. Know any takers?

Cheers, mate!
Ronny

Carl shook his head. Ronny's knack of spreading joy seemingly knew no bounds.

He tossed the card into the wastepaper basket and stood up.

"Why's it so important we drive out there, Rose? Can't see the point, if you ask me."

She was standing behind Assad in the corridor, helping him on with his jacket.

"Because Assad and I need to, OK?"

"You get in the back," she commanded five minutes later, having picked up the minuscule Ford and parked it half on the pavement outside Police HQ.

Carl spluttered invective, requiring two attempts before managing to squeeze himself into the Ka. Marcus Jacobsen and his sodding budget.

They drove for ten nerve-racking minutes in heavy traffic that respectfully made room as Rose experimented with novel rules of the road and lunged through the gears.

Eventually, she swerved on to Kapelvej, almost hurling the vehicle sideways into a space between two unlawfully parked cars, even smiling as she removed the key and announced they were now at their destination: Assistens Cemetery.

Thank Christ for that, Carl mused, extracting himself from the Ford.

"She's over here," said Rose, and took Assad by the arm.

He walked rather slowly in the snow, but the last couple of weeks had seen progress on that count, too.

"There," she said, spotting the grave from a distance. "Look, Assad, they've got the headstone up now."

"I'm glad," he replied.

Carl nodded. The case of Nete Hermansen had taken its toll on all three of them. Thinking about it, he could see why they needed some kind of closure. File No. 64 was now once and for all to be consigned to the past, and Rose had decided it should be done with a Christmas wreath of spruce, pine cones, and red ribbon. What else?

"I wonder who that might be?" she said, indicating a white-haired woman crossing over to the grave from an adjoining path.

In times gone by she must have been considerably taller, but age and the burden of life now weighed upon her spine, her neck thrusting almost horizontally from her shoulders.

They stopped for a moment and watched as the woman rummaged inside a plastic bag, producing something that from a distance looked like the lid of a small box.

She bent down and placed whatever it was against the headstone.

"What's she doing?" Rose said out loud, tugging the two men along with her.

They saw the inscription from ten meters off. "Nete Hermansen 1937–1987." That was all. No date of birth or death. No mention of her married name. Not even an RIP. This was what the administrators of her estate had mustered.

"Did you know her?" Rose asked the old lady. The woman nodded her head as she contemplated the slushy snow on the grave.

"Is there anything more pitiful than a grave without flowers?" she answered.

Rose stepped up to her. "Here," she said, handing her the tawdry wreath with its garish ribbon. "It's Christmas, so I thought it might be all right," she explained.

The woman smiled and bent down as far as she could to place it by the stone.

"I'm sorry, you asked if I knew Nete. My name's Marianne Hanstholm, and I was Nete's teacher. She was very dear to me. That's why I had to come. Of course I read all about it in the papers. All those dreadful people they arrested, and the man behind it, who was to blame for all Nete's suffering. I so wish we could have found each other again, but we lost touch." She spread out her frail arms. "That's life, I suppose. And who might you be?"

She nodded, eyes mild, a warm smile on her lips.

"We're the ones who found her again," said Rose.

"May I ask what it was you put down just before?" Assad asked, stepping up to the grave.

"Oh, just a little reminder I thought she ought to have with her."

Again she bent down with difficulty, picking up a small wooden tablet that at first blush looked like a buttering board with writing on it.

She turned it over in her hands and held it up toward them.

I'M GOOD ENOUGH!

Carl nodded to himself.

He was in no doubt she had been.

Once.

ACKNOWLEDGMENTS

A warm thanks to Hanne Adler-Olsen for daily inspiration, encouragement, and wise, insightful contributions. Thanks also to Freddy Milton, Eddie Kiran, Hanne Petersen, Micha Schmalstieg, and Karlo Andersen for indispensable and painstaking comments, and to Anne C. Andersen for her keen eye and astonishing energy. Thanks to Niels and Marianne Haarbo, and to Gitte and Peter Q. Rannes and the Danish Center for Writers and Translators at Hald Hovedgaard, for hospitality. Thanks to Police Superintendent Leif Christensen for generously sharing his experience and for corrections concerning police matters and procedure. Thanks to A/S Sund & Bælt, the Danmarks Radio Archive, Marianne Fryd, Kurt Rehder, Birthe Frid-Nielsen, Ulla Yde, Frida Thorup, Gyrit Kaaber, Karl Ravn, and Søs Novella for their contributions to my research on the Women's Home of Sprogø.

A **150**-YEAR PUBLISHING TRADITION

●───────────────●

In 1864, E. P. Dutton & Co. bought the famous Old Corner
Bookstore and its publishing division from Ticknor and
Fields and began their storied publishing career. Mr.
Edward Payson Dutton and his partner, Mr. Lemuel Ide,
had started the company in Boston, Massachusetts, as a
bookseller in 1852. Dutton expanded to New York City,
and in 1869 opened both a bookstore and publishing
house at 713 Broadway. In 2014, Dutton celebrates 150
years of publishing excellence. We have redesigned our
longtime logotype to reflect the simple design of those
earliest published books. For more information on the
history of Dutton and its books and authors, please visit
www.penguin.com/dutton.